L.A. Johnson Jr.

I0671316

Yolanda The Enchantress

By

L. A. Johnson Jr.

Mamba Books & Publishing

L.A. Johnson Jr.

Fifst Edited   Percy A. Johnson Sr.
First printing

ISBN: 0-9817448-2-6
Published by: Mamba Publishing
Surry Virginia

Printed in the United States of America

Yolanda The Enchantress

L.A. Johnson Jr.

In 1765, Congo was a tiny jungle island of white settlements threatened on every side by African nations, which held the entire region north of Yoruba River, and south of Redwood Trail. Congo's only connecting link with other settlements was to the east. Separating the settlements was more than two hundred miles of jungle, full of exotic animals, threw that jungle ran a narrow elephant path known as Congo Road.

L. A. Johnson Jr.

Yolanda The Enchantress

Table of Contents

Chapter 1
Leave Her

The sun low in the south beamed through heavy fog making everything look hazy and bleak, it looked as if a thin vale had been cast across the jungle village and the Zambezi River. The hazy patches of vanishing mist, the sandy blood-stained riverbanks revealed a glistening metallic gold. The huge bloodstained palm and banana trees. The slushy paths trees and flowing streams, the holes in burning huts made by Portuguese cannons, made the village looked depressing. Anything that moved in the gloomy, hazy light stood out like a horse fly on its gleaming white sand.

Liberia Biometry with his camels was carrying buckets of rubber from one of his rubber trees to big wooden barrels behind his hut. From the African village on the edge of the settlement two Nicola women were paddling a raft across the Zambezi River towards a tall African waiting on the other side, with the carcass of a crocodile around his shoulders.

Captain Cordoba was wading in the marsh south of the village hunting ducks and ostriches. Captain Satan and Lieutenant Trinity were sharing a bottle of white bubbly palm wine in the galley of a wrecked ship anchored in the river. Soldiers not on duty were wandering restlessly through the village, flirting with African women, looking for someone to spend time with. Out side of the main gates of the stockade stood an angry pack of Nicola chiefs waiting to talk to the officer in charge. None of the Portuguese officers were in sight.

In side the stockade the enslaved African prince, Amid Kudzu, paced frantically thinking about his people within the village he had surrendered. He was a striking sight wrapped in

Yolanda The Enchantress

his copper blanket smoking his long pipe in the shadows of the palisade. Paulo Dais Novas was standing above on a rifle platform leisurely puffing on his pipe in full view of the Africans below. He wanted them to know that he was keeping them waiting another day, and he was in no hurry to listen to their complaints. The young colonel from Portugal and his rag-tag army had just won their greatest victory. They had won it because his men knew him and they were willing to follow him anywhere, no matter what the hazard. Now to hold what they had won he had to maintain that same unyielding attitude to the enemy.

All this Dominique de Salvo saw with one glance from the edge of the jungle. Then, eagerly, he looked to see if a jug was sitting on Zephyr's window cell; it was there as he was certain it would be. There was still an hour before dark. He had spent the day pretending to hunt, he had killed nothing but a snake that had gotten fat eating mice, uncovered by thrashing banana leaves. The snake had eaten so many mice it could no longer move. He was about to toss it aside when he noticed how fat it was. It wasn't much of a present; still he decided to take it to Zephyr. The Nigerian woman who lived with her could certainly cook it. He cleaned the snake and washed his hands in the stream.

While wiping his hands dry against his game bag ripples in the stream smoothed out. His reflection mirrored back at him with watchful brown eyes. The faint lines around them, weathered by seasons of wind and sun, gave him an older, more distinguished look than his thirty-eight years. He took an uneasy second glance at the reflection. In his thin woven gown, head shawl, goat-hair crown, wide trousers, and gold-embroidered aba. Which he often wore since reaching Mozambique? His form revealed the slender outline of a Portuguese soldier. He lifted the crown and head shawl uncovering his curly black hair, his muscular neck trusted up from his shoulders, which looked even wider, when covered with a flimsy garment. He smiled. A week's carrying on with a Nicola woman had given him the stuffy attitude of an African chief.

The jungle grew dark. The sun dropped behind thick gray clouds; Dominique ran his fingers along the line of his jaw. He

7

hadn't shaved today after getting up, now there were many rough spots. He dabbed his face with water from the stream, with his hunting knife he shaved his face smooth. Since his beard had started to grow as a young man could he remember shaving more than once a week? Now he had to shave everyday. These weeks in Mozambique had made him do that. He leaned back on his heels and reflected with satisfaction about.

The first time he broke into Zephyr's hut it was during the attack in order to fire from her bedroom window into the Nicola strong-hole. Every time after that there was a jug on her window cell, and she open the door to let him in.

He was a part of a great military victory, which had filled his pockets with gold. He had experienced a greater pleasure with a woman by far than he had ever before experienced. A man couldn't ask for more than that of any week. He would be a fool to catch himself wondering how it would be, if he were somewhere else, doing some-thing else. It was twilight now. It would be dark by the time he reached the outer shore of the Zambezi River. He would be foolish to have anything on his mind other than reaching her hut the minute darkness covered the village. He picked up the snake and bent low angling across until he could walk in the tracks left by Liberia's camel.

Skirting the African section of the village he noticed that the old chiefs had given up for the day. They were huddled near the council fire speaking softly, shaking their heads vigorously, like men who had endured much suffering. Warriors stood about restlessly, in groups whispering, watching their chiefs. Women were keeping their camels and elephants hobbled within close reach. Their personal belongings were packed so that the whole tribe could make a break for the jungle if the order was given. A crocodile had been killed and dressed, splashed with dabs of blood and decorated with silver shillings and strips of pine were tied on a pole above the fire. The pit below the pole was covered with burning coals. A rack connected to the pole was covered with baskets, and strips of dried meat that had been pounded and seasoned with melted fat. From time to time a log was thrown into the fire. Ordinarily a crocodile feast with all these trimmings was offered as a special offering to the gods to fight off some contagious disease or greater threat to the tribe. Novas' temper

Yolanda The Enchantress

was the disease that these Nikola chiefs feared. Dominique enjoyed their power.

He walked along the riverbank, veering away from it keeping out of the light cast from the fire behind Ray Aspirin's trading store. There, most of the men in the Fernandez Company were barbecuing an ox. They had purchased a keg of whiskey from Ray Aspirin. It was early in the evening, some of the men were beginning to get rowdy. Frightened Nikola families in huts were peering from windows through slightly drawn bamboo curtains because of their concern. All were watching this disturbing example of Portuguese behavior. Because of those inquisitive eyes, Dominique had to be careful; he circled more widely around the mosque and trading post.

The huge mosque had been attacked and ravished more than any other building in the village the nights of the assault when Portuguese cannon blasted wildly at the sleeping African villagers. Hector Moralize and Peter Hernandez were somewhere among the tangle of fallen timbers, each had a bottle of brandy. In the darkness Dominique could tell who they were, by the sound of their voices.

"You know what we have bin doing the whole week we have been here," Peter was saying. "Doing nothing but sitting, after we took this place. Now what do we do? Just sit and wait. We should be halfway to Elephant Falls by now, that's where we should be."

Peter's disgusted voice changed to uncertainty as Dominique moved away. Every man in the company was more anxious than Novas to fight the next battle in the campaign. Dominique worked his way down in the shadow of Raven Mateo's lumberyard, sneaking pass the warehouse, and back to the riverbank. Here he looked for Mario Goalie. This was certainly no time to let Mario see him sneaking past. Mario had asked him where he had been spending so much of his time every night; the distribution centers door was closed. Mario was somewhere else. Dominique headed downstream, keeping close to the bank, below Rendi Garcia's garden. He crept among the pilings supporting the boat ramp of Chico Hillsdale, and sneaked pass the voodoo woman's hut. He circled around pilings that supported the boat landing in front of the hut of Ibo Boca

9

L. A. Johnson Jr.

the fisherman's home.

Ibo, Zephyr's husband had left Mozambique four weeks ago with a cargo of elephant tusk, and crocodile hides to trade with Pygmies in the Congo River Basin. On the other hand, there were other reasons to be careful. The family of Kalahari Sahara, Ibo's brother-in-law, shared with Zephyr a connecting double hut. His sister-in law did a lot of snooping, to keep track of what Zephyr was doing. There was no way of telling whether she was protecting the interests of her brother-in law, or was suspicious of her own husband.

Dominique crawled through pilings, until he was near the section of the hut that was built near the shore; there he paused to listen. The Guineas, in their part of the round double hut on the other side of the central storeroom were quarreling as usual, and one of their children was crying. From Zephyr's kitchen he could hear the cheerful chatter of Sophia, the Nigerian woman chatting with a friend. In the adjoining hut Zephyr was pacing up and down in her bedroom. Her sudden stops and quick turns were like those of a trapped animal in a cage.

The sounds in the adjoining hut mingled with those more distant. The sounds of the night varied, mingling with distant yells. Then suddenly the tap of a drum announcing a change of guard at the fort. The sound of conversation in the Romania boathouse, where Orlando Rumania's sons were preparing for their voyage tomorrow to the Ivory Coast. Dominique squatted, listing, thinking this is a moment worth savoring.

The sound of her footsteps echoed, there was the added excitement of the risk they both were willing to take. They had to be careful of more than her family. There was not a man in this village that wouldn't envy his presence here; most of them were Portuguese soldiers. Any of them if they had a chance, would gladly take his place. He knew that his reckless actions could trigger new battles between the African people.

He reached up and pulled the palm mat. Instantly the woven palm mat across the window was pulled aside. He tossed the meat through the opening, and shoved his rifle in after it. He swung himself up and in. As always the room was dark except for a single candle glowing on the table in the corner. The smell of palm leaves and fresh berries surrounded him. Turning, he

10

leaned his rifle against the wall and embraced her in the darkness.

This had always been the moment she would retreat. She would act like she didn't want to see him. Her sudden flight took them all around the room, each being careful not to knock over anything or make any sound that might be heard by Sophia in the adjoining hut. Even after he had caught her she would resist for a while. She knew how to handle him, and how to control the situation.

Tonight was different. She rushed to him and embraced him as if she had a feeling he was going away. She was breathing hard, shaking all over. She pressed against him as hard as she could, kissing him over and over again. Backing up a step, he stepped on the meat on the floor. He pushed her away to pick up the meat and gave it to her.

"Meat I bought you," he whispered. There was no purpose, or reason to say anything, because she didn't speak Portuguese, nor did he speak her language. "Snake meat," he said again in Portuguese, knowing she knew a word or two.

She reached out to take the meat, when she realized what it was she let out a gasp of surprise. Then a sigh of satisfaction, She grabbed the bag turning, looking towards the kitchen as if she were thinking, how to cook it. He reached over and started to unfasten the tie string around the waist of her skirt. She pushed his hands away. She was looking towards the kitchen.

"There," she whispered with sudden determination.

She had made up her mind about something, whatever it was she wasted no more time. She pushed the sack of meat back into his hands, grabbed him by the wrist, and pulled him forcefully towards the door, which opened into the storage room. When he realized she was taking him out of the bedroom he resisted. "Come, come, come," she kept saying. He picked up his rifle and followed.

She guided him swiftly and silently the length of the dark storage room, between barrels of rubber, and around hanging coils of rope. They brushed, against racks of smoked goat and huge slabs of Cape buffalo. When they reached the door leading to the outside, she unbarred it. After unbarring the door, she spoke loudly with surprise and excitement. She slammed against the door noisily. She pulled him towards another door in the storage room the door opened, her sister-in-law stepped out. Zephyr laughed as Sophia pushed her kitchen door wide open, to let the light shine on them.

Dominique was beginning to understand. The meat had been important after all. She had some reason for making it known that he was in her hut tonight. She had taken advantage of him bringing it as an excuse for letting him in. She was setting the seen when she made the commotion. She was performing her greatest act; she took the meat, thanking him, than held it up for Sophia to inspect. Dominique was not prepared to see the other person he heard Sophia talking to when listening outside the hut.

It wasn't a neighbor. It was his friend Mario Goalie. Mario was comfortable with his situation up to the minute Dominique came in. This was the only hut in Mozambique; no Portuguese soldier had visited after dark. He was so comfortable, he felt as if he were at home. His feet were stretched out under the table. Mario was nodding and grinning at Sofia's big round buttocks while placing his hand in his pants. His round, face was wrinkled, with an expression of satisfaction, his mouth fell open when he looked up and saw Dominique standing in Zephyr's doorway.

"Why are you here?" Dominique demanded.

Mario leaned back in the chair with the innocence and surprise of an honest man. he said, "I was walking past just before dark, the woman there" he glanced at Sophia, "invited me in."

Dominique glanced at Sophia. "She speaks Portuguese?"

"She speaks Latin." Mario glanced at his half empty plate. "And she can cook." He didn't ask why or what Dominique was doing here. He kept looking at Sofia's big round buttocks and then, stared at Dominique. Dominique sat down.

"You can see for yourself," he said. "I bought 'em meat."

He wasn't deceiving Mario. Mario knew how many nights he had spent away from the lumberyard this past week. The longer Mario looked at Sophia the more his eyes bulged. He was licking his lips as if some of Dominique's good luck had switched to him.

Yolanda The Enchantress

Dominique glanced at Zephyr hiding in the shadows over by the lantern; it was the brightest light he had seen her in. She had curly black hair and brown eyes. She looked like a goddess, her skin was medium brown, and how she was built was enough to take a man's breath away, with a single glance. Mario was sitting at the table drooling. Zephyr and her sister-in-law were the best-looking women in Mozambique; and you could throw in all of Africa and Europe, if you wanted too.

The woman's voices dropped to a whisper, they had forgotten the fresh meat, now their excitement had increased. Zephyr was insisting on something. Sophia was objecting vigorously. Zephyr shook her head angrily. She kept insisting. Sophia threw her hands above her head and pulled a vale over her face and began to cry. Zephyr shook her head angrily again.

Sophia surrendered. She turned her tear-streaked face to Mario and began to speak to him in Latin. Mario had spoken Latin all his life. As a child, he had learned to speak several languages. Dominique began to realize why Mario had been asked in. There was something Zephyr wanted him to do. She could tell it to Sophia in their native tong, and Sophia could tell it to Mario in Latin, then Mario could tell him in Portuguese.

"They know I'm your friend," said Mario. "She," he pointed at Zephyr, "wants to know if you can trust me."

Dominique had known Mario most of his life. They were the best of friends, but there wasn't anything he wanted Mario to tell Zephyr for him. "Tell her with my life," he said.

Mario began to explain to Sophia. Listening to the sound of his voice while watching his sudden gestures explaining that the two of them were the best of friends.

Zephyr and Sophia talked from time to time glancing at Mario with doubt. Finally Sophia turned to Mario and told him something.

"No! No! No way!" Mario shouted.

Sophia continued with her story. Mario began to smile. Sophia ended with harsh words of disapproval.

"You better find a place to hide," Mario told Dominique. "Her husband's coming home tomorrow."

"What are you talking about," said Dominique. "By now he's in the Congo River Basin."

13

"Nope," said Mario. With every word the news got worst. "At Dome Palm he heard about Nova's conquest. He started worrying about his village, and turned around and started home. One of his wife's brothers took the short way threw the jungle when they reached Dome Pine. That's how she knows." Back in the shadows Zephyr was acting as if her life was about to end.

"Tell her this," said Dominique. "Tell her she has nothing to be afraid of, if he raises his voice at her; I'll kill him."

Mario thought all this was funny. "From what I've heard," he continued, "her husband is six seven, and as mean as a man can get."

"Tell her what I said," said Dominique.

This message triggered another argument between Zephyr and Sophia. Sophia burst into tears again. She wiped her eyes and turned to Mario. This time, he didn't think what she was saying was funny. He looked at Dominique with a stare, revealing confusion.

"She's not afraid of her husband," Mario said. "He worships her. He will do whatever she wants. She doesn't like him as much as she likes you. She wants you to take her away."

"My gracious!" said Dominique. "Where?"

This discussion, between Mario and Sophia, produced an immediate reply from Zephyr.

"She said anywhere," said Mario. "Anywhere far away. She's heard you're from Portugal, she wants you to take her there."

"Well," said Dominique, "that's far away."

Zephyr was staring hard at his face, watching his expressions, anxiously, for the first hint of how he felt. Her face moved closer to the candle. She was leaning forward, gripping the table. The light was bouncing off her face. Her skin had drawn tight across her cheekbones and around her mouth and at the corners of her eyes. She was much older than he thought. Young or old, he had never wanted her more than at this moment. She knew what she wanted and she wasn't afraid to go after it. He didn't want this affair to end this soon, but it was ending. He leaned back in the chair. Then stood up.

"Tell her I'll be back before dawn," he instructed Mario.

Yolanda The Enchantress

Before dawn he would make sure that Novas would send him out to join one of the scouting parties going to Elephant Falk. Mario pondered over the importance of his message. The two women embraced. Sophia was weeping again. Dominique reached for the door.

"Wait a minute," Mario said. "Don't rush off before you eat something'. Might be the last good meal you'll eat for a long time."

When he realized that Dominique was really leaving he rushed after him. "That big butt one," he said when he caught up with Dominique outside the door, "she's got a pot of crocodile stew on the fire that's tastier than any crocodile I've ever eaten."

"If you give her what she wants," said Dominique, "she'll cook that snake for you."

"Takes more than a snake," said Mario. "She's got a big butt and she knows how to use it." He looked at Dominique, trying to read his face in the moonlight. "You're going to take her with you?"

"Maybe. Maybe not."

"Running off with Zephyr?"

"Why not?"

Mario shook his head, torn between envy and concern. "I would do it too," he boasted, "if I had a woman with a body like that to rub against me. I wouldn't mind being' chased no matter how far I had to go. No sir, if I had her in bed with me every night." He kept breaking into trots in his anxiety to get Dominique back to their quarters where they could talk. He dropped the key twice before unlocking the door to the lumberyard. Dominique watched him fumble thinking about what would happen to Mario if some woman took him in hand. Women threw themselves at him. Mario was tall and muscular, and slightly bowlegged. He was clever as hell, with an honest face, and he made friends easily. He didn't scare easy in other ways, but there was something about women unless they were old fat or unattractive, that scared him.

There were coals burning in the fireplace in the huge bunkroom that sat in one corner of the distribution center. Mario stirred the embers, to get a small blaze started; he placed a pan of water over the fire. Afterward s, he opened a jug of white

15

palm wine. Then he opened a bucket of honey and a tub of butter.

"She said something I didn't tell you," he grumbled. She said something' about Zephyr leaving' a wealthy husband. He owns a fleet of fishing boats. She said with your money you'd be able to take good care of Zephyr. She's after your money."

Dominique sat down on the bed, now that the excitement and novelty that had made this week so wonderful had come to an unpredictable end. A familiar restlessness was gnawing at Dominique again. Mario's teasing him wasn't much help. "Why have money if you don't buy what you want with it? What do you want to buy with yours?"

"A few camels, some horses, and six real good pack burros, that's what I'm going to buy with mine. I'm going to Eagle Landing. There you can buy good camels and Arabian stallions from Arabs for very little money. With more people coming to Congo all the time and Africans always stealing' the few camels and horses they have. A man could do well with a camel caravan and a string of pack donkeys for hire."

"Do you know when you're going' to Eagle Landing?"

"Yep," said Mario, "As soon as I can get out of the army. Earlier today I thought it would be tomorrow. That conversation came up while you were hiding in the jungle. I haven't had a chance to talk to you about it. Novas' has decided to send Prince Kudzu, Octavos and his Nikola slave Swami, with thirty other African troublemakers, to Eagle Landing. He wants to get them far away from here, and then he won't have to worry about 'em escaping, and having to recapture them. I think he wants to prove to people down east, how strong his army is. Anyway, when I heard about his plan I asked to be sent along as one of the scouts but Novas said no. He's picking men to go, that's sick, or having' family problems at home, or those he wants to get rid of." Mario bent down and dropped a lump of honey in each jug. He added white bubbly palm wine, some boiling water, and a small slice of butter, and stirred the hot mixture with his knife.

Dominique was gazing at the fire as if he could see through the flames all the way to Eagle Landing where the guards, and prisoners of the escort party would be traveling. He could see every foot of their journey down the Nile River, up the

Yolanda The Enchantress

Yoruba, across Congo Basin, and over Congo Road. It would take months, but from the moment they set out they would be on their way to Eagle Landing. Every morning they would be starting a new adventure, every night they would be nearer their journey's end.

Suddenly excitement gripped Dominique. The opportunity was so perfect that it seemed like something he had planned himself. The impulse to take advantage of the opportunity was overpowering. He wasn't thinking clearly. He had made up his mind to quickly. Even an ignorant, or the most savage African, moves were influenced while hunting by the fight of birds, or by the movement of grass, the shapes of clouds; The thrashing of waves, or splashes of fish. At least they were influenced by something. There were Portuguese escudos in the bottom of his game bag. He took one out. Heads he would go, tails he would stay. It was tails. He dropped the coin back into his bag and took it out again. Tails again, before he could flip it another time Mario handed him one of the jugs and sat on a wooden crate near the fire.

"What I don't understand," said Mario, gripping his jug tightly, "is why did she decide to tell me this tonight."

"She doesn't speak any Portuguese?"

Dominique nodded and took a drink. Mario smiled and laughed uneasily, and said. "You got to know her that well without talking'?"

"She knows a few Ashanti words like snake," said Dominique.

Mario's eyes brightened and his mouth opened.

"I never thought about it that way before," he admitted, "but I can see how it could work." Mario would never have approached Sophia without being invited in and there was nothing he liked to talk about as much as the way he imagined she would have behaves. His face began to glow in the flickering light that had cast a thin shadow over him. "Imagine how long it takes. When you have a woman of your own kind. You have to waste time talking', no matter how she feels she'll keep pushing your hand away, because she's ashamed to come right out and say yes. When she says no she pretends to act like she means it, but when you get with a women that don't know your language,

L. A. Johnson Jr.

there's nothing to say, or you can say. You just keep on moving in, because there's no easy way for her to protest before it's too late. Dominique said, "I hadn't thought of it, that way."

Mario smiled appreciably, as if this situation mirrored some of his own unpleasant experiences. He picked up Dominique's half empty jug and poured another round. "When you show up…. in Eagle Landing with Zephyr your fathers eyes will pop out of their sockets."

"What happened to them?"

"Africans killed them. When I was ten."

Mario handed over the refilled jug. "I'm sorry," he said.

"My family's not in Eagle Landing, any more."

"Don't know if I've ever told you what happened to mine, either. All but my father, they died after catching a contagious disease, when I was eight. He married a woman that was mean as hell; far too mean for me to stay." Mario sat down continuing to nurse his drink. He shook his head a few times painfully remembering the heartbreaking times. The lost of whole families to African warriors, or contagious diseases were not an uncommon event. He returned to the present. "If you have nobody there, why are you taking Zephyr to Eagle Landing?"

"No good reason," said Dominique.

Mario lifted his jug not to drink, but to stir the honey melting in the steaming palm wine. "No matter where you go," he said, with pleasure, "she'll be the best looking woman they've ever seen."

Dominique flipped the coin again. It was still tails. "No," he said suddenly. "I'm not going to Eagle Landing. If I were going to Eagle Landing, I would go to see someone I've always loved."

Mario rose quickly. "You never told me about her."

"I'm not saying anything now."

"If I understood what you just hinted, that, whoever she is, she's even more beautiful than Zephyr."

"Let's not talk about her."

Mario took a sip of his drink, but in his frustration, he took to big a swallow, it choked him. "You have told me many times you haven't been back to Eagle Landing since you were eighteen."

18

Yolanda The Enchantress

"That's right."

Mario stared at him. "What you're saying is crazy." Mario was frustrated even more; his curiosity was controlling his thoughts, now. "What happened, her father didn't like you?"

"I've said too much," stated Dominique.

"No."

"She wouldn't have you?"

"I never spoke to her."

"That," surprised Mario, "I can't believe what I'm hearing." He said.

. Dominique took another sip. He knew he had said too much but he couldn't stop now. Some of this he had to tell somebody, hoping that telling the tale would help him regain control of himself

"I never spoke to her," he said. "I was an apprentice that year to an old man named Hector Mendoza. He had a general store at the lower crossing of the Nile River in Santiago Coca border, Angola. He worked the hell out of me all day and made me sit up most of the night reading, and writing. When I learned enough to keep his accounts, he sent me to school to be a lawyer. The girl rode past the store every day, she turned eighteen the same summer, I did. I was arms and legs with a vast thirst for knowledge, but she had developed into a fully-grown woman. She road past almost every day She and her father lived up the road one-way, her older brother the other. I got to know the pounding sound of her horse. Whenever I heard it, I would makeup an excuse; I'd find some reason, to go out front to look at her. After a while she began to nod and smile."

It was remarkable how clearly he could remember leaves of the lotus and pickerel-weeds that grew along the riverbank, the feel of the sandy earth clinging to his bare feet; The smell of blossoms on mangrove trees, in the rear of the store, The approaching pounding sound of her horse's feet pounding against the hard sandy road, and how well he remembered his secret. At this moment he remembered and felt, that same old overpowering lustful exciting feeling he had while waiting for the first glimpse of her. Never since had he been able to see, hear, smell or feel anything quite as clearly as he had that summer.

"What happened?" asked Mario, by now more curious

than interested.

"That summer she went somewhere over in the Old Kingdom Of Benin to visit with relatives. When I heard she had come back home I couldn't wait for her to ride past. That night I sneaked over to her father's plantation, and climbed a tree and looked in her bedroom window. The window was about ten yards from the tree. She was undressing and going to bed. When I saw her necket body, I nearly fell out of the tree but I didn't stop looking."

Mario's interest increased. "What happened?"

"Nothing. Even, now I remember the way she looked that night just as clearly as if she were standing over there by the window."

Mario glanced at the window, and back at Dominique. "Did you open the window?"

"It was open. When she blew the lantern out I climbed down the tree and went home."

Mario uttered his dissatisfaction with the story. "It's over, no good talking' about it now. That was a long time ago. If she's as beautiful as you say, she's married by now and has four or five children."

"I don't know about children, but I know she's married. She got married the next week to a businessman she met down at Gangland. Everybody was happy and dancing at the wedding. I left that night." He thrust down his empty jug with a sudden rage of unexpected anger. "I ran away and joined the army with a broken heart."

"The same night she got married," asked Mario.

Dominique reached for the jug and leaned back. I better stop drinking and talking, the palm wine is packing a wallop tonight. Mario changed the conversation. "You haven't told me how you got next to Zephyr so fast."

"That," said Dominique, "was an accident."

Mario sat waiting patiently. Dominique said nothing.

"Well," said Mario calmly, "what are you going to do now sit and wait for another accident?" Mario rose to his feet with the attitude of a man compelled to take charge of the situation. "You'll need a boat and some food. You better start looking' for them. You should be miles from here, by dawn." He

Yolanda The Enchantress

gave in a little. "All you have to do is ask, if you want my help."

Dominique didn't flip the coin again. He had told Mario his story to keep himself from doing something he would regret. He knew what he was going to do.

"Yes, there is," he said. "Lopez is in command of the guards tonight, isn't he?"

"That's right."

"He's a friend of yours. Go and talk to him like you're asking for his advice. Act like you're upset because you're afraid I'm thinking about running off with an African woman."

"That's crazy. He'll tell Novas."

"I know. I'm not going to run out on Novas without giving him a warning. I owe him that much."

"He'll throw you in the guardhouse. That's how he'll stop you."

"When I get ready to go nobody can stop me. Now go and do as I ask."

Mario walked out shaking his head and muttering. Dominique stretched out on the bed. For the first time in many years he rested peacefully.

It seemed to him that he had hardly fallen asleep before Mario was waking him up. Novas didn't send for him. He was standing beside Mario. Dominique stretched once and stood up.

"Got a lantern?" asked Novas, very grimly. "I want to see his face clearly."

Mario found the lantern and lit it. Novas took it from him and held it near Dominique's face. Novas, was as tall as Dominique. He looked Dominique straight in the eye. Novas unbuttoned shirt fell apart in front showing his nightshirt, tucked into his pants. His long red hair stuck out around the edge of his wide-brimmed hat. He had jumped out of bed to come here, and his angry green eyes were wide open. Their gaze pierced at Dominique with the sharpness of a recently sharpened knife.

"What makes you so sure I can't take Elephants Falls?"

Dominique didn't say a word. When Novas asked you a question you answer without asking what he meant by it.

"I don't think you can."

"Why?"

"You can't, unless you give the Belgian settlers time to

21

build a strong army, to help."

"That's what you think?"

"That's what I know."

"Everybody here but you, tells me want they think I want to hear, not what they think. Is that what you're doing?"

Dominique was beginning to understand. "No. What made you jump out of bed to find out if some kind of gossip was going around? I can settle that for you, too. I've heard things too but none you would like to hear. I don't know of a man in this army that's not ready to start for Elephant Falls tomorrow if you gave the order. If you don't believe me ask Mario. He gets around more than I do."

"I don't give a damn about what Mario thinks. Tell me what you are thinking."

"I've told you."

Novas lowered the lantern and turned to put it down. He dropped the lantern in a pale of water splashing water all over the table, and picked up the jug of palm wine. Mario started-mopping up the water from the table.

"Never mind the water," ordered Novas.

He sat down at the table and poured wine from the jug into a mug, washed it around in his mouth for a moment, and leaned back to look at Dominique again.

"Tell me what has gotten into you tonight that makes you feel like running our on me?"

"Nothing that has anything to do with you or Elephant Falls."

"I don't have a man who doesn't want to talk about Elephant Falls, including you."

"Congo Basin is full of white men that could releave some of us."

This was a subject that bought anger back into Novas' face. "Given an indirect response." Novas got angry. "Settlers are running around claiming land while soldiers are ramble through the jungle keeping, angry Africans off their backs."

A surge of pride replaced the anger in Novas' voice.

"There are a lot of men that would like to take your place, all right, but none of them are as smart as you. I don't have to tell you that, you know that as well as I do. You were one of the first captains I chose. You joined before Dome Pine and you've given me good legal advice. You've helped me make important decisions. You have been more help to me than higher-ranking officers. What... do you want me to do? Raise your rank."

"Dominique didn't answer."

Novas drew a slow deep breath, looked at the ceiling and glanced down at the floor. Then stared at the mug on the table near his elbow, his lips quivered as if he were upset. He picked up the mug and took a drink.

"He sat down on a crate."

Dominique sat on the edge of the bed.

"There must be some way to get to the bottom of this," said Novas. "There must be something important on your mind, all of you think you know more than me. I'll tell you why I'have stayed here. I knew staying here while the Nikola were wondering what hit them. The men could rest and we would have a better chance to take Elephant Falls. Nobody likes taking chances more than I do, but with a settlement as important as Elephant Falls. I can't afford to take chances I don't have to take. It's a fact that Nakoma, and British are plotting to kill us. But there's a reason for our waiting here. Dino and Victor Conti will be here within a month with a thousand armed men from Congo Basin settlements. With their help we'll roll right over those Africans. We'll take Elephant Falls, back."

"I don't doubt that for a second," agreed Dominique.

Novas leaned over and touched Dominique's money belt, the leather pouch was stuffed with silver escudos. "You haven't done so badly here. Imagine how much better you will do at Elephant Fall."

"Far more."

"Does that make any different to you?"

"No!"

Novas stood and walked over to the fireplace staring into it, and kicked a fresh log onto the burning coals. Than he sat on a crate and took another drink. "Enough of these games," he said, "Who is she?"

Dominique shook his head. "If I told you, you'll think of some way to stop me."

L. A. Johnson Jr.

"Married woman, eh?"

Dominique shrugged.

"No good that can come from it.

"You're right!"

I'll think of some way to stop you." Novas threw his hands above his head and folded is arms. He grinned and for a moment he looked younger than his forty-nine years. "I could beat the hell of out you... by myself."

Dominique glanced at Novas, thoughtfully. "I don't think you can," he said. "But I wouldn't be surprised if you tried."

"Another way would be to lock you up and keep you locked up. Or perhaps let the men know, you like African women. Some of them wouldn't like that," said Novas. "There are ten Africans for every one of us. As long as we're here, we have to be careful, when dealing with them. They've rebelled twice in the last two months. They don't dislike us, as much as they dislike some of their neighboring tribes. Nothing can bring them together quicker than fooling with their women. On top of that you've chosen the woman, with a husband that can bring all the tribes together. With his fishing crew of fifty men, and a village full of relatives and friends, Ibo Boca has more power and courage than most people. When he returns and finds his wife gone, we'll have a war on our hands we can't win."

Dominique turned to argue with Mario, then stood and started for him. Novas smiled. "You have no reason to be angry with Mario. He didn't tell me about your woman. It wasn't hard to guess who she was. You're no fool; there's only one woman in this village that could make you run." Novas, was still smiling. "You have made up your mind; you have to have her."

"Some things once you start you have to finish."

Dominique sat down and waited. Novas stood, and now he had stopped smiling.

"Stand up. Captain de Salvo." Dominique rose.

"I'm your commanding officer. Will you refuse an order from me?"

"Not a military order, Sir."

"I'm sending some prisoners to Eagle Landing. They're leaving first thing in the morning; I'm assigning you to the guard detachment. This is a direct military order, Private de Salvo,

24

Yolanda The Enchantress

Will you disobey it?"

"No Sir

Novas said. "I owe more to you, and Mario, and a few more like you, than any of you will ever know."

Mario returned after escorting Novas out, walked over to Dominique and pulled him around. "You tricky bastard," he said. "You were counting on him sending' you to Eagle Landing." He sat in the window and complained. "You tricked me. You tricked me. You're slicker than a fox in a hen-house." His annoyance showed. "And *me*, who has a good reason to go to Eagle Landing. I'm stuck here in the jungle. I'm going to get drunk." He reached for the jug and stared at Dominique. "You better sneak over there and tell Zephyr you're leaving without her in the morning."

"No, said Dominique. "Anything I say would make her angry. It won't kill her to stay with a husband who loves her. In the morning tell Sophia, Novas sent me to Eagle Landing with the prisoners."

Mario forgot about the jug and stretched out on his bed, he groaned. Followed by a weird glance glancing up. "With your luck, you'll run into that woman in Eagle Landing again. I wonder if you'll have the same luck with her you had with Zephyr." Dominique didn't answer. Mario sat up. "So that's it. I've never underestimated you but this takes guts. So many years and this far away, you start thinking about a woman you've only seen on a horse, or through a window that's married to another man."

Dominique poured, himself another drink and slowly set it down. he said. "I'm sick of fighting wars, and killing innocent people for their land. Most of us are. Now that my pockets full of money, I want to go somewhere I can spend it. What's wrong with that?"

"Nothing'. Only if that were true you would head for Mali. That's the place you can get the most fun for your money."

"Lisbon is where I was born, but I grew up in Eagle Landing. Why shouldn't I want to visit Eagle Landing again?"

"No reason. That woman is in Eagle Landing and you're going to see her." Once he had staked out a position in an argument Mario stuck to it.

"You don't understand," said Dominique. "I just want to

25

see how she looks now."

Mario glanced scornfully into the fire. "If that's all there is to it, wait 'till the wars over."

"A man could get killed in this war." Said Dominique.

"A man could get killed fooling with a married woman." Answered Mario.

Dominique walked over to the fireplace, and kicked a log into the fire. Mario was watching him with the concern of a man whose best friend has suddenly begun to show signs of stress. Dominique cleared his throat. He thought, maybe if he explained in his own words Mario would understand. Mario had a wealth of knowledge mixed with unyielding principles and good sense.

"This is something I have to do. It's like scouting back over an old trail to look for something you missed the first time. I have to do it."

Mario shook his head. "You're going back and looking for a married woman! Married women, that's trouble. "

Chapter 2
Figueroa Station

Dominique left Hippo Path and trotted down the shoulder of the ridge towards Figueroa Station, this was familiar country. The year the settlement was founded he had hunted with Dino Figueroa. Five years ago it wasn't much of a job to keep the settlement supplied with meat. There wasn't a settlement in Congo Basin more than five years old. Before the settlers came gazelle, and hippos wallowed in the Zambezi River with in sight of the stockade. Today he hadn't seen fresh gazelle prints for the last eight miles. Wild big game was rarely seen near the settlement, and settlers had to guard their cattle because Africans kept killing them when they let them graze.

The amount of African trouble in Congo surprised him, and all the men of the escort who had spent the last year with Novas in Xhosa Country bragging about the easy life people in Congo Basin were having. When they entered Port Eden Ton they began to realize how wrong they had been. There had been no big attacks this month. All year, small parties of Pygmies and Bantu warriors had attacked Congo Basin settlements. People spent most of their time cooped up in their homes behind their palisades, cut off from news from other settlement. At Port Eden Ton, the whole year had gone by without them learning of Prince Kudzu's recaptured of Mozambique. They had heard of the battle the day before word had come that Novas had taken Mozambique again, along with the Masai prince.

Dominique walked out on the mountain above Figueroa's Station. The place hadn't changed much. It was still the same log stockade built in a small valley. The houses were built against the inner walls facing each other. In the center the roofs were slanted inward to make it easier to bring water to fires started by Pygmies blazing arrows. Figueroa had to fight constantly to keep this place from the day he built it, but most likely he hadn't changed much either. This little valley was the one stretch of land in Africa he was determined to keep.

To the north two horsemen rode out of the jungle into the smoky charred valley. There maize had been burned to deny Pygmies cover, in the fields surrounding the station. Captain Satan in command of the escort kept scouts on the trail ahead and behind. Every since they left Port Eden Ton the scouts patrolled wider; they acted as if Congo were enemy country. They were always on guard thinking some war party might decide to attempt to rescue the prisoners, or some angry settlers might try to kill them. Everybody at Elephant Falls had heard the story that the Masai Prince had paid handsome rewards for Portuguese heads mounted on long poles. The fact that Prince Kudzu was now a prisoner of war made him even more an enemy.

Dominique slid down the ravine that separated the jungle from the grasslands and started across the opening heading for the station. People were running out to staring and shouting at the soldiers, and African prisoners strutted proudly in the open.

Captain Satan hadn't been able to requisition horses or camel from other hard-pressed settlers of the Congo Basin. He sent runners ahead to carry the news. Despite the fact that the prisoners were not in sight, but you could hear them rebelling, singing, and chanting African war songs. Some of the stations women were shouting threats and insults. Dino Figueroa standing in the gateway saw Dominique coming and rushed out to meet him. His thick brown beard had turned gray since Dominique had last seen him, but his tall powerful figure was as erect as ever.

"I knew you would return one day," he shouted with amiable calm, "but I didn't count on you turning up with the Headhunter as your prisoners. How is Novas?"

"Mad as hell when he realizes you're not on the way. What happened to your arm?"

Figueroa glanced down at his arm dangling in a sling. "A spear," he said. "I was out hunting for ostrich, a Pygmies spotted me first. Same damn arm that got shot in a few years ago. Let's go to see Anita before the crowd returns."

Most of the people had wondered out along the trail to get a closer look at the prisoners. Figueroa placed his good arm on Dominique's shoulder, and walked with him through the gate. After breathing the fresh air of the jungle from which Dominique had come, the lingering odors of fresh manure and ashes, the stench of the station sharpened in his nostrils. The unpleasant scent of soap and soiled bedding, mingled with the unpleasant smell of decaying hides.

"How did you know?" asked Figueroa. "Conti's been talking?"

"Not to me. We saw him at Sea Pen. He sucked up to us a lot, and said nothing."

"Why do you think we're not joining Novas?"

"Conti would have had more to say, and so would you, if that was what you were planning."

"Novas thinks nothing is more important than taking back Elephant Falls." Figueroa took his hand off Dominique's shoulder, and suddenly stopped. He turned to face Dominique, waiting for his response. Dominique shrugged. Novas, Conti, Figueroa, Gonzales, San Diego, De Torrential, and Serrano were all good friends. They were in charge of Portuguese colonization in Africa. If they couldn't make their minds up on something they could agree on, nothing would be gained by any white man in Congo Basin. For some reason Figueroa seemed uneasy, but anxious to explain his position. "Novas don't understand that there are settlements more important than Elephant Falls."

"What settlements?"

"All of Congo Basin. If we keep letting Africanc, keep us hemmed in like they have been doing; our people are going to leave and go back home to Portugal."

"How Novas looks at it is; take Elephant Falls and that will keep them off your backs. That's where the tribal leaders meet and plan their next move."

"Even if we helped Novas take Elephant Falls it wouldn't last long. The Masai with the help of Wagnerian warriors will take it back. The settlers are out there separated from us by miles of rough jungle."

What Figueroa said was so convincing that Dominique started to get angry. "You said that you're going to get pushed out of Congo Basin if you don't do something; what are you going to do?"

"We haven't done anything yet. Nor have we changed our minds about joining up with Novas. We'll do something that will help all Congo settlers instead of wasting out time fighting to keep Elephant Falls. After our folks get their land plowed, and crops planted, they won't have so many excuses. That's when we'll get all the men we need. We'll destroy Pygmy villages, Bantu villages, Ashanti villages and Lozi villages on Dung River. That's where most of them; that have been attacking us come from. We'll burn their villages and kill as many of them as we can. That'll keep them off our backs for a while."

Before Dominique's eyes flashed a picture of Novas face when he heard that he was to get no support this year from his most trusted officers, and he had lost his chance to take Elephant Falls because his friends had decided instead to burn some African villages.

Dominique had a sudden, overpowering impulse to return to help Novas, but he dismissed that idea, because it was too late for Novas' plans to work this year. The design of Congo settlements had already committed Novas to spending this season hanging on to Mozambique, Zambia, and Dome Palm. Dominique knew Figueroa was waiting for his comment, a comment from him he wanted to hear.

"Novas will do something," said Dominique. "He's use

to going it alone."

"Dominique de Salvo," came an excited cry from behind Dino. "Come and give me a hug."

Standing on the porch of Dino's house Anita Figueroa stood, gesturing, Dino grabbed Dominique's arm and pulled him towards the doorway, immediately more concern with pleasing his lovely wife. "I was on my way to tell you Dominique has returned," he called out to her.

"So I see," said Anita. "After you've stood there talking for an hour, with me the last person on the minds of either of you." She looked at Dominique with concern. "Come into the kitchen where I can kiss you without giving my nosy neighbors anything to talk about." She pulled Dominique away from her husband, and walked through the doorway with him; Dino followed.

"What kind of ideas?" Dominique said. She put her arm around his shoulder and pulled him down to her and kissed him, and stepped back to look him over with critical affection. "You've gained a few pounds."

"For now," said Dino.

"How many times do you have to kiss a man before he begins to look good, too you?" said Dominique.

"As crude as ever," Anita said.

Into the gateway the escort were entering the yard with the prisoners, angry yells, whistles and alarming gears from the accompanying crowd took on a new and more threatening note.

"There's a lot of unhappy people out there," said Dino, walking towards the door.

"I've got plenty of meat and potatoes for any that need it." Anita told him, pointing at a large cast iron pot of stew dangling on a iron pole above the fire. "Send somebody in to get the pot. I don't want any of those African's in my kitchen."

"A fine way to talk about a Masai prince." Dino turned in the doorway and grinned at Anita, and winked at Dominique. "Fact is–she's scared to look at a strange African. Last week we bought in a Lozi warrior we hunted with dogs over near the border of Zulu Land. She took a good look at him and she couldn't sleep that night." Dino walked out the door.

"He's right," admitted Anita. "I don't trust them."

Yolanda The Enchantress

The commotion outside had risen to a roar, accompanied by the sound of blows and yells of pain.

"I know most of the people out there, soldiers and settlers." said Dominique.

"Dino will handle it," said Anita. "Listen?" The uproar began to calm down. Her eyes brightened. "The Holy Bible says pride leads to sin, but how can you keep from being proud when you have a husband like that?"

There came a wail from the cradle in the corner, the silence had awakened the child, but the noise outside had not. Anita rushed to the cradle and lifted the one-year-old boy until he could stand holding the railings,

"Hush, Dino Jr.", she said, the child stopped crying.

"This is Dino Jr.," she said to Dominique. Then to Dino Junior, "This is Dominique. You don't remember Dominique; he rode all the way from Sea Pen through a storm to get your father when you were born. Watch himlittle man while I prepare something for him to eat before he rushes off again."

"Looks as much like his father as Alberto did his age.... where's Alberto?" asked Dominique. "

"Somewhere out there in the crowd," said Anita smugly. "And probably yelling louder than anybody, he's as tough as Dino already. Day before yesterday he was determined to shoot Dino's rifle, its kicked knocked him flat on the ground. Dino thought that had cured him but when he offered to let him try again, he was just as eager as the first time.

Sit down." She placed before Dominique a plate of turkey smothered with gravy, with chunks of onions. Fresh greens and a bowl of tomato soup. "Bread will be ready in a minute. We ran out of coffee a few days ago....Don't know how I can get along without coffee much longer."

Dominique was about to bite the first chunk of turkey, when he looked up and saw someone that took his appetite away. Mario was standing in the doorway smiling.

"Hello, Dominique." Said Mario.

Dominique said to Anita. "He's a friend and one of Novas men, meet Mario Goalie."

"Please to meet you ma'am," said Mario.

"A good friend of yours?" Anita asked Dominique.

31

L. A. Johnson Jr.

"Sometime he act's like one, but I don't know why he is here unless he has deserted the army."

He's wrong ma'am," said Mario. "I didn't desert. I was sent here to make sure he doesn't."

"Novas gave you written orders?" asked Dominique.

Mario replied. "Day after you left."

Anita put another serving on the table. "If you're a friend of Dominique's you're welcome here. Help yourself. Little Dino's ready for his dinner." She lifted the baby from his cradle, and started for the next room, her fingers beginning to unbutton her dress. She turned in the doorway. "If you see Dino before I do tell him, I'll eat with that, Prince Kudzu. If he thinks it's best for him to eat in this house."

Mario fumbled on the table for a fork, his admiring glance still staring at the door through which Mrs. Figueroa had walked. He turned to Dominique, shaking his head in disbelief. "You're always in a kitchen...with the best looking woman in the settlement."

"What are you saying, she's Dino's wife." Dominique said.

Mario helped himself liberally to the turkey and began stuffing it down. "There's no harm in looking at her," he said with his mouth full.

Dominique's stare was cold and suspicious. "Well?" he demanded.

"I'll tell you what happened," said Mario. "The next morning Zephyr went to Novas to find out what happened to you. She made up some story about how you owed her money for something; she wanted you bought back to pay for it. Perhaps I should say first that night in the warehouse Novas thought you just wanted to visit Eagle Landing like most of us. He thought you were using Zephyr as an excuse to get away, but after he talked to Zephyr, and took a closer looked at her, he started thinking he was wrong. He didn't think you could forget her so easily. That's why he sent me."

"Wait a minute. You told her to talk to Novas."

"I wasn't sure," admitted Mario. "But everything turned out fine. Novas ordered me to catch-up with you as fast as I could, he sent me to watch you, because he didn't want you to

Yolanda The Enchantress

come back to Mozambique."

"If that's true, why did it take you so long to catch up?"

"I knew you didn't need watching," said Mario. "So when I left Port Eden Ton I took the long way around through Chimpanzee Valley."

"Why?"

"I was looking for Alonzo La Rosa. You remember old Alonzo. He bought a boatload of meat to Dome Palm last year. I remembered hearing Alonzo say he had traveled down the Nile River to Santiago Cacao Country, I knew it was somewhere near where you worked as a lawyer."

"You went out of your way to see where I lived nearly twenty-years ago?"

Mario didn't answer, undisturbed by Dominique's question; he chewed and swallowed a huge chunk of meat. "Hasn't had meat so tasty and tender since I left Belgium Congo. I was trying to help you, because you're not thinking clearly. Didn't seem to me you were making the right moves." That's how I see it. So I got Alonzo drunk with a jug of brandy. When he was drunk he started talking, and he began to remember everything. He told me he used to work for a man named Silver Hernandez that ran a small lumberyard twelve miles south of Hector Mendoza store. He didn't remember you but he said he heard old Mendoza died of dysentery ten years ago, that was the year Alonzo left to come out here."

Dominique's anger diminished for a moment. "I planned on looking up Hector Mendoza when I got there," he said softly. "I owe him more than I could ever imagine when I left."

Mario ate for a while in silence, but he didn't keep quiet long. "Old Alonzo remembered a family by the name of Gomez, they owned a farm on the Nile River." He glanced up while eating to look at his friends face. "Does that name mean anything to you?"

Dominique pretended that it didn't. "Keep talking," he said. "I was sorry to hear about Mr. Mendoza, is there more bad news about people I knew?"

"Did you know Antonio…. a big redheaded man, one of the four brothers?" Dominique kept eating and pretending he wasn't paying any attention to the question. Mario continued;

L. A. Johnson Jr.

"Alonzo said he heard Antonio was coming out here sometime this year to look at some land on Lake Tanganyika, the Gomez family bought."

"What's unusual about a rich man coming to Congo Basin to look for land, or going on a safari," said Dominique. "Have you found out something that's worth talking about?"

"Mario smiled. The more Dominique pretended he wasn't interested, Mario talked even more. "If you don't remember Antonio, here's a Gomez you remember.... Old Alonzo remembered a girl named Liana that married a doctor who owned a gunsmith shop in Guam Land. He remembered that because they had a big wedding, people for miles around came to it. He remembered it was eighteen years ago because it happened the same year Francisco Serrano was nearly killed by a Zulu warrior. Mario paused on this note of triumph. Dominique continued eating. "If you want me to tell you more," He said, "you better stop eating and go to see Alonzo La Rosa. You will be glad I visited old Alonzo," said Mario, who was disturbed by Dominique's continued calmness. "You won't be so calm when you hear what I'm going to tell you next. This guy, Edwin Copula, her husband; he was killed 5years ago when his ship sank in the Atlantic." He leaned across the table and gripped Dominique's arm. "Do you know what I'm saying? Her husband is dead!"

Dominique stood. "I've known that since last summer. I read an article about it in a Guam Land newspaper Raven Macho bought back with him from that trip he took to Mali."

It didn't seem to surprise Mario much to find out all his prying had revealed nothing new. Instead, he looked as pleased as if he had finally realized what his friend was thinking.

"Now I know," he declared. You have known for five years she was a widow, eh? And you did nothing. You just went on dreaming and fantasizing like you did before. You were patient, and practicing because you thought you weren't ready. I remember that Belgian woman at Sea Pen, every time you walked pass her house she would come out to look for something. She wasn't bad looking, but she wasn't good enough for you. Then there was the Italian's daughter that ran to put on her best dress every time she saw you coming'. Do you remember

Yolanda The Enchantress

that redheaded Kingdom of Buganda beauty on the beach at Dome Pine? Your luck was good, and getting better, but none of them were good enough for you. It took Zephyr to make you realize your worth, and now you think you're ready. She was use to men trying' to get her, but you didn't want her. She was even ready to leave her husband and go anywhere with you. That's when you made up your mind; you knew and you didn't have to pretend anymore. You knew you were ready."

"Think whatever you wish," said Dominique, "you are lucky I don't give a damn about whatever you think."

Dominique walked to the door, because he was uncomfortable with Mario's questions. Mario talked as if a man's thoughts were as simple as those of a wild animal in the jungle, but there was no denying the truth. When he first read that article in that Guam Land newspaper he started thinking about Liana, but he didn't think about seeing her again. Mario was right about that. That came later, after his romance with Zephyr. He had become more comfortable around beautiful women as he matured. Dominique stood in the doorway thinking about what Mario had told him. There was no one piece of Mario's news that made a difference to him. Until now he had planned to stay with Hector Mendoza.

He had hoped he could eventfully buy Mendozas' business, where he once had worked, and could again until he retired. He felt like it was a good place to stay while he decided what to do. Now he had to think of another excuse to return to the settlement where he had no good reason to visit. He couldn't just ride up to the Gomez house uninvited and say that he had come to see Liana.

The answer was in another part of Mario's news, it was revealed to him almost at once. It kept reoccurring to him, each time with an awaken flavor of comical satisfaction. While helping Mario carry out the huge pot of turkey soup to feed soldiers, and prisoners, he talked to some of his old friends around the station. Dominique spent nearly a half an hour telling Alberto about the capture of Mozambique. He sat at the table that night in Dino's kitchen with Dino, Anita, Captain Satan, and Lieutenant Trinity. They sat with the imprisoned Chief Koala, Prince Amid Kudzu, they talked peacefully.

L. A. Johnson Jr.

Dino had insisted on Dominique joining them. "God all mighty," he declared. "If Anita and I will let those butchers come into our house, we won't throw out our friend." Satan and Trinity didn't want a busted military officer to eat with them. Prince Kudzu by now was surprised of nothing the Portuguese did. Dino over ruled the objection of Major Octavos Vega, second in rank only to the prisoner Prince Kudzu, among the prisoners. Vega was a Baule warrior from Sierra Leone who had become a prince by marrying Chief Kudzu's youngest daughter.

"I can put up with Prince Kudzu," Dino said. "He was born a prince, but that Sierra Leone turn tail is lucky we didn't let him eat with our dogs."

Chief Koala spoke up quickly when he heard Dominique telling Alberto how Hector and Peter pulled the Masai Chief out of his bed, the night of the surprise attack. And used him as a shield in a ditch twenty yards from the village, they crawled there to shoot through one of the gun ports of the Masai stronghold, every since that night Chief Koala has been extremely nervous.

"You couldn't repeat that trick again," said Dino.

Prince Kudzu was wearing a elegant gold dust shirt, made out of a cloth called *kente*. It had been folded, and taken from the only sack he was allowed to bring with him. The shirt was given to him by one of his Ashanti cousin. The stunning defeat he had suffered at Mozambique, and the personal humiliations to which he had been subjected to while traveling through Congo Basin; made him harsh and insensitive. After bowing to Anita upon entering he maintained an unyielding composure.

"Be careful, Dino Figueroa," Anita said. "You and Dominique behave yourselves. No matter how you feel about your prisonere you'll not going to harass him at my table."

The meal began in a strained unpleasant silence. It wasn't easy for soldiers to find much to talk about that had no connection with the war, or Africans, or the daily struggle of staying alive. The silence became awkward.

"Very tender meat Mrs. Figueroa," said Prince Kudzu.

"Thank you, " said Anita. "Usually I like to make my stew a little richer than this, but we've been short of butter."

Yolanda The Enchantress

Dino grabbed his broken arm. "It's been hard lately finding a safe pasture for our cows and goats." he said.

Anita gave a stern warning glance at her husband, and quickly changed the subject. "The laugh was surely on me when I was out in the jungle hunting these turkeys," she said. "There was an old turkey making a terrible to do because she thought she had lost one of her chicks. She couldn't find it though the chick kept chirping like it was in trouble. I started to help her look but I spotted a leopard in the tall grass. It was making sounds like a scared chick to trick that old turkey."

She looked at her husband to keep the conversation going now that she had started it. Leopard's can make mostly any kind of sound there is," said Dino.

"I saw one that could make a sound, like pulling the plug out of a jug," said Dominique. "Bother my father because he was always doing it when he walked out of the house."

"There was a young Ashanti guide hunting with me a few summers ago," said Prince Kudzu, "who could imitate an impala so good, he had lions lurking in high grass, and impala running to him."

"Most Africans are sneakier than leopards at making tricky noises," said Captain Satan, with a sudden, unexpected harshness from a man usually silent. "I have never forgotten the first trickster I ever saw. I was ten, out in the jungle looking for our cow. I could hear the cow's moos, and, I followed it farther and farther into the jungle. The moos kept starting', and stopping', like the cow was eating, picking' at one thing and another. When I caught up with it, it was a Pygmy warrior. Pygmy warriors make all kind of sounds."

Dino glanced reflectively at Satan's head. "You still have your head."

"Prisoners were worth more than heads those days," said Satan. "Took everything my people had to buy me back."

Lieutenant Trinity seated beside Satan gave him a bump with his elbow. Satan's face turned red, he stared without emotion at his plate ashamed to look at Anita. She glanced angrily at her husband because his remark had led Satan astray. She turned swiftly smiling at Prince Kudzu. "What a striking shirt, Prince Kudzu," she said, leaning closer, to look at the *kente-cloth*. "An

L. A. Johnson Jr.

uncle of mine had a shirt made out of that kind of cloth."

"There's only one like this, madam," said Prince Kudzu.

Dino coughed and then met Anita's piercing stare with a look of innocence, she forced another phony smile. "Dino passed the platter of turkey around again. Now, please eat and enjoy yourselves, eat as much as you wish. There's more in the pot."

Dominique had been watching Alberto. The boy had left his bed in the loft, and crawled to the head of the ladder where his solemn gaze was fixed on the imprisoned Masai prince. Dino noticed him, and nudged Dominique.

"Find a place to hide," Dino whispered. "Alberto's about to explode."

"Mom," he shouted out clearly in his childish voice from directly over Anita's head. "Why are you calling him Prince? I thought his name was Headhunter?"

Prince Kudzu slowly laid down his knife and spoon, his smiling face slowly wrinkled.

"Alberto," said Anita sternly, though she was looking not at Alberto. She was looking at Dino as if this were in some way his doing, "go to bed this minute." She turned facing Prince Kudzu. Her voice was regretful, but not apologetic. "I hope you'll forgive him, he's a very foolish young man."

"Madam," said Prince Kudzu, "these past days I have become insulated from insults from white people, of all ages."

Silence returned to the table, this time not broken even by Anita, Prince Kudzu glanced defiantly around. Chief Koala, who knew too little Portuguese to understand what was being said, continued to stare straight ahead. Every once in a while, he lifted his hand to calm the twitching muscle in his face. Satan was mopping gravy from his plate with maize-bread. Trinity with equal vigor was wiping his mouth with his handkerchief. Dominique's attention was fixed on the gold dust *kente cloth* shirt; only Dino met Prince Kudzu's stare.

Have some beef?" Dino asked cheerfully.

"No, thank you," said Prince Kudzu. Beads of perspiration flowed from his forehead. "I know what you think. You have taught even your babies to hate us. This crime that you charge me with, let's talk about it. Colonel Figueroa, if you were invading any part of Europe, and we offered you our support

38

Yolanda The Enchantress

would you accept it?"

"You're damned right I would." Said Dino.

"You are the first honest white man I have met this side of the Yoruba River," said Prince Kudzu.

Anita gasped as if she had been struck. She sprung up, her angry eyes turned first at Prince Kudzu and then at her husband. Her face was pale except for a faint trace of color above her cheekbones. "Honest, you call that honest," she cried. "Dino Figueroa, I'd sooner see you hanged, as you very likely would be if you were caught collaborating with a them, as any Portiguse soldier should be who dared to turn those murders loose on our people."

Prince Kudzu rose eagerly, smiling as he confronted Anita. "Thank you madam for your plain honest speaking, I welcome the opportunity to give an equally plain, honest answer. Would you hang Portuguese soldiers that have inflicted suffering on their enemy? Or have you forgotten the first duty of a soldier. Or purpose of war, in fact, is to inflict suffering on your enemy? Do you agree or not, when our witch doctors or one of your doctors remove a leg. It is less painful if the cut is done quickly?"

"All my life I've heard soldiers talk," said Anita, breathing hard, "Nobody thinks like a good soldier, but so often they are wrong. Right or wrong, war is war and war never changes. Its only purpose is to kill."

Dino nudged Dominique's leg under the table, watching his wife's eyes brightened. "Well," he said, getting to his feet, "I think we've talked enough tonight. Prince Kudzu, I don't have to tell you, we're kind of   crowded here in this house. It would be safer if you sleep here by the fireplace along side Dominique, or in the stable with your warriors?"

"The stable," said Prince Kudzu. "I've had enough of your hospitality." He bowed to Anita. "For which I hope you will believe me. I'm deeply grateful."

Captain Satan and Lieutenant Trinity walked out with their prisoners. Dino smiled at Anita, and winked at Dominique. "It's good you're staying the night with us. If it wasn't for your company, Anita would be arguing all night."

"Takes more than a wagging' tong to straighten out a man," said Anita. She placed her hands on her hips and leaned forward looking at the pile of dirty dishes. "A man thinks he can say whatever he wants, because he can swing an ax harder and lift a heavier load, but sometime he doesn't understand right from wrong." A speck of gravy was on her cheek. "But right or wrong, he has to be a man or what good is he to you?"

She began to clean and stack the dishes. Dino and Dominique sat at the table and smoking their pipes.

"I'd like to change the subject," said Dominique.

"Go ahead," said Dino. "Anita will be keeping me up all night for the next few days, telling me what she thinks."

"That's right," said Anita. "The only time you will have any piece is when the children are asleep. Now I'd like to hear what Dominique has to say. He's had something on his mind all day."

Dominique glanced at Anita as she continued stacking dishes. "I heard today about some people in Eagle Landing, that's looking for land in Congo Basin," he said.

Both Dino, and Anita were interested, as he knew they would be.

"What kind of people?" Dino asked.

"A very wealthy family that farms five or six hundred acres. They had about six hundred cows, thirty to forty horses, nearly twenty camels, two big elephants, and one-hundred-eighty to two hundred slaves." He could tell without looking how Dino felt. So substantial and important family would be a great addition to any Congo settlement.

"Where are they planning on locating?"

"One of the sons is coming out this summer to look along Lake Tanganyika."

"Plenty of good land there," said Dino. "But mighty easy for Pygmies and Bantu savages to attack you on Lake Tanganyika. But to near the Yoruba River, all they have to do is cross the lake, and come down Elephant Trail, and they're in your backyard." Dominique listened. Dino brushed his beard nervously. "They should look for land around here before making up their minds. There's a nice piece over the hill near Zebra Valley that's better than any I've seen on Lake Tanganyika. They'll be much better off here."

Dominique agreed. "I think they would."

40

Yolanda The Enchantress

"Will you see them when you go there?"

"I might!"

"If you do, tell them off they'd be here."

"I don't know them that well," said Dominique. "You have to know people real well to give them advice, or not know them at all."

Dino grunted regretfully. "Well, you know best. They sound like the kind of people we need here."

"You could write them a letter telling them about your place here and the kind of land they could expect, and I'll make sure they get the letter."

"That's a good idea," said Dino. "Anita, see if there's any of that letter writing paper left." Anita was no longer in the room. "Anita," he called. When she came back, she had paper, pen, and ink-horn in her hand. Dino glanced at her suspiciously.

Anita smiled. She pushed aside the dishes and sat down at the table. "Tell me what you want to say. I'll write it down." she glanced at Dominique and said, "Dominique will deliver it."

"Address it to Legacy Gomez," said Dominique, "He's the oldest the brothers."

He didn't have to worry about what Anita was thinking. It was when he got to the Gomez plantation he had to be careful. At least, with this letter in his pocket, he had an excuse to ride up to her door.

Chapter 3
Burgle Ferry Crossing

Leaving Figueroa Station, African people called this hostel region, of brush-covered slopes, vine-choked gorges, snakes, monkey's, huge cats, and untamed mountains full of gorillas and baboons. *Africans called it "Congo Road." White people called it "Dead Mans Journey,"* because it was the only way to get to the settlements beyond Eagle Landing. The road was a narrow game trail that ran for miles through the jungle. An accidental linking of ancient elephant and rhinoceros trails. When riding camels or horses you had to ride single file. The road was no better now than when the first Portuguese trackers first traveled it.

Africans traveled it for thousands of years before the first white man arrived. For three hundred miles they climbed rocky ridges where storms howled. They dropped into soggy bottoms where bamboo grew twenty feet high, nearly as thick as small trees. The trail surged between and around huge trees covered with vines. Colorful birds flew from trees again and again.

The flowing rivers could only be crossed by swimming, or on rafts. Anybody who knew Congo Road, or had heard of it, traveled it with a special dread. It was a region where any kind of problem could be expected; a misstep could mean a fall from a cliff. A horse or camel's stumble could mean a broken leg, or any thicket could mean danger.

This was a party of soldiers, Dominique, each day scouted the trail miles ahead. From time to time he found African signs or footprints, but no sign of Africans in numbers large enough to fight with Novas' experienced veterans. He enjoyed the hard and lonely going; it gave him time to think. When traveling through dangerous country you had to think about what you might be walking into. Now they were heading for country more dangerous than Congo Road, because of the danger they couldn't spend scouts ahead into Santiago Cacao to let them know what to expect.

Since hearing about old man Mendoza he realized he couldn't hang around after he arrived to think about what he was about to do. When he reached his destination, he had to keep going. The letter would take him only to the door. After that, there was the possibility, which he didn't want to think about. Eighteen years was a long time. By now she could be fat or sickly or the mother of a half dozen children. If this were so all he could do was walk away. If so he would return to Novas and be in good soldier.

For days, the peace and calm was unnatural along Congo Road. Soldiers and prisoners faces brightened with every step they took because they were leaving the jungle. Every step they took they moved closer to Eagle Landing.

The bad luck they expected on Congo Road caught up

Yolanda The Enchantress

with them, at Gun Road. Colonel Domingo San Diego had come from Nova Gala settlement. He was waiting at the fork of the road to take command of the detachment for the rest of the journey. As the tired column straggled in off the trail to the campsite he was shouting his first command: Fall in." The confused, disgusted men pushed and elbowed into a semblance of company formation.

"What's wrong with you? Haven't you stood in formation before?" The colonel inspected them with a disapproving faultfinding eye. "Have you forgotten you're soldiers, damn-it, from now on you'll remember."

All evening Captain Satan moved from fire to fire, trying to comfort his tired men. "Be careful." someone said. He's from a wealthy, very influential family in Portugal with powerful folks in Nova Gala settlement. They are determined to make him the governor of Congo settlements. He thinks he can get greater recognition from the politicians in Eagle Landing, if he marches into Guam Land with the Headhunter and bunch of African warriors in chains. But nobody's going to forget that it was Novas that captured them."

From the moment the headstrong young military officer took over it made quite a different. He often remembered that he was a lieutenant, and his military experience at its best was family connections, all the way back to Portugal. He valued his own judgment so much above any other man's, a year ago; in the course of a difference of opinion over defense plans, he assembles a formal court in order to drop charges against his friend and neighbor. Francisco Serene, who had suddenly, became a friend, and defender of local Africans'.

Now he was refusing to listen to any suggestions of Captain Satan, or the complaints of the men. He continued to insist on the most rigid military formality, despite the fact that they were deep in the jungle. So deep that an unarmed prisoner would starve or be killed by a hungry animal if he escaped. In fact, some prisoners and soldiers were so frightened of the dark, dense jungle they couldn't be driven away. The stubborn colonel required a full complement of pickets at every campsite; soldiers of the escort who had marched on foot all day were forced to stand guard all night.

L. A. Johnson Jr.

"Only the strong will survive," San Diego bellowed. Men preformed their duties reluctantly, they argued over the slightest thing. Domingo San Diego had bought with him bad weather, and an unpredictable temper. The mild tropical weather turned stormy and cool. Huge drops of rain blinded them, and frost covered their blankets at night. They struggled out of rivers with their clothing soaked with mud. Men got sick. Their boots were wet and their feet were swelled, slowing their progress, and because of the slow pace their rations ran out.

All welcome the moment when they came out of the jungle at Lions Din. This was open country along the Niger River. They saw houses, barns, fenced fields and well-kept orchards. Here settlers had lived in peace for many years. Yet even here their troubles hadn't lessened; they were different. Though miles from the fighting the inhabitants here were more hostile to the prisoners than the people of Congo Basin.

The Niger River settlers were eager to lavish acclaim and their hospitality upon the soldiers of Novas' army. They were as equally eager to show their hate to the Masai and Nikola prisoners. People were so hostile to the African warriors they didn't offer them a crumb of bread or a drop of water. At every settlement there were riots; the soldiers had to fight the crowd to protect their prisoners.

Dominique paid little attention to their many trials, but San Diego relished the brawls. He didn't care if the prisoners were hungry or not. Dominique was occupied with his concerns, he was thinking about the moment he would reach the Gomez mansion. He could foresee the welcoming interest the letter would assure him, but he could also picture himself arriving in his weather-beaten clothing, looking like a good-for-nothing soldier, that drifted back and forth out of the jungle every season. He imagined that he would be welcomed and treated kindly, only, because of the letter. He didn't want to be bedded, and fed out back somewhere with their slaves.

From what he remembered of the road ahead, there wasn't a store on this side of Santiago Cacao Settlement, where he could buy clothes that might pass, even in a pinch. He could go to Guam Land first, but he was too impatient for that. A new set of clothing wasn't what he wanted. He would be better off wearing his old weather-beaten uniform, than to make the Go-mez family think he had dressed up to impress them. More and more his mind kept drifting on two garments he had seen two men wearing at Dino's house. He knew they were neatly packed in the baggage. Major Octavos Vega, breeches, and Prince Amid Kudzu's shirt. They might not want to sell them, no matter how much he offered. He didn't want to pay more than they were worth, either. He needed Mario's advice. Mario had worked for an ivory trader when he was young; he always knew the right price to pay for things.

Mario understood immediately, and took an immediate interest. "It'll be better if you let me do your bargaining," he said. "You'll pay too much. Or if they don't want to sell, you'll make them angry, and you'll achieve nothing."

He had approached Mario while they were still in the jungle during the worst of the storm. That same night when he returned to camp Mario had the pants. They looked new but not too new. Dominique was very pleased with them. He folded them carefully, and wrapped them in an oiled impala skin to keep them dry, and put them in his backpack.

"How much?"

"Nothin'."

Dominique started taking it out of his backpack. "You stole them," he said.

Mario laughed. "I meant no money Octavos been cold the last few nights, so cold he couldn't sleep. I traded that orange copper blanket you bought from that Xhosa warrior when we were in South Africa for the pants."

The blanket was bulky and heavy, he never used it, and Dominique was satisfied. He always rolled up in his military blanket when it was cold. He was glad to get rid of that heavy old blanket. The only reason he had kept it so long was because Dino liked it so much.

The next night they camped at Servile Valley, Mario waited until they were alone. He made sure they weren't being watched, and handed him a watch. It had a heavy gold case, a loud thick, and a gold crest on the back, a very expensive piece of jewelry. "A mighty good-looking' watch!" said Mario.

"That's San Diego's watch. What are you doing' with his

watch?"

"Not San Diego's anymore," said Mario. "It's yours now."

"Mine? I don't need a watch."

"It's what you need. A nice watch makes a man look important. Like clothing' that's hasn't been wrapped and pressed, is like, like keeping' the same old dingy uniform on. People like them expect you to look a certain way. You're saying you have made it, and you have nothing' to worry about when you wear jewelry like that. Ever notice how San Diego was always taking it out to look at it? When you take out a piece of jewelry like that people notice."

"How much?"

"Fifty escudos, and its worth twice that. Solid gold mounted with precious stones. Look at the embroidery on the crown and on the back. And every hour she plays a tune to let you know what time it is, even in the dark."

Dominique continued to stare at Mario. "How did you get it from San Diego? That stuck-up prick would never deal with a common soldier like you."

"I didn't buy it from him. Captain Satan bought it from San Diego for me." Mario was disturbed by Dominique's lack of enthusiasm. "If you don't want it, give it back. In Guam Land I can get twice that amount for it."

Dominique looked at the watch again. He liked the feel of it in his hand. He had never owned jewelry this valuable.

"No," he said. "I'll keep it, but get this into your head. Don't come up with any more ideas about what you think I should have; now all I want is that shirt."

Mario sulked for a while but by the next day his interest was stronger than before. More than a went by without Mario making any effort to approach Prince Kudzu.

"I have to wait for the right moment," Mario explained. "He's been tied up and gagged most of the time, and he's been threw than any of us. He's a proud man. He doesn't want to show up in Guam Land in dirty clothing'. At this moment, he wouldn't give his only shirt to his mother, if she were naked." The night they reached Port Amboy near the Niger River, Mario placed the shirt on Dominique's shoulder.

Yolanda The Enchantress

"How did you get it?"

"By waiting' for the right moment."

"When was that?"

"When he got angry enough?"

"What made him that angry?"

"Watching'. Watching' his men starve while the rest of us had more than we could eat. San Diego did what he could; he tried to get people to give a little more, but every time Prince Kudzu complained about his men not being fed. San Diego told him, he wasn't going' to spend a dime to buy food for, head hunting prisoners. So Prince Kudzu decided to buy food for them himself, but the settlers wouldn't deal with him, or any African. That's when he got mad enough to sell me his shirt, and I agreed to buy the food he needed."

"How much?"

"One hundred escudos. That's more than the shirt's worth. I made the deal because I knew you wanted it."

Dominique put the shirt into his backpack. Now on he had nothing to worry about except, how slowly the column marched. They walked on well-traveled game trails; still they made no better time than in the jungle.

May passed, now it was early June. The weather turned then hot, and prisoners were hungry. Their feet were sore and swollen. Suddenly the prisoners refused to be hurried. Mario was taking advantage of the slow pace. Whenever off duty he visited farms along the road to look at elephant's camel's burros and horses.

"I'm not going to buy 'em yet," he told Dominique. "I just want to see what they have for sale, and, the prices they're asking'. You don't know what you can buy with Portuguese money anymore, its worth less every day."

"If you happen to see an Arabian stallion for forty or fifty escudos," said Dominique. "Buy it for me. When we reach our destination I'm going to show my discharge papers to San Diego and pull out. I'll need a horse or a camel."

At Fort Kalahari, Mario returned to camp riding a young Arabian mare. She was a ruddy-colored bay with a white blaze and four white hairy hooves, she moved as gracefully as if she were a feather drifting on a gentle breeze.

47

L. A. Johnson Jr.

"I see you have found an old mare to lead your camel caravan." said Dominique.

"Nope," said Mario. "She's too fancy for me. I bought her for you. What do you think of her?"

"Not bad."

"She's the best mare I've ever seen," said Mario.

"How much?"

"Try her," said Mario. "You've never set on a horse that moves like she does."

"How much?"

"She's just turned three and she hasn't a blemish on her. Look at her quarters. She's really built."

"How much?"

"Two hundred and fifty escudos-saddle-and bridle thrown in."

"Silver coins."

"Real escudos."

"Take her back."

"Whatever you wish," said Mario. "I thought when you went to see that woman you'd want to ride up on something that's nice." He dismounted and handed Dominique the reins. "Hold her a minute. Before I take her back I want San Diego to see her, he's been looking for a good horse."

The horse took a step nearer to Dominique and sniffed at his shirtsleeve. She had been gently raised. She didn't shy when he lifted a hand to stroke her neck. She was wide in the chest and wide between the eyes and her nostrils were large enough to take in plenty of air when she needed to. Everything about her was right. She moved nearer, with her ears forward and nudged his shoulder.

"What's her name?" asked Dominique.

"People that raised her named her Brandy. If she was mine, I would call her Ruddy."

"I like Ruddy better than Brandy," said Dominique.

The next morning as he was saddling her Captain Satan walked over. "A beautiful horse," he said, looking her at the mare favorably. "Like a chance to try her out? Ride ahead to Burgle Ferry Crossing and tell them we'll be there before dust. Pueblo Plato likes to take good care of people passing through,

48

he'll be disappointed if we don't tell him, we are coming so that he can prepare."

Trying out Ruddy was a pleasure. Her gait was smooth. She liked to gallop, and she had no bad habits, and when he let her out she flew like an eagle. Her swift fluent movements, after weeks of tramping through the jungle most of the time on foot, convinced him. Traveling alone on this horse he could reach Santiago Coca in six days, seven at the most. Staying with the detachment would take him a month to getting that far downs the Ubangi. Now that they were well into Eagle Landing the scouts were no longer needed. Tomorrow he would leave the army and go on ahead.

He found things had changed at Burgle Ferry Crossing since he had last come through here going the other way. The original Plato home was now a large mansion on a huge plantation. It was surrounded with orchards, barns, hundreds of acres of maize, rice and, even tiny spice gardens had been planted. His place had a huge well-manicured lawn in front of the front porch. Down the road there was a tavern and a general store.

Fifty yards from the ferry, there were huge stables for travelers who were driving their overloaded wagons up and down Jungle Road as if it were the highway between Guam Land and Gulf of Guinea. Pueblo Plato was one of the first early settlers who had grown and prospered with this country.

The man who told Dominique where to find Pueblo Plato said, Plato's businesses were grossing more than ten thousand dollars a month. But no matter how well Plato was doing he had paid for being the first to build here thirty years ago when this section of the country was no safer than Congo Basin was now.

His wife has never been the same since she got back after the Lozi carried her off, and two of her half-breed children died in captivity and another was found, crippled after years of searching. Mr. Plato remembered Dominique at once, from the time he and Novas stopped at his general store to purchase some rifles. He was intensely interested in what Dominique had to say. Having done his share of African fighting his main interest, unlike most, was not in the Masai or Nikola prisoners, he wanted to know about the men who'd captured them.

"Novas attacked the Masai village so fast Prince Kudzu

49

was still sleeping on his palm mat," he was thinking. "Can't blame the Masai for not counting on an army wading through miles of crocodile infested water to get him. We haven't had much good news lately; news like this is welcome. One thing I don't understand. You say you didn't have a rifle with you, but they had spears bows and arrows, and over a hundred-fifty warriors in the village. What made them give up without a fight?"

This was Dominique's first chance to talk to some-body that hadn't heard about Mozambique and it was a pleasure. "When we approached the village it was mid-night, he said. "When it got light, Novas ordered them to surrender; he talked and acted like he had the whole Portuguese army with him. He gave Prince Kudzu thirty minutes to make up his mind. While we were waiting something happened that helped. A group of Bushmen, Pygmies, and Masai warriors were returning from Congo Basin with heads on long poles, nudging white prisoners. Instead of the big reception they were counting on they walked blindly into our army. Novas had them beaten and kicked viciously in their heads in front of main entrance to the village. After that Prince Kudzu stopped arguing about terms and surrendered."

"That Paulo Dais de Novas, he's a man you don't play with," said Plato. "I remember the last time he came through here; he was on the way to talk to some important people down there in Gangland to ask them to send help to Congo Basin. He had only one man with him, that man was you. He knew the people out there were nearly out of gunpowder, but listening to him you'd think he already had the Masai in chains. Come in and shove your feet under my table."

"Mrs. Plato's troubled eyes didn't brighten as she listened to the news, but when their three daughters ran in to learn who was coming they were as excited as their father about planning an appropriate welcome.

"We'll barbecue a pig," said Plato. "One of you run tell Nero to butcher and season a buffalo right away. Roseann, get, Dominion and Leonardo. Have them ride up and down the river and let everybody know soldiers are coming with prisoners. They'll all want to be here."

Yolanda The Enchantress

The girls were already planning the party; they wanted to do something special. They had their own ideas.

"We'll have the slaves sweep and scrub the floors in the big red barn, there will be more room there to dance, Francisco Brunt's working at Thousands Oaks, we'll get him, he's the best banjo picker in this country, remember him at Angela Lair's wedding. We'll send for Tony Columbia to do the calling, nobody can call like he can. And we'll set up tables under the arbor and hang lanterns along the trellis...and...."

"I'll get a barrel of rum and whiskey from the tavern," said Pueblo. "Get a jug of wine for those that don't like rum or whiskey." He turned to Dominique, "Tell Colonel San Diego to lock his prisoners in the stables down by the ferry. We'll count on him and his officers and that headhunting Prince Kudzu. I think he should eat in the main house with us, and we'll want everybody in your outfit here to eat and drink and dance with the women. We'll let all of you how we feel about you."

"Pull up a chair," said Mrs. Plato to Dominique.

While the others had been talking she was taking canned and dried food from her pantry. On the table before Dominique was a platter piled with thick slices of baked gazelle, buttered wheat bread, and a bowl of wild berries. Mrs. Plato poured a cup of fresh cream over the berries.

"You get hungry when you are traveling'. Here's something' to hold you until supper."

"Since Mrs. Plato got so hungry in the jungle when she escaped from Lozi," said Pueblo, as casually as if she were not in the room, "she likes to see people eat." Pueblo and the girls left the house.

Mrs. Plato watched Dominique eat without expression; she watched each bite he took until he had finished, some time forgetting his presence.

He rode south along the road to a meadow with a stream running through it. He unsaddled Ruddy, rubbed her down, and turned her out to graze. He took a leisurely refreshing swim in the stream and slept under a bush. It might be a while, Dominique thought, after having such a peaceful afternoon.

"That's mighty nice of Pueblo Plato," said Colonel San Diego, when Dominique told him of the reception they were

51

planning. "Ride back and tell him we'll be pleased to eat with him."

The men at the head of the column pass the word back and a ripple of cheers traveled with the news, suddenly the stern military frown returned to San Diego's face. "Which squad goes to the party and who guards the prisoners "You and Lieutenant Trinity deside," he said to Captain Satan,

Galloping towards the village Dominique heard the distant ringing of a hammer on an anvil. It was a welcome sound, because Ruddy was barefoot, if she wore shoes she would walk better during the hard riding that was to begin tomorrow. After leaving word at the Plato house that the column was near he rode towards the sound of the hammering.

Around a bend in the road beyond the tavern, there was a log fence. A blockhouse and a section of the back wall was still standing in front of the fence. A small stone house and rows of outbuildings now occupied the rest of the site. Under a shed near the center stood a forge at which two gigantic young, Wagnerian, slaves poked into the bed of glowing coals with tongs, lifted a iron grating, and placed it on the anvil and continued their hammering. Both were naked above the waist and perspiration poured from them in streams over their tall muscular bodies.

They lifted the heavy iron grating as if it were no heavier than a twig. Between the ringing and sudden strokes of their hammers they talked to each other in some strange tongue. Neither of them spoke or glanced at him, he was beginning to get annoyed. Finally the hammering stopped and with that same graceful ease as before, they placed the grating back onto the fire. One of the young men began to work the bellows, the other walked over to Dominique. Standing erect his height was even more impressive, towering over Dominique at least six inches he looked down directly into Dominique eyes without any of the uneasiness usual in enslaved Africans addressing a white man.

"May I help you sir?" he inquired.

"Can you shoe my horse?" asked Dominique.

"Yes sir. I'd be proud to. First thing in the morning." His speech was proper and direct.

"I'll be leaving first thing in the morning." said Dominique.

Yolanda The Enchantress

The giant looked past Dominique at Ruddy. He shook his head regretfully. "We promised that grating to a man who's waiting over at the tavern, he's taking it with him tonight. It will take my brother and me until dark to finish this job." His regret seemed genuine. "If you really need it, ask my father." He glanced at the door of an adjoining building. "He rarely shoes any more. If you ask him he might help you."

"Thank you," said Dominique. For a second he had forgotten that he was talking to a slave, leaving Ruddy Dominique walked over to the open door. The father of the young African giants was bent over a rifle barrel locked in a vise on a gunsmith's bench. A thin rope running through the barrel was kept taut with a strong stick; he was sighting along it to get an accurate line on the bore. All Dominique could see of him was his broad back across which his white cotton shirt was stretched.

"Can you shoe my horse?" asked Dominique.

The man turned and straightened, removing his thick spectacles to look at Dominique. He was taller and wider in the chest and shoulder than his sons. The same dignity, strength, and intelligence that had been bread in his sons were in him. Every line of his powerful dignified face screamed that he was aware that he had found his place in this settlement and that he was equal to any man. In his deep-set, brown haunting eyes, revealed spark of his ancestors'; his manner were that of a king. Even the remaining black and gray specks on his balding head made him look even more distinguished.

He walked over to the door and looked past Dominique, staring at the horse. Again he glanced at Dominique.

"When I finished straightening the barrels," he said. He looked at a bench against the wall outside the door. "Make yourself comfortable while you wait."

"My name is Dominique de Salvo," said Dominique.

"They call me Jumbo."

"Please to meet you, Jumbo."

Dominique unsaddled and unbridled Ruddy, and tied her to the hitching post and sat down on the bench. By the time he had smoke his pipe the head of the column appeared in the bend of the road, marching at a faster pace. The prisoners must have guessed that even for them there might be something to eat.

L. A. Johnson Jr.

Dominique walked to the edge of the road. Colonel San Diego was not in his usual position out front. Dominique pulled Mario out of line.

"Where's San Diego?"

"He stopped at the Plato mansion. Didn't expect to see you here, both times you rode off ahead today, I thought you'd keep right on going."

"No reason to sneak off when all I have to do is tell Colonel San Diego I'm finished," said Dominique. "I'm leaving in the morning. How long are you staying?"

"Just a little longer. I'm looking for horses and camels along the road. I'll let the army paid me while I'm looking."

Dominique walked back and found Jumbo examining his horses' feet.

"I'd like to see her gait," said Jumbo.

Dominique mounted her bareback and put the mare through her paces up and down the yard. Jumbo nodded and went to work. Whether or not he was the best gunsmith in Beguiler Ferry Crossing he was certainly the best horseman. Dominique told him, then paid him and saddled, then led Ruddy out to the edge of the road. Never having had shoes on before she was confused; she kept shaking her feet.

The warm spring evening was growing dark. People were streaming past on their way to the Plato's party. Families from miles around were riding in, men were shouting out greeting to friends, their wives and daughters smiling and chattering. A bright orange moon slowly climbed over the ridge, and from up the road came the sound of a banjo and a fiddler. They started playing "old Portuguese songs." It was the same dance tune Dominique had heard, the night of Linda's wedding. Again it seemed to taunt him.

So fine a moonlit night could better be spent on the road than staying here. He swung into the saddle, stroked the mare and watched her prance around on her new iron shoes, then straightened her out. There was no reason to stay any longer. He had to find San Diego and be on his way. The Plato's yard was filled with people eating and talking, though some of the younger people were dancing in the barn. The officers and the Plato family were in the mansion eating. Impatient as he was, this wasn't a good enough reason to interrupt the Plato family's dinner. He pushed through the crowd around the rum, and whiskey barrels, and pored himself a drink. The burning tingling sensation had hardly started to cool in his throat when a group of people came out of the Plato's back door to dance, laughing and talking, towards the barn. In the shadows he saw Captain Satan and the older Plato girl but he didn't see Colonel San Diego. Captain Satan stopped near the barbecue pit to light his pipe. Dominique went over to him.

"San Diego's still in the house?" asked Dominique

"Why do you want to see San Diego?"

"To tell him, I'm leaving."

"Satan laughed. "You don't need to see him for that, unless you want to kiss him good-by. He's known about your discharge, and Mario's, since the day he took command." He put out his hand. "All you have to do is shake hands with me and leave." He gripped Dominique's hand. "Hope you'll return to the regiment next spring, and bring Mario with you." He slapped Dominique on the back and walked toward the barn.

Dominique had everything settled in his mind since leaving Mozambique, in Eagle Landing he would get out of the army. Yet now when the separation came, it made him feel uneasy. He had a surprisingly odd feeling, pleasurable enough, but disturbing to realize that he was completely released from the army. For years he hadn't been able to come and go as he pleased. Now he could. His first impulse was to get on his horse and start riding. This was his first moment of freedom, as he turned to go, he saw her.

Liana was coming out of the mansion, she stepped into the light cast from the lanterns hanging above her head, dangling from the arbor and stood. She wasn't more than ten feet from him glancing around the yard looking for someone. Then she saw him and for a second she was startled. He stared and hoped; during that second it was he she was looking for. Then she looked past him, and left the circle of light and walked towards the barn. He stood still, too stunned to go after her. He was surprise to find her here, a hundred miles from Santiago Coca County. He was too busy thinking about how she looked. She looked exactly as he'd remembered. She didn't look much older except for the body of a full-grown woman. That alluring glance she still had, but she had lost that shy smile of a young girl. The red tint in her glossy, reddish, brown hair, made her hair look silky. The spark in her brown eyes was still there. The white softness of her skin looked softer than ever, the shape of her face; everything was just as he'd remembered.

When he looked around to see where she had gone she was standing in the shadows cast from the light in the barn doorway, talking to Mr. Plato. A fight had started over by the rum barrel. Mr. Plato left her and rushed towards it. Dominique approached grabbing his arm.

"The woman over there, the one you were talking to...."

"Know her?" asked Plato, oddly interest.

"She looks like someone I once knew," said Dominique.

"Funny," said Mr. Plato. "She had the same feeling when she saw you, but she couldn't remember where. I told her your name, that didn't mean anything to her."

"Why is she here?"

She's a friend of my daughters. Wait until I break up that fight, I'll take you over and introduce you to her."

Dominique didn't wait. He didn't want anyone to introduce him to her. She had noticed him talking to Plato and she was coming. She took a few steps forward to meet them, and she was beginning to smile politely. Then the thought of the letter crossed his mind, the pocket watch, and the printed shirt, the pants, all tucked away neatly in his backpack. It was too late now for any preparations. The moment had come, as so often in battle without warning, h-e walked towards her.

Chapter 4
Who Are You

She was looking intently up into his eyes, giving him a chance to study her.

"I rarely approach strangers," she said. "I mentioned to Mr. Plato that I'd seen you somewhere, but I didn't think he would tell you."

Yolanda The Enchantress

She must have learned years ago that with most men she could pretend to be interested as she was doing now. Her voice was calm, low keyed, yet harsh lending to each word an odd note of importance.

"I've seen you before," he said, "Do you remember me?"

"Do you?"

"Perhaps we should forget the past and start over again. That other time if there was one, couldn't have amounted to much."

"Then I'd better remember, where and when."

"She had been on guard from the instant he started to speak. She had been startled, not so much by what he had said but by the way he said it. Since he was one of Novas men she treated him as a military hero, but she didn't expect from him the manner that placed him on an equal status with her. That was the problem with meeting a stranger on the road from Congo Basin. You couldn't tell by sight weather he was just another country-boy or a gentleman like Dino Figueroa, Major Conti or Novas. They would be carrying the same kind of rifle and game bag and wearing the same old stained military uniform. Tonight he was really better off by far, than if he would have been if he had dressed in his new clothes.

People moving back and forth through the barn doorway were shoving them. Standing between the dancing and the barrel of rum in the yard. He took her hand and steered her towards a bench under the big incense tree at the end of the arbor. The warmth of her hand surged through his skin.

"Eighteen years ago," he was saying, "were you on a ladder picking mangroves behind a stone fence fifty yards from the road, wearing a dress almost the same color as the one you have on, and the ladder started to tip?"

"It's your story. Isn't it?"

"It is, but what I remember, that girl's hair was red. Or perhaps it was the summer before at a place on the Nile below Gorilla Mountain where your camel stepped in a hole, and threw you into the river; you hung your clothes on a lime tree that had fallen near a curve in the road?"

They stopped beside a bench. She didn't sit down.

"What happened next? Tell me you don't remember."

L. A. Johnson Jr.

"Please sit down. I'll remember where I saw you." She shook her head. "You're trying to hard."

"Give me a minute. I've seen you somewhere."

"Well, you are not making much progress. First you pretend one thing-but you can't remember what or where."

"Its not that you look like somebody else, I've seen you somewhere. Don't worry; I'll remember where and when, any minute."

"You'll probably remember later." She was starting to leave.

"Just one more chance. I remember something. Do you have a small brown spot below your waist on the right side, if I remember, on your hip?"

She sat down with a gasp. "Who are you?" she said.

He sat beside her. "My name is Dominique de Salvo," he said. "I...."

"How could you have know," she broke in, "about that, that, that spot?" He smiled. "Perhaps, I've gotten you mixed up with someone else. Lots of women have small spots one place or another."

"Answer me," she insisted.

"Something to drink," asked Dominique. He stood. "Don't leave."

"Don't worry," said Liana.

He came back with two mugs of rum.

"Want some water?" saked Dominique.

She shook her head and swallowed the drink with one big gulp.

"Now," she said.

He sat down beside her again, taking her empty mug and placed it on the ground. Then he leaned back against the incense tree, and watched her in the deepest of thought making her feel very uncomfortable.

"This moment, reminds me of when Novas first reached Mozambique," he said. "He didn't have enough men or guns to take the village. So he had to make Prince Kudzu do what he wanted him to do."

"I can't imagine what you're trying to make me do, or remember, if that's what you're trying to do. I sat beside Prince

Yolanda The Enchantress

Kudzu at supper tonight. It's hard to understand that man."

"Prince Kudzu's not so bad. Remember we've taken his country."

"He's a bloodthirsty man, and tonight I was glad to give him something else to think about. He asked me what was wrong with Mrs. Plato. I told him! I told him there was nothing wrong with her except she couldn't stop thinking; thinking of a baby she had by one of his people. They weren't his people.

They Africans; Africans burned her house and carried her off; and when she had a chance to get away from them, she got away but she couldn't take her baby, she had to leave her child behind if she wanted to see her husband again."

Dominique looked at her with new interest. "Is that what you would have done?"

"Of course, if I had a man as good as she had waiting for her. Just like Melanie Plato, I wouldn't be able to stop thinking about my child. For heavens sake, how did we get on this subject?"

"I was telling you about Novas and Kudzu."

"Instead of answering my question."

"About the spot?"

"Yes."

"That's what I was trying to say. I was telling I was in the same fix Novas was. I led the platoon that captures those Bushmen returning to his village."

"That's not an answer, to my question."

"He shook his head regretfully. "Perhaps you are making more of this than you should, think of the most common, ordinary answer that could be."

"For example." asked Liana

"Well, like I said at first it could have been just a guest, or I could have heard one of the Plato women mention it."

"Then why mention it at all?" she said.

"I had to say something. If I hadn't you would have been polite, and that would have been the end of a more interesting conversation. Now we're beginning to get acquainted."

"Pretend you are Novas and I am Kudzu. What village are you trying to take?"

"Right now I'm just observing."

59

"I'm sure of one thing. We have never spoken to each other before tonight, because I wouldn't have forgotten a man that says so many annoying things."

She stood. He rose and stood beside her, fighting off an impulse to grab her arms to keep her from leaving. Then suddenly she began to laugh. He watched her thoughtfully.

"How can you stand there looking so solemn?" she smiled. "Don't you. Don't you understand what is so funny?"

"Depends on what or who you are laughing at." He said.

"Myself, of course. You are a romantic good-for-nothing soldier. A charmer, you prey on innocent women. It was that crossing my mind, which made me laugh. Here I stand long since married and widowed, becoming an old woman. Look at the pleasure you've given me tonight. *Who are you? Where did you come from?*" she demanded

"I told you. My name is Dominique de Salvo."

"*Please* don't repeat that again." She said.

At that moment over her shoulder he saw a pale, blond young man. He was tall and thin, remarkably hand-some in spite of his eerie green eyes and puffy cheeks, dressed with unique elegance in a brown waistcoat and a silk shirt. He was slapping his leg with a riding crop while prowling with nervous impatience through the crowd, searching for someone. Then he caught sight of Liana and headed towards the incense tree.

"Is he looking for you?" asked Dominique.

Liana turned. "Monty!" she exclaimed. "He's looking for me." She ran to the man and into his outstretched arms. The man didn't seem even a little curious about Liana's companion. Keeping an arm around her he pulled her with him into a slow strolled along the perimeter of the arbor away from Dominique. He was telling her something that Dominique couldn't hear, but he heard her reply. "Really, Monty!" She said, "Wait, I'll get my shawl." She was turning towards the mansion. It was obvious that the good will that he had been building had taken a sudden turn for the worst; He walked over to join them.

"I'm still here," he said.

Liana turned to face him. "So you are," she said. "How could I have forgotten? Monty, this is Dominique de Salvo, one of Colonel Novas' men. Mr. de Salvo my brother, Monty."

Yolanda The Enchantress

She said, to Monty, "I'm certain it was with Novas that he learned to be so impulsive."

"Can't blame you, Mr. de Salvo, you have to take control of the situation or she'll control you. If you don't she'll run over you." Said Monty; Unexpectedly friendly.

"Very disappointed, you taking her away," said Dominique.

"We've met somewhere before and we were just beginning to figure out where and when it was."

Mr. de Salvo's imagination is most unusual," said Liana hastily. "Monty if Legacy just got here he's had a long day. I'll ride out first thing in the morning."

"Good enough," agreed Monty. He glanced at Dominique with a spark of new interest. He kissed Liana and nodded to Dominique, "Best of luck to you." There was a gleam in his eye as he said it. He rushed across the yard with that same air of nervous impatience he had when approaching.

"I concede," said Liana, "you have won the first battle."

"No," said Dominique. "Only a skirmish."

One thing he could see. She was fond of her brothers. He remembered how often in the old days she had ridden past the general store to visit Legacy. Tonight she was here with him, her hand on his hand, strolling affectionately along beside him towards the incense tree.

"Monty bought a place last year he calls it Thousand Oaks," she was explaining. "He came to get me because Legacy, my older brother has just arrived from Santiago Coca."

The letter was addressed to Legacy, but Dominique decided to say nothing about it for the moment. He might have need for it tomorrow if things don't work out tonight. The banjo and fiddler players played and stomped there feet with renewed spirit.

"I've never heard that tune before," said Liana. "What kind of music is it?"

"An old African dance tune," said Dominique. "I for-got-its- name."

"You remember and forget things at will."

"I'll show you how the Zulu dance to it?"

"Why not?" she agreed.

61

L. A. Johnson Jr.

Instead of leading her towards the dance floor in the barn, he took her arms. "More room here in the yard," he said. "We need plenty of room; it's that kind of dance."

She took a quick look up into his eyes leaning forward. He swung her around on the hard-clay earth, between the incense tree and the arbor, the music was swift like a fast polka. The Zulu danced to this song with a lot of jumping, bending, twisting, and whirling. At first he was content to dance at half time. He was happy to be holding her in his arms.

"You dance very well," she said. You're full of surprises." He started twisting her around very fast, holding her firm against him; he kept whirling and twisting her until she was breathless. He slowed holding her firmly against his body. The rapid movement made their clinging together more intimate. Her thighs rubbed against his. Her body seemed to yield but she resisted. Slowly, her breath rose and fell, again she resisted. Her face moved as near his as if she were about to whisper something to him.

"In Zulu Land, where they danced like this, what kind of village did you say it was?"

"A small village," he said.

The fiddler and banjo picker suddenly stopped and then excitedly started once more at the beginning. The laughter and chatter from the barn seemed to drift away from the distance, leaving them entirely alone in the shadows under the incense tree. They danced even slower, now they were embracing; they were no longer dancing. The silence made the moment enchanting. The enchanting moment had become erratic. Willfully prolonging their lustful feelings. They were embracing in an agreeable sensation. The music stopped. He didn't release her nor did she push away. She leaned back to look up at him. A spark of moonlight drifted through the shadows and lingered on her face, as he bent down her lips parted. He could feel the sudden stiffness in her fingers digging into his shoulders. Her lips were soft and sweet.

His only thought was to kiss her again, but near by a child giggled. Some other couples had now sought the solitude of these shadows. The lighted noisy yard was just beyond the trees, Dominique edging farther and farther away, guiding Liana

Yolanda The Enchantress

with his arm around her. He was surprise of her willingness to go with him. The significance of what he was doing rushed upon him. They walked in the shadows of a camel pen surrounded by date palm trees. Ahead in the moonlight a huge rock stood. They climbed over it, still without a word, their silence becoming even more erotic than when they had pretended to dance. Beyond the rock and hill a path meandered toward the stream flowing through shadowy clusters of huge coconut tree.

When they entered this cluster of trees he paused and drew her against him again. She looked over her shoulder at the lights and the people and shook her head. This time she pushed him away. They crossed the stream stepping on stones and, entered a cluster of pineapple trees. They came upon a fern-covered with vines only seen by a reflection of moonlight. They entered another thicket, leading to another stream. Again he stopped, this time she kept walking. This stream splashed gently over its hidden rocks. This path led into deeper patches of darkness where he couldn't see her at all. She took his hands, while holding them she placed them against her breast and led him on. They walked under a huge African tulip tree and stopped under its outspread branches.

Suddenly he realized that the brushing against him wasn't a branch, it was a section of the stockade. The path had led to a narrow opening in the log wall, and they were through it. Embers in the forge were glowing, casting an ashy red reflection competing with the moonlight casting shadows over the yard. The figures of the three giants rose from the bench where they had been resting. A tall, middle-aged beautiful, dark, African woman walked out of the house.

"You are home early, Miss Liana," she said. "I was going to send Osceola up to the Plato mansion to wait for you."

"Thank you, Else," said Liana. She turned to Dominique. His eyes were as wide and as innocent looking as the two young girls. "Thank you, Mr. de Salvo, for escorting me home."

Dominique pretended not to hear her.

"This is where you live," he said.

"Since last year," she said. "It's a good location with so many new people traveling along Gorilla Passage. We make and repair guns and all sorts of iron work."

"I know. I had shoes put on my horse, here earlier today. A very good job it was, too."

"I'm sure of it," said Liana, smiling at her huge slaves. "They're as good as they are tall. My husband gave them to me. Thank you for a most interesting evening. Good night, Mr. de Salvo."

Instead of saying good night he took her arm and walked with her towards the door, softly singing several bars of the Zulu dance tune. "What time tomorrow?" he asked, when they reached the door.

"Time for what?"

"For me to see you."

"This is good-by, Mr. de Salvo. I'm going to my brother's house, first thing in the morning. This has been an unusual evening. You have told me things I shall always remember. She went in and closed the door.

Chapter 5
Haven't We Suffered Enough

The chatter of the banjo and the whining of the fiddle rose above the clamor of stamping, and clapping in the barn. There was uproar centered around the rum barrel and a fight in the tavern across the road, where men had gone to talk, drink and talk without their wives and children.

Dominique put Ruddy in the stable behind the tavern, watered and fed her, and spread his blanket on the ground. He was too excited too mingle with people or sleep. There was the moon to watch; by the time it vanished the sun would be welcoming a new day. Each hour the moon seemed to move more slowly. As soon as it was light enough to see, he knocked on Apollo's door, the old freed-slave who ran the general store for the Plato's. Apollo didn't like being awakened so early but when the bargaining began he didn't mind. Dominique bought an egg-shell colored shirt and necktie, a fancy hat, white socks and riding boots.

At the sight of Dominique's escudo's Apollo change his

Yolanda The Enchantress

prices, and after bargaining Dominique's money belt was much lighter. Dominique washed and shaved in a bucket behind the tavern, after washing he went into the stable to change into his new clothing. Everything fit well; his shirt and pants were rankled from being folded in the backpack. On the other hand, the new shirt and hat were without wrinkles. The general effect was that of a man who owned good clothes, which cared about how he looked at the end of his journey. This was the effect he wanted.

He led Ruddy out and was lifting her saddle when Mario came in, breathing hard and staring.

"My gracious, I hardly recognized you."

"Sir, who are you?"

Mario grunted and said. "I wanted to let you know, you can count on me. I'll buy a few camels, donkeys and horses; I'll be back by the end of the week."

Dominique grabbed him before he could get away looking at him suspiciously. "Back here? Why here?"

"I don't know," stated Mario. I don't know why I worry so much about you. Somebody's got to because that luck of yours is goin' to change sooner or later. I'll meet you here."

"I didn't see you last night," said Dominique.

"I was around," said Mario. "I saw you. I saw you led her into the bushes. If you want to know, I'll tell you what I saw. I was late getting' to the party because I went to a settlement across the river where I was told a farmer had some donkeys for sale. The donkeys were no good, but I happen to overhear some men talking about a widow living here. I looked for you because I didn't want you to go to Santiago Coca for nothing. By the time I found you, you'd found her. She was standing beside you under the arbor, hanging on to you like she was in love. It took no more than a glance for me to see there was nothing I could tell you. So I went to the party to get something to eat. From there I couldn't help seeing you and her in the shadows under the incense tree, because the light in the barn reflected on you." He moved away a step or two and said quickly: "I didn't see anything after you and her climb the hill behind the rock."

"You watched us while we were under the incense tree?"

"I wasn't watching' you"

65

L. A. Johnson Jr.

"You said that before," said Dominique. "Were other people at the food table watching'."

"Nope. Nobody. Nobody but Nero, he was the cooking the food. Pueblo Plato walked over to make sure I had enough to eat.

His oldest daughter stopped and looked on her way to the mansion to get a bandage for the banjo pickers finger. A chubby woman they call Aunt Amanda, who's kin to one of the women, that's married to your woman's youngest brother. Nobody else."

"Nobody but family."

Dominique's reaction caused Mario to step back again.

"I've got to get to the ferry before the last boatload leaves or I'll have to pay my own way. Like I said, I'll be back in a week, by then you'll need my help."

Dominique saddled his horse and went into the tavern. He bought huge slices of ostrich leg, and a jug of ale. He paid his stable bill so he could leave when the right time came, but he was in no hurry. Liana wouldn't leave for Thousand Oaks until the ferry had transported all the soldiers. She wouldn't cross with a boat full of soldiers and prisoners, and surely not with a chance of seeing him among them.

Before hearing Mario's story he was going to Thousand Oak's to deliver the letter to Legacy. Now because of what so many people had seen last night, he had to think of a different way to handle the situation. Up and down the Atlantic River Valley there would be talk today about how the widow Copula had carried on at the party with the soldier from Congo Basin. The story would have reached Monty's house by now.

He left Ruddy in the stable, cut across the field below the bend in the road, and hid behind a cluster of trees lining the road. From here he could see down into the yard between the blacksmith shop and her house, what he saw gave him time to relax. He started eating the ostrich and drinking the ale. Liana was wearing a brown suit, that matched the color of her hair and eyes and, pacing nervously about in front of her door, from time to time pausing to sip coffee from a cup on a tray held by Else. The old woman was watching her with concern and disapproval. Osceola, equally concerned but sympathetic, was holding the bridle of a beautiful black stallion, whose restlessness revealed that he

66

had been saddled and waiting a long time. Deep hoof-prints indicated that much earlier she had set out at a gallop towards the ferry and suddenly had returned to the yard at a slow gallop. Most revealing of all, one of Osceola's sons was down near the river where he could see the ferry, now taking off with the last boatload of soldiers and prisoners, the other son was across the road where he could see anyone coming around the bend from the tavern.

Dominique watched Liana and wondered what was the reasoning of all this. She had come back to wait. She had taken every precaution not to be seen waiting, and she wasn't waiting patiently. She was angry, impatient, and annoyed with herself and with everybody around her this morning. He tossed the meat aside, drank the last swallow of ale and placed the jug on the ground. The ferry was returning. The giant at the river was running back to tell her the furry was coming. Dominique ran across the field, mounted and then rode out of the tavern yard. He timed it so that he would approach the bend after Liana. She dashed out of her yard on her black stallion galloping down the road towards the ferry.

He let Ruddy all the way out to catch her before she reached the landing. She heard the hoofs behind her, but after a quick glance over her shoulder she didn't looked around again. It wasn't until he was riding alongside of her that she knew who it was, and the sight of his face caught her off guard. For a second there was no mistaking the sudden light in her face, a look of both relief and delight. Then, before she could force her face into a frown, the nearness of Ruddy startled her horse. Dominique pulled Ruddy to a slow gallop, and watched. It took a while to get the stallion under control; she knew how to handle a horse.

"Didn't mean to scare you," he said.

Getting her horse under control heightened her anger and patience. "You didn't."

He looked at her face. "You are angry, eh?"

"I don't like being followed."

"I was following you, that's a fact!" he admitted. "Only after I saw you on the road ahead."

"Why?"

Dominique's horse was trotting. Her horse, tilting his

eyes and bobbing his head was keeping pace. "I remembered you saying you were going to Monty's house today and it seemed like a good excuse to have you show me the way."

"Why, why do you want to go out there?"

"Just to be sociable, I liked your brother, when I met him last night, and since your brother Legacy is here, I'd like to meet him, too."

She bit her nails nervously, and then she apparently decided there were safer topics to pursue. "How did you get away from the army? Did you Desert!"

"I didn't desert, and I'm not in the army any more."

They had reached the landing and the ferry conductor was watching them with unwavering interest. Liana remained silent during the crossing; and Dominique wasn't eager to talk. Neither said a word until they turned off the main road onto the road leading to Thousand Oaks. Liana pulled up.

"You are really going there?"

"Why not?"

"About some things, my brothers have a poor sense of humor when it's about me. No matter how they act if you insist on going out there with me. I promise you I'll make it difficult for you. I'm warning you."

"I'll take my chances," said Dominique.

She glanced up the road ahead.

"Want to race?" asked Dominique. "The road's wide enough."

She glanced at Ruddy. "No."

Dominique placed his hands on the saddle horn and, grinned. "Certainly is a fine morning."

"You not as stupid as you are trying to act. Surely you understand there's a difference between flirting with a soldier at a dance, and the next morning finding him following you around dressed up like; like a shady lawyer."

Dominique unbuttoned the collar of his shirt and took off his necktie. "The only clothes I had with me except for my army uniforms... I'm going with you, if I ride beside you, you won't have to worry about me following."

Liana shrugged, struck her horse and took off at a gallop. Ruddy drew alongside and kept pace. Liana continued to look straight ahead, paying little attention to him. The road climbed a hill and gradually slanted down-wards towards a stream. She broke stride, swaggered, and pulled into a slow trot.

"We're almost there," she said. "What are you are going to say to my brothers?"

"I'll think of something." He replied.

"Why were you laughing when you said that?" she asked.

"It'll take to long to explain."

They turned into a in a peaceful meadow, and rode down a road that veered away from the river, and entered a cluster of mangrove trees.

"I don't. I was married a long time, and I've been a widow long enough to know I liked having a man around the house."

"Got one?" he asked

"No!" she replied.

"Looking for one?" he asked.

"I'm in no hurry." She ansewered.

"Everything but a man." He said.

They rounded the cluster of mangrove trees and were approaching a huge mansion, still under construction. This obviously was Monty's home. The Gomez's were doing well. Even her youngest brother had a larger plantation than their parents had twenty years ago. Dominique scanned the grounds as if he were more interested in what he could see than in what she had just said.

"More new mansions in this country," he whispered. "African prisoners from Perez's army," she explained, watching his face. "Last year up and down the valley people hired friendly Africans to build houses."

An African stable hand approached from the corner of the house to take the horses. Dominique dismounted and reached up to help her down. She started to lean forward and suddenly drew back, staring down at him.

You worked at Mendoza's!" she said.

He said. "I thought you knew all the time."

"I didn't. It just came to me this minute." She said.

She dismounted and handed the reins to the slave.

"Where's Mr. Legacy?"

"Somewhere out back with Mr. Monty and Miss Monica."

She stepped up on the porch and turned to look down at Dominique again.

"Looking down at you makes the difference, that's how I always saw you, out in front of the general store."

"Now where do I stand with you? He asked."

"About the same, with one tiny difference. I'm beginning to remember there was something about that young lawyer I liked." She looked at him, as if she were willing to give him the benefit of doubt. "I have to admit that I like you even now more than I should. Let's call a truce for the moment. I have important business to discuss with my brothers today. Please leave now and call on me here tomorrow. Will you?"

"Are you hiding behind some kind of excuse?" Her eyes glared. "Good-by, Mr. de Salvo."

"I'll come back tomorrow, but I need to see your brothers today."

She stared at him. "You couldn't have some silly idea or something you should discuss with me, first, do you?"

"I think they have something to say to me, without wanting to wait another day. You may not know it but your neighbors were watching us under that tree last night."

"Good by, Mr. de Salvo."

She went in and closed the door, like she had the night before. This time he was at ease with her rudeness. He saw two men coming from the direction of the camel pen. It would be easier to explain everything to her brothers without her around.

He could see that one of the two was Monty and he took it for granted the other was Legacy, though Legacy looked nothing like Monty. He was a foot shorter, stocky built, dark instead of fair and with an air of superiority that bordered on arrogance. His left arm dangled in a sling, and he limped slightly. Probably no more than fifty, his black hair had turned gray. As he moved closer Dominique saw the gleam of his gray eyes. Under his heavy gray brow revealed a sharp penetrating glance, stronger than any he had ever met. His piercing eyes were scanning Dominique, his apparel, his demeanor and his horse all in one swift, decisive glance.

"Mr. de Salvo we were talking about you," said Monty, still several strides away. "I was telling Legacy, pardon me Mr. de Salvo. Major Legacy Gomez; I was just telling him that, perhaps you'd run into Antonio on the trail. Antonio's our brother, if you had you would have said something about it when we met last night."

"I would have," said Dominique, drawing long breathes.

Legacy took command of the conversation. "There's only one trail between here and Congo Basin, isn't it?"

"That's right." Replied Dominique.

"When you came over the mountain did you see, or hear anything about a redheaded man wearing new denim clothing. A big man, big and tall, as Monty but much heavier riding a Wooly Bactrian camel traveling with an old elephant hunter named Rosario Vales?"

"No." replied Dominique.

"The imbecile's got lost somewhere in the jungle."

"Not likely with old Rosario along. How long have they been gone?" said Dominique?

"Left Santiago Coca the last week in June."

"Did they come through here?" Dominique asked Monty.

"Nobody knew," said Monty. "I found out only an hour ago, when Legacy told me. If they came through here he didn't stop."

"I told him to stay away from you," said Legacy. "I didn't want you to go with him."

"Where was he headed for?" asked Dominique.

"Lake Tanganyika." said Legacy.

"That's why we didn't meet him. They turned north at Gun Road, two men traveling on camels could have easily taken a game path through the jungle before we got there."

"Sounds reasonable," agreed Legacy, "if there was any trouble to get into Antonio would find it." He looked at Dominique. "Know that part of the country?"

"Excuse me," said Monty. "If we're going to start asking Mr. de Salvo about Congo Basin, let's go into the house and find a bottle of spirits and settle down where we can talk with him in comfort. Where is Liana?"

L. A. Johnson Jr.

"She went in the house," said Dominique. "I rode out with her to deliver a letter from Colonel Dino Figueroa to Major Gomez."

"You don't say!" Monty took Dominique by the arm. "and said better and better." He took the letter, and gave it to Legacy and hung onto Dominique's arm.

"Could have given it to you to bring to your brother when I saw you last night," said Dominique, "but I didn't think of it."

"We can thank Liana for that." Monty's eyes were bright again. "We're glade you didn't. Come on in, and around dinner-time we'll know more about Congo Basin than we've learn all summer."

A slim, very pretty woman in a brightly colored dress stood in the open doorway. Her hair and eyebrows and eyelashes were raspberry colored and her eyes such a clear blue that they looked almost without color, except when looked at Monty they glowed. She was Monty's wife, Crystal. By the time Dominique had been introduced and everybody had walked through the doorway it was she instead of Monty who clung to his arm. In the hallway she held him back to talk to him. Liana came rushing through and angrily slammed the back door. She was so angry she barely noticed Dominique. "You made quite an impression on her last night." Said Crystal.

"Last night?" replied Dominique.

"Don't pretend you don't know what I'm talking about, we didn't go to the party because we were expecting Legacy; but everybody else in Thousand Oaks did." She stepped back to look up at Dominique. "It's time she had some good luck with men."

"Where's Liana?" Legacy was asking.

"Out back looking for you and Monty," Crystal said. "I'll get her."

Dominique looked around quickly, you could tell a lot about people by observing the furniture inside their house, and how their fields were worked. The way they cared for their stock and, treated their slaves. The section of the house to the right of the hall was unfinished, but the room, to the left, into which they were walking, was a huge room, with hardwood floors covered with very expensive hand-woven rugs. Everything matched and all made out of mahogany. On the tables and cabinets were brass candle-holders, all well worn and highly polished. They looked like pieces that had been in the family for a long time.

Dominique had lived most of his life among people who considered any old bed with a headboard elegant of furniture. Here it wasn't the things themselves so much as the way they were arranged. Even in this partially house the furniture fit in with the people who live here. He was glad that he had ridden up to this house on a horse good as Ruddy, and he was entering it wearing good clothes.

The people here confused him even more. According to what Crystal had told him, everybody knew about last night, and still her brothers had made him feel welcome. It couldn't be that they didn't care what she did. It was even more confusing; Crystal acting as if Lanais showing favor to any man other than her brothers. Suddenly he realized her brothers were clever. They were glad he had come. They were interested in Congo Basin, like most white settlers in Eagle Landing and Kingdom of Buganda, and they were taking advantage of the opportunity to question him.

Monty took the letter from Legacy, he open it and handed it back to him. Legacy sat down and started to read it.

"Have a seat, Mr. de Salvo," said Monty. "What's your first name? We'll be addressing you that way, after the third drink, might as well start now."

"Dominique."

"Sit down, Dominique." He raised his voice grunting "Osceola, brandy."

Osceola, an old Africa with a smooth dark brown face the color of the dining room table, walked through the door from the kitchen with five tall glasses on a wooden tray. He had not only foreseen the demand but by some mysterious intuition he knew the exact number. Dominique took one of the frosty glasses. He wondered how they made ice in this tropical country. He could hear Crystal calling: "Liana, Legacy and Monty are in here." Three of Monty's hunting dogs had come in with Osceola. Two of them stretched out lazily on the floor but the other drifted over to sniff Dominique's riding boots.

Legacy glanced up from the letter. "I've heard a lot about

Colonel Figueroa. He must be a good man."

"He is," said Dominique.

"He speaks very highly of you."

Dominique knew there had been no reference to him, when Dino dictated the letter that night; Anita had slipped that in. He could hear the voices of the women in the hall. Then Liana came strolling in and walked over to Legacy, dropped on her knees and placed her arms around his neck before he could move.

"I'm trying to read an important letter," Legacy said.

"It's been ages since I've seen you." Said Liana.

"Is that why you didn't come to see me last night?"

"If I had I would have found you sound asleep, and grumpier than you are now."

She kissed him on the top of his head, took a glass from Osceola's tray and glanced at Dominique, and down at the dog which now stood beside Dominique's chair with his face resting on Dominique's knee. "Well," she said. "I see you have even managed to charm the dogs."

"Liana," asked Crystal, "why didn't you tell me that Mr. de Salvo came out here to bring Legacy a letter from Colonel Figueroa?"

"I didn't know, he didn't tell me. Mr. de Salvo is full of secrets, some of them unpredictable." You should have told me." She took a sip of her drink glancing at Dominique, while turning appealingly to her brothers. Saying. "You wouldn't believe how he's taken advantage of me."

"We heard," said Monty smiling.

"Always ready to listen to gossip." She turned back to Dominique. "My brothers think that I fall in love easily

"Actually," said Crystal, "there's not another woman in Eagle Landing, or Burgle Ferry crossing that's harder to please. She compares every man with her brothers. I keep telling her that her brothers are not the only good men in Africa."

"Leave us alone a minute," Legacy told Liana. "Or sit down and listen, you have as much to loose or gain as we do! This is an interesting letter, and Colonel Figueroa was kind enough to take the trouble, he tossed the letter on the table, but since Dominique is here I'd rather hear what he can tell us."

Yolanda The Enchantress

"Colonel Figueroa's more than kind to tell us about the land around his settlement station," said Legacy; "but we have already purchased twenty thousand acres somewhere along Lake Tanganyika, none of us has ever seen it. We bought the rights to it from the Portuguese government ten years ago. Holding the title didn't amount to much then, it's probably worth less now."

There's only one title in Congo Basin that amounts to anything at all," said Dominique. "You must build on as much land as you can hold onto yourself."

"That's why Antonio went out there this spring."

"Did you know about that? Liana asked Monty.

He shook his head. She looked angrily at Legacy. "Did you tell him to sneak through here after dark?"

"You couldn't have stopped him any more than I could," said Legacy. He turned back to Dominique. "My brother was bound to see for himself if this land was worth hanging onto."

"It'll take a lot of people to hang onto that much land," said Dominique. "The problem with taking settlers out there is that, they always decide after they've fought off Africans, and tended the land, they'll keep it for themselves."

"How good is Congo Basin land?"

"Some is the best you'll ever find anywhere."

"Then it might be worth making an effort to hang onto all of it."

"All Antonio needed was an excuse," said Liana. "If you don't watch out, he'll want to move out there. You and Antonio still live in Santiago Coca, Monty and I here."

"I think," said Legacy, "we' would be better off closer together, once we find the right place."

Crystal sprung up, "Legacy," she cried. She turned looking unhappily at Monty. "Monty. You can't let Antonio move to Congo Basin. After all we've heard, everybody out there in the jungle has to fight all the time, just to stay alive. This family has suffered enough. Look at Monty, he hasn't gained a pound since he caught that contagious disease at Cameroon, and you, Legacy, look at what the war has done to you. Think of Ironic and Edwin As for Antonio, big and strong as he looks, he's still spitting blood every day since that time he was left for dead in Angola..."

L. A. Johnson Jr.

Liana's voice broke. Monty reached up and pulled her down onto his lap where she hid her face against his shoulder.

"Ironic was my other brother," Liana whispered to Dominique. "He was killed on the Ivory Coast. Edwin was my husband."

"It's a fact," said Legacy, "The Gomez family has played a major roll in conquering Africa." He walked to the window, looked out, then came back to sit down. "Congo Basin's not the only place in Africa that war is being fought."

Monty was stroking Crystal's hair. He looked at Dominique. "Novas' taking Mozambique and catching Prince Kudzu is going to make a big difference in things out there?"

"Only for a while," said Dominique. "Africans will fight to keep their land as long as the Bantu and Masai live in Eagle Falls. The problem you'll have on Lake Tanganyika is if they deside to cross the Yoruba River, they'll come through your land first."

Crystal lifted her head to look at Legacy and lowered it again when she noticed he said nothing.

"Congo Road I've heard so much talk about," he said. "What is it like?"

"Just a wide rocky elephant trail." Said Dominique.

"Hard going?" asked Monti.

"Well, when you leave the Niger River you climb Tribesmen Mountain, tramp through shallow places in Tribesmen River, climb snake infested hills and wade through streams of crocodile infested water. Then you march down Redwood Trail and from there down Gun Road through the dark jungle. From there on the going gets really hard and dangerous!"

"How far have you traveled by that time?" asked Monty

"About a hundred and fifty miles from the last settlement on the Niger." Said Dominique. "No White-man has ever settled in that area, and there are no white people after you leave the last settlement this side of Lions Din; till you are in sight of Figueroa's Station or Nova Gala Settlement."

"It's at Gun Road you said the trail forks?" said Monty.

"One way you go towards Figueroa Station, about another sixty miles and through Sea Pen, or Port Eden Ton. The other way is go to Nova Gala, about eighty miles and, then fifty miles farther is Lake Tanganyika. Nothing but Africans, jungle too thick, gives them too many places to hide, and makes them too hard to kill. Gorilla Passage is the main road."

Crystal changed position on Monty's lap so that she could watch his face. Suddenly she jumped up.

"We've been shut up in here for hours," she said. "Let's go outside to get a breath of fresh air before dinner."

"What we have been discussing is important," said Legacy. "We have more to talk about."

"Dominique might be interested in seeing your giraffes and zebras have you forgotten. We have to get out of Osceola's way so he can set the table?"

Liana came to her support. "Come on. We've the rest of the day to talk about Congo Basin."

Legacy and Monty looked at the women, exchanged harsh glances, and reluctantly yielded. The five of them walked out to the camel pen in the rear. Most of the herd was in a distant field. There were a few camels, zebras, and young giraffe in a nearby field. Monty pointed out a Woolly Bactrian camel he bought from a herder while visiting the Gobi desert of Asia, but no special importance was attached too it. Crystal was linking her arms with those of Monty and Legacy, and steering them back towards the house. "Liana," she said over her shoulder, "before you come in, show Dominique the spring?"

"I'm sure he's just dying to see it," said Liana. "Come, Dominique."

"Half hour," shouted Monty. "We'll hold dinner no longer."

"Liana placed her hand on Dominique's hand and, walked beside him. They walked down a long path towards a cluster of African tulip trees at the base of a slope. Crystal was looking over her shoulder, watching them.

"I can't complain," he said. "She's very nice, but what is she up to?"

"She couldn't stand all that talk about Congo Basin, she wants you to tell them that Congo Basin is the most dangerous place in Africa. She doesn't know them as well as I do. Telling them that would only make them more interested."

"You are not against Congo Basin as she is." He asked.

L. A. Johnson Jr.

"Our family that sticks together, there's plenty of time to destroy Antonio's Congo Basin ideas. Legacy's the one who will decide, and he's not as reckless or emotional as Antonio or Monty. He will stop to think; he'll listen to his wife, Brittany and me. Crystal is getting nervous too soon. Nothing will happen until Antonio gets back. I'll have the rainy season to work on Legacy."

"Are you always able to work things out the way you want them?"

"I wish I could."

"Why did you leave Santiago Coca if you were so anxious to keep your family together?"

"There wasn't enough land for all of us."

"So now you plan to get Legacy and Antonio to sell their homes and settle here. Then you can move your blacksmith shop next door and you'll have everything the way you want it."

She smiled. "Nearly everything, but a man, that will come, sooner or later."

Approaching the creek, water was flowing over moss-covered rocks. The dark green palm and banana leaves seemed to have closed in around them. The air was sweet with fragrance of rose-colored blossoms. It was a place in which only lovers should linger. A short-lived breeze brushed across a cluster of flowers, releasing a new wave of scent. An exploding ray of sunlight drifted across her hair and down into the hollow between her breast. Probably he was a fool to make a move on her so soon, but it was too late to back away now. "Well?" he demanded.

She was looking up at him in wonder, as if as much surprised at herself as at him. "How can I be certain, so soon?"

"Why not?"

"I'm more or less certain," she admitted, "more curious than I've ever been before."

He put his arms around her shoulders and pulled her closer. She moved without resisting into his embrace but she didn't respond as she had last night. This time her lips resisted his advance. Perhaps she was thinking of what they had already said, and what they were about to say. For the moment her actions increased his desire, because she seemed quite willing to indulge him. His arms tightened around her, but she refused to share this moment with him. Holding her shoulders looking at her face, Dominique shoved her away his anger vanished. She was lovely.

Smiling he said. "Your brothers and Crystal like me. Even your brothers' dogs like me. Why can't you?"

"I do. Everything is happening so fast, I'm not thinking clearly."

"You will have time to think," he said seriously. "I've never liked making plans myself, but I have to make some now."

She placed her hands on his chest; she understood what he was saying, "No, Dominique, that's one thing, that's something we don't have to worry about." This was dangerous ground and it was her turn to smile. "I wouldn't marry, to get a man to run my business; but I need a manager."

He stepped back, his hands dropped to his side. His voice was harsher then he had intended, "and when you get him you'll have everything... just like you want it.

A woman seldom gets everything the way she wants it," she replied.

He hadn't imagined anything as bad as this. It was an issue too serious to discuss without thinking. Better to evade it, and pretend they were joking. "Sounds like you need an overseer, not a husband." He murmured.

She was more anxious than he was to not discuss the subject lightly. "Should I wish, for a shack on Lake Tanganyika?"

Pretending that they were joking was no good. Every word each said was evasive but still cracking like a whip. The sudden clang of the dinner bell came from the direction of the house. Both welcomed the interruption, without word they turned to go. She placed her hand under his arm as they walked along, she kept looking up at him, inquisitively, but he stared straight ahead.

He had to have her, he was certain of that now. After dancing with her at Plato's, last night, he could have her. Last night she made that clear enough. To have her he would have to marry her, but he wouldn't be marrying her, she would be marrying him. He would have to spend a few hours' everyday giving orders to her slaves'. He'd have to settle down, and live in her house, and take his place as one of the lesser members of her family. The rest of the day he'd have to do things to make her happy. It would be an easy life, a very favorable one, but not what he had in mind. They opened the back door and walked down the hallway into the dining room.

"Next week," he said to Legacy, "If you want to see your land–I'll take you there."

Crystal gasped. Monty looked past Dominique at Liana smiling.

"A very generous offer," said Legacy. "So good a one, in fact, I don't see how Monty and I can afford to refuse it." Legacy glanced at Monty, who promptly nodded back at him, and then at Dominique. "We welcome your help, but I need to ask one question, a very friendly one. What do you want?"

"Hoping you will decide to move to Congo Basin," said Dominique. "I want to live in the Congo, as white-men increase in numbers there, we'll control more of the country."

He looked at Liana. She was angry. "Don't treat me like I'm one of your African women that you control by cracking a whip?

Liana placed a, comforting, arm around her shoulder. Crystal was crying. Liana told Crystal, "if I had a gun I would shoot him."

"To keep him from getting away." Monty said smiling.

Chapter 5   **Part 2**   A week later:

"Nobody's luck can last forever," said Mario. "Nobody's. Not even yours."

"What's so good about it?" demanded Dominique.

"How could it get any better?" Mario shook his head, marveling in awe. "That blacksmith business of hers, with those big, smart slaves running it, there isn't another business that could make more and make it faster anywhere you settle on this side of the Atlantic; they're moving'. When men like them decide to do something, they do it. Sure as my name is Mario Goalie they're going to move to Congo Basin. They are dry behind the ears, they know, you know, the country out there and they don't. Out there they'll need you. They'll need you and she'll need you. You have them where you want them. Luck, my friend, how much luck do you need."

There was no doubt about the luck that accompanied them on their passage through the jungle. The mild haze traveling through the rain forest hid the most for-bidding heights and uncertainties. Their days on the trail and their nights in camp were hot, cold or wet. The river had fallen since the spring floods making it easy to cross, they were traveling light. Mario's camel caravan and four burros were loaded with a few axes, shovels, saws, surveying instruments and camping equipment. In pleasant weather moved much faster and reduced the risk of running into Wagnerian warriors.

They stopped only occasionally to satisfy the Gomez brothers' passion for hunting. Here, too, the luck held. Legacy saw his first mountain gorilla. He followed it on foot into a ravine and killed it with his rifle. Monty's dogs flushed an enormous aardvark out of an anthill and he followed bringing the beast down with a single shot from nearly a hundred yards away. The brothers were equally delighted with the weather, the scenery, and the swift progress.

"Prettiest country I ever seen," declared Monty.

"I've seen rougher going," said Legacy, "on the Ivory Coast after a few days of rain."

They reached Gun Road and turned inland. Each day they traveled longer hours and more miles, as Monty and Legacy's eagerness to see their land increased. After losing sight of the last village in eastern Eagle Landing they came out on a ridge from which they could see sprawled out on the bank of Congo River below, sat the big stockade of Nova Gala. Ten days had passed. They rode through fields of maize nearly ten feet high, and people farming ran out to meet them. In this, their first encounter with white people who lived in Congo Basin, the talk was all of favorable news. Conti and Figueroa had invaded Lozi country, destroyed crops, stolen their donkeys and killed nearly a hundred warriors and burned their villages. They said since that attack there has been less trouble in Congo Basin. To Legacy and Monty there was another piece of news that was even better.

L. A. Johnson Jr.

To the north of Nova Gala, Torres had built a Trading Station on Lake Tanganyika, and Grasper was building a new settlement station, lest than fifty miles from the lake.

"With two stations between our land and the Yoruba," Legacy said, "sounds like we'll only have to worry about warriorrs coming from the direction of Gorilla Passage or the trail to the east."

"Those station could be helpful," agreed Dominique.

They spent the night at Nova Gala, listening to stories of this tropical wilderness, white men would settle. They set out in the morning more impatient than ever. From here on there were no longer any good trails to follow. The scattered settlements of Congo Basin all lay to the north and west of Nova Gala. They were turning to the northeast. They rode over rolling hills and walked down bush-covered valleys towards the Congo River, camping that night on the shores of a stream flowing northward into the south fork of Lake Tanganyika. Rising at dawn, Legacy and Monty too excited to wait for breakfast, started on. Their luck still held. In the first hour Monty's dogs started whining with eagerness recognizing a familiar scent. The dogs led them straight to the camp of Antonio and Rosario Vales. Old Rosario was dressing a gazelle. After one quick look, he waved casually, as if visitors from Eagle Landing riding into camp had been expected this morning, and continued with his skinning. Antonio was bathing in the stream. He reared up, his red hair and beard and huge white body gleaming in the sun, stared and then began to scream with wild unrestrained delight.

"Get down," he shouted. "Get off of those camels."

He pranced around them like a crazy-man, and hugged Legacy and Monty while dripping, after hugging them he started leaping and gesturing.

"Come," he demanded. "Come with me."

Without stopping to dress or even to dry himself, he ran along the stream bank gesturing for them to follow. He led the way around a bend, plunging through patches of wild-berry vines, paying no attention to briar's brushing against his skin. "Come on," he kept shouting. "Follow me, just follow me." Clusters of bananas trees stood along the path, and flocks of colorful birds dashed from under foot. Flocks of ibis were

chattering angrily in a field, and dashed through the undergrowth ahead of them. Antonio broke out into the open at the top
of a slope beyond, turning to confront them.

He said in triumph, "Take a look." The stream was arch-
ing below, dipping over huge limestones and rocky ledges. It
rambled to the north through miles of breath taking green valleys. Beyond on the encircling hills the jungle gave way to vast
expanses of grassland. Across which wind had carved waves in
its thick carpets of elephant grass, rye, and clover. The valley
bottom and meadows were dotted with huge African tulip trees.
There were huge clusters of banana, mango, pear, pineapple, and
coconut trees. All bordered by belts of towering bamboo, lime,
orange, lemon, and cane. Another stream was flowing through
the jungle towards the heaven, it looked like a shimmering rib-
bon of blue drifting towards the clouds, and in the distance you
could see green splashes of water casting whitecaps towards the
shore. "You are looking at land that's just as rich as it looks,"
said Antonio waving his arms. "Look at the ledges of limestone,
the size of the trees, the color of the grass, the height of the
bamboo. That's how you tell good land out here. Look at everything, everything in sight belongs to us."

"I see nearly eighty elephants in sight, thirty rhinoceros,
and more impala than I can count," said Monty. "No, over one
hundred elephants."

"That heard in the distance," said Legacy, "they are giraffe, look over there, Cape buffalo, and there's some fair-sized
fish in the stream. Look at that, crocodiles in the stream below
the second fall, must be at least ten pounds. What's the name of
the creek?"

Antonio bent to pick up several small sticks, which he
began to break hastily. "No White-man has ever seen this land
except a few ivory hunters. According to Rosario they call it
Rhino Creek, because of the rhino trail that crosses, just beyond
that grove of mangrove trees. There's a big hot, fresh water
spring down there." He straightened up. "If I'm right, as far as
you can see, our land covers all of this valley and more. Everything you see from here and beyond belongs to us." He faced
Monty and Legacy, holding out one hand from which ends of the
sticks stuck out.

L. A. Johnson Jr.

"Take one."

"Why?" Asked Legacy.

"For first choice of a place to build. If I win I plan to build there in that bend."

Legacy looked and shook his head. "That's going to be the town. Spot for a lumberyard at one falls and a flower mill at the other."

Antonio let out another scream of delight. "Hear that, Monty? Hear that? One look and old Legacy is convinced. Already he's talking about mills and towns. Looks like we're going to live here."

"Slowly Monty, agreed" grinning.

Mario dug his elbow into Dominique's ribs. Legacy's keen eyes seldom missed much.

"I suppose the two of you are use to the way a newcomer acts when they get their first good look at the land out here," he said.

"It's a mighty pretty valley, that's a fact," said Dominique.

Legacy's attention returned to the view. "Get dressed and saddle your camel," he told Antonio. "Let's take a closer look."

For the next month the three brothers explored there land, ran survey lines, marked trees and moved huge rocks to mark their boundaries. The others hunted, cooked, and watched for unfriendly visitors.

At night in camp there was much talk of Arabian stallions, exotic animals, cooking, and tall tails, Legacy said, "The Yoruba people carve beautiful statues to honor their ancestors, mothers and children. The statues are called Ibeji, celebrates the birth of twins. If one dies, the Ibeji takes his place." Mario motioned and said; Wagerian people walk on catwalks above Congo River. Many kind of fish, thousands of them fill the river, some weigh more than three hundred pounds.

Fishermen check to see if there are any fish in their huge hand-woven bamboo traps. Many traps were ten feet high and fifteen feet long. Young boys clean and repair them." Then out of no where he said, "The Nile not the Zambezi is the longer river." Dominique talked about his great, great, great grandfather Magellan, and how he died searching for the Northwest Passage, which did not exist. Mario complained about the prices he had paid for his camels and burros, while bragging about the handful of spices he had dumped into old Rosario's impala stew, when Rosario turned his head. Rosario's stated with conviction that a baboon was endowed with greater human intelligence than most people.

There was no talk of the land in the green valleys of Rhino Creek or of the Gomez brothers plans regarding it. After days of planning they were deeply absorbed in the exploration, examination, and surveying of their land, at night they avoided that subject. The decisions, which were in the making, were to be theirs and theirs alone. When any important decision had to be dealt with the Gomez's closed ranks. The family was bound together by blood and strong family ties which excluded all outsiders from their councils.

Weeks went by slowly. Again and again Dominique watched the three brothers pause to talk in the course of their daily surveying, soil testing, and boundary marking. He could see them pointing to areas of meadows or woodland, gesturing with differences of opinion, while nodding their heads up and down in agreement, coming to conclusions which Legacy entered in his notebook.. Never once did they stop and ask him a question, or seek his advice, as they had so often done before reaching their land. Anxiety began to gnaw at Dominique. He had made a regrettable miscalculation if they had already decided they had no further need for him. He thought about his parting from Liana. After her first fit of rage she seemed to realize that she couldn't hold him entirely responsible for her brothers' obsessions with their Congo Basin land. When the time came to say good-by, she didn't resist his kisses. She smiled; her fingers clung to his arm tightening for a moment.

She whispered a vague statement, "When you bring them back safely...."

Bringing them back safely was not going to be enough if thereafter he was thanked for his help and left with no future part in their plans. Then, too, his respect for her three brothers was growing as he came to know them. He could barely remember any of his relative. He began to think of what it would be like to be a part of this family, so loyal to each other. Being accepted, as one of them wasn't a goal that he could pursue as he had pursued Liana. There was nothing to do but wait.

At last came a day when his suspense was relieved. Returning to camp late one evening with two geese, and an ostrich when he saw Legacy, Monty and Antonio, standing by the falls. For the first time since there arrival here they were sitting down during daylight.

"Dominique," yelled Antonio. "Come down here."

Dominique joined them. The time had come. They had made up their minds about something and were ready to talk to him. It was odd to remember how recently he wouldn't have felt concerned about anything anybody had to say to him. Now his outward calm was like that of a young Masai warrior waiting outside the council lodge to learn weather or not he will be inducted into the society of future chiefs.

"Sit down," said Legacy. "You've had time to look around. What do you think of this section?"

"About as good as there is."

"That's what we think. We are going to build on this section of land first. We don't want to go off half-cocked, and we certainly don't want to rush out here with our families until we're certain we have everything, as it should be. First we want to build on what we need, and plant enough crops so nobody will go hungry and brings in enough people to keep unfriendly African's away."

"That's the way to do it," said Dominigue.

"It's too big a job for us to handle alone," said Legacy. "So this is how we have decided to do: We are going to keep the land on the east side of the creek for ourselves, and we are going to form a company and sell ten thousand acres on this side. We will sell shares in the company and with each shareholder will have an acre here at the town-site, ten acres to the north and a thousand acres of farmland. We're selling shares, the price a thousand escudo. The money will be used for building the stockade, mills, general store, and whatever is necessary to make a new settlement successful.

We'll but four of the shares and sell six. The other six we don't want to sell just to anybody who happens to have a thousand Portuguese dollars. We want only men that have something

Yolanda The Enchantress

useful to offer, men we know we can count on. For example, Silva Hernandez back in Santiago Coca who has runs a lumberyard all his life. A lumberyard is one of the first things a settlement needs, when its up and running you can build homes and barns much faster. By the time the first maize crop has matured we'll need a flower mill, and a general store. A doctor and a lawyer, he smiled at Dominique, if we can get them. Maybe even a preacher. You have lived in this jungle quite a while, and you have seen new settlements get started. Is there anything wrong with our plan?"

"No," said Dominique.

"Good. Because the first share after our own we would like to offer to a lawyer, do you. Want it?"

Dominique clung to his outward calm. The most he had expected was a job, as a guide, hunter, or African fighter or general advisory. Instead they were making him a partner. They didn't know he had only eighty dollars to his name. They were making him an offer in good faith. They were looking forward to him becoming one of them. It was the first step before the negotiation of an engagement contract. Somewhere, and quick, he had to get a thousand Portuguese escudos.

"I'd be a fool if I didn't," he replied.

"Good," said Legacy, this time with unexpected added warmth. "While he was talking Dominique could see Monty and Antonio squirming with delight."

All three shook hands with him. There was no doubt that this was more than just a business deal.

"How soon will you need the money?"

"We won't start building until next spring, after the rainy season. That will give you time to make any arrangements you have to make. One more thing, there's no way these days to count on what money's going to be worth. So we will calculate each escudo at the rate of twenty-five cents a bushel of maize."

Four thousand bushels of maize, you could raise that in a year on fifty acres of good cleared land, he didn't have time to raise it, if he had the land. People were wary of talking escudos because they never knew what they were worth. But four thousand bushels of maize was more than eight elephants pulling eighty huge wagon-loads.

L. A. Johnson Jr.

Dominique searched the jungle to the north looking for Mario, because it was Mario's day to watch the game trails for African warriors, he found Mario at the lower freshwater spring. Mario didn't think Dominique had problem raising the money.

"I can get you five hundred escudos for your horse, the watch and the shirt," he said.

"How about the other five?"

"Borrow it from your future brother-in-laws. They'll loan it to you."

"No," said Dominique. "I am not going in begging."

"Don't forget," taunted Mario. "You'll be in as deep as they are."

"Anyway you look at it," said Dominique soberly, "it's a good deal for me."

"It surely is," agreed Mario. "You can't afford not to take it. Now where will you get the money?"

They both thought for a while. What is magnesium sulfate worth a pound?" asked Dominique.

"Not bad," exclaimed Mario. "Not a bad idea, at, all. I knew you'd come up with an idea, but I didn't think you would have such a sensible one. Magnesium sulfate's worth twenty, thirty, forty cents a pound, depends on how short the supply is. If it's real short you can get whatever you ask for it. You know where you can find some."

Dominique nodded. "A cave down on the other side of the jungle, near Victoria Falls where I lived the first year I came out here. There's mineral salt a foot thick covering the ground. I will need buckets, kettles, and tools for digging. How much will those things cost me?"

"More than they're worth, anywhere in Congo Basin, near as bad along the Niger River. Closest place to get a good price, a price you can afford is in Surrey. Buy them there."

Dominique thought for a while longer.

"Help the Gomez's pack, and get them home to Thousand Oaks," he said. "With Antonio and Rosario you'll have a stronger party than when we came. Old Rosario's sharp but keep your eyes open. I promised Liana, I'd get them back safe."

"Don't worry about them," said Mario. "After the trouble I took finding those burros of mine, I want let anything happen to them."

"Take care of Ruddy for me."

"Wait," grumbled Mario. "While I'm doing your work for you, what will you be doing'?"

"I'm going to Surrey. I can move faster on foot through the jungle traveling along the border of Baeda Land, I'll head down the White Nile. I'll bring the supplies up the Yoruba by boat. Meet me in two months at Port Eden Ton."

"I'll be there," said Mario, seeing nothing unusual in a man's setting out to travel alone through miles of jungle.

Chapter 6
Unnatural Weather

"Two Months to the day," Mario was at Port Eden Ton. "You've been traveling' fast."

"I was in a hurry, said Dominique.

Mario said, "let's get going'."

Mario inspected the supplies and approved the price Dominique had paid. They packed and set out at once, though it was already midday. "Only a few hours of daylight left," said Mario. "Might as well use it."

"Five days later, moving south each day every minute of daylight, the little caravan was winding through the rugged jungle above the upper section of Victoria Falls. Dominique was to spend the rainy season in a land, which was even lonely than anyone could imagine. It was wilder and more deserted then the land he had traveled on his way to and from Surrey. From Figueroa Station and beyond Congo Road, no settlements were anywhere in this section of this country to the south nearer than Tupelo on the Zambezi River, nearly five hundred miles away.

"It's been eighteen years since I was through here," said Dominique. "Suppose I can't find the cave."

There was little chance of that. A young man's first season in this jungle was not something he was likely to forget. Riding ahead of the caravan he circled to the west of the stream and over a hill, keeping on through until he reached a stretch of coconut and mangrove trees. They climbed the next ridge, descended into a valley of bamboo. Here they turned onto a wide well traveled rhinoceros trail. That was the only way by which packed burros could travel through this section of the jungle. They couldn't see rhinoceros but they heard them grunting and splashing in the stream. The trail crossed a wide rocky stream. Dominique turned down that stream, for the next five miles the caravan splashed through crocodile and python infested water, leaving even less signs of their traveling than on the well worn game trail behind.

The valley narrowed, and the stream veered near the ridge on the south. Then, as they rounded a bend, the jungle opened disclosing a wide meadow running down to a long, flat rock standing in a pool of deeper water, the lower edge of the rock slanted and revealed an array of fish darting to and fro. Along the north bank a wall of colorful trees, bamboo, and cane was nearly impenetrable. Suddenly the ridge rose and changed into a sheer cliff. The only approach was to wade along the stream, after a quick glance Mario gave his approval. "You picked a hell of a spot to spend the rainy season in," he said. When they dismounted Dominique had more to show him about the value of this spot. Behind drooping branches, and vines at the foot of the cliff, there was a door to a cabin built in the cave. Dominique twisted a dried bush into a torch and led the way, they entered cabin with a low roof, and the floor was clay. To one side lay the ashes of the last fire Dominique had built. On the other side stood a framed bed upon which Dominique had slept.

"Nobody's been here in years," said Mario. "How did you find this place?"

"On my way out my first season I ran into an old ivory hunter, people in Servile Valley called him, River Rhino," said Dominique. "He wanted some company, somebody to talk to and so did I. Anyway, we started traveling together, and one day we came here. One morning while I was cooking fish he went out to kill an impala, he climbed the falls and went into the jungle. When he didn't return I went out to look for him, but I couldn't find him, no matter how loud I yelled, he didn't answer.

90

Yolanda The Enchantress

It started to rain so hard I couldn't track him. I never saw him again alive, only what was left of his remains when it stopped raining. He had fallen into a crack between two rocks, lions and hyenas had eaten him."

"It will be a long year for you, in the jungle alone," remarked Mario. He looked around. I don't see any magnesium sulfate." He said.

Dominique walked out of the door of the cabin through a huge opening. He took an abrupt turn. Mario followed looking past Dominique. The light from the torch uncovered the darkness in the enormous cave, far as you could see; the floor of the cave was white.

"God all mighty," said Mario. Somewhere back in the darkness there was bubbling and splashing.

"That's an underground stream," said Dominique. "It runs off to the southeast. If you follow it to the end you'll come out on the other side of the mountain above the falls. If Africans ever walk in the front door, I can go out the back. Look at this." He lifted the torch. The flame was bending away from the outer entrance. "That's fresh air and another way out. Year round the wind blows in like that. There's no chance for smoke from my fire to drift outside where it might attract attention, year round the cave sucks wind in and blows it out. That's why African's call this-- the Land Where Caves Breathe."

Much as he would have liked to stay, at least long enough to help Dominique get settled in this most interesting place, Mario had to leave as soon as his burros were unloaded. At Figueroa's he had been hired to move a group of discouraged settlers to Eagle Landing.

"I have to get back to Eagle Landing before the rainy season, to pick up the lumberyard equipment, some sawmill gear, and supplies for Legacy," he explained for the last time. "I'll get paid going and coming."

"You're doing the work, you should get paid both ways," said Dominique.

"When should I come back to pack up your mineral salt?"

"Early spring."

"Should be able to make it right early, Legacy wants that

lumberyard equipment at Rhino Creek as soon as we can get it through the jungle."

"That will depend on how long the rainy season last. I'll be looking for you, when the ground dries up enough for a wagon to carry a heavy load."

"That's when you'll see me," said Mario.

Dominique hated to see him go, but working alone was better. He threw himself into this work with, fierce unrestrained energy, with as much enthusiasm as if he were building the house in which Liana and he were to live. His hopes and expectations had become so defined that in his mind it seemed almost unreal. His first need was timber for building and logs for fuel. He waded miles up stream to do his cutting. Zulu hunters often circled around Victoria Falls countryside. Even if no Zulu warrior heard the ring of his ax, sooner or later some Zulu would notice the chips, or broken branches. He didn't want any unwanted attention to his cave.

The logs and firewood were rafted down the stream. With some of the logs he built a pen for Ruddy surrounded by mangrove, palm, and cottonwood trees near a huge maple at the lower edge of the meadow. A hundred feet from the mouth of the cave, he built a shed to shelter her from wind and rain. With the other logs he built a wall across the mouth of the cave and fitted it with a new door that could be barred, making the dwelling into a refuge stronger than any cabin and one that could be defended, by one man. The firewood was stacked in the main cavern. Keeping four big pots boiling would take a lot of fuel, and once he had started purifying mineral salt to make magnesium sulfate he didn't want to stop to get more.

He paid attention to the slightest detail with his preparations. This morning, he was transporting his last raft of wood down stream, the sky got cloudy, and it turned very cold. It started raining. He thought little of it at first because occasionally, slightly cooler weather wasn't uncommon in this section of Africa, in late October. By noon there was a blizzard of such ferocity; one like Old Rhino had told him about. The kind of weather, that happens frequently on mountains of Morocco. One like the Old Rhino said he had experienced on the Kilimanjaro Mountain, in Tanzania, each hour, the weather got colder.

Yolanda The Enchantress

The last stacks of wood were covered in ice before he could drag them into his cave. He tied his extra blanket over Ruddy and fed her. After she was sheltered in the shed, he staggered against strong gusting winds to his cabin door. He had been working for days, often to the limits of his strength. Now that he was sheltered and warm within, he welcomed this moment.

He slept soundly from late afternoon through the night, stirring only occasionally and noticing that the wind was still blowing against the door. It was an intensely cold, a bone-chilling breeze creeping across the dirt floor that awakened him at dawn. The wind had stopped. His first thought was of Ruddy. He was moving hastily to put logs on coals, smoldering under the ashes of his fire. Before he could get the flames going, he heard a gunshot. The sound was so close; he picked up his rifle, and rushed to the door. Before he could open the door to see out, there was a louder blast even nearer. With a quick glance, he saw the white blanket of snow was unbroken. No tracks were anywhere; even at the edge of the jungle was one thick sheet of white. To his astonishment, the cold had been so severe that the stream had frozen. He heard more shots and cracking sounds in the distance.

He began to think there was some other reason for the cracking, blasting sounds. There couldn't be so many people wandering about, in the cold, not this far from any of the Congo Basin settlements or African villages. He saw a tree that had fallen by the horse pen; the trunk was split wide open. The cold was so intense it had frozen sap in the trees; everywhere trees were splitting, and sounding like guns were firing. He opened the door even wider; it was so cold the air burned when it struck his face. Stepping into the open he could feel the cold rushing through his clothing. It felt as if he had stepped into a pool of ice water. Under the dark sky the whiteness of the jungle revealed the whiteness of death. Only the crushing of snow under his boots, and the cracking of trees broke the lifeless silence. He tramped through the snow and rushed to his horses' pen.

Ruddy stood in the doorway of the shed and whinnied her usual morning welcome. Vapor shot from her nostrils as she breathed. Beads of ice hung under her muzzle, she hadn't suf-

93

fered at all. He threw an armful of elephant grass and cane in to her. One of the many virtues of cane was that the lesser leaves remained green all season making it good winter-feed. As for water for his horse, and his own use he had to chop through the icy stream. In only one night, two inches of ice had formed.

On his way back to the cave he thought of the advantage the unexpected cold had bought. The impala he had killed, and hung in a tree had frozen; it was as hard as a rock. As long as this weather lasted his meat would keep. He could cut off what he needed each day and wouldn't need to stop working to hunt. He decided with a sudden zest of impatience, its time to start working.

After eating breakfast he went into the main cavern, and filled his pots with water and started his fires. Purifying the powder on the caves floor, which he would call magnesium sulfate. He knew only what he had been told. It was not a complicated process. It was shoveling and gathering the white dust from the floor of the cave. After scooping the minerals up, he washed the substance with water. He boiled the powdery substance until crystals formed, than let them cool. His first attempts were unsuccessful, but when he washed and boiled the powder longer, to his satisfaction clusters of magnesium sulfite crystals appeared.

It was slower work than he had anticipated, but by the third day he was able to improve on that, come spring, he would certainly have accumulated as much magnesium sulfite as Mario's donkeys could carry. The long waits while the solution boiled was what took the time. He stopped sleeping through the night and took his rest in short segments, getting up as often as was necessary to keep the fires going and the water boiling. He was shut off from the weather outside. Here in the heart of the mountain there was no way of telling weather it was hot or cold. Each time he emerged he expected to find a change, but there was none. Occasionally the wind had bought more snow. The northwest gales were never succeeded by the flow of warmer air from the south which usually follows storms. Each day, the bitter weather increased even more. He could imagine the shock, of such an unnatural cold spell in the settlements, and African villages in Congo Basin.

Yolanda The Enchantress

On day sixty he discovered that the stream had frozen solid. The water of the stream in the cavern was now too bitter to drink. From then on, to get water for himself and his horse he had to melt snow. The following day he ate the last of his impala and he realized that he had to stop working and go hunting, but with the morning came another problem that took the thought of hunting from his mind. Ruddy didn't appear in the shed doorway. When he reached the stable he found her inside lying on the ground. She was nearly unconscious, breathing sporadically, struggling and gasping; there was blood on her lips and body. Her body was rigid and cold, except for her throat, which was swollen and hot. Prying her mouth open he saw cuts on her tongue and shreds of cottonwood bark between her teeth, he knew what had happened. With the stubbornness of a horse she had ignored the cane or elephant grass, she had stretched through the fence to eat bark from the cotton-wood tree. Normally cottonwood bark is good for horses, they could feed on it through an ordinary season with no other food, but when frozen hard it was dangerous. The sharp-edged shreds had cut her throat and stomach, if he didn't do something fast, she would die.

He remembered that salt was commonly used to treat such a disorder. Desperately he forced salt into her mouth, and down her throat, trying to choke her. He wanted to stop her labored breathing. He built a fire in the shed, and kept her covered with a heated blanket while he warmed the other. He put his spare shirt in boiling water and placed it on her throat, and rubbed the swelling with chunks of ice. Night came, and another day. She showed no improvement, the horse's spastic breathing never stopped. He grasped at one faint hope. A horse that was going to die usually died right away. When they hung on like this they had a fighting chance. He shoved a handful of cooked mush far enough down her throat for her to swallow. With a long hollow reed he forced warm water into her rectum to make her have a bowel movement.

After a second day and night without sleep he was nearly as weak as his horse, but he was saved from further starving by an old ostrich, which had frozen on its perch during the night. He cleaned the frozen carcass and cooked it, keeping little account of time because of his concern for his horse, his hunger

95

made him eat a large portion of it before it was done. Already tense and exhausted, his gorging on the half-cooked meat made him sick. He was left with so little strength that it was only by painful efforts that he managed to get the last of the ostrich into the pot and keep the fire burning. Now he was as sick as his horse. When he sipped the hot broth he noticed something that did more to restore him than the hot soup. Ruddy lifted her head and looked at him.

The next day she stopped resisting, and swallowed the mash. The day after she stood. The third day, though trembling and shaky, she walked unsteadily, he moved her into the cave to keep her warm. The effort tired her so much that she barely made it through the door, but after he bedded her down. She stopped panting and she was eating more than she had eaten in days. Confident at last that she would live, Dominique slept until he was rested. Awakening, he was delighted to see her standing, her ears pricked forward watching him with interest. There was no longer the slightest doubt of her getting well. He leaped out of bed, refreshed, eager to return to his work, only to encounter moments later another crushing blow. The sound of water running in the cavern had stopped while he slept. Not believing, he ran to look. The underground stream had dwindled to a trickle. He ran to the door to discover that the cold outside was more intense than ever. What happened was obvious. At some point near the cave's source the stream had frozen solid. Until the weather changed there would be no water to boil.

For a short time he refused to submit to this unbelievable disaster. Realizing he couldn't carry enough snow to be melted. He chopped slabs of ice from the stream, and carried the chunks in to melt. After a day of effort he realized that he could never carry the amount of water that was needed for washing and boiling. He was too sick, and each day he got sicker.

Storms came and went, the cold weather continued, but the need to hunt for food was not a problem. Within sight of the cave there were frozen carcasses of two impalas, and three ostrich. Several times he searched the land more widely, curious yet reluctant to see more of the destruction, and effects of the unnatural weather. Everywhere trees had split and white mounds where animals had given up their struggle to exist dotted snow-

Yolanda The Enchantress

covered landscape. Much of the grass and bamboo had been killed. The jungle would be a long time recovering, from the effects of this unnatural storm of 1765.

Depressed by what he had seen outside, Dominique spent his days gazing at the fire. This season, upon which he had depended on so much, was drifting away. The approaching spring, of which he had expected so much, when it came, would welcome him with very little accomplished. He dreamed constantly and in his dreams he was as frustrated as in his waking hours. His dreams were vivid and disturbing when he was neither quite awake nor asleep, therefore his most frightening nightmarish portions constantly blended with reality. He couldn't sleep without dreaming of running water, boiling pots, and the jungle green and sunlit, Mario's donkeys loaded with magnesium sulfate and; yet without ever entirely losing the consciousness that it was only dreams.

Often Liana appeared in his dreams, at first always near smiling with her arms outstretched, and her lips parted waiting to be kissed. When he reached for her she seemed to drift just beyond his grasp. She would drift to him again when his arms dropped, to taunt him, until the harshness of reality woke him up. The sudden surge of longing gave in to reality, when he realized how far away she was, and, how unsuccessful he had been trying to bring her closer. He was equally haunted by his desire for the weather to change, and his constant thoughts of spring. In spring, Legacy, Monty and Antonio would return to Rhino Creek, and he wouldn't be there to keep his appointment with them, unless he went empty handed. His only comfort was that of his horses' health continuing to improve. He had lost count of days, but he knew the stream had been frozen for more than three months. Now there was very little time to do the things he had planned. At least three months had been lost.

Suddenly the weather changed without a warn ing. In the middle of the night he heard water splashing in the cave. It was a sound he had heard so often in his dreams, for a moment he didn't believe what he was hearing. He listened, and clapped his hands to be sure that he was awake. He still heard it. He lit a torch and ran into the cave. The stream was flowing again, and water was gathering in its hollow beds. He rushed outside. The air was hot and snow was melting, and trees were dripping in the middle of the night. He was so happy he yelled, until he could barely make a sound. He rushed back to the cavern and rekindled his fires. Within an hour there was water enough to start one pot and by the next morning all of them were boiling. Deeper in the cavern the impregnated earth had formed thicker layers of gleaming white powder, on the ground. The floor of the cave was now whiter and much richer. Making the longer trips, there was a greater increase of crystals at the bottom of each pot. Raking and shoveling the powder gave him something to do, while the pots were boiling. Now that he was working again, he was driven by that same strange restless impatience that had tormented him during the forced idleness of the unusual winter weather.

Spring coming at last came with such a vengeance, it was as if Mother Nature was apologizing, in days the snow was gone. Flamingos flew in from the south, and grass grew in the meadow. Ruddy quickly recovered and played in the sun, leaping and rolling in the grass. Every plant tree and creature of the wild that hadn't been killed by the cold, stirred. Mangrove buds appeared, swelled and slowly burst into bloom, still Mario hadn't come. At first Dominique thought little of his failure to return at the time agreed upon. The unusual weather must have delayed his travel schedule, even a man who plans every move as carefully as Mario, could have run into unforeseen problems. At first, the delay was a relief, because Dominique wasn't ready. When Mario returned he would have had to wait, he would complain about the money he was losing from paying customers.

After a second week, and then a third week went by, with no sign of Mario, Dominique began to worry. Perhaps something had happened to Mario, he would never be this late. The more Dominique thought about it the more he was overwhelmed by one possibility. Going to and from Eagle Landing Mario traveled with a large party, his greatest risk was traveling alone from Figueroa's to the cave. Dominique hung around a few more days, then he saddled Ruddy and set out to search the trail leading to Figueroa Station. No one had traveled it since Mario had taken it north the autumn before. Nor was the slightest sign that Africans had been anywhere in the region after the snow had melted. Af-

Yolanda The Enchantress

ter such an unusual season most people were busy hunting to keep their families from starving. They were too busy to look for trouble...

An irritating possibility occurred to him. Mario could have left Congo Road when it merged with Gun Road, and traveled westward through the jungle. If Mario were coming from that direction he would come out on the other side of the ridge that swerved to the east. The more Dominique thought that Mario might be on the way, to the cave, or waiting there, while he was wasting time searching for him on the road leading to Figueroa's Station, the more annoyed he became. He decided before going any further, to search the game trail to be sure. The thick vine covered rocky ridges were much easily climbed on foot. He tied Ruddy in a vine-covered tree and set out. Three hours later he climbed down the other side to discover Mario had not passed along this old African trail, which followed the creek westward. After more hazardous hours he returned to the spot he had left his horse, and here he discovered that he had lost even more.

Ruddy was gone, it was apparent that African warriors had taken her. After examining the ground near and around the vine-covered tree, he knew what had happened as clearly as if he had witnessed it. There were two of them, both Zulu. The heavier one left foot has been recently broken and the other had a injured leg because his right foot dragged. They were traveling south, fast, probably from a northern village in Zululand, and had come upon his horse by the purest chance. They traveled up Congo Basin, instead of taking Gorilla Passage, to steal a horse or camel. They had failed because they were still on foot, and were surprised to find a horse tied up waiting for them.

The two Zulu warriors, one riding and the other running behind, were heading south, towards Swaziland. Dominique's impulse was to pursue. There were many reasons for his going to any length to recover his horse but none of them crossed his mind. His rage was reason enough. To let a couple of Africans take something from him was not to be endured. The Zulu warriors pulled away from him that first afternoon. They kept changing places in the saddle so that the one on foot was always fresh. Dominique was tired from running and climbing. When

99

night came he rested, and lost more distance. To follow their trail in the dark he had to feel for hoof-prints, for many hours, moving as fast as the landscape permitted.

The next morning, luckily, they slept well past dawn. He gained on them again at the crossing of Redwood River; because Ruddy didn't like water, they lost time getting her to swim the river. In the afternoon they slowed up a little and stopped changing places in the saddle. Thereafter the warrior with the injured foot did all the riding and the other all the running. He no longer clung to the horse's tail but kept a safe distance. Dominique assumed the warrior running was in better shape.

The next morning ashes in their campfire were still warm. Before nightfall, he began to think with a little luck he would catch up with them. But early that afternoon, just after crossing a wide stream running northwest towards Redwood River, they met another African, and after talking with him they turned east, instead of keeping on towards Swaziland.

They walked slowly, following an old hippo trail, walking alongside each other where the going permitted. The first two chewing dried gazelle that the other warrior had given them. One of them dropped apiece, which Dominique picked up and ate. Several times they stopped to talk. The Africans were waving their arms, pointing and talking, gesturing with emotion in Dominique's direction. There was no doubt; this was an important message that was being told to the two warriors from the north. After observing the conversation and pointing, Dominique kept a safe distance behind them. Before dark they would stop, and darkness would bring him his chance. Now he had three instead of two to deal with, but on the other hand, more than likely with three in camp they would be less watchful.

Later in the afternoon something happened that disturbed Dominique. Vultures circling overhead were noisy, and excited. Over a distant hilltop more vultures were hovering low, as they did when attracted by something dead. In the old rhino trail he came upon deep prints where a gazelle, running at full speed had dashed headlong into the warriors' camp, and suddenly wheeled away. The gazelle was running towards them when he spotted them. This was a section of the jungle that had recently been hunted. The stream widened revealing a glimpse of grassland ahead. He climbed a tree and saw the stream circling around the edge of a meadow. In the middle of that meadow was a Zulu hunting camp with more than a dozen families. Since the moment he started the chase he knew what he was going to do, when he caught up with them. He would creep in and kill the two while they were sleeping, and take his horse and leave. Even if they reached one of their villages before being overtaken there would be an opportunity to do some-thing. Horses and cattle had to be taken out to graze during the day, to a pasture some distance beyond the maize-fields. Young boys could be out-witted or dealt with much easier than a man, but this hunting camp was a problem. There was plenty of grass in the middle of the camp, and too many hunters to creep in upon at night.

There was no use hanging around worrying about what to do. An opportunity of some sort might turn up. He had to do something, but whatever attempt he made in the coming darkness he needed a closer look. He had to see the way the camp was laid out while it was light. He climbed down the tree and waded up the steam under shrubbery hanging over the bank. He swam until he was able to crawl into a cluster of bushes from which the camp was in full view. Smoke from meat drying on racks, and cooking fires in the camp circled and drifted over the brush huts becoming more visible in the still evening air. Most of the hunters had returned. Women were laughing and yelling at each other while skinning, butchering, and cooking. The whole camp was buzzing with excitement. The arrival of the two warriors from the north had created a stir of excitement, and their horse was the focus of their attention. They were pretending that stealing the horse was nothing special, and, talking very big. The two warriors were strutting, nodding, and making hand gestures. They were telling the others about the great things they had done while they'd been away, of which the horse was mentioned only once.

The hunters and women listened for a while, then they leaped, bend, and twisted, Zulu fashion. The men bragged about everything they had done since they had killed their first lion. The group of them would sit up all night, eating, bragging, singing and dancing. Dominique watched, getting frustrated and angry; getting Ruddy tonight wouldn't be easy. The luck of which Mario had so often spoke, was gnawing at him with a vengeance. The sensible thing to do was to wait. All he could do was wait. Tomorrow night, after tonight's excitement, the camp would be more approachable, or the camp would break up, and the hunters would scatter to search for better hunting. The two warriors might decide to go on alone to show their prize, and tell their story to a bigger audience, in their village. The problem was that Dominique couldn't afford to wait. He couldn't afford to be patient or do the sensible thing. He had to get back to his cave to find out what had happened to Mario, and to do everything else he had to do. He couldn't wait a day. Whatever he was going to do, he had to do it tonight. If he got the chance, he would take her and go.

A dry stick snapped, not far from the bushes he was hiding under on the other side of the creek. This near the camp before dark no wild animal big enough to break a stick that size would be wondering, Dominique stayed still and listened, there was a crunching of dry leaves as of a bare foot. He drew his feet in, turned on his side, bent his right arm, drew his ax and held it in his hand for a quick throw. He was hiding in a cluster of bushes unseen. If whoever was approaching happened to see him; he had to be certain his ax reached its mark, before any outcry that might be heard in the camp. He waited, tensely.

Across the stream only a few paces away a branch moved. The branch was drawn aside, and a young African woman stepped into view. She was slender, well shaped and graceful even on the slippery bank. Her beaded headband reflected in the vanishing sunlight. The furry goatskin bands on her legs and arms, complimented her short goat skirt. She moved with the lightness and grace of a cheetah, her wrist was tiny and her hands were small. Her braided hair was wet. There was red, white, and black paint on her forehead, and cheekbones. She had just finished washing, and painting her face in a nearby pool. A snake slivered from under her feet into the water. She paused to watch. She smiled, as it swam away, and began to stroll along the bank in Dominique's direction, glancing about leisurely, enjoying the evening.

Dominique's fingers tightened on the handle of his ax. He wasn't sure he could bring himself to make the throw, even if she discovered him and screamed, even if it came to be a choice of her life or his. She was so young, so innocent of any intention to threaten him, and so defenseless. Her movement along the bank bought her out of the shadows. Under her painted face her skin was mediumt brown. He knew Portuguese and Spanish people who had tanned as dark as she was. She turned towards him, not to look on the ground where he was, she was looking over the bushes in the direction of her camp. He saw then that her eyes were odd, in striking contrast to her curly, braided black hair, and that paint on her face. She was probably a half-breed daughter of some white trader, which had left her behind to grow up with her Zulu relatives.

She stood directly across from him, only a few feet away. The wild grass scent of her hair, and the skimpy garments she was wearing taunted him. Her skirt brushed against a thorn and she turned to free it. Her upper thigh was revealed for a moment when her skirt was pulled above the top of her goatskin thigh bands, they were as firm as any Portuguese woman. She could be Portuguese, Dominique decided, and moetlikele she was certainly a prisoner. She moved on. He was safe from her discovering him, if she was a prisoner she would be willing to help him. She would be glad to do anything to annoy her kidnaper's. All she'd have to do was to get up tonight, and bring his horse to him. Whatever the risk of approaching her it was a far lesser risk than any other that faced him.

He rushed across the stream, and ran up behind her, keeping low making sure he couldn't be seen from the camp over the top of the bushes. She turned and saw him, her eyes widened, but she didn't scream. He smiled, and made reassuring gestures as he moved towards her, still she didn't scream. She turned and started to run. He lunged, and caught her by the arm and pulled her around to face him.

"S-s-h," he warned, putting a finger to his lips.

She began to struggle and broke free. He slipped the strap of his rifle over his shoulder, grabbed both arms and shook her to bring her to her senses.

"Stop shouting," he said. "I'm here to help you."

The sound of his voice speaking unknown words bought her head up. She stared into his face. He was a white man, when

103

she spoke it was not to him, but to scream the Zulu alarm. He placed his hand over her mouth, and straightened up enough to look towards the Zulu camp. The warriors in the campsite didn't hear her scream, but two women carrying jugs of water from the stream heard her scream. They started running and screaming. Dominique hit the young woman and brutally shook her.

"You fool," he said. "I'm not going to hurt you."

She sank her teeth into the hand he was holding over her mouth. He snatched his hand away and punched her on the jaw. In his anger he punched her harder than he had intended, the blow knocked her off her feet and senseless.

The women had given the alarm, and warriors were reaching for their weapons. There was no hope now of getting Ruddy. The only thing that he could do now, was to make sure that he didn't get caught. He turned to run, but after thinking he returned. He bent down, and grabbed her again. If he left her here they would find her, and she would tell them the direction he had taken. It was better to keep them looking for her forcing them to spend as much time as possible circling trying to figure out what had happened. He threw her limp body over his shoulder, jumped into the water and started running in the stream.

Dark clouds gathered, over trees, it began to get dark. In the distance he could hear signals, whistles and animal calls of the searching Africans. He thought they would have discovered by now where he had hidden in the bushes, and jumped in the stream, but they were not sure of what had happened to her. They wouldn't catch him tonight; it would be dark in minutes.

Near the stream was a hippo trail on which he could travel much faster, but there he would leave footprints that would be seen in the morning. His prints would reveal the direction he had taken. Daylight tomorrow the real danger would come. After running behind his horse the last few days, and not sleeping at night, he didn't have the strength to outrun them if they picked up his trail before noon tomorrow. His only chance to get away was to keep them guessing about the direction he had taken. He kept to the stream, stumbling over rocks, and often falling headfirst. The sudden plunges into cold water woke the woman up. She started struggling to break away. For a while she fought and struggled silently, with the vicious energy of a trapped cheetah. Because of his superior strength he forced her into a position where she could no longer move, then she started yelling. He placed his hand over her mouth, this time avoiding her teeth.

"Listen," he whispered. "There's nothing you can do. You're staying' with me, and you'll be quiet. When I'm a safe distance away, I'll let you go, you can go. Until then behave yourself and nothing will happen to you."

She gave no sign that she understood, or heard a word he said. The moment his grasp relaxed she tried to break away from him again. She was a burden, but he couldn't let her go. She would have the Zulu after him in no time at all, he didn't want to knock her out again, and leave her. He took the rope he had in his pocket, and tied her up, forcing one end of the rope between her teeth, knotting it in position to keep her gagged. He shoved and forced her into the middle of an incense tree. Tomorrow the Zulu would search both banks of the stream, and before the day was over some sharp eyed warrior would spot her. But it would be too late, for her to tell them anything that would help them.

He started down the stream, a lion roared on a distant hilltop. He thought it was a Zulu warrior until the call was answered from another slope to the west. It was natural for lions and other large cats to gather in a section that had recently been hunted. Wounded impalas got lions as excited as any other animal that was injured, or trapped. When blood was spattered on leaves along trails, or where carcasses had been picked drove lions into frenzies, they would look every-where for whatever they could find. Another lion growled. Dominique continued a few steps, stopped, slowly turned and rushed back to the tree. He picked her up, and threw her over his shoulder, and started down stream.

He kept moving until he reached a wider stream, wading shoulder deep at times, until he reached a tiny island made of piles of driftwood, and debris. He struggled to dry ground beyond the driftwood and, dumped her limp body and dropped to his hands and knees.

Fumbling in the dark he checked to see if the rope tied to his prisoner's ankles and wrists were tight. They were and while drying they would tighten even more. She would have an uncomfortable night. He was glad of that. She was lucky to be alive. She was getting out of this unpleasant situation with only a nasty scratch and a night's discomfort. Her stupidity had cost him his only chance to get his horse.

It was because of her, that his horse was still in the hands of Zulu warriors. He was left with nothing to show for all his suffering and effort but a slim chance of getting away unharmed. Wrapping the loose end around his wrist, he jerked savagely on the rope. He started to get up, and kick her around for a while until she feared him, but he was too tired. He dropped to the ground, and placed his face on the damp sand, and fell asleep.

Chapter 7
Zulu Woman

At dawn Dominique opened his eyes long enough to survey his situation. Dense belts bamboo and mangrove trees lined the banks on each side. Very little of the island could be seem from anywhere beyond the bamboo and trees. Only hunters coming down could see him the stream. He felt fairly safe because of that. The hunters in the campsite didn't have a boat, and would never think of building one. He jerked the rope to make sure the woman was still fasten to him, and turned over and went back to sleep.

When the sun, rose above the eastern hilltop, he turned over again. He was stiff and sore but less tired than when he had reached the island but, much too restless to sleep any longer. There was little for him to do the next few hours but to sit and wait. He was deciding his next moves. Zulu searchers would press hard today and tomorrow, making traveling overland too much of a risk. Instead of running that risk he would build a raft, and drift down the stream under cover of darkness. Entering upper Victoria Falls, after reaching Red-wood River. Having left no trail behind him, the next day it would be safer to travel through the jungle to reach his cave and then, if Mario hasn't arrived, he would go to Figueroa Station. He sat up looking at his prisoner, she had moved as far from him as the rope would let

Yolanda The Enchantress

her. She lay on her side with her bounded hands and feet thrust towards him. She had managed to slide the gag from her mouth, but the knots on her wrists were too tight for her to untie. Her eyes were closed and her face showed no emotion; she was pretending she was asleep. She was waiting for him to fall asleep.

It angered him that she was so stupid, she was trembling with fear of what he might do next. He glanced at the slender shape of her arms, they were smooth and shapely. Her black eyelashes hid under her long thick hair. Her hair fell across her face; it was so long that he couldn't tell if she were watching him. Her eyebrows had been trimmed, keeping an old Zulu custom. The way she braided her hair and the shape of her body, those exotic features haunted him. They contrasted with the paint on her face, which gave her the appearance of a woman. She was younger than he had thought at first, probably not more than eighteen or nineteen. Her womanly figure stirred an unexpected lustful emotion in him. After all the trouble she had caused him, and no matter how ignorant and savage looking, he couldn't let her go. Her wrists were swollen and raw under the leather rope. He knelt beside her and loosened them. Her eyes opened and there was no emotion in her haunting gaze to indicate what she might be thinking. She just watched him.

"Your fault," he told her.

Without a warning she leaped on the pile of driftwood and leaped into the water. He jumped over the driftwood and plunged into the water after her. She was a stronger and much better swimmer, than he. Had she not struck a submerged sand bar she would have gotten away. Now the water was shallow standing upright, he thrashed through knee-deep water leaping from sandbar to sandbar until he caught up with her. He took a desperate lunge and grabbed her by the ankle. He dragged her to the sandbar but she refused to stand up, when he pulled her up she fought him every way she could, clawing, kicking, biting, until he hit her. She collapse and he carried her back to the island, dropped her on the ground and stared at her angrily.

"One more trick." he threatened, "I'll kill you."

She was squeezing water from her hair and shaking her head. After she finished she sat erect with her hands folded on her lap. The paint on her face had smeared and run. Her stern

Zulu composure, and stubborn refusal to give the slightest hint that she knew he was talking to her. The paint smeared across her expressionless face.

"Wash your face," he shouted angrily. "Then you won't look so much like a dirty, stinking, Zulu."

He might as well have been talking to a rock or a piece of driftwood. River water had flowed under the driftwood forming small pools near where she was sitting. He grabbed the back of her neck, bent her over and washed her face. She didn't resist, even when he used muddy water, to scrub her face clean.

"There," he said, leaning back, "now you look better."

She calmly picked up a handful of red clay, and dabbed it across her face. He was sorry he had started so foolish a game, but he was committed to win it now. He bent her over and washed her face again. She reached for the mud; he grabbed the back of her neck. Without looking at him she dropped the handful of clay, and washed her hands, sat back, and folded her hands on her lap and gazed up the river. He continued twisting the rope. He had won another round but it hadn't given him much satisfaction. He watched her. Now that it was clean, her face had a certain fineness, very pleasant features. Her eyes, her nose, her mouth, each in itself was pleasing to look at, but showing an absence of feeling. That stern, senseless Zulu look no longer went with her face.

"Hungry?" he asked.

She paid no attention. It was like talking to a stone.

"Well, I am," he said. "I'll catch a fish."

He rose and walked over to the bamboo and cut a pole. Then he came back and sat down and began trimming it to make a spear, he tied his knife on one end. She never glanced around to follow any of his movements. Her refusal to acknowledge him made him determined to get some kind of response from her.

"I told you I would turn you loose," he said. "I'll do it, when the time is right."

Nothing he said bought a response. She continued to sit without emotion, giving no indication that his words were understood. It could be that she didn't understand Portuguese, but even a trapped animal would have responded to the sound of his voice. She didn't so much as bat an eye at the sound of his voice. There was the other option that there was something wrong with her hearing. "Look out," he shouted loudly. She didn't move. Without a warning he threw his knife into a branch above her head. She was looking in another direction; she couldn't have seen the movement of his arm when he made the throw. When the knife plunged into the branch she turned, he laughed and said, "You are not deaf."

He was getting up to retrieve his knife. She snatched the still quivering knife from the branch above her head, and started for him. He was caught off balance and off guard; it was by the narrowest margin that he avoided the blow, which was aimed at his throat. He grabbed her arm and twisted the knife out of her hand while holding her off.

She angrily stared without remorse or hesitation. There was an expression of renewed life in her face now. It was easy to predict what she was thinking and feeling. She was glad she had tried to kill him; and sorry she had failed, but eager to try again.

"Be careful little lady don't push your luck. I warned you, I'll kill you," he said. With the bamboo pole he was holding, he began to beat her. She didn't flinch, cringe, or cry out or move to avoid the blows. She stood still, and after each stroke she smiled at him scornfully. He threw the pole down in disgust. Beating didn't help. It was like beating a wild animal. The thing to do is to get rid of her, he would release her before the day was over; she wasn't his responsibility. He picked up the rope and tied one end to her ankle, and the other around a tree. He searched the area around her for anything she could use to cut the leather, before he started fishing.

He returned with a huge catfish and carved half a dozen slices from it. He split pieces of dry driftwood into slivers, kindled a very small, very hot fire and cooked the slices of fish on a green stick. The first slice he offered to her. She ignored him. He put it on a leaf within her reach. He ate until he was no longer hungry.

After a glance at the sun to determine the time of day, he stretched out in the shade and slept for hours. Awaking refreshed he saw the woman biting the rope, with persistence and determination. He smiled, and let her chew. It was tough old crocodile hide, and long before she could chew it in half, he would be turning her loose. He pretended not to notice what she was doing. He started searching for huge stalks of bamboo the right size, shape, to build a raft, and for vines strong enough to hold it together. She was no longer staring up the river; she was watching his every move. A fatal flaw in his plan suddenly struck him. He wasn't sure of the distance to Redwood River, and he had to take advantage of every hour of the night. He had to start building the raft now, if he wanted to leave at dust. She was watching him and she had seen enough to know what he was doing. When she told her Zulu relatives about the raft they would know the direction he had taken, they would be able to catch him by running along the ridges, and they would reach Redwood River before he did. He had to keep her with him another day.

She watched him prepare for the journey, by now he knew her well enough to be constantly on guard. He was careful that his rifle, ax or knife was never placed within her reach. He never became too preoccupied with his raft building to keep an eye on her. She sat and watched. At nightfall, he was ready to go. She showed no anger or resentment. He tied the end of the leather rope that had been tied to the mangrove tree around his waist. She didn't resist, but when the raft was launched, and they'd started down the river she stood up, and grabbed a branch hanging over her head, and leaped from the raft to the tree. The rope, tightened around Dominique's waist making him lean against the bamboo pole with which he was guiding the raft, and jerked him into the water. The raft bobbed and drifted downstream. It was at this point that he was tempted to kill her, nearer than he had been at any time. He dragged her ashore and tied the rope to a branch high enough so that the ankle to which the rope was tied held her off the ground. Leaving her in this awkward suspended position dangling in the air, he swam after the raft.

After a hard swim he returned with the raft, and found her dangling uncomfortably in the air waving the untied leg. When she boarded the raft she curled up like a wild cheetah, and fell asleep. For him it was a night of never ending labor, constantly freeing the raft from obstructions. Dragging it over sand bars, pushing it away from sandbanks. While she slept through everything, at dawn when he slept she would be awake; rested and plotting her next move. They had not reached Redwood

Yolanda The Enchantress

River, as he had hoped. At the first glimpse of dawn he poled into a reed covered inlet beyond a merging stream. There they would stay until nightfall, hidden from watchful eyes scanning the open river, from the surrounding hills. He pulled the raft onto the bank, and offered her some of the fish. She refused it. After her refusal he ate all of it, and pulled the slack out of the rope to keep her from moving, without him knowing. He placed his weapons under him so that she couldn't reach them, and then prepared to sleep. She continued to show no emotion as usual, but there was a roving gleam in her eyes.

Defensively shielding his face with one arm, he watched her though sleepy eyes. She was scanning the area with cunning, alert eyes; looking at everything near and far. She looked up at flashes of light, and shadow cast by the canopy overhead. Than down at the water flowing past the raft. She smiled, at a school of colorful fish swimming under the roots of mangrove trees. She glanced at a pair of flamingos that were incredibly brilliant gracefully dancing in the sun. She smiled at two hummingbirds, hovering over her head, before dashing away. She winked at monkeys and tiny apes, and from time to time, she glanced at Dominique, with evil intentions. Suddenly, her eyes became fixed on something behind him. He turned, and looked.

About thirty feet away a huge turtle had come to the water's edge to eat. Dominique slowly moved his ax from under him. He untied the leather rope. "Turtle for supper instead of fish," he thought. The throw was from an awkward position but it was true. The turtle fell backward kicking. Dominique untied the rope, and gestured to her woman to retrieve his kill. To this orders she obeyed. She never stopped to think. He watched her tramp along the bank; if she dashed for the jungle with the long rope trailing behind her. The tide was retreating, making water near the bank to shallow to swim in. He hoped, when she picked up the ax, she would throw it at him. He would enjoy showing her how easily he could catch it, but she ran back with the huge turtle; and gave him his weapon, and climbed back on the raft.

He tied the rope around his waist and settled down again. He had almost fallen asleep before noticing what she was doing. Placing her fingers in the gash in the turtle's throat and using the water beside the raft as a mirror, she was painting her face with blood. Dominique rose and took the carcass away from her, and washed her face. Submerging her, thrusting her head downward into the water, the strap to her top came untied. When lifted her upright the top fell down exposing her breast. They were hard and well formed the breasts of a fully-grown woman. He quickly placed her top back into position.

For the first time she laughed, it was a taunting, bone chilling laugh filled with hostility. She deliberately took off all her clothing for him to see her. He realized that from her strange, heathen point of view there was nothing obscene in her gestures. It was his actions that uncovered her breast. It was because of his actions she had seized upon this as another way to fight him. She was flaunting her contempt for him.

He stepped back and turned away, hoping she would stop, when she realized, she was nothing to him. Instead she took off her beaded headband. Now she was wearing only white goatskin bands on her arms and legs.

He grabbed her clothing and threw them at her. That provoked another senseless challenge. Everything about his actions was contrary to his character; this was like a bad dream. He was struggling to keep her covered, but she kept taking her clothing off. Her taunting laughter continued and his swearing became more and more violent. Escaping his grasp for a second she snatched her clothing from hem, and threw them into the water, and watched them float away. She confronted him without clothing, with her arms flung upward. Her eyes glowing like those of a wild cheetah, her laughter was gay with even more of a haunting sound, this time with malicious triumph. He was so blinded by rage that he could hardly tell weather or not, she was a wild animal. He ripped off his shirt and forced her into it. This cloth was too strong for her to tear. To make sure that she didn't take it off, he sat on her, and tied strips of leather around her from the bottom to her shoulders. He tied knots in the ends of the shirt-sleeves. He took another strip of leather and tied the knots together to keep her arms, and hands from being free.

He stepped back, and looked at what he had done. This was the first moment of satisfaction he had. This effect was worth all the problems, and misery he had been through. She was safely out of mischief. And she was bagged and tied in a

Yolanda The Enchantress

sack. He wished he had thought of this sooner. She scrambled to her feet, and looked down at herself. Struggling helplessly with her hands imprisoned in the folds of the shirtsleeve. Now bounded at neck, feet, and knees with strips of leather. When he laughed at her, the hostility in the look she gave him was even more deadly than when she had tried to kill him. She wanted to fight, but she couldn't hit him; she was helpless. She regained control of her emotions, and did what a Zulu warrior would do under these circumstances. She started thinking and acting like a Zulu warrior. She straightened her back, and moved to the edge of the raft. There she sat, her knees drawn up under her chin. She hunched her shoulders inside the shirt, which hung over her like a collapsed tent, and avoided all contact with him.

Delighted by the advantage he gained; Dominique stretched out and slept until past noon. He awoke full of energy and new ideas. Though he hadn't reached Redwood River he would make better time if he carved out a dugout canoe this afternoon so that he could travel faster tonight. He looked at the young woman. She hadn't moved. He tied the end of rope to the raft and went ashore. Finally finding an elm of the right size, he cut a ten-foot strip of bark from it in a single piece. After bending the bark into the shape he wanted, he filled the ends with heated bark. He filled the hull with strips of cedar, and sealed the stems with tar. Then he softened the tar on the flat heated stones he had placed beside the fire, after roasting the turtle. Well before night had come the dugout was finished. It was crude and shaky, but it was a boat.

He ate a portion of the roasted turtle and wrapped the rest in a green banana leaves for later. While eating he glanced up and saw a cluster of young trees well up towards the top of the hill above them. He had intended to carve a paddle from a piece of driftwood he had seen near the shore near the raft. Cedar would make a better paddle, and he had completed the boat early enough to give him time to make a good ore. He ran up the hill towards the trees. When he reached the crest of the hill, he dropped to the ground as suddenly as if he had seen a Zulu warrior. It was almost as bad. Along the crest of the ridge, just beyond the trees, ran a well-traveled African trail. This must be the new Zulu trail he had heard talk about. The last year or two most Africans had gone out of their way, to avoid contact with white-men, they circled west of Congo Basin settlements when traveling to and from northern African villages, instead of taking Gorilla Passage through the eastern mountains. This path crossed Redwood River Trail near the stream; he was following, and merged with the main river.

He crawled forward to examine the surface. No one had come down it today or yesterday, but one thing was certain. Before giving up their search the Zulu would search the jungle trail as far as Redwood River. It was strange they hadn't already done that. He was convinced of something else now. When he turned the woman loose to night she would head for this trail. She probably knew about it and even if she didn't, she would find it, and run to meet her Zulu relatives in time to head north to Redwood River to catch him. The satisfaction he had experienced after wrapping her in his shirt, and building a dugout canoe vanished. He couldn't let her go tonight. He had to keep her another night, at least until he had crossed Redwood River Trail, and that was on the other side of the river.

He spent an hour carefully removing evidence of his approach to the trail, there was no use trying to cover up carving around the sight where he had built the boat, and the fire. If or when they came along, they would never search that far down the embankment; there would be no reason for it. Unless they came during the remaining hours of daylight they wouldn't know he had built a boat until tomorrow morning, by then he would have enough of a start on them.He carried the dugout out and set it in the water along side the raft. It would be a relief to be able to travel faster tonight. The woman hadn't moved and he wanted nothing to do with her, and now he had to think of himself. Her wrists were swollen and raw; she didn't even look at the dugout. He unties the sleeves of the shirt to free her hands, and gave her a piece of turtle to eat.

"Eat it," he said.

She wouldn't touch it, she continued her stubbornness. Again he had an impulse to force her to eat, but he didn't have time to fight with her. He started carving an ore from a piece of driftwood he had seen earlier. While carving he listened for sounds on the trail, the peaceful sound of the jungle continued;

Yolanda The Enchantress

and clouds gathered overhead.

There was a distant whistle in the east just before night-fall. The woman pretended she didn't hear it. He loosened the end of the rope and tied it to an opening on the raft. He jerked on it gesturing for her to get in, but she didn't move. He picked her up and dropped her in the bow, and pushed off.

The boat heeled to the left a little, he corrected it by shift-ing his weight. At the mouth of the creek he paused a moment to listen. The jungle behind them was still quiet. It was dark now. He shot out into the main stream. It was a pleasure to feel the smooth swift glide after the sluggish pounding of the raft last night. The only danger in moving so fast was that he could run into something submerged, and rip a hold in the bottom, that was the chance he had to take. He needed to get further up the river before daylight. The woman hadn't moved since he had dumped her in the bow. When she moved, it was quick. She lifted her legs suddenly into the air, and swung them over the side. The sudden shift in her weight turned the boat over instantly. With a desperate grab Dominique managed to hang onto the oar, and his rifle, as well as the boat. She swam downstream with the current, but the rope tied around his waist stopped her.

The water was only shoulder deep. Dominique pushed the boat onto a sandbar, and dumped the water out of it. While pulling his prisoner against the current she fought, and struggled like a fish on a hook. When he got her to the boat she was chok-ing, and gasping for air, she had almost drowned. This time he placed her in the boat where she was within his reach. Afloat again, he leaned forward and gave her a solid whack with he oar.

"One more trick," he threatened, "and I'll give you a beating that will keep you quiet the rest of the night." He hit her again to make sure that even if she didn't understand his words she understood his intentions. Apparently she did. She took a long deep breath, which ended with a yell.

Leaning back to dip his paddle again, he realized the cur-rent had changed direction. Around the next bend the expanse of sparkling water ahead suddenly widened, they had reached Redwood River. He headed for the shore. He was traveling al-most as fast as he had hoped. He kept in the shadows of the shore, following the bend in the river. After following this course he had passed the point of greatest danger. Still any second might bring a sudden yell, followed by hissing arrows and flaming spears, but nothing happened. There was no strange animal signals or whistles. There was no smoke from campfires, nor was there any smell of smoke in the air. He deepened and lengthened his strokes. It would be harder going from now on, they were traveling against the current, but at last he was headed for his section in the jungle. They were out of Zululand.

He could see a faint gleam in her eyes when she looked up at the stars, the slight tilt of her head as she listened to the sound of water thrashing against the side of the boat. She knew that they had entered Redwood River, and they were traveling northeast towards Congo Basin. To her this was enemy country.

Her foot moved, barely visibly, she wiggled her toes and inched them along the side of the boat. Slowly edging her legs sideways, inching them upwards. Since the rope was still tied to them she couldn't escape, but she was determined to do something, whatever the cost. Hardly breaking the rhythm of his strokes, Dominique lifted the oar, and bought it down hard across her thighs. She didn't scream or make a sound. Her legs slamming against the bottom of the boat. The blow broke her skin and there was a cracking sound. Dominique took a few more strokes regretting he had hit her so hard, thinking he had broken one of her legs. He stopped paddling and bent forward to check her leg. There was a crack in her skin, which he could feel through her leggings. The flesh on each side was swelling, but after some vigorous twisting and prodding he knew the bone wasn't broken. She didn't make a sound when he lifted her and turned her, face down.

"Stay there." he told her.

She didn't move the rest of the night, still he kept a steady pace not pushing too hard. With daylight approaching, he would be on foot traveling through the jungle; and he might have to run. The first streak of light he hadn't reached the big bend. This section of Redwood River twisted and turns with long, lazy curves. The currents was so strong, it made it seam as if he were paddling two miles for one. He landed at the northern border and pulled the boat ashore after him. The woman lay stretched out face down in the bottom of the boat, shivering in the morning mist, giving no sign his landing made any difference to her. Tied up in the oversize shirt she looked lost and abandoned.

"Get up," he said.

She was resisting. She didn't move. He bent down and turned her over. She looked up at him angrily. There was a slight hint of a smile on her face. The woman hadn't caught on yet that he was letting her go here.

"Have it your way," he said.

He chopped a hold in the bottom of the boat, and dropped heavy stones in it; and shoved it out into the river. The boat drifted down stream and sank.

"Get up," he insisted.

She didn't move. He grabbed her by the shoulder and jerked her to her feet. When he let go her legs went limp, and she tumbled to the ground again.

"You picked the right place to pretend you can't walk," he said... "I hate to give you my shirt, but I have too." He picked up his rifle. He backed away a couple of steps, with gestures indicating that he was leaving. Gesturing she could go wherever she pleased, she didn't believe him. He walked a few more steps, repeating his gestures. She still didn't believe him. She thought he was trying to trick her into getting up. He remembered the remains of the turtle in his game bag. He walked back, tossed a leg to the ground beside her, and walked away again. This time he kept walking until he was out of sight. He dropped to the ground and crawled back to watch her, to see how she was going to act when she was certain he had gone. She lifted her head but only to listen. She thought he was trying to trick her. Leaning on her elbows she looked towards the river, then in the direction he had gone, considering whether or not she could reach the water before he could catch her. The turtle caught her attention. She picked it up and ate it. She was hungry because he hadn't eaten for days. After a few bites, the greasy meat made her sick. Dominique laughed. This alone was worth him coming back to see.

Slowly she mustered enough strength to limp down the riverbank. The shirt flopping around her, she was a sad looking figure against the incoming tide. He was sorry he had hung around to watch, because there was more to this than turning her loose. She had no way too hunt or make a fire, she was badly injured, Because of the unusual winter season this section of the jungle offered little to eat; there were no fruit or berries. She would get much hungrier than she is now, and she had a long ways to go. He couldn't live with the thought of leaving her to take care of herself. He stepped into the open.

"Come here," he shouted.

She didn't look around at the sound of his voice. She limped over to a patch of elephant grass, to lie down. That, same old stubbornness had started again. She was angrier with herself, than she was with him; he walked over to her.

"Get up," he shouted.

She looked at him. He had weakened but she hadn't. He slapped her lightly across the thighs with the handle of his ax. Watching the angry glare in her eyes he realized that it made no difference to her which end of the ax he hit her with.

"You're going with me," he said.

He squatted down with his back to her, and pulled her legs around his waist, tied her ankles together in front of him, gripped her arms, placed them over his shoulder, pulled the long shirt sleeves tight, crossed them and tied the ends together. She was anchored to his back now, like a knapsack. His arms were free while her hands were encased in the heavy cotton sleeves so that she couldn't scratch him, or poke his eyes or reach any of his weapons. . He stood and shifted her weight into a comfortable position, bent, and picked up his rifle and set out

He was so angry the first hour or two, he didn't notice the extra weight, but she got heavier and heavier as the day wore on. There wasn't much she could do... but what she did was worst. She slumped down inside the shirt and became an anchor, she was dead weight on his back. He didn't think the Zulu would search for him north of Redwood River. Nevertheless until well past noon he took every precaution. He stepped on rocks, and walked on stony ground, tramp through creeks, he did whatever he could to make it hard to be followed. After miles of covering his tracks he was certain that they were safe, except from some unforeseen encounter, an accidental encounter like that, which had cost him his horse. He swore every time he thought about his horse. What a mess he had made, instead of riding his horseback, he was returning to his cave carrying a woman.

Yolanda The Enchantress

Late that afternoon he shot a wild boar. Before they reach his campsite he needed to eat something if he wasn't too tired to swallow. Paddling all night against the current, and carrying a woman all day over hills, and through the jungle, was more punishment than any man should endure. He wouldn't have had the strength to keep going the last hour if he hadn't been so anxious to find out if Mario had come. He was barely able to keep his footing as he stumbled down the stream leading to his cabin. The falls came in sight, and the meadow came soon after. He saw at a glance Mario's burros were not there. He staggered on until he reached the door and kicked it open. No one had been here since he left. Crushed by this final disappointment, he bent to his knees and untied the woman. He untied the sleeves from around his chest, and lifted her over his head before he entered the doorway. Turning his back to her he examined his feet. His boots were worn out, and his feet were raw, and blistered.

A commotion in the cabin caused him to look around. The woman was up, she was still weak but her eyes were bright, she was looking around the cabin with quick, intent glances. Looking out at the meadow, stream and walls of bamboo, she walked out the door. She was looking at walls of sugarcane and elephant grass, she was glad to be at this isolated dwelling.

She spoke to him not in words, but with vivid questioning gestures. You live here? You live here, alone, no one else live near? He nodded watching her. She looked out at the jungle, and at the lonely wilderness without, now at the cabin that was built in a cave, he drew a long breath of relief. He was confused until he remembered that she was an African. Africans when captured, expected their enemies to make a show of them, and she would cooperate as little as possible. She was relieved to find this cabin in a cave her destination. Her fear had been of public indignities, and dishonor of which she had anticipated upon her arrival in a white settlement.

"Don't relax too soon," he said angrily. "Like it or not, tomorrow I'm taking you to a settlement"

He got up walking with difficulty into the cabin. She went in before him, and sat down on the floor with her back against the wall, watching his every move. He scooped a handful of boar's grease out of a wooden bucket he had stored away,

119

rubbed it on his feet and took out a clean pair of socks and another pair of boots. There was barely enough strength left in him to put on his boots, he wanted to throw himself down on his bed, and sleep until he had regained his strength, but he knew he would feel better if he ate something first. Moving stiffly in pain with fierce determination, he started a fire. Got a bucket of water from the stream, and set a cast-iron pot over the fire. He skinned and cleaned the boar, and bought the meat back, and dropped it in the pot, and threw in a little salt.

"This is something you could be doing," he said, "if you had enough sense."

She listened trying to understand, watching everything he did, but she looked away when he looked at her. She studied objects hanging on the wall, which caught her attention, such as: the ax or the cast-iron pots. Her gaze lingered longest on the crocodile-skin hanging on the wall. He had dressed it during the winter season. Noticing her looking; he took down the skin, and looked for his ball of thread. He took his knife out of its case, and dropped every-thing in her lap.

"My shirt fits me better than it does you," he said. "Make yourself something to wear." She understood instantly. She was happy to have the chance to return his shirt to him. She would have taken it off that moment if he hadn't stopped her. She started working on her new clothing.

He sat down on the other side of the fire, dozing and nodding until the smell of the stew told him it was ready to be eaten. Scooping out a cup of broth, he gave it to her, and told her to sip it slowly to keep from getting sick, again. His graphic dramatic performance, referring to her early morning disaster on the riverbank, bought a brief flash of anger into her eyes, but she relaxed and began to sip. He drank three huge cups of broth without stopping. The food revived him a little; it was bringing him out of the sluggishness of exhaustion, and helped him to start thinking. He could hear the stream in the cave; his fires had been out for nearly a week. The fires would stay out for another week, if not longer, while he went to Figueroa Station to find out what happened to Mario. He was forced to do nothing all winter, and now he was being forced to waste the spring. Now after all his other bad luck he had an angry Zulu woman on his hands.

Yolanda The Enchantress

He scooped out a huge chunk of meat, and started eating it. He wasn't as hungry now. He liked wild boar roasted better than boiled. He had only stewed meat to give to her. His belly was full and he was getting sleepy, but before he could go to bed he had to close the door. He said to himself, why close the door; let her escape. He would pretend to doze off by the fire, she was busy making a skirt, sewing the crocodile hide. The moment she would see him drop off, she would rush for the door. He picked up a slice of meat and nibbled at it, and slowly let his hand drop into his lap; he nooded and a few times. He closed his eyes, and nodded, and pretended to snore. He couldn't tell if she was watching him, but everything was working just like he planned it.

Chapter 8
Don't Leave Me

The familiar dreams of Liana haunted him; she was coming to join him. A gust of wind brushed against her hair, and pressed the folds of her dress against her. Be-hind her stretched the green slopes of Rhino Creek. The splashing sounds of water flowing over ledges were no longer the sounds of Rhino Creek but of his own stream in the cave. He was tossing logs on his fires, with the feeling that he was accomplishing all and more than he had set out to do. Liana was there. She wasn't helping but she was standing at his side, watching him.

He woke up with a sudden jerked. He had slept beside the fire pit and he was sore from yesterday's adventure. He had slept for hours on the unyielding earth, and there was a scar across his rib on which he had rested. The thought of Liana's presence slipped away from him, but the other person was still with him. Suddenly he was able to account for it. The door was wide open, and the sun was drifting in the doorway. The Zulu woman was gone, he had fallen asleep and by now she was miles away.

He struggled to his knees and looked around, with concern, to see what she had taken with her. After sleeping as

soundly the way he had he deserved it if she had stolen everything he owned? He was lucky that she hadn't slit his throat. First
he looked for his rifle; to his relief it was leaning against the wall
where he had placed it. As long as she hadn't stolen that, whatever else she had stolen didn't matter, but as he continued to look
around he saw his knife, ax, powder horn, flint and steal, all still
in sight.

The moment he fell asleep she must have sneaked off,
like a scared cheetah. Then, he realized his shirt had been placed
across his shoulder. Before sneaking off she had taken it off, and
placed it over him as he slept. That didn't fit too well with his
scared cheetah theory. The crocodile-hide, too, was gone, except
for a neatly folded bundle of leftover trimmings, suggesting she
had waited until she had finished the garment. Continuing to
look around he noticed one thing that was missing. His machete
was no longer stuck in the logs beside the door. He would have
given her that knife. He leaned back on his thighs, while settling
his only thread of satisfaction was beginning to unravel. It was a
blessing that she was gone, but there were no other blessings for
him to count. There was nothing else of which he could think of
because his horse was still gone. Mario hadn't come, his fires
were still out, and they would have to stay out. Be-fore lighting
them again he had to go to Figueroa Station to find out what
happened.

After all the time he had lost he had to loose even more.
He slowly and stiffly struggled to his feet. From head to toe, his
body was covered with mud and perspiration. His beard was a
cake of mud, mixed with grease. He smelled like a skunk. If he
went down to the stream, and washed he would feel better. He
hobbled to the doorway, as he reached it, even that one tiny
thread of satisfaction vanished. The woman was oming across
the meadow to wards his cave. She was carrying an armful of
dry sticks, for the fire, and a string of fish. The crocodile-skin
had become a very short, sleeveless dress, barely covering her
slender figure. Even though it covered from neck to her upper
thigh, it didn't cover much.

Her hair was damp, and her skin was glowing. She didn't
look at him when she strolled past, without expression, like she
was unaware of his presence. She walked over to the corner of

the cabin to where the machete was kept, and put down the machete she had used to clean the fish, dropped her load of twig. She laid the fish on a flat stone beside the fire pit, and stirred the coals into a blaze. Her movements were quick, and organized.

"Why did you change your mind?" he demanded.

She looked at him when he spoke watching his lips until he had finished, and then watched his hands, waiting for him to make some gesture to indicate what he was saying. In her attitude there was still no great eagerness to please him, only a willingness to consider his views if he could make her understand. When he stared, and holler at her, she concentrated on her cleaning and cooking.

He walked down past the horse pen to the stream at the foot of the meadow. He took off his pants and boots, wondering angrily, what had made her stay? He had to take her with him to Figueroa Station; there was nothing else he could do. Traveling alone he could make it the same day. Now it would take him an extra day, he sat in the stream. There was no comfort even in the warmth of the water thrashing against him. Still the water was refreshing, submerged in the water he thought more clearly, and the longer he thought about his situation, the more discontented he became. He stood at the water's edge to dry in the sun while he shaved. After all, the woman was only one small problem among many. The more he thought, the harder he tried, and he got even more confused. He hadn't the faintest idea of how much things had changed in the settlements, while he was working in the cave.

There was the war, for one thing. All Congo Basin settlements could have been taken, for all he knew. Or the terrible weather could have been worst than any African attacks. This tropical country had gotten so cold that trees split, rivers froze solid, and animals had frozen in their tracks. This was no land of promise. The Gomez's could have given up further thought of moving to Congo Basin. Even people living in Congo Basin could have decided, that such an unusual winter, combined with all their other problems, was too much. Last year there was a lot of talk about abandoning some settlements until the war was over. Now, after so many years of trouble, they could have done it. There could be nobody at Figueroa Station, when he gets there.

The bushes parted behind him, the woman was running swiftly, and noiselessly to his side. He stood up angrily, grabbing his pants. She was paying no attention to his nakedness. She had her finger to her lips looking upstream. His rifle was in her hands; she was shoving it at him. He took it and listened. There was a faint splashing, and the sound of horses coming down the stream. It was hard for him to keep his mind on the approaching threat because the woman running to warn him confused him. Then he heard the ringing pounding sound of iron stepping on rocks. That meant, men were coming on horses. It could still be Africans with horses they had stolen, or it could be Mario. He called, and whistled the signal of geese, breaking in the middle of the second phrase: "Honk honk, honk." Immediately their came a response, the signal broke on the first note: "Honk, honk honk." It was Mario. Dominique transferred the rifle to the hand that was holding his pants against him, and gave the woman a hug. "It's a friend of mine," he said. "Thanks for bringing the rifle."

She showed no response to the statement. Her face had taken on that stern Zulu look. The geese calls had told her that whoever was coming was someone Dominique knew, and expected. She started back to the cabin. Dominique put on his clothes, and ran to the flat rock at the foot of the meadow. Mario came into sight, riding his horse with his burros stringed, galloping behind. The burros were fat; they had gotten a good long rest before coming through the jungle. Whatever Mario had been doing he hadn't rushed to get here. Dominique tried to control his anger. Because Mario had taken his time, he had lost his horse, and he was living with a Zulu woman. All this had happened because of Mario's failing to return when he was supposed to. His anger grew even more when he saw Mario's grinnning. He was happy to see his friend, and glad that he was alive, but he was angry. Dominique sat down on the rock, and tried to hide how happy he was.

Mario dismounted and turned his burros loose to graze in the meadow; Dominique's doubts began to return. Taking a closer look at his friend, and he noticed something about Mario was different. Instead of work clothes he wore a waistcoat, and a tan store bought shirt, brown dress pants, fancy boots, and a new, tan, wide-brimmed hat. His hair had grown long, and it was tied in the back of his neck with a leather strap. Even his face looked different. He grinned a lot, but there wasn't that tenseness beneath his grin. He looked at peace with himself, as if he had just bought, a good piece of land for a third of what it was worth. After kneeling on the bank to take a drink of water, he walked over, and sat down on the rock beside Dominique.

"Figured you had given up on me," he said.

Dominique glanced at Mario grimly. He didn't act concern about being so late, nor did he act or look uneasy. Dominique was getting angry again. Mario took off his hat, and looked up at the sky shielding his eyes from the sun.

"Fine morning," he said, casually, as if this were just any morning. "Seems like after the last few months a man can't get enough sun." He took out his tobacco pouch and offered it to Dominique. Dominique shook his head, looking at Mario coldly. Mario began filling his pipe. Dominique noticed his waistcoat had been altered, and made for a man much larger than Mario. It was neatly altered. Mario was as calm, and well fed as his horse and burros. Wherever he had stopped to rest someone had taken good care of him, too.

"Knew you' would worry some," said Mario, with anther good-humored grin. "I got tied up." He laughed as if there were something unusually funny about the way this had come about.

"I think its worst than that," said Dominique. "How could you get so tied up, it took you nearly a month to think about a friend." He glanced across at the well-fed horse, and burros. "Or was the weather so bad you couldn't feed your horses, and donkeys."

"Sure was an unusual winter, wasn't it?" said Mario. "But it wasn't bad enough to keep me, from coming through the jungle. When snow melted folks stopped worrying about it, and said we'll never be another one like it, not in this country. You'll never believe how many people are coming to Congo Basin, more this season than all the years before this put together. Congo Road's full of 'em from one end to the other. The day I left I heard three hundred ships docked in Port Eden Ton since the ice melted in the Atlantic."

L. A. Johnson Jr.

"You've been busy," asked Dominique, "that's why you're a month late."

"That wasn't what made me late." Mario laughed again, his fingers with which he was holding the flint, and steel to light his pipe were all thumbs, he never looked up to meet Dominique's stare. They kept talking anyway. "New settlements being built everywhere, there's a new one down the river, they call Mamba Land, right on Redwood River. And in your back yard, Domino Median's, uncle is building a settlement station near Victoria Falls, forty miles west of where we're sitting. Land out here is going to be worth more than land in Eagle Landing."

"That's an interesting story," said Dominique.

"There's more," said Mario. "Thing's have been happening, while you've been stuck back here in the jungle.

Can't blame you for not understanding. What got every body so excited all of a sudden was the way the wars going, its been mighty good. Novas knew what he was doing, when he sent Prince Kudzu to Guam Land; and let people up and down the road, see the headhunter in a cage. Not long after that, Major Cordoba, and Colonel Figueroa burned Lozi villages. When they finished, Colonel Perez gave, General De Gamma half his army, and De Gamma burned down hundreds of villages in Nigeria, and then he headed for Mali.

The same time Colonel Lara killed hundreds of blacks in Angola, and burned villages, in Sierra Leone on the Atlantic. They chased Ashanti warriors all the way to Guinea. We've taken everything from Mozambique to Senegal. On top of all that the British have taken Egypt, and they're heading east. The French have taken Algeria; they're heading west to Gambia, they've already taken Morocco. The Belgian army is heading for the Congo. White people just about own all of Africa. On top of all that our Portuguese government has sent land commissioners out here to keep track of land owned by the Portuguese. Our people better hurry and get as much land as they can, before it's all gone, or the Belgian army will steal it."

"That sounds fine," said Dominique. Now what's the bad news you are not telling me"?

"Nothing," said Mario. "The lumber yard and sawmill is set up, and we have been sawing timber over a month. The

126

stockades finished, and most of the houses are under construction. Legacy, Monty, and Antonio, they're going to be a few months late, because they're bringing their families with them instead of waiting until next year."

Dominique took a deep breath. "Nothing kept you from coming, that's good to know, because it will be a month before we can get out of here."

"A month?" Mario jumped up as if he had been bitten. "A month?" Here! I... I can't stay a month. I've got to get started right away."

Dominique shook his head. "Be another month or more before I'll have a full load."

"What have you been doing?" Mario demanded.

"Most of it I spent waiting for the stream to thaw. Some of it was wasted chasing the Zulu warriors that stole my horse while I was out looking for you."

Even after hearing his explanation, Mario didn't seem to care or believe that excuse, which Dominique was suggesting it was Mario's fault his horse had been stolen. "He said. I'll leave the burros with you. Then you can pack out whenever you're ready. I have to get back."

"Why?"

Mario took off his hat, and wiped his brow. "I'm sorry your horse was stolen," he said. "The kind of people that's moving to Congo this year, I could have easily gotten you five hundred dollars for her, but there's something that might make up for it. Last fall when Colonel Trinity was coming' up the Yoruba River with five boatloads of military supplies from Mali, pirates, robbed him. My guess is you'll find magnesium sulfate is worth more than it's ever been before. Won't be much gunpowder in the settlements this year except for what settlers make themselves."

"Why are you in such a hurry?" asked Dominique.

"Cause I said I would," said Mario, suddenly defiant. "That's why. If I don't, Cindy she'll...." He broke off, when he realized he had spoken her name aloud. Cindy? Stop questioning me," said Mario, "I'll tell you, what happened. She's Silva Hernandez daughter. She came with him when I packed his sawmill, equipment, over the mountain and through the jungle." Mario

127

was sweating now. "Snowbound for nearly a month. Just this side of Servile Valley we got stuck. That's when Cindy and I got to know each other really well. Anyway, this spring when I got ready to come to get you she started worrying' about something' happening to me. Silva, he had that same feeling."

"I have to admit," said Dominique, "that's a better excuse than I thought you'd have. Can blame a man for wanting to stay home the first month he's married."

"Married? Who said I'm married? I didn't say I was, yet."

"You don't have to take it so hard. You're not the first man that has been trapped by a woman's father."

"It's not like that," protested Mario. It wasn't his idea it was Cindy's. I mean it was mine, mostly."

"How do you like it?"

Mario sat down on the rock again, with a sigh of relief. "I like it," he confessed. "What's so good about it? Cindy, she's known Liana since they were little. You and me being' friends like we are, that's going' to make everything work out just right." He suddenly grabbed his jacket, fumbling at an inside pocket. "Talking about Liana made me remember something I had forgotten. She wrote you a letter."

"Well," said Dominique, "Where did you put it?" Mario grabbed the envelope, heavily sealing with wax, and tossed it to him. "When did it come, and, how long have you had it?"

"Little over a month ago, last time I heard from Legacy. Legacy's overseer Shameless Romero delivered it, when he came out this spring, along with his three sons and their families, and a few dozen of the Gomez slaves to clear land and plant maize."

The envelope was wrinkled and dirty from being carried in various pockets of his saddlebag, but there was his name, Dominique de Salvo, elegantly written clear and precise. Dominique's imagination took over; he could see her strong, fingers writing the letter, her head bent, and her eyes fixed on what she was writing. She must have written it while his stream was frozen, during his lowest point. He opened the envelope:

Dear Dominique:

Yolanda The Enchantress

Legacy, Antonio and Monty are back, safe and well, for which I am most grateful. Their enthusiasm for Congo is Boundless because of that, I fear, I must become reconciled. I sincerely hope that you will keep yourself safe and well until we meet again.

Liana

She had spoken as directly as her brothers when they'd offered him a share in their land company. She didn't waist time with words. She had taking the time to write him a letter at this great distance, and her admitting that she was no longer opposed to the Congo Basin venture, was the same as admitting nothing longer stood between them. If Mario hadn't been sitting there, watching him, watching his every expression, he would have leaped into the air. He started reading Liana's letter again.

Mario gave an unexpected jerk that caused Dominique to look up. The Zulu woman was coming out of the cave, carrying a banana leaf heaped with fruits, and baked fish. With humble downcast eyes, while maintaining her most rid-get stone-like Zulu calm, she walked over to them, bent, and placed the banana leaf covered with fish and fruit on the rock between them. She straightened, without glancing at either and stood as if for some sign from her master to say something. She was playing the role of a female servant. Mario stared at her, open-mouthed.

"My God," he stammered.

She gave him a look so cold, so hostile that he placed his hands over his mouth.

"Excuse me, little lady," he muttered hastily.

"You don't have to worry," said Dominique. "She doesn't know a word of Portuguese." He gestured for her to go back to the cave. She retreated obediently. Mario couldn't take his eyes off her, he watched her, until she walked through the doorway.

"My Gracious," he repeated. He stared at Dominique, blinking. "Way out here in the jungle, sixty miles from nowhere, and I find you in another kitchen just like you were in Mozambique, with a woman feeding you and looking after you, not just any woman but as fine and sweet a piece, a man could find in any large, city in Europe."

"I ran across her when I was trying to get my horse back.

129

She's just another savage." said Dominique."

"She looks a little wild, but she doesn't look bad to me," said Mario.

"I was going to take her to Figueroa's today," said Dominique. "Since you're leaving, you can take her."

Mario's grin couldn't have vanished any faster. It was as if a spear had pierced his shoulder blade. "Me?" he cried. Me! A man that's just got married, come out of the jungle with a young African woman? That story would be told all over Congo in a month. Cindy is real easy to get along with, but she wouldn't be after that. Oh, oh no. Not me!" He picked up a fish and began eating it nervously.

"You expect me to continue living with her in a cave? That will make quite a story." said Dominique

"You're not married, yet," said Mario. "You're already living with her, here in that cave; you're already stuck with that story. Since you have to spend another month here, you might as well make the best of it, and let her help you."

"I have never touched her," said Dominique. He stared at Mario until Mario stopped grinning.

"I believe you," said Mario. "Just like everybody in the settlement, will, once you make them listen."

"It's the truth," said Dominique bitterly. "You don't know her. She is not as old as she looks. She is barely a woman. She is a heathen. She is really wild."

"You're saying you can't handle her?" snickered Mario.

"No," said Dominique. "I'm telling you she's," he hesitated, and then said, "innocent."

When Mario realized Dominique was serious he started grinning again. "Innocent, you say? She's an Africans and you think she's innocent?"

"I said it and I mean it," said Dominique. "That's one thing a woman can't fool me about."

Mario shook his head scornfully. "A season alone has softened you." He leaned towards Dominique, speaking with the concern of a father educating his son. "There's something else, a man has to remember my boy. When you get around enough you're learn. That underneath, when you get to know them, women ain't no different from men. Their desires and needs are the same as a man, sometime a little bit more." He glanced towards the cave, "She's probably angry with you for being so stupid, she probably thinks something wrong with you." When he realized what he was saying was making no impression on Dominique he stood up, and wiped his hands on his pants. "Just give me five minutes and I'll prove to you how innocent she is."

He started for the cabin doorway. Dominique watched him, marveling. A month, married had changed him. Mario walked through the doorway. It didn't take him seven seconds to prove that fact. In less than five seconds he bolted out again. Yolanda appeared briefly in the doorway, with machete in her hand.

Mario slowed to a walk as he approached the rock. He wiped his brow. "She's wild, all right." He picked up his rifle and game bag. "Well, I've got to get started back."

"Tell them at Rhino Creek I'll be there in a month."

Mario nodded, shook his head and said. "I won't tell nobody about your Zulu woman." He looked at Dominique solemnly. "You want my advice?"

"What is it?"

"If I were you, I would let her go back to her people today."

Dominique watched Mario splash up the stream and out of sight. She came out and looked around to make sure Mario had gone, picked up the banana leaf, rinsed it in the stream and returned to the cabin. One thing was certain, Dominique decided. Mario was right about the gossip that would follow when he appeared at Figueroa Station with her. If she looked homely or old it wouldn't be so bad. There was no telling how Liana would react when she heard about her. She might try to understand, but she wouldn't like it. Mario was right about something else. He was already stuck with whatever name they'd give him because of her, whether he took the woman to Figueroa Station tomorrow or a month from today. He needed to settle down and get his work. Then when he took her out of the jungle to leave her with Anita he could get to Rhino Creek ahead of the gossip. Besides, there was always the chance that during the month she might decide to run away.

Two young impalas wandered into the open, nibbling at

patches of grass that had sprouted around stalks of sugarcane. They were chewing stems near the bank of the stream, Dominique picked up his rifle. Enough meat to last a month was walking towards him. The first impala dropped when the shot was fired. While reloading, the other sniffed curiously at her fallen companion, and turned suddenly, to gallop away. He shot recklessly in a hurry hitting the impala too far back of the shoulder, making him track the impala for miles before it finally fell. He came back to get a burros, and saw that the woman had the first impala skinned. She was carving it up in slices. She was working hard. She never looked up nor did she give any sign that she wanted or needed his approval. She seemed to regard this as a task, which was natural for her to under-take. Nevertheless, he welcomed her help, and before going after the second carcass, he hung around long enough to cut sapling to make a drying rack.

When he returned with the other impala, she had set up the drying rack, and a fire was burning under it. Instead of erecting it outside in the meadow, she had put it up in the cabin, leaving them very little room to get around. The cabin was filled with smoke. He protested. She walked to the door, and motioned up, at the sky, clouds were gathering. Rain when it came would have spoiled the meat if the rack had been outside. Without hesitation or a wasted motion, she started cleaning the second load of meat; and cut wide flat strips, and spread them on the rack to smoke. She worked swiftly; she had turned out to be very helpful. She had been doing things for him since early this morning,.

"Look... he pointed towards himself," he said. "Let's stop acting like enemies."

"Dominique," she repeated.

He pointed at her.

"Yolanda," she said.

"Did you say Yolanda?"

She nodded and went on with her work. "He held up his knife, then said knife.

"Knife," she repeated.

They continued working; from time to time he named other articles. She was trying to learn while working, glancing up only when he gestured with his hands to some new object. Her voice was low and clear.

Yolanda The Enchantress

Dominique set the ribs of the impalas in a pot to cook above the fire. Before their work at the drying rack was finished, the ribs were browned and sizzling, ready to be eaten. They sat at the fire and began to eat.

"Sit down," he ordered her impatiently.

He cut off a huge section of rib, very meaty, and gave it to her before taking any himself. She gorged like a wild cheetah, tearing at the meat with her sharp teeth, gulping and reaching for more. They ate steadily and silently, until they could swallow no more. Dominique walked over to the water bucket, and washed the grease from his hands and mouth. When she finished, she did likewise. He took out his pipe, and returned to the fire. Since Mario had left they'd been busy every minute. Compared to their former silence, the exchange of a few spoken words had been a pleasant relief. Even eating together both of them tired and hungry. They had earned their evening meal, they weren't friends but they were now trying to be sociable.

"Pipe," he said, holding it up.

"Pipe," she repeated, with somewhat less than her earlier interest in his speaking Portuguese words.

She sat looking into the fire with an expression of contented on her face. Seldom, during the language coaching, had she looked directly at him? She did now. Her hands folded in her lap; she continued to stare into the fire.

He walked over to his bed and picked up an armful of straw, and carried it to the opposite side of the drying rack and dropped it against the wall. Over the straw he spread a blanket. Then he walked to the door and slid a log into a slot to lock the door, and stood near the fire. She didn't move or look up.

"I'm going to bed," he said.

She didn't move or look up. She sat there quiet and still, nearly as pliable as a piece of straw.

He went over and sat down on his blanket, loosened his belt, placed his rifle, powder horn, and ax within reach, took his priming horn, flint and steel out of his shirt pocket so that he wouldn't roll on them while sleeping and stretched out. She continued to stare into the fire with that, unusual stressful air of waiting that was becoming each moment more distrusting.

The air was heavy with an oily greasy scent of smoking

meat, and the smell of burned fat that had dripped from the meat and the odor of burning wood. Rain was pounding against the door, but within there was complete stillness, and the shut in feeling of the huge cavern. They were surrounded and enclosed by Victoria Falls.

"Go to bed," he ordered.

She looked at him with a questioning glance.

"Bed," he said.

"Bed," she repeated, as in an earlier language lesson. After she spoke her eyes brightened up. "Bed," she said again, for the first time speaking the word as if it were her own instead of repeating what he had said. Suddenly, in a clear voice, she added: "Go to bed."

Dominique rose on one elbow and stared at her. "You remembered that," he said.

The glow had gone from her face. She shook her head vigorously. She looked frightened, but Dominique was excited. He knew she was intelligent. He knew that she had faint memories of her childhood. No matter how she acted she wasn't a savage.

"You sleep here," he said.

She looked up at him understanding. She didn't act angry or disappointed or relieved but just agreeable.

Dominique went back to his bed. He was breathing hard. He could hear a faint rustle as she made herself comfortable. This is never going to work, he thought. Not for a whole month. He had to take her to Figueroa Station after all.

He got up and went to the door. The rain had stopped, and light from the moon was glowing through thick gray clouds. Everything was moving slowly for him. No matter how hard he pushed, the trip to Figueroa's would cost him three more days. It would take at least that time, and a lot of talking to Dino and Anita. He didn't like that part much. And there was no predicting how she would act, not that she had been any trouble since they reached the cabin. Except for that flair-up against Mario, for that she could hardly be blamed. Still, she could change any second.

Suddenly He remembered Mario's telling him about the new settlement Dominion Median's uncle was building, on the lower end of Victoria Falls. Median's was half as far as Figueroa

134

Yolanda The Enchantress

Station, and it was not on Congo Road. It was deep in the jungle; gossip would take a while to spread from there. Dominion might be there; he and Dominion had always gotten along well. Median's was the place to leave her while he finished his work here. This decision was so practical that he was able to go to bed and soundly sleep.

Early the nest morning he took his watch out of the wooden box in the crevice where he had hidden it, along with his bag of silver escudos. By the time he had fed and watered the burros, Yolanda had the cooking fire going, and the leftover ribs were warming. She moved about quickly keeping out of his way, except for when they were working together. Her being around was not a problem, most of the time. He enjoyed her company after being alone in the cave for so long. She never looked at him except when he spoke to her. After they ate breakfast he picked up his rifle, and motioned for her to come with him. She followed him out, taking the machete as she walked through the doorway.

They tramped off to the west at a good steady pace. In country as rough as this they would make better time on foot. Occasionally he gestured naming things along the way: shore, eagle, Cape buffalo, monkey, lion, giraffe, elephant, and clouds. Each time she repeated the word and after she said them over and over again she remembered them. When they paused for a brief rest she was able to repeat the name of everything he had taught her the night before, rifle, boot, nose, face, ear, hand, gorilla, and finger. They started walking.

"Mamba," she cried suddenly. "Black Mamba."

From under a rock, over which Dominique had just stepped, slivered a deadly snake. The snake was of no interest to him, but what she had said was.

"Black Mamba," he stated. "

"Mamba," she whispered, shaking her head helplessly, looking a little afraid, like she was remembering something she couldn't understand. She was shaking her head in confusion, troubled, she became even more confused because she didn't understand most of the words he was saying.

"Well, come along," he said impatiently.

The next hour they came upon a carved trail, a white

man's trail carved by medal prints of horses' shoes and wagon wheels. This trail was coming from the direction of the main Congo settlements on to the southwestern coast. They had entered Pygmies country. The trail was too well traveled to be leading only to a single settlement station. It was leading to that new settlement on Redwood River that Mario said, they called Mamba Land. Dominique lengthened his strides. Every approaching path or new settlement reminded him of how much he had to do, and how far he was falling behind in getting it done. Shortly after noon they came out on a ridge, below them stood the other side of Victoria Falls clear blue water. The water was sparkling in the sunlight, in a meadow near the falls stood six or seven, dozen cabins within a half-finished stockade. Yolanda's eyes narrowed, and focused the instant she saw these cabins. She stopped in mid-stride like a cheetah that has caught the first whiff of a threatening scent.

"Come on," ordered Dominique. "That is where we are going."

She stood still. Her face had taken on that same, old stern Zulu look.

Do as you wish," said Dominique. "I'm going down there."

He tramped off down the trail. Immediately he could hear soft pounding of bare feet just behind him. He kept on, without looking around pretending that he didn't care if she followed or stayed behind. The path twisted and turned bordering the edge of the jungle that entered the lower slope. She was still at his heels. When he reached the clearing at the edge of the meadow he stopped, and called out. It was never a good idea to get too close to a settlement station until you were sure the people in it were sure you were a friend.

The shouting back, and forth revealed that old man Median, had gone to Figueroa Station to trade with ivory hunters, but his son Dominion was somewhere around. He's fish in the river, somebody said. Then almost immediately Dominion came scrambling up from the riverbank.

"Take it easy, Dominion, and don't load your rifle," yelled Dominique, referring to the time in Doom Palm when, drunk one night, Dominion had relieved himself in his own rifle

Yolanda The Enchantress

barrel. Dominion recognized the voice at once. "It's the gorilla killer himself. What are you waiting on, Dominique? Come out of those bushes where I can get a better look at you."

Dominique started walking towards the open grassland. Yolanda followed behind; so close that he could feel her breathing on his neck. Yelling children and barking dogs rushed out around the end of the uncompleted palisade. The uproar increased, then suddenly condemned by the elders, because children were throwing stones at dogs in a useless attempt to quiet them. Dominion, still favoring the leg he fractured when he fell off an elephant that first night at Mozambique, limped towards them with out-stretched hands.

"Come in and make yourself at home. We have beans and greens, what we have you are welcome to."

"This," said Dominique, is Yolanda, "I stole her from the Zulus."

The women of the settlement pressed forward, looking over Yolanda with mingled curiosity. Janice, Dominion's Nairobian wife he had courted the year when he served Novas as town major at Nairobi tried to take her hand. Yolanda drew back and edged closer to Dominique.

"No use standing here surrounded by nosy children, and barking dogs," said Dominion. "Come on in."

He led the way to the nearest cabin, everybody held back until Dominique and Yolanda walked in. Then all tried to get through the doorway at once. A small boy was knocked down; he let out a furious outcry. Janice bent down, lifted him up and began soothing him. Yolanda's eyes brightened. She spoke to Janice, and Janice quickly replied.

"You're speaking Old Swahili, mingled with Zulu and something else," cried Dominique.

Janice nodded, confused by his sudden excitement. Dominique grabbed Janice by the arm, and pulled them from the crowd in the center of the room to a bench along the wall. When they were seated he knelt facing them. Everyone in the room was silent. Even the child in Janice arms, held back his tears, and stared at Dominique.

"Look," said Dominique to Janice. "So far I haven't been able to find out a thing about her. I don't speak Zulu, and she doesn't speak Portuguese."

Janice asked Yolanda and both women shook their heads.

"Then how come she knows that old form of Swahili?"

Janice questioned Yolanda again. Yolanda answered immediately, apparently impressed by Janice's friendliness, and more than that by Dominique's sudden interest.

"Her father's Bantu and her mother's Zulu," said Janice.

"When her mother died," explained Janice. "She was adopted by her grandmother, who lived with a trader? Her grandmother's people spoke Zulu and Swahili mixed with Zulu and Pig Latin.

"How long has she been with the Zulu?"

"From the time she was so," interpreted Janice, cradling her arms indicating the size of a newborn baby.

"How did they get her?"

"I don't think she's Zulu." Dominique said.

This created a much longer discussion between Janice and Yolanda, during which Janice several times shivered with fear.

"She is Zulu," stated Janice. Now, Yolanda was no longer answering readily. The subject had become a painful one, no doubt, but she didn't appear to be unhappy.

"These eyes what she say," repeated Janice. "Long time ago, very many years, when I was a baby I go with man, and Zulu woman down the Swaziland River. At place where the water go round rocks very fast, heading to a place my grandmother call Kingdom of Buganda. A small boat, she sinks. Everybody die. Only this one, so small, survived, wash up on bank in wooden box."

"What was the name of that family?"

Janice questioned Yolanda, who kept shaking her head, defiantly.

"She doesn't know."

"The Zulu chief tried to find out, so he could ask for a ransom. Did he?"

"Maybe so, maybe no. No one tell this one nothing'."

"Where was the family from?"

There was another long discussion between Janice and Yolanda, but it revealed very little.

Yolanda The Enchantress

"Judy never says. Jade one time, long time ago, when in *Zulu infants tournament* they call me *'Little Kingdom of Buganda.'*"

She must know more than that about who she is," insisted Dominique.

"She knows only her Zulu name," reported Janice after more questioning, "Yolanda. They call her 'Slivering Cheetah'. The Zulu name her when she was a baby, so very small, after she slivered out of the water."

Dominique stood, thinking. One of the women shoved into his hand a bowl of wild greens sprinkled with ham and olive oil, the bowl of greens seemed to be in his way, he put it down.

"I bought her here," he told Dominion, "because I'm camped alone in the jungle, and can't take care of her. Sounds like she has family in Kingdom of Buganda. I want to leave her with your
woman until I can figure out some way to send her there."

Dominion's smile vanished. "Another mouth to feed,"
Dominion said.

Dominique took out the watch and placed it in Dominion's hand. Dominique had already taken time to wind it. Dominion listened to the tick and then, suddenly, the watch started striking the hour and playing a tune. The room was so quiet that everyone could hear, the delightful musical clang, followed by a soothing sound. To cover up how much he wanted the watch Dominion shrugged his shoulders and laid it on the table.

"Well," said Dominion, "a watch ain't what we got the most need for around here, but I'll take care of her for you, until you finish your work."

Dominique turned to tell Janice to break the news to Yolanda, but he saw in an eager whisper she was already doing so. Yolanda jumped up.

"No," she said frantically in Swahili.

"Tell her that she has to wait here," said Dominique. "Until I take her to Kingdom of Buganda."

"No," said Yolanda, without waiting for Janice to tell her anything.

Dominion's aunt, a huge woman big enough to make two

of Yolanda, wobbled over to Yolanda, and put her arms around her.

"We'll look after you just like you're one of our own, Zulu lady," she said, hugging Yolanda, holding Yolanda in spite of her struggling to break free.

Yolanda snatched the machete from her belt. The big woman jumped back, the big woman grabbed Yolanda again.

"Tell her;" said Dominique to Janice, "she has too stay!"

His voice quivered. He was just as angry as Yolanda. He turned and pushed his way out of the door. Dominion followed hastily.

"No," Yolanda cried once more in the house behind them.

"We'll take care of her," said Dominion.

"Make sure you do," mumbled Dominique. He started across the meadow, walking very fast. When he reached the jungle he found himself running. He slowed down to an ordinary pace, feeling there was no reason he should feel as if he was running away. When he came out on the open crest he didn't look back until it occurred to him that this was only another sign of her foolishness. He came to a sudden stop and turned to look at the settlement station.

He was startled when he saw Dominion's cabin on fire, men were on the roof with pails of water. Dominique started to run back but he stopped. There were no gunshots or a sign of an attack. The men fighting the fire had gotten the flames under control. Perhaps there was an accident. There was a fire in the fireplace when he was in the house. Probably a burning log had rolled against the wall or the clay chimney had caught fire as they so often did.

He turned to go; there came a low broken call of a goose: "Honk, honk, honk." It was Mario's call but not Mario's voice. He moved from the trail and hid in the woods. Yolanda was standing just beyond a cluster of lime trees. She was breathing hard from running, but her face was remarkably serene, almost enchanting. She glanced down in the direction of the settlement. Then over the hills in the direction of his cave, and then up at him.

"They will never take you in again," said Dominique.

"Not after setting their home on fire. You might as well come with me."

They walked east, and she was walking behind him. After a while he turned around, and confronted her.

" He said, "I gave my watch away for nothing."

"Watch?" she repeated.

"Yes, watch," he said.

She shook her head, and reached into the waistline of her skirt and took out the watch and handed it to him.

Chapter 9
Savage Warrior Vow

Dominique scraped the magnesium sulfate crystals from the bottom of the pot, and scooped them into leather sacks; and tied them tight. This was the last sack. His cargo was complete. His work here was done. Beyond the distant gleam revealed the never-ending darkness of the cave beyond the barren cold cavern where he had worked so hard. Where he had done his back-breaking labor, sometime in frustration, more difficult than any labor could ever be. Now it had suddenly become a wonderful new world, a world that had yielded huge benefits.

He sat down relaxing a moment for the first time during the month, realizing that the month had ended. He summoned the image of Liana as he had seen her in dreams, this time deliberately. What he had done was for her, now he could have her. Tomorrow he was leaving for Rhino Creek to claim the land, which was to be their home; there would be no end to his journey until he married her.

During the month the watch had played an important role in their life in the cave, it divided their days into equal periods. He slept afternoons, and she slept nights, there was always one of them awake to keep the fire burning. Bedtime no longer posed an awkward problem.

"I'm coming," he said, rudely.

He followed her out. The aroma that rose from the pot above the cooking fire in the cabin lightened his ill humor.

L. A. Johnson Jr.

"What are you cooking?" he asked.

She had collected berries and wild vegetables, caught crabs and shrimp, snared waterfowl, quail, and ostrich, but this as something new. Then he saw the discarded shells. She had improved their regular diet of dried impala and fish.

"Turtle," he exclaimed.

"Kasa," she said, nodding in Swahili.

That was the name she called it, but he didn't longer paid attention, when another word came to her. It made her angry when he didn't comment. Sometime, when she wanted to say something, and didn't stop to think, whole sentences would come to her at once. New words were spoken daily; those times had become more and more common. When she herself noticed what she had done she was always upset. She would stop speaking words, and talk with signs, but he would refuse to answer. Whatever the circumstance, he would stop at that moment until she spoke the word she was trying to say.

She wanted to learn Portuguese because she could speak broken Swahili, Tswana, Zulu and Ndebele; and she was eager to learn Portuguese words from him. It was the sudden unexpected flashes of memory that confused her. With her knowledge of broken Spanish, and what she had learned from him, he could hold a conversation with her in Portuguese, she understood most things he said, and this last week she started saing words that surprised him.

Before serving the main dish she gave him slices of smoked ostrich that had been soaked in olive oil. The main serving was stew, with large slices of onions. She had thrown in wild green peppers to release the sharp fragrance of the richness of turtle. The tang of wild spices, parsley, celery, and other wild herbs were strange to him. On the ground beside him sat a platter of wild plumbs, peaches and strawberries. She had done well enough before, but she had done even better today.

"Eat with me," he said. By the time he had eaten all the turtle in the gumbo stew, there wasn't any room for strawberries. He lit his pipe, relaxed in the rocking chair, and stretched out his legs. "Well," he said. "Tomorrow we go."

She nodded solemnly. Her smile vanished before he spoke. Perhaps it was because she always seemed to know what

142

he was going to say before he said it.

"Is it far?" she asked.

"Not very." She covered her face with her hands. "How long, you stay there?"

He pondered over the question in his mind. He would leave her at Figueroa Station, and go to Sea Pen to sell his magnesium sulfite, and then cut across to Rhino Creek to settle with the Gomez's. If the sale hadn't netted him the amount he needed he would borrow the difference from Mario. Mario would certainly be repaid because there was always more mineral salt to be mined. In any event the transaction shouldn't take very long.

Then he would go to Beguiler Ferry Crossing to see Liana. On the way back he would pick up Yolanda at Figueroa's, and take her to Kingdom of Buganda. That would cost him even more time, but that is what he had to do. If he left her stranded in Congo Basin she would run back to the Zulu's. If she stayed in Congo Basin among strangers it would be even worst. Either way, people would never get over talking about how he had taken advantage of her, and left her to make it on her own. Getting her permanently settled somewhere she belonged, was his responsibility, he had to face that, and this was a commitment he had to finish.

"Perhaps three, four weeks," he said.

"Where you go then?"

"I'll take you to Kingdom of Buganda, to look for your people."

"Kingdom of Buganda is very far," she said, smiling. In Zululand they talk about Kingdom of Buganda where, Zulu once lived. "It is over the mountain far down the river." The thought of so long a journey still before them seemed to leave her with no further concern.

She stood picking up the crocodile-skin shirt she had made for him. She held the shirt up to show it to him, she was pleased with it, as she had a right to be. He liked it because it was simple, plain, and strong. He liked it, because he had once attempted to make a shirt for himself, but he couldn't master the straight precision of the stitches. She gestured for him to stand; she held the shirt against him to see if it would fit.

"Wait, I'll try it on," he said.

L. A. Johnson Jr.

He pulled off his old shirt and put on the one she had made. She walked around him tugging at seems, and her head was bowed just enough for him to glance down at her face. Her skin was glowing. There couldn't be smoother, fresher-looking skin then that on her face neck and arms. Her face was thin, but her lips and nose were wide. The way she braided her hair with two huge braids, gave her an enchanting, Zulu look. Her eyes were another good feature. Her long trimmed eyelashes matched her golden skin. They looked larger and brighter now that her eyebrows had started to grow out. Her brown face wasn't a face he would have taken a second look at even during those roving years before he and Zephyr were together.

She looked too much like what she was, too independent, too different, too African, too much like herself, yet her features made her look inviting to any man. He had told Mario the truth. Her presence had been almost like having a servant around, and a month of her company had made very little difference in his opinion of her.

She backed away, her head tilted, lookit at how the shirt hung on him, then she gestured for him to take it off.

"You bigger than I think," she muttered.

She sat down and ripped out a seam, while he smoked his pipe. Normally at this hour she would have gone into the cave to tend the fires. He rubbed his hand over his chin. They would be leaving too early for him to shave in the morning; he might as well do it now. One of the many comforts of Yolanda's housekeeping was the jug of clean hot water, kept hot by heated stones; beside the fire. There was sensed soap, too, she had made with grease and ashes.

Outside it was hot and muggy, after the pleasant coolness in the cave. He shaved slowly and carefully, enjoying the scent of this afternoon, for once; there was no need to hurry. When he finished shaving and splashing warm water on his face his hair hung down in his way. It had grown much too long. He took out his knife and started cutting it off, a handful at a time. Without a mirror it was an awkward process. Yolanda came over and stood watching, and laughing. She seldom laughed; he enjoyed the sound of her laughter. After watching a few moments she took the knife out of his hand, pulled him down to his knees, and began to cut his hair. So personal a service made him feel uneasy, but he surrendered rather than admit his uneasiness. She worked swiftly, pushing his head, this way, and that.

He shivered, slightly as his hair dropped on his hairy shoulders, and chest. She laughed again, while brushing him off. She could not have been behaving more congenial, yet the feel of her fingertips lingered. She continued cutting his hair; her encircling arms were at times so near they brushed against his face. Her breasts were damp from heat and perspiration. The faint scent of her body was pleasant. He resisted an impulse to sniff the perfume, perfume she had splashed all over her body. That was certainly one of her good features. Everything about her was fresh and sweet. She slowly moved in front of him and her upraised arms revealed the curling clusters of black hair in her armpits. He was aroused as he looked. She had given up many of her Zulu ways.

He remembered her slender naked body that day on the raft. That savage and heathen hairless body no longer existed. Her dark slender fingers were revealing the unmistakable features of a woman of another race. He could see this as vividly as if the modest covering of her crocodileskin and top didn't exist. Desire, lust, overpowering desire, seized him. There was no good reason to deny them. He couldn't understand why he hadn't felt this way before. There was no sense in his being so foolish, she was beautiful.

Everyday this whole month she had been ready, and he had probably disappointed her as Mario had said. He didn't have to any longer. He didn't even have to make any awkward approaches. She was so near that they were on the verge of an embrace. All he had to do was reach out and grab her. There would be no talk, no argument, and no struggle, just a sudden, lustful, passionate, release for both of them.

"So," she said, stepping back to survey her work.

She moved closer again and brushed his hair briskly dislodging the loose ends. Again and again she moved closer brushing off his shoulders, chest, and back. He rose slowly to his feet.

"Come," she said, handing him his knife while grabbing his arm guiding him towards the doorway. "It's time for you to sleep."

He jerked free. "Maybe," he said. "But not there."

He leisurely walked off towards the stream behind the horse pen. That had been about as narrow an escape as he ever had, and he had plenty of close ones. After having kept his mind on what he was doing for a whole month he almost made a fool of himself the very last day. It was the way she brushed his hair that bought him back to reality. She was acting as if they had lived together for years.

The air was getting stuffy, heavier and denser by the minute. There was a grayish haze in the west, beyond the clouds were darkening bulging drifting clouds. Chances were there would be rain before sundown. He took a swim, put on this pants, and crawled under a cluster of bushes surrounded by banana trees just beyond the elephant grass and, went to sleep.

He was awakened by Yolanda's frightening call. "Dominique, Dominique." She was running in the stream, searching for him, searching desperately with fear. "Dominique!" she screamed. He rose to his knees; there was no sign of danger. The donkeys were restless, but they weren't looking in a specific direction. She hadn't bought his rifle as she had done when she heard Mario's approach. She spotted him and rushed to him. She grabbed his hand, when he was slow to rise she hit him with her fist.

"Run," she kept shouting. "Run."

He rose to his feet, looking at it coming over the trees under which he had been lying. It was not a threat against which his rifle would have been any help. A huge black cloud had formed in the west covering the sky. Suddenly around them everything became calm; in the west the jungle was whipping, snapping and trees were leaning towards the clouds. Then from the clouds a long gray funnel surged towards the earth. Its lower tip was bending, twisting, and swaying, like an enormous python searching for something to eat. The tip touched the crest of the ridge a mile away, and their roots jerked huge trees up. The trees flew upward into the cyclone's interior, and then there came a roar that swallowed up the thunder. A sudden gust of wind rushed across the grasslands, and meadows throwing Yolanda against Dominique. After touching the ridge, the tip of the funnel took one long searching bounce, and settled again. It rushed down the slope towards them, tearing and whipping through the jungle as easily as a heard of elephants running through soft soil.

"Come," Yolanda was pleading. "Come now."

He ran with her to the door of the cabin. It was too late to save the donkeys, but they were safe in the cabin sheltered by the cave. Now he and Yolanda would be safe no matter how near the cyclone came. They stood in the doorway clinging to each other watching as strong winds and hail continued its onward rush. The cyclones roar was earth shaking, surging, rising and falling with a deadly sound and bouncing motion.

Trees and huge boulders drifted upward into the cyclones belly. The donkeys were frightened, and throwing their body's against the walls of their pen. The animals' screams were drowned out with the sound of howling winds, and violent cracks of thunder. The split tree by the stable gave way with the rising winds and rushed upward into the belly of the storm. The violent twirling funnel pressed on until its tip reached the stream just below Dominique's cave. The upward current sucked up water and mud. Then after a slight hesitation, with the impulse of a wild animal it veered away from the donkeys. The cyclone swerved to the north hopping, the funnel dangled in the sky above the waving jungle dumping buckets of water on the earth, creating islands of destruction.

"It missed the donkeys," Dominique shouted.

Only then did he realize that he had drawn Yolanda against him protectively. He was stroking her hair. She was trembling, unable to get over her fright. Her arms were clamped around him, her eyes were closed, and she was rubbing her face against his hairy chest as if trying to reassure herself that they had come through safely. She was still trembling, beginning to smile, and whispering something in Zulu, he didn't understand a word. The whispering was a combination of chanting and odd sounds in Swahili He stopped stroking her hair and started to let her go. Her arms tightened, she slowly turned her face and pressed her lips against his chest. He could feel the warm, moist tip of her tongue. "No," he said, pushing her away. Wild eyed, not in anger, trying to understand. She looked up at him.

"Why?"

L. A. Johnson Jr.

"It's wrong."

She asked. "Wrong for me or wrong for you?"

"Wrong for both of us."

He walked into the cabin. She followed, looking ashamed.

"I forget," she said.

"You forgot what?"

She tried to tell him what she had forgotten but she couldn't find the words. Before he could say anything she had started making signs. In swift succession she made the one for warrior, for fasting and prayer, for woman, and for complete absence. She thought he had taken a warrior's vow. It was known that Zulu men stayed away from women while planning war or engaging in serious hunting or trying to understand the meaning of a dream.

He pretended he didn't understand what she meant to give himself time to think. He tried to understand how being alone in the cabin with her had changed her so quickly after she had tried to kill him. He didn't understand why she wasn't angry, or resentful of his refusal of her. Suddenly he knew that a warrior's vow was the only possible explanation.

"Vow," he said. "Warrior's vow."

"Vow?" she repeated.

He nodded.

"How long?" she asked.

"For quite a while."

She picked up the shirt she had been working on.

"I'll check the donkeys," he said, walking out the door.

The donkeys had already settled down and were eating the remains of their morning feed. He cut more cane and threw it in to them. Now that the cyclone was over he realized how close he had come to losing the donkeys. He would have had to pay Mario for the donkeys before he did anything about his own affairs. What frightened him most was that the cyclone had come on the very last day. It was as if he had been given a warning. There could be Zulu warriors somewhere in the neighborhood. And it reminded him that it was on the way to Figueroa's when he lost his horse. You couldn't stir a single pack donkey out of a walk. Six of them would leave a trail wide enough a blind Afri-

148

can could spot a mile away. All day tomorrow, they would be traveling through the jungle, inviting trouble every step they took.

The rain decreased to a drizzle. It would be clear before dark and there would be a bright moon a little later. If they got started before dusk they could be past the worst stretch of jungle before daylight. He started carrying out sacks of magnesium sulfate, stacking them near the door. The sacks were too heavy for Yolanda, she started packing the equipment. Each time he came into the cabin with another sack on his back she was bent over the cooking fire, or folding blankets, or packing a basket of food. She was doing her part and he was deceiving her. It wasn't fair to let her think, all she had to do was wait. This hiding behind that Zulu warriors vow story was no good.He put off saying anything until he had finished carrying out the merchandise, and surveyed the sky, which was clearing up as he had expected, he didn't say anything until after they had eaten. Even then he found it hard to begin.

"When I get to Congo Basin," he said, "I'm going to buy a farm."

"What is farm?" she asked.

"A place where you grow maize, beans. Goats and oxen are kept in a fence. Like your people have rice, and maize fields, something like in a Zulu village, but this won't belong to everybody, it will belong to me."

She listened intensely with keen interest, as she always did to anything he said about himself. "Then you will stay, all the time, in one village?"

"No. In a house I'll build on my farm."

She looked around the cabin. "That house, it will be better than this?"

"Much better."

"Who will plant the maize?"

"I'll plant it myself, at first.

She was more suspicious about this than the house. "You will work very hard."

"That's right."

"Why?"

This was a simple question, but he had to stop to think to

give a truthful answer. "So I can have what I want."

"What you want?"

This seemed as good an opportunity as any. "What I want is a woman in Eagle Landing."

She was confused.

Where is Eagle Landing?"

"About as far as Kingdom of Buganda, only more to the north."

She pondered with a faint smile. "You are here. She is not here. You do not want her very much."

"I've wanted her since I was a teenage boy," he insisted.

Yolanda was more than ever confused. "You take her then, you want her now?"

"No, I've never had her. I came to Congo."

"You never forget her?"

"Never," said Dominique, hoping he was finally making some progress.

"All this time nobody else want her?"

"Of course they did. She was married, but she's a widow now." He was beginning to sweat and fumble with his pipe.

"Widow?"

"A widow is a woman whose husband died."

"Widow," repeated Yolanda. "She cut off her hair and make scars on her face?"

"No. Portuguese women don't do that. She's been a widow a long time."

Yolanda thought about the many statements, questions, and answers. "This woman you never forget, she is old now."

"She's my age."

"She has many children?"

"No."

"Yolanda rose, strolled thoughtfully about the cabin and came back to confront him. "This woman, I do not like. What does she look like?"

He stood and faced her. He had to handle this problem now. "She has red hair, and light blue eyes, she's taller than you," he held up his hands a foot over Yolanda's head, his hands moved down making clear gestures describing female curves, "more of this than you." His hands dropped. "She's beautiful and she's Portuguese like me."

Yolanda glanced down at her own shapely figure, with her hands repeated his gestures, though somewhat enlarging upon it, indicating considerable more breast and hips than she. "She is more tall than me, more breast and hips than me, and more like this, than me." She said smugly. "She is already old. Soon she will be fat." Her interest in the topic diminished. She picked up the shirt. "Your shirt is finished."

"When I get to Eagle Landing," said Dominique angrily, "I'll to marry her."

"Marry?"

"She will be my wife, and she will live with me."

Yolanda considered this statement. For a moment there was an unstable sparkle in her eyes, for a moment only.

"First we go to Congo Basin?"

"Yes."

"And then we go to Kingdom of Buganda?"

"Yes."

Her calm was fully restored. "It is vary far to Congo Basin, and to Kingdom of Buganda." She held up the shirt for him to put on.

Chapter 10
I am Zulu

They reached Figueroa Station an hour or so after dark. Miles before they were in sight of the settlement they had spotted a glow in the sky that made them wonder if the settlement was on fire. It turned out to be only campfires of new settlers, too many settlers to crowd into the station. Settlers were camped up and down Congo Road for miles outside the gate. One war cry from any African would have sent the lot of them running for the rest of the night. There were at least sixty families, their children, slaves and livestock, were standing around big blazing fires. There wasn't a man among them who had ever seen a Bushmen, or Zulu warrior. People were running around acting confused, no one noticed him approaching with Yolanda. There wasn't even a curious glance, nor had she been given the faintest excuse to start shivering or hanging onto him as she is now.

She had even less of an excuse when they reached Dino's house. Anita and Dino were in bed, they got up, and let them in with as warm a welcome as Dominique had expected. But, after one look at Yolanda, and then at him, and back at Yolanda again, Anita's smile faded. Yolanda continued acting as if he were the only person in the world, her only friend in the midst of enemies. She refused to eat, talk, or do anything except stay as close to Dominique as she could.

"Well, that's about all," he finished. "Then we came here."

Anita glanced down at Yolanda with a worm smile and whispered. "She's scared."

"She's not as young as she looks," said Dominique. "I mean...."

Dino laughed and coughed hastily when Anita looked at him. Anita's stare returned to Dominique.

"You mean?"

"I meant she's as much a child as when I first stumbled into her." The conversation wasn't going the way he had planned. "I suppose you think she would have been better off if I'd let her go back to the Zulu's."

"I'm not sure."

"That's because you don't know as much as Dino or I do about Africans I took her to the nearest Portuguese settlement, but she wouldn't stay there."

"Then you took her to your cabin for a month, and now that the month is over you want us to take her off you hands?"

"Only until I can go to Sea Pen and Rhino Creek and back."

"She's counting on your coming back?"

"*I'm coming back.* I've told you, I'm going to take her to Kingdom of Buganda."

"That's what she wants?"

"Yes."

Anita looked at Yolanda crouched by Dominique's leg. "She has an odd way of showing it."

Dominique yanked his leg away from Yolanda's roaming

fingers. "Don't be fooled by the way she's been acting since she's been here. She understands every word we're saying."

"That's good," said Anita, "because we're not saying anything that should be kept from her."

"Nobody's been keeping anything from her. She knows I'm going to Eagle Landing to get married."

"And you think that's OK with her?"

Doesn't make a difference what she thinks. Nothing happened to make her think she belongs to me." In spite of his attempt to satisfy Anita, Dominique's temper flared. "I can't take her with me all over Congo. I have to leave her somewhere; if it's not here it'll be somewhere else."

"You have no reason to feel that way," Anita said. She looked at Yolanda again. "We'll take care of her for you, there's nothing else we can do, but I would like to know how she feels about it."

"You'll know, when she decides to tell you," said Dominique. "She's probably saving her strength for the hell she is going to raise when I leave in the morning. Remember what I told you she did at Median's."

Anita rose. "She won't have to start any fires here. She'll be free to come, and go as she pleases, we're not going to lock her in a room." She bent over Yolanda. "Speak up for yourself. Do you want to stay?"

The haunting expression in her upturned face, the faint quiver of her lips. The silent pleading in her weeping eyes, spoke more clearly than any words she could say. She would rather die than stay, but if Dominique wanted her to stay she would stay. Yolanda's only answer was to look up at Dominique and he nearly choked. This attitude of helpless sub mission was worst than anything she had done to him on the island or on the raft. He shoved her away and stood up. "If it's up to me it's settled. She stays."

A flicker of hope rose in Dominique as he watched Anita. She was too smart to be tricked by this last performance of Yolanda's, but the eyes of the two women had suddenly met in a strange, concentrating absorbed focused look. Anita bent and touched Yolanda's shoulder reassuringly. "He will come back," she said. "Even if we have to send for him." Standing tall, the look she gave Dominique was haunting and strangely speculative, as if, in spite of having known him for so many years, she was just beginning to understand him.

"Well," said Anita, suddenly and very casually, "time for bed. I'll get some blankets." She went into the other room.

"Don't take Anita too serious," said Dino. "She will be OK in the morning. She always gets angry when she thinks somebody's being treated unfairly."

"Who's been treated more unfairly than me?" demanded Dominique.

"I don't see how you could have done anything other than what you did., now what are you going to do? Only one thing bothers me. If you don't know the name of her folks, how do you figure on finding her relatives in Kingdom of Buganda?"

"Couldn't have been so many people in Tupelo that long ago. Somebody will remember."

Anita came back, caring two blankets and dragging a thick straw mat. "We haven't all the room we need, yet," she said. She dropped a mat and one of the blankets beside Yolanda. "You can sleep on the mat until we have time tomorrow to find you something better." She handed the other blanket to Dominique. "You can sleep up in the loft with Alberto."

Dominique took the blanket and started for the ladder.

"No," said Yolanda, jumping up.

She overtook him at the foot of the ladder. There wasn't any doubt she was overdoing it now. Anita would never put up with this nonsense.

"I can tie her up," said Dominique.

Anita's calm was broken by nothing more than a tight-lipped smile. "I never thought I would stand for anything like this in my house," she said. "But after a month living in a cabin in a cave together, I don't think it will make a difference if you spend one more night together in the same room."

She left the room. Dino followed, reluctantly. He turned in the doorway. "Hasn't had a chance to tell you, I saw Novas in Sea Pen week before last."

People shouted his name so loud it sounded like an echo from another world.

"How is he?"

Yolanda The Enchantress

"Meaner than ever, he hung on to Xhosa country through that wintry spell all right; scared off the Masai and Belgian. He clashed with the British, at African Oak, too. The Belgian and British claim to be helping us, but they will betray us if they think nobody's looking. Then he went to Congo Basin and tried to raise an army to go to Elephant Falls. He couldn't get more than five men to join up. Most of the settlers think the war is just about over and they are searching for land and filing claims. Novas swore and argued and afterwords he couldn't wait any longer. He headed west to build Fort Novas on the Ivory Coast."

"On the Ivory Coast?"

"That's right. Just below the mouth of the Yoruba River where it dumps into the Atlantic. Good place to keep the Spanish, from traveling too freely up and down the Atlantic, or the Yoruba River. And keeps the British, French, Belgian and Germans remembering that that section is ours.

When he got back that evening the five men he had recruited had wandered off, thinking they should grab what they could, before anymore-new settlers filed claims on all the land that was left. After that Novas closed the land office to keep people from filing land claims. He said he would keep it locked until he returned from Elephant Falls so that settlers that stayed behind couldn't take advantage of the men fighting the war. Good many said he had no right to do it, but Novas said Congo land would be no good to any of us unless we drove the French and Belgian out of Elephant Falls.

No way to tell how closing the land office worked, because a few days later, word came that Costar with fifteen hundred angry men attacked African villages on the Zambezi. They took back Panda Via, and African Oaks. They burned every African village on the way to Mali. Novas had to drop everything and head west again to join Colonel Costar."

Until last spring that was Dominique's world, this is more than echoes from another world. Campaigning with Novas keeps a man fighting and feeling that he is always in the middle of whatever is happening. He found himself wishing that he were in that ship, heading west with Novas with nothing on his mind, going wherever Novas had to go. "Good thing Congo has Novas," he said.

That's a fact," said Dino. "Could be we made a mistake not joining up with him last spring. Anyway, what I was saying he told me to tell you something. He heard about your new settlement on Lake Tanganyika. He said don't worry about coming' back to him. He said there isn't a better place for you to be; you're better use to him and Congo, their. Make sure that that settlement so close to Gorilla Passage is successful."

"Dino," called Anita.

"Coming'." he replied. He withdrew and closed the door.

Dominique looked disgustedly down at Yolanda. The message from Novas had been a great comfort to him. Many times during the snowy season he battled with himself, thinking uneasily about parts of his plans of which he was not satisfied. Obviously what he was doing prevented any thought of returning to military service with Novas. He had been sent a message from Novas that what he was doing was even more helpful. At the moment he wasn't helping anybody hold any thing. He was in a kitchen with the most annoying female ever born.

Yolanda was no longer pretending. Her harsh Zulu look had settled over her.

"Might as well go to bed," he said. "You have caused all the trouble you can for me tonight."

She got up, walked over to the mat, wrapped her blanket around her and sat on the floor against the wall. He kicked the woven mat nearer to her. "It's for you," he said. "Use it."

She shook her head.

"Whatever you wish," he said. "You always do."

The mat lay on the floor between them. He blew out the candle and rolled up in his blanket against the opposite wall. They hadn't slept the night before because they were traveling, and tonight he was too annoyed to sleep. He could tell by her breathing that the same was true for her. Still, it could have been even worst, he decided. As bad as things had been with the reception of his story by Anita, he was glad that he didn't have to tell it to a more suspicious person. He shuddered when he thought of the Gomez brothers, and their wives listening to his story, while watching Yolanda's backstabbing antics. One thing was certain, neither Anita, nor Yolanda needed to worry about his getting back here as fast as he could, to take Yolanda to

Yolanda The Enchantress

Kingdom of Buganda.

The door to Dino's bedroom opened. "Dominique," came Dino's harsh whisper.

"Yes?"

"Don't know why I didn't think of it before. Old Oswald Peruse has a cabin on the headwaters of Zebra Valley."

"Who's he?"

"About as no 'count as they come, but for years he traded with the Zulu, before they ran him out when the war started. He could have been around when that boat capsized or heard about it. He might know something about her family."

Dominique sat up. "Where did you say he was?"

"I'll take you to see him... first thing in the morning."

Dino closed the door. Dominique leaned back on his blanket, but felt less than ever like sleeping. It didn't seem possible that something even faintly helpful should have turned up. However little the old ivory trader might know about Yolanda's family, if he knew anything at all it would simplify the search and any saving of time would be a stroke of luck. He sat up and looked across the dark room towards Yolanda's shadowy figure. She must have heard Dino. She should be excited, too.

"Ever see that trader-Oswald Peruse?"

"No."

"Ever hear of him?"

"No."

"Dino said he lived in Zulu country for years."

"Many men trade with Zulu, there are many Zulu villages. My village was in Zululand. These traders never come."

"What makes you so sure?"

"When white men come, everybody knows. This Man never come."

"Just the same, I'm going to talk to him in the morning."

She didn't reply. He was irritated by her lack of interest.

"Are you afraid of what he might know about you?"

"I not afraid."

"Then what's wrong?"

Her calm broke; here voice flowied towards him out of the darkness was suddenly cold and harsh. "You speak to me as I am nothing. I know who I am. I am me. I am Yolanda. Always, I have been Yolanda. With Zulu I belong to a clan. I am Zulu, one of the Cheetah people. The earth trembles with the thunder of stomping feet, when our warriors dance too war drums. My people "talk with drums, we send messages to people miles and miles away. Our drums talk on special occasions. The drums tell us what dance to do. I know who I am! My mother is Zulu. That makes me Zulu! My grandmother, she is my mother now. In the Woman's Council nobody stand in front of my grandmother. I am proud to be Zulu, I am Zulu! Why do you want to ask a white man who I am? With white people I am nobody."

"You can be prouder of belonging to the poorest white family," said Dominique angrily, "than to the best Zulu clan."

"I am Zulu!" said Yolanda. "I have no family in Kingdom of Buganda."

"The hell with that," said Dominique. "Tomorrow I'm taking you with me to see this old ivory trader. He might know more than you think. And if he doesn't we'll still keep trying. We'll keep searching and asking questions until we find your people. Now settle down and get some sleep."

Before dawn Anita had a kettle of coffee brewing, and bacon was sizzling in the frying pan. They ate hastily and were halfway over the ridge before the sun rose.

"Anita had suddenly announced at breakfast. I'm going with you," It was good she had, as it turned out. When they reached Oswald's shabby little cabin they found the old ivory trader in bed with his fat, cross-eyed Quittance wife. He came scrambling out, scratching, and grinning, and pulling at his hat, to greet them.

"Well, what a surprise, it's Colonel Figueroa, and his wife. Come in and have a seat." He turned to yell into the cabin behind him. "Yuma, throw together a pot of foufou and fry some of this gazelle meat for these folks to eat." There was a quarter of ant infested, and fly-dotted gazelle hanging from a tree. It had started to spoil. Oswald gazed at Yolanda with modest interest, while fumbling thoughtfully with one crusty, scar-riddled grimy old hand at his silky gray beard. "Nope, Colonel, never seen her before," he said, regretfully.

"Are you sure?" Dominique asked Yolanda.

Oswald's African woman, accompanied by as many flies

as were clinging to the gazelle meat, wobbled into the doorway to look with sudden curiosity.

"Have you seen her?"

Yolanda shook her head again. "Quittance," she said scornfully.

After a quick glance at the dirty cabin, and the people living it. Neither Anita nor Yolanda dismounted Anita carefully stroked her horse's mane to keep from looking again. Yolanda kept staring scornfully at the old ivory trader, chanting Zulu words under her breath. Dominique moved a step closer to Yolanda. Her bare feet in the stirrup pressed against him, he could feel her leg trembling.

"Ever been to Zululand near the Indian Ocean?" he asked Oswald.

"Been there once or twice but never spent no time there."

"Where was your store?" asked Dino.

"Near a Zulu village called Mohair."

"That's near the Swazi River, isn't it?"

"On the southern bank, Colonel."

"You must have seen settler's, on the way to Tupelo."

Oswald overflowed with eagerness to talk. He continued to answer readily sometime enthusiastically. "Every year, Colonel, every year. Not so many at first, but when word got back about the good land at Tupelo more settlers came."

"Perhaps you remember something about a ship wreck that everybody drowned, but one little girl," asked Dominique.

Oswald stopped scratching, and grinning, giving this question serious, and solemn consideration. He seemed to be searching his memory, anxious to be helpful. "Nope. Never heard nothing about that," he said, blinking, and scratching while shaking his head despondently.

"Must have heard a good deal of gossip around that time. You living right on the river seems like you would have heard something about it."

The old ivory trader shook his head, saddened even more that he couldn't answer the question truthfully. "Seems like I might-for a fact. Africans do a lot of gossiping', but you never know when they are telling the truth. Besides, Levee's more than a hundred miles down the river from where I was. The story had probably changed many times before it reached me."

"If you heard nothing about it, how did you know it happened at Levee?"

Oswald smiled complacently. "Reason I remembered Levee was that's the most dangerous place on the river, where anybody ship could run into trouble. Once when I was down that way looking for a no-good black that owed me, I saw six ships in a row sink."

"You never said a word."

"No. Never did." A sound of defiance was in his voice.

Anita leaned over and placed her hand on Yolanda's shoulder. "I'm sorry," she said, sadly.

Yolanda was anxious to leave. She looked down at Dominique.

"You have more to ask him?"

"No," said Dominique.

Again refusing the old ivory trader's invitation to share the gazelle, they started home. They rode on in silence. The trip had been a failure, after the excited interest with which they had set out that morning. Dominique was beginning to foresee similar frustrations that would probably await his inquiries when they reached Kingdom of Buganda.

"He was living in Zululand the year it happened you would have thought the old fool would have heard something about it Dominique," said Dino."

Anita pulled in her horse. "He was lying," she said.

"What makes you think that?" demanded Dino.

"He was lying," repeated Anita.

She turned her horse around. Oswald heard them coming and rushed out to greet them again.

"Glad you changed your minds." he said."

Anita rode up to him' "We didn't come back to eat with you," she said. "We came back to find out why you lied to us."

"Mrs. Figueroa you have no reason to speak to me like that," protested Oswald."

"He knows something but he's afraid to tell us." said Anita to Dino and Dominique,

"What a man can't remember," argued Oswald stubbornly, "nothing can make him remember."

Yolanda The Enchantress

"I'm not sure about that," said Anita. She moved her horse a step towards him, forcing his back against the wall of his cabin. She leaned down in her saddle. "You're living among white people now.

Unless you start telling us the truth, this minute, I'll tell you how I'm going to help you remember. The very next time an African shoots a cow, or steals a horse anywhere near this settlement, I'll remind every white woman in the settlement that you lived with Africans for years, and that you still have one living with you here. You can guess how long it'll take those people to come out here, and burn you out."

"Dino Figueroa," begged the old ivory trader. "You're a colonel and the law in this section; you've got no right to let her talk to me like this."

"Takes more than a colonel," said Dino slowly, "to keep women from gossiping."

Oswald put one hand on his head, the other to the center of his back as if he were stressed by pain in both places at once. "I'm too old to live in the jungle again," he whined. "Some days my arthritis is so bad, I can hardly move around." He studied the faces of his neighbors, and exhaled noisily when he saw no sign of sympathy. "Ain't no use you bearing' down on me so hard. That was a long time ago. Like I told you, I want to help but a man my age can't remember every little bit of gossip he might have heard so many years ago."

Still he saw no hint that his inquisitive visitors might give in. he said ."Come in and have a seat, I've got a jug of homemade rum. After we've pass it around a few times something might come back to me."

Nobody moved. His eyes shifted helplessly to the ground at his feet, and then to the jungle, then to the sky over the surrounding hills, as if he hoped against hope aid might come to him from someone. He finally glanced nervously at Anita's horse. Again he sighed deeply, and his shoulders dropped more despondently than before. "What year was that?"

"How long did you live with the Zulu's?" Dominique asked.

"Eighteen seasons."

"That was the summer of 1761."

161

L. A. Johnson Jr.

"Hum," grunted Oswald, beginning once more to put on a show of trying to remember. "The year settlers began to travel around. The Zulu had been peaceful for a while and people from Kingdom of Buganda was starting' to tramp through their country taking their land, especially at Tupelo." Suddenly he placed his hand on his brow. "Now, it comes back to me. That year I heard something about a Zulu shipwreck down the river, almost the first one that came through. Everybody died but one little girl." He smiled flatteringly at Yolanda. "Well, well, are you that little girl?"

"We already know what she can tell us," said Dominique coldly. "We want to hear what you know about her father."

"Nothing, I know nothing'. I never laid eyes on him." Oswald leaned forward grabbing her bridle. "Give me time to think. Things are beginning' to come back to me in little pieces. Perhaps she was with a Zulu man, and woman I saw coming pass my store at Mohapi. The man that owed the ship was talking' crazy, so crazy that I thought he was drunk. The woman was pretty. This gal here looks like her. That's the only reason it's coming back to me. They had a very young child with them, maybe nine, ten months old, and several warriors. The boat was floating awful low in the water."

"Was that why the man stopped to see you?" asked Dominique. "To sell you some of his cargo?"

Oswald stepped into the trap. "Nope. He didn't want to sell me nothing. He...."

"Yes. Go on," said Anita. "Why did he stop to see you?"

"He didn't. I only saw the boat going past."

Dino's voice was as cold as an icicle hanging in a frozen cave. "Oswald Peruse, you're the worst liar I've ever had to listen to. Damn it, I'm not going to wait for women gossip-in, to get around, when I can burn you out right now."

The ivory trader leaned back against the wall; bolder men had collapsed from the look that was coming men from Dino's face. "I'll tell you, exactly how it was, Colonel Figueroa," he said, his last shred of resistance collapsing. "He stopped to give me a message to take to his brother in Zulu Land the next time I went over the mountain."

"So he gave you a message," said Dominique. "Then you

162

Yolanda The Enchantress

know his name."

The ivory trader nodded. He was dazed. "Qukeza," he said.

"Qukeza," whispered Yolanda. "Qukeza." Her expression never changed. "He's making this up," she whispered. "So nobody will kill him."

"Be quiet, said Dominique. "What was his name, and the child's?"

"I don't know," said Oswald, helplessly. "Only name I was given was Qukeza the letter was addressed to, his brother in Kingdom of Buganda. That was Rendi Qukeza." Finally he is telling the truth. "He had five boys and as many girls. I went there that summer on my way to Mateo to buy supplies. Rendi Qukeza was awful sick and in no shape to travel to get the girl."

"How much did he give you?"

"One hundred gold coins." The trader's spirit was completely broken. "When I got back I went to Zululand. The young child was being taken care of by her grandmother, an old woman they called, Eon. She was the head woman of the village. She was the widow of a Zulu chief named, Kafka Bissau, he had left her well off. She kept her granddaughter, and she wouldn't sell her for no amount of money."

"You kept the money."

"That's right."

"What did you tell Rendi Qukeza?"

"I sent them word the little girl was dead." Dominique looked at Yolanda. "Now you know something about your people," he told her. "They didn't forget you. And you belong to a big family. You'll find Kingdom of Buganda is full of Qukeza's."

"Qukeza," she said again, as if trying to sound it. "Yolanda Qukeza."

"What's wrong with that?"

"I am still me," she said. "I am still Zulu."

On the way back Anita rode ahead with Dino, Yolanda remained grave and silent. "Are you wondering about how you'll get along with your Kingdom of Buganda relatives?" he asked.

"No. They are far away."

"Not as far away as they were yesterday."

She didn't reply.

L. A. Johnson Jr.

"Then what are you thinking about so hard?"

"I do not know what I think."

They rode on in silence. Feeling alarmed, and annoyed, this time he had something else on his mind. He didn't understand what it could be. This time was different. A heavy burden had been lifted. Thanks to the luck of encountering, Oswald Peruse he could once more be sure of what he was doing, and where he was going. He wouldn't have to wander all over Kingdom of Buganda asking questions. He knew exactly where he was headed, Sea Pen, Rhino Creek, Figueroa Station, Rotshidzwa, and then Beguiler Ferry Crossing.

The trail winding down the lower slope of the ridge began to offer occasional glimpses of the open grassland below. A man was riding out from the station towards the foot of the trail. From time to time that man pulled up, and scanned the wooded slope above. When Dominique, and Yolanda came out of the jungle onto the grassland. They saw that Dino and Anita had rained in their horses, and were talking to him. Then he realized that man was Mario.

Mario's reappeared again, because something had happened, something unforeseen and most likely disturbing.

"Thought I'd come back to help you with the pack train," Mario said, as Dominique and Yolanda approached.

"So you could make better time."

"What's wrong now?"

Mario laughed, "I've come to help you. Before you say hello you ask what's wrong. Nothing is wrong, my friend." He laughed again. "Nothing," he repeated. "Rhino Creek is in better shape now than most new settlements that's been around for years."

"What happened?"

"Day before I left Legacy, Monty, and Antonio returned with their families. They bought so much stuff with them, it took twenty elephants pulling huge wagons; and thirty pack donkeys to carry everything."

"You told me they were bringing out their families later this year."

"I didn't tell you this', because I didn't know. Nobody knew. That's what I've come to tell you now," he glanced at

164

Yolanda The Enchantress

Yolanda, "you need to get rid of her. Your woman, she came with them." He added with emphasis: "She's at Rhino Creek, waiting' for you."

"The woman from Eagle Landing," said Yolanda in a clear unsympathetic voice.

Mario nearly fell off of his horse. "You told me she didn't speak a word of Portuguese," he stared at Dominique. "How was I to know she understood what I was saying'?"

Dominique didn't try to explain to Mario. All he was able to think about was that Liana hadn't waited for him to come to get her. She had come to join him. She was in Congo Basin, and he had only a few miles to travel to be with her.

"You don't have to worry about her. Said Anita. "Nothing is being kept from her, and, nothing will be."

"You're right ma'am," agreed Mario politely. He turned to Dominique, excited to report his information. "She bought her forge, and them big black smooth talking' slaves, and their wives, and all her stuff. When the new land company had the land drawing she drew for her piece of land along with the rest of them." He leaned over stroked his horse's neck as if what he had to say was of little importance. "Because you weren't there to draw for yourself. She drew for you, too."

Anita leaned over placing her hand on Dominique's shoulder. She was studying his face with the first flash of warmth, and sympathy she had shown since he had walked into her house with Yolanda. "Is this the woman you wanted the letter for?"

"He nodded, yes."

"You're in love with her?"

He nodded again.

"I'll tell you how much he is," said Mario. "He's so much in love that he hasn't given another woman a second look since the dance at Pueblo Plato's plantation nearly a year ago."

"Well that is that," said Anita. "Nobody's to blame, and nothing can be done about it." She turned to Yolanda. "We'll keep you with us-and, when we can, we will make sure that you get to your relatives in Kingdom of Buganda."

Yolanda shook her head. "I will wait for Dominique. He will take me."

165

L. A. Johnson Jr.

"Why do you think that?"

"Because he said he would, many times."

The horses, restless from being held in one place, were stamping and kicking. "She's right," said Dominique, as surprised as the others with a sudden quiver in his voice. "Making sure she gets there is my responsibility."

All at once Anita was more disturbed, than she had been about their feeding Africans in her house, the night Prince Kudzu was bought to her home for dinner in chains.

"I don't think this other woman is the one for you. If she is, go to her and stay. Your plans what you want, and what she wants, even the land you're buying, all that goes together, and probably belongs together, but there is one thing that couldn't be more wrong. You riding off leaving Yolanda here, thinking you'll come back to take her to Kingdom of Buganda. Tell her the truth now, Dominique; tell her that she'll never see you again. Tell her the truth, and stop fooling her, you have to do that."

"I haven't fooled her, said Dominique. All there is to it is this: I took her away from her Zulu relatives, and I'm going to take her to Kingdom of Buganda. I owe her that and nothing else."

"You owe her more than that," said Anita. "She's the same as in a trap, and you have got to let her out, and let her go. That's what you owe her."

"Call it a trap if you like," said Dominique.

Anita's angry voice reached a new pitch. "It is a trap and, whoever set it, you're the person that is keeping her in it. You know in your heart when you see that woman you're so stuck on, you'll never going to leave her again. You'll embrace each other, and neither of you will want to let go."

Dominique's sudden rage was not directed towards Anita. She was telling the truth, and what she was saying suddenly angered him. Taking Yolanda to Kingdom of Buganda was certainly no way to spend the first half of a marriage, which should be spent with Liana, but if he didn't his words would mean nothing. He would be a lowdown scandal, and he couldn't live with that. Anita saw his anger, and was she got angrier.

"Let me tell you this," she stated. "If you go, leaving her

here waiting and wondering, and you haven't come back within two weeks, Dino and I will bring her to Rhino Creek, too you."

Mario straightened up with a jerk. "Wait a minute." He spoke with a note of authority Dominique had never heard in his voice before. "It's not my business and surely none of yours, ma'am. If you feel like keeping' the woman in your home, that's your business, but when you threaten to bring her to Rhino Creek, that's different, then your problem becomes my problem, too. I have a family there and there's a lot of other families all working' hard getting' a new settlement started." He was talking to Mr. and Mrs. Figueroa now. "This other woman of Dominique's from Eagle Landing has a blacksmith shop; her slaves are probably the best iron workers anywhere.

There's nothing' a new settlement needs more than that kind of business. If something foolish happens to make her pull up stakes, and return to Eagle Landing, two hundred people that have absolutely nothing to do with Dominique's problem, one way or another will be loosing something they can't afford to loose. Right or wrong the way Dominique treats this woman, you know as well as I do, even better, most likely, because you have been through it. You know that it's wrong to bring trouble to a new settlement. "I have nothing else to say."

"Now I'll have mine," said Dominique. "I'm getting sick of all this talk about my two women. I have one. All the talk about what I have done to Yolanda will continue and get worse. If I leave her here the lies will simmer, and spread like a wild fire? The three of you are my oldest friends; look at how you're carrying on. A man can only guess how big this story will grow, when it spreads. The only way to stop the talk and make people understand there is nothing to it. There's only one way to do that. The woman I intend to marry is at Rhino Creek. To make it entirely clear where I stand, and what I think about all this gossip. I'm not going to leave Yolanda here, are any-where else? I'll take her with me. I'll settle this before we leave for Kingdom of Buganda. If anybody has anything to say, I'll face it in the open and get it over with. I can't think of any other way to get it through everybody's head that I haven't done anything that I have to be ashamed of."

"You have gone crazy," shouted Mario.

"You would actually take that girl into a hornet's nest like that," cried Anita. "I won't let you. I won't let you."

Dino spoke up for the first time. "All of you have been doing a lot of talking. Nobody has asked, Yolanda what she wants to do?" He looked at Yolanda. "Do you want to go with Dominique?"

Spots of color appeared in her cheeks and sparks in her eyes. "Yes," she said promptly.

"You don't know what you are walking into?" protested Anita.

Yolanda seemed to know quite well. "Before we go to Kingdom of Buganda," she explained, "I would like to see this woman from Eagle Landing."

Chapter 11
A New Red Dress

Towards night Dominique dropped behind to be certain they were not being followed. No war parties of any kind had been seen anywhere in Congo since the snow had melted. You could always count on a few young warriors hanging around in the jungle alone, or in small war groups. Young warriors were anxious to earn a reputation by stealing a horse, or a camel or killing a white man and mounting his head on a long pole for all to see. Warriors would hide in the jungle for weeks, often until they nearly starved for to kill a white-man straggling behind. In this unsettled country between Green River, and Congo Basin, the most prosperous settlements were built on each side of Congo Road. This was the perfect place to be attacked.

He stretched out on a hill and waited. Monkeys, snakes, parakeets and giraffes quickly ignored the movement of the tiny caravan. Animals high up in trees continued their ordinary playful, aimless confrontational pursuits. Secretary birds stopped their squawking, and not a single bird of any kind made a sound anywhere within hearing range along the jungle trail.

Dominique moved higher up the slope to a point he could see the open meadow they had crossed nearly an hour ago.

Yolanda The Enchantress

hippos and lions were grazing peacefully in the meadow. At least, the tiny caravan wasn't being followed yet.

Mario unloaded the merchandise, and tied the donkeys and horses in a cluster of trees. He cut enough cane to keep them quiet through the night. Dominique circled the campsite, recorded every natural detail in his memory so that he could move about without difficulty in the coming darkness, if necessary.

The afterglow faded above Dungeon Landing, in the western sky. The three settled down around the food basket from which Yolanda was taking out what they had to eat. Dominique's nerves were on edged as he approached the end of his journey. He put out the fire. They had their pick of Yolanda's cape buffalo jerky, smoked ostrich, goose liver, together with wheat bread, slices of ham and hard-boiled eggs Anita had given them.

No fire while they ate. The hostility between Mario and Yolanda continued even when making idle conversation. Dominique had too much to think about to be a peacemaker, or say anything he didn't have to. The darkness deepened in the jungle surrounding them had overwhelming their fire camp.

In the silence the munching, and neighs of the horses, and chewing of donkeys was the only sound. There was chirping, and rustling in the surrounding jungle as animals in the undergrowth began their nightly search for food. The sudden woo of owls and birds singing. Frogs leaped as they chatter, and played in the stream. Ducks quacked, and splashed wildly before leaping from the water. In the distance hyenas howled, lions roared, and cheetahs cried. Majestic animals like elephants, gun, giraffe, jackals, hippopotamus, leopards, and mountain gorillas splashed in a mangrove swamp.

Dominique remembered the cry of the cheetahs the night he left Yolanda tied up under a tree. He had to go back and get her then, and she's been hanging onto him every since. The cheetahs' cry was a reminder that he had never been able, even up to now to find a place in which it was right to leave her behind. She was sitting there, silently, listing to haunting sounds in the darkness. Her face was turned in his direction, it revealed only a faint blur, and she was looking at him. He knew that she was waiting for him to say something to her. It could be that with all her heathen ways she feared darkness and needed his reassurance. She

169

moved. He could see her arm reaching towards him as if she had a sudden impulse to touch him, but she was reaching for her blanket.

She picked her blanket up, and retired under a large African willow a few feet away. Mario yawned, stretched, and moved to a place beyond the horses, and donkeys this way if there were any disturbance he and Dominique would be on either side of them. After some time Dominique followed, and squatted behind him. Mario had fallen asleep. Dominique shook him. "I've been thinking," he said.

"You don't say," said Mario. "About what?"

"Drifting in on Liana all of a sudden would be too much of a surprise," said Dominique.

"Whatever could have put that thought in your head? You don't have to worry about that. Like it or not she'll see you coming out of the jungle with a wild woman on your arm. She'll think things like that go on all the time out here."

"Yolanda's not as wild as she was at first."

"She still looks it." Mario sat up. "We should have asked, Anita to give her some of her clothing. Then she might look a little more respectable."

"Anita wanted to. I wouldn't let her."

"You wouldn't? Why not?"

"My story is, I stole her from the Zulu's where she had been enslaved for years. Part of it is true, but it doesn't hurt when you're talking about someone; if that person looks, talks, and dresses the way you described her to them."

Mario thought a moment and grunted suspiciously. "You can paint her face, and place colorful beads on her nappy hair, and nothings' going to help you. That's what you woke me up to tell me you have been thinking?

"I've been thinking that it's a mistake to surprise Liana. It's only fair to give her a chance to think. For that reason and that reason alone. You should get started before dawn and ride into Rhino Creek. You'll be there before dark tomorrow. Tell her that I'm coming with Yolanda and tell her why. "

"What else do you want me to tell her?"

"Tell her everything. Tell her everything you know, but leave out things you've been assuming. Tomorrow night I'll

Yolanda The Enchantress

camp where we found Antonio, and Rosario camped that day, and I'll come into the settlement the next morning. That will give Liana time to think."

Mario stared at Dominique so hard he took a step back. Then he shook his head so hard the bones in his neck cracked. "She's your problem not mine," he said. "You have been making a lot of mistakes, now you're making another one. The trouble with you is that you never pay any attention to the way a woman acts except when you are plotting to get her in bed. You're always doing something to make her angry and the longer you give her to think about it the angrier she gets."

"Liana's got more sense than that."

Why did I ever think you knew so much about women?"

Mario rebelliously set out an hour before dawn. Dominique, followed leading the caravan at a much slower pace, he swung wide around Nova Gala Settlement to avoid curios eyes seeing Yolanda's appearance. They reached Antonio's old camping place on the shore of Rhino Creek. Late in the after noon, a steady drizzle of rain started. The bush and sapling thatched roof was sagging. He started working propping it up repairing it, and adding a lean-to. The leather sacks would shed water for a while, but they wouldn't keep the mineral salt dry if the rain lasted through the night. He tied the donkeys and horses in a cluster of trees where they could gnaw on the bark, and piled the sacks in the hut. After he finished, he crept away in the darkness to the top of the hill. He could barely see the valley below through the haze, and pounding rain. Then a faint glimmer of light appeared in the stockade.

He sat on the ground, wrapping his arms around his knees. There was an overpowering need for him to cling onto himself. Liana was down there so near if he rose, if he started walking he could be with her in a few minutes.

He tried to imagine what she might be doing in the faint glimmer of light behind those log walls. Mario must have told her, he's on his way. She could be talking it over with her brothers, while her family considered their options, or what stand was right for all of them to take as a family.

On the other hand, she hadn't told any of them, yet. She could be alone in a room, pacing back and forth making up her mind. Or she could be sitting in a rocking chair, thinking. Possibly, she could be setting by the fireplace cooking. He liked that thought. He imagined the gleam of the firelight across her face, bouncing on her hair, and reflecting in her eyes. Perhaps, she was already in bed. This thought was even better. The overpowering feelings that accompanied them were strangely comforting. She had to understand how he felt about her. He had a passion so strong and overpowering that she had to know how strong it was. Women knew things like that.

There was a rustle behind him. He reached for his rifle, but it was only Yolanda. She squatted beside him and stared at the dim glows in the settlement.

"Get out of the rain," he said harshly.

"She is down there?"

"Yes."

"Mario tell her about me?"

"What makes you think that?"

"Last night when you talk to him, I come close. I hear what you say." Her low laughter was haunting. "Maybe tomorrow I feel very bad, but tonight she feel bad."

"Go back like I told you."

"The rain, the jungle and the dark, they are good. We sit here and think. That is good, too."

He grabbed her by the wrist and pulled her back to camp. It was too dark in the hut to see anything at all. He felt among his sacks of magnesium sulfate to make sure they weren't leaking. The remaining space was so small they had to stretch their blankets side by side. For a second Yolanda's head and shoulders were faintly outlined, when she leaned into the doorway just beyond his feet to wring water from her hair. She leaned back into the complete blackness beside him. He could hear a faint, slivering and then a whisper.

"What are you doing?" he asked.

"My close are wet, I take them off."

"No," he protested.

"It is all right," she replied calmly. "You not see."

It was true he couldn't see, but it was almost the same as seeing because she was so near, he couldn't help hearing and knowing every move she made. She dried herself with her blanket, spread it out on the ground, lay down upon it, and squirmed about in search of a comfortable position.

Again came her low haunting, laugh. "She is down there alone. She is thinking about us up here together. She thinks that we are closer than this." She reached out and touched his face. "She will never believe that nothing happened. That is good."

"Shut up and go to sleep."

She was quiet for a while. "No," she murmured. "It is not good, but it is better than nothing."

"I guess tomorrow you'll make all the trouble you can."

"I do not know how I will feel tomorrow."

"If you make things worse I'll ring your neck."

"My neck is here," she whispered. Wring it now?"

Dominique turned away from her placing his blanket around his shoulders. His shirt and pants were cold and soggy. There was no reason he should spend an uncomfortable night, he decided angrily. Swearing under his breath, he sat up, took off everything including his underclothing, and pulled his blanket around him.

There wasn't any use in trying to get any sleep; with everything he had to think about, at least, he didn't have to shiver all night. He wished it were morning. He could no longer find comfort in thinking about Liana, as he had on the top of the hill with Yolanda lying so near. He could hear the erotic, alluring sound of her breathing, near his ear. He remembered how near he had come to taking her that day she trimmed his hair. What a good thing it had been he had resisted that time. His thoughts became more confused.

She was crouched in the doorway looking out, and listening. It was still raining but the clouds had lifted, and the moon shone bright above the campsite. There was light enough for her shapely figure to stand out clearly. Her black breaded hair was flowing over her shoulders, making her naked body look appealing. She shook his foot again.

"Somebody come," she whispered.

He sat up, reaching for his rifle, was so annoyed when preparing to go to bed, he forgot to load it. The powder in the pan was dry. Somebody was coming, all right, and it certainly wasn't an African sneaking into the camp. Whoever it was, was tramping through the bushes, sounding like an elephant pushing away heavy bushes covered with vines.

"It is Mario," said Yolanda.

She moved out of the doorway, and stepped back into the darkness beside Dominique. From Mario came the familiar geese call, a little weak this time because he was winded. A moment later he appeared in the doorway, stumbled over Dominique outstretched feet and tumbled forward, putting out one hand to protect himself.

"My gracious," he cried, jerking his hand back as if he had put it into a fire. "She doesn't have any clothes on." He stepped sideways to get Dominique between them, saying in the darkness beyond Dominique. "I can't see a thing, don't attack me in the dark with a knife."

"Nobody's going to attack with anything," said Dominique.

"What's wrong with you? Why are you here?"

"I don't trust her," said Mario, grabbing Dominique's arm. His grip made him suddenly aware that Dominique was also bare. He stepped back slapping Dominique joyfully on the back. "Well, well, hitting it for the last time, eh? I don't blame you."

"We got wet," said Dominique. "We're drying off."

"Bad to sleep in wet clothes, all right," agreed Mario. "Could make you sick."

"Go to hell," said Dominique. "Why are you here?"

"Thought I should warn you," said Mario. "You better finished what ever you're doing before dawn. Liana is coming out here first thing in the morning."

"She knows you came to tell me?"

"Nobody knows. Not even my wife."

"How did Liana take it when you told her about Yolanda?"

"I couldn't tell what she was thinking', no more than you can tell, what Yolanda's thinking'. She listened until I finished talking and asked some question."

"About what"

"Sure is a mighty wet night, you're always doing something' to make me leave my home. Yolanda." Mario started to

Yolanda The Enchantress

back out. It'll be a relief when I don't have to travel so far to keep you out of trouble. It will take a load off of me once you get settled one way or another while I still have a wife to run home to." He stuck a hand out to test the drizzle. "A night like this, I could stand a little drying off myself. Wait a minute." He squatted in the doorway. "There's something else you should know.

There's a doctor named, Diesel Avila that came out with the Gomez's. He has bought a piece of land, and he's a partner in the land company. I didn't think much about it the first day they got in, or before I came to Figueroa Station to see you. He's awful close to the whole Gomez family.

They talked like they grew up together in Santiago Coca, but Cindy's noticed something while I was away. She said this doctor is with Liana morning noon and night, and Liana seams to be enjoying his company, too much. Don't get upset. Chances are that once you're back, you'll have nothing' to worry about. Why I'm telling you is because his flirting could be good for you. When she says something about Yolanda you can ask her about the fancy doctor. Well, this time I'm gone."

Mario backed out of the door, muttering words of profanity, when he stepped into a muddy puddle. He rushed pass the donkeys, and entered the entanglement of wild berry bushes below the grove of orange and date trees. Dominique sat down on his blanket.

"This man," said Yolanda, "he will take her."

"Go to sleep."

"He follow her here. She did not tell him to go back."

"I'm going to sleep whether you do or not."

"I say this. Maybe everything, it will come out all right. Now I sleep."

The rain stopped, it turned warmer. Now the air in the hut was stifling. The blankets and the pile of clothing beside them were wet. Dominique wanted to go outside to walk around, but he didn't want Yolanda to know how much he was troubled. There were no stars out yet; making it impossible to tell how much longer darkness would last, probably a good many hours. Hours later he hadn't realize that he had fallen asleep until he was awakened, this time by the sun breaking over the crest of the eastern mountain. Bright beams of light flashed across his eyes.

L. A. Johnson Jr.

Yolanda was no longer beside him. He crawled to the doorway, and looked out. The first thing he saw was her crocodile top and bottom spread out drying on a bush up stream not far away. Then he saw Yolanda bathing in the pool beyond. Her wet hair, arms, and shoulders glistened, as beams of sunlight bounced off the lake, reflecting on her naked body.

"Put your clothes on," he yelled.

"Don't worry," she called back. "Nobody come yet."

He stood up looking towards the wild-berry patch, and beyond the grove of orange and date trees, putting his clothes on. They were damp, which was perhaps just as well, since the only way he could have kept dry during the night was to have spent it in the hut with Yolanda. He took his blanket to the stream, dropped it in the water and rubbed mud on it before spreading it over a bush to dry. Having doing this he got angry folded the blanket and placed it back in the hut. He started to build a fire, and suddenly remembered his beard, and instead went down to the stream to shave.

When Yolanda came back she was dressed in her old clothing with her hair neatly braided. The furry bands on her legs and arms, every-thing about her was glowing with her usual morning cleanliness. There was another kind of glow in her eyes this morning, but her outward manner was serene and cheerful. She took out the food basket and started folding the blankets and packing for the day's move. She found his blanket soaking wet on the bush he didn't say anything, and she didn't either as she folded it.

When he came back to the hut Yolanda was slicing strips of meat on a rock by the fire pit. He considered building a fire but decided there was no use. Now the slightest decision was an enormous task.

He hadn't eaten since yesterday morning. He was hungry, weather he had sense enough to know it or not. He crammed a slice of cold dry meat into his mouth, and dragged out the sacks of magnesium sulfate. He stacked his cargo out on a strip of grass along the stream, and then he loaded the donkeys. Still Liana had not appeared.

"Maybe she not come," suggested Yolanda. "If she wanted to come she wouldn't tell Mario."

Yolanda The Enchantress

"This time you stay here," said Dominique. He started for the wild-berry bushes, just below the date, and orange trees. From the hill he could see weather or not she was on her way up from the settlement. The second he reached the top of the hill overlooking the grassland he dropped flat.

Liana was bareheaded, wearing a yellow dress riding her gray stallion, she was almost to the top, but he couldn't rush to meet her or even take a second look because beside her was a man. A man with black-hair, and brown-eyes. A lean, long-legged man wearing a light brown shirt, brown pants, fancy, expensive silver-trimmed boots, and a brown, wide brim hat, it was the doctor. The two had pulled their horses into a slow trot, riding very close together, talking seriously. He was begging her to do something, but she wasn't agreeing, she was listening. You couldn't help seeing how he felt about her.

Dominique started to rise to face them and dropped again. At first sight of them he instinctively dropped to the ground, as a soldier would do when catching sight of something unexpected. Now it was too late for him to show himself, no matter how stress-free he tried to look, he would look like he was hiding in the bushes, watching them. He crawled backwards into the wild-berry bushes. Bent and crawled through the tangle of vines and bushes, and ran for the camp.

"She's coming," he warned Yolanda.

Yolanda was watching his face as he came rushing towards her. She smiled. The worst things were for him today the better she liked it. He could hear their horses approaching. He strolled down to the donkeys and pulled their tie ropes, Now that they were near, they were coming faster. Yolanda knelt down by the food basket as if she, too, were busy.

"Dominique," called Liana. "Dominique."

They pulled up their horses in the open space between two pine trees on the opposite side of the hut, near the doorway. Dominique ran towards them. There was a sound of unquestionable welcome in her call.

"Liana," he yelled, echoing her greeting. "Liana."

He hoped he was sounding surprised. He hoped he didn't sound as if his throat were as tight as it felt. She hadn't changed, and she was looking down at him as he approached. She didn't look angry, she was glad to see him.

"You have lost weight," she said. Her horse wheeled restlessly, she pulled him back. "Dominique," she said, "this is Diesel Avila. He insisted on coming along," she laughed, "to protect me from your Zulu woman."

Diesel lifted his hat. He had been watching Dominique with sharp curiosity but now his grin was stern and phony. If he had been anyone else Dominique would have liked him on sight.

"Glad to meet you, Dominique de Salvo," said Diesel. "What I have heard about you has been so good that I thought I would be disappointed. I might add, I'm annoyed, just a little because I'm not disappointed."

Diesel wasn't bashful at all. Before he had come to Rhino Creek, he was staking out a piece of whatever land was going to be cleared here. Dominique couldn't stop looking at Liana long enough to give him more than a polite nod. She had quieted the stallion. Dominique moved forward her to lift her down, but she was looking pass him. Yolanda was joining them and she was wearing her Zulu look, her face looked like a stone mask.

"This is Yolanda," said Dominique, "the young girl Mario told you about."

Liana looked at Yolanda with perfect composure. "Mario said she was young, and scrawny, but she's a woman, and a beautiful one."

Yolanda came closer, her expressionless stare fixed on Liana. Dominique held his breath, afraid to scold Yolanda too soon because it would only make her harder to handle. She walked slowly circling the stallion, studying Liana from every angle. A speck of color appeared in Liana's cheeks as she exchanged an amusing glance with Diesel. Yolanda completed her inspection.

"She doesn't look old," she said. "Like I said, Dominique, soon she will be fat."

"Good heavens," said Liana. "She speaks Portuguese. Mario didn't tell me that. She's crude, she's a little dark."

"She's half white," said Dominique, glancing at Yolanda. "She's so ignorant and so mean you would never guess it."

Yolanda remained emotionless. "I am young," she said. "I can wait. You will not stay with her."

Yolanda The Enchantress

"Liana, you have a rival," cried Diesel. Yolanda had turned away facing the fire pit as if for her the incident was over, but she turned back to look at him. He took off his hat and bowed low in the saddle to Yolanda. "Take care of yourself Zulu woman my best wishes, hopes, and prayers go with you."

Yolanda continued to stare at him with a interest.

"If you want her why do you not take her?"

"A challenge most passionately to be under taken," he replied, "but on shaky ground."

"Diesel was at Lisbon College with my brother, Ironic," Liana explained. "As you can't help from noticing, he loves to flaunt his learning."

"So brief a biography scarcely does a subject justice, my dear," protested Diesel. He addressed Dominique. "I pursued my thirst for knowledge in medicine at the University Of Lisbon College Of Medicine, and later was dismissed from the Portuguese Army because of a most unprofessional dislike against bleeding men already wounded. So now you see before you a heart broken physician."

Yolanda resumed her examination of Liana. She told Diesel. She is strong. She will be able to work hard and she is a widow, she no what to do in bed."

"Shut up, Yolanda," threatened Dominique, "before I take my belt to you." He glanced swiftly at the two on horseback. He didn't know what to do when he saw they were amused. "She's not stupid like she pretends to be, she knows what she's saying. She likes to make trouble."

"Mario said it was your decision to bring her here," said Liana, "so we could judge for ourselves how much trouble she has been for you."

She's lived all of her life with the Zulu," said Dominique. "She's an African. You can see that."

"I can see that." He couldn't be sure weather the gleam in Liana's eye's was just amusement. "She's the reason I came out here this morning." She reached into a saddlebag behind her, and took out a package, which concealed a red bonnet, and a plain red and white homemade dress. "Most people in the settlement have never lived with a wild African. That makes them very unpredictable. Some of them even rejected old Rosario Vales because of the story; he once had a Xhosa wife and children. I think we might have a more successful entrance with her, if your Zulu woman looked a little less wild. Get her to put on this dress."

Dominique took the package she was handing to him, swung around and gave it to Yolanda. She examined it cautiously, with critical suspicion.

"Take it," said Dominique.

She took the bundle, examining it as if she thought there might be a snake wrapped up in it, carefully unfolded the dress and looked at it. The dress was plain. Red with edging of white sowed around the neck and sleeves. She started to give it back to Dominique, and then paused to take a second look, first at the dress, then at the bonnet.

"A new dress," murmured Diesel, "a tribute to soothe the savage, female, Zulu beast."

"Put it on," said Dominique. "Do as I ask for once."

"Yes, Dominique," said Yolanda. Yolanda slowly walked into the hut.

Dominique turned, looking up at Liana. Liana was watching him suspiciously. He reached up and helped her to the ground. When she was standing facing him he didn't release her arms, and he could feel that she too, was not letting go of his. Their eyes met. They didn't waver. He could see suddenly that she was trying just as hard as he was to figure everything out.

"We have come a long ways, Dominique," she said.

"Quite a distance?"

"If you are going to kiss him," said Diesel, "let me know …I'll turn my back. I don't want to see it."

She kissed him, it was a good one, as good as that first kiss under the acacia tree. For a moment she embraced him as firmly as he was embracing her. His arms tightened even more encircling her. She pulled her lips away from his.

"Still breathtaking," she whispered.

"Enjoying it," he insisted.

"Be careful," said Diesel. "There's an unhappy woman."

Over Liana's shoulder Dominique saw Yolanda in the doorway of the hut. Yolanda had changed into the dress and was coming out of the hut to let him see her in it. Liana and Dominique were embracing. The bonnet she was carrying by its straps slipped from her fingers, she bent swiftly and picked up the long bladed knife she had been slicing meat with. Dominique released Liana and rushed towards Yolanda.

Drop it," he demanded.

Yolanda stepped to one side so the she could see Lianas pass him. Her eyes narrowed and her teeth were showing, when Dominique reached for the knife she dropped it, and looked up at him and smiled. She glanced down at the homemade dress as if there were nothing else on her mind. It was so long it dragged the ground. It was too big, far to large for her.

"This dress," she said. "I do not like."

"You are going to wear it."

"No," she said, with finality.

Liana walked over to them. Like Yolanda, she was concerned only with the dress.

"Don't be silly," she said. "It fits you quite well."

She picked up the bonnet, slipped it over Yolanda's head, and tied the straps under her chin. Yolanda didn't move. Liana stepped back to take a look.

"You look lovely. Doesn't she, Dominique?"

Yolanda took off the bonnet, ripped it and dropped it on the ground and ran into the hut.

"Come back out here," shouted Dominique.

When she didn't return he went in after her. She was pulling the homemade dress over her head. He picked up her crocodile-skin clothing. She reached and snatched it. He yanked it away from her, took it out with him and tossed it high in the nearest orange tree. Liana and Diesel were watching amused, and getting more fascinated every minute.

In the silence there came from within the hut the sound of tearing cloth. Tnen the ripped homemade dress came flying out the door.

"Something tells me, my friend," said Diesel, "you are going to climb a tree."

Liana was laughing. All the time Dominique was climbing the tree her laughter ring in his ears. After climbing down, he threw the crocodile-skin outfit through the doorway into the hut.

"I'm glad you bought her, Dominique," Liana said drying

her eyes. "I'm just beginning to understand what you've been through."

Before he could reply she began to laugh again. Dominique turned to see what Yolanda was up to now. He was relieved to see she had put on the crocodile-skin clothing again.

At least she hadn't come out naked, but, he had to climb the tree, and she had painted her face. He grabbed her, and dragged her to the stream, and washed her face with muddy water and dragged her back again.

Liana stopped laughing. She was watching thoughtfully.

Dominique released Yolanda, and watched wondering, what she might do next.

"He treats her like a child," Liana said to Diesel.

"True," said Diesel. "She's a child with rather interesting dimensions."

Yolanda suddenly pulled away rushing in the direction of the donkeys shouting war chants, in an earsplitting series of whoops. The peacefully grazing donkeys and horses were startled into frenzy. They broke their ropes, and bolted away. Before Dominique could control Yolanda the whole caravan had stampeded. Liana's quick thinking saved Dominique's magnesium sulfate from being scattered over miles of untamed jungle. Leaping into the saddle, Liana called ordering Diesel to help her while galloping in pursuit. They managed to catch the donkeys and horses and soothe them, and bring them back to camp.

Dominique was tying Yolanda's hands and feet. Liana rode up sitting in the saddle looking down, at the conclusion of the grim and efficient process.

"Well, that's a relief." she said.

"What?"

"To know that's the only way you can handle her."

"How else could anybody?"

"I don't know. Maybe I'm wrong; I think after a month in a cabin in a cave with you, I would be quite submissive."

"I doubt it," said Diesel.

Dominique stood up, walked over and pulled Liana out of the saddle none too gently. He held her firmly gripping her shoulders, forcing her to look at him.

"Have you another rope for me?" she asked.

Yolanda The Enchantress

"Let's have it out here and now," he said. "Nothing happened between me and her in that cave or anywhere else."

"I believe you," she replied. "Not that it would have made a difference to me?"

"What would make that difference to you?"

"Nothing that's happened so far."

"Are you saying it depends on what happens down there in the settlement?"

"No, Dominique. It depends on what happens between you and me."

"If you are working up another kiss," said Diesel, "may I suggest postponing it until a more appropriate time. The restrained young lady and I are not a sympathetic audience."

Dominique released Liana.

"Get down off that horse," he said.

"I'm not fond of being told what to do, especially in that tone," said Diesel. "But under the circum stances, I'll be delighted to oblige."

He leaped to the ground and moved towards Dominique. He was just as ready for this kind of trouble as he was ready to speak his mind. "Some other time, perhaps," said Dominique impatiently. "All I want is your horse," he pointed at Yolanda, "so I can tie her in the saddle. That will keep me from dragging her by her feet all the way to the settlement station."

Diesel smiled. "I surrender," he said, "under protest after watching your rough and ready, distasteful, display of male dominance over a tiny half breed woman."

"Dominique," said Liana, "that won't do at all."

"What now?"

"Taking her down there tied up."

"Then how will we get her there?"

"People will never understand."

"Wait a minute," said Dominique. "Maybe we haven't settled everything, after all. Why are you so afraid of what people down there think? What do they have to do with it?"

"Since my chief function today seems to be that of an observer," said Diesel, "perhaps I can help."

"I would like to know," said Dominique, "what do you have to do with this."

"I'll tell you," said Diesel. "I sincerely wish it were in a manner that could cause you more concern. I'm here instead of one of Liana's brothers, to keep the introduction of your Zulu woman from giving the impression of a purely Gomez venture. There are other families living in the settlement, they aren't Gomez's. You know how people crowded together in a settlement station make everybody's business his or her own. What we're trying to do is to make your arrival with the girl, as normal as possible."

"Leaving the Gomez's free," said Dominique, "to decide among themselves what they're going to do."

"Why not?" asked Liana? "Why did you bring her here?"

Yolanda was watching, and listing with intent interest. She sat up stretching out her bound hands to Dominique. "No more today," she said, "I will do whatever you want me to do."

Dominique quickly untied her.

"How do you know the performance won't start again?" asked Diesel, astonished.

"Mean as she is," said Dominique, "you can trust her. She'll do whatever she says she'll do."

"When we get in sight of the settlement," suggested Liana, "she will ride beside me? Can you get her to do that? "

Dominique looked at Yolanda. "Do you want me to?" she asked.

"Yes."

"Then I will."

"Beware of strangers with gifts," murmured Diesel.

"What do you mean?" demanded Dominique.

"Only thinking out loud carelessly. I was thinking about your new friends, from which you have been receiving gifts."

Dominique walked over to the donkeys to string them, and Yolanda tied the food basket on the back of Diesel's horses' saddle. She mounted and wheeled the horse around beside Liana's. The tiny convoy set out with the two women riding slowly ahead. Dominique and Diesel followed leading the donkeys.

When they reach the top of the hill Dominique stopped. Just about everybody in the settlement, were assembled on a strip of flat grassland in front of the open gate. There was a faint clinging of a banjo and the squeal of a fiddle. The carcass of an impala was hanging over a barbecue pit. A camel race was in progress. Other men were engaged in a turkey shoot, and others were watching a wrestling match.

"Last night Maria Renaldo, the miller's wife, had a boy," explained Diesel. "Everybody decided not to work today to celebrate the first child born in this settlement."

"You bought them here, to watch the Zulu woman come in," said Dominique.

"No. It gives them something else to think about."

Dominique took a careful look at the way the station was laid out. There was much to approve of. Hundreds of acres of land along Lake Tanganyika, and along the lower stream had been cleared and cultivated. Maize had been planted, and crops were doing well. A pasture for horses, camels and other live-stock had been fenced in. The stockade was high and strong with stables, and blockhouses at each corner. The houses inside were bigger and more substantial than in other new settlement. The trading post was built on flat land in the center of the bend be-tween the two falls. There were building, with an overhanging, unrestrained under story at the lower falls with a mill wheel turn-ing beside it. Another mill of equal size was under construction. At the upper falls another structure was being built.

"Carlos Renaldo is building his sand-mill right along-side Silva Hernandez and Mario's lumber yard at the lower falls," explained Diesel. "There's power enough from the one big wheel to run both. That's where Liana is building her home and businesses. She's building them at the upper falls because in time she'll have waterpower too, she'll add a tilt hammer to her forge. As you can see, the mills are within gunshot of the stockade. They'll have guards at night, and they'll serve as outlying fortifi-cation, adding to the strength of the station."

Dominique nodded. The Gomez's had planned well, and they had carried out what they'd planned.

"As you know," Diesel continued, "the Gomez's kept the land on the east side of the stream. They turned the west side over to the company and small farmers they bought in. Most of the farmers they financed, to add to the population for the sake of defense." He glanced at Dominique. "We're on Liana's land, it stretches from beyond her mill-site all around this section of the

185

valley?"

"Where's mine?"

"In that direction, along the west slope, not the next the one beyond Liana's boundary."

"Who has the land in between?"

"I have. You see I drew before Liana drew for you."

"How about trading?"

"You seem to be laboring under some delusion. Don't be deceived. I'm a dreamer and incredibly hopeful, to the end. If the occasion arises, I'll buy you out."

"You want have to buy my land. I'll give it to you as a wedding present." Said Dominique,

"If it goes the other way you expect me to do the same?"

"Whatever you wish."

Diesel smiled. "You're a bold fellow, you give me hope. It's a pleasure to know you, Dominique. Liana's never liked being dominated." He thought about what he said. "At least, she never thought she did, until now."

Chapter 12
Everything is up to Liana

People kept doing whatever they were doing, without paying any attention to the approaching caravan.

"Gate wide open and nobody lookin'," Dominique grumbled. "How do they know whose coming?"

"The Gomez's know," said Diesel. "If you know Legacy you know the station's being guarded. Guards are posted every night at the gate, and around the pasture. Every morning before dawn, Rosario Vales takes five or six men out to search the edges of the jungle; He'll do it as soon as he can get around to it, later today Legacy's going to organize a militia company. Just about every man here has been in the Portuguese army or navy."

Liana and Yolanda rode ahead galloping through the stream, and turned towards the gate. Several women on the nearer fringe of the crowd glanced around. It was only after a second look that they seemed to realize that Liana's companion

Yolanda The Enchantress

was a stranger. Had Yolanda been wearing the red dress, and bonnet, Liana might have slipped her into the stockade without being noticed. Yolanda's crocodile-skin, bare feet, and braids made people suddenly curious. More and more of them were looking around. Then, as if timed to cover the woman's entrance, a bell ring, drawing everybody's attention the other way. Liana and Yolanda rode through the gate without attracting further notice.

One thing was clear. The Gomez's had closed rinks, and adopted a plan. Liana and Diesel's coming to meet him was a part of it, the red dress and bonnet. The bell, even the barbecue was all part of a deliberate their plan. They had told nobody Yolanda was coming, or that she had been rescued from the Zulu's. They didn't want anybody outside that close family circle to know or help. With Yolanda safely in the stockade and in one of their houses, they could deal with this situation any way they chose.

The caravan was crossing the stream; three men were coming out to meet them. The crowd moved towards a table under a huge baobab tree where the bell was ringing. The men coming were Monty, Antonio and Mario. Antonio reached them first. He shook Dominique's hand, and punched Dominique on the shoul der with a friendly slap.

"Dominique, good to see you," he shouted. "Mario told us you had a hard winter. I knew you'd never let a little cold weather slow you down." He glanced proudly toward the stockade, the mill and the maize-fields. "Been a few changes since you were here, eh?" Ever seen a finer location?

Monty was not as loud but his welcome was just as warm. "Big day for us, he said. Bought the station its first child, nd the company's last partner."

Big day for me, too," said Dominique. "Been a couple of times I wasn't too sure I'd get here."

"I'll take the donkeys and horses," said Mario.

He gave Dominique a wink warning him to be careful. Antonio was pulling Dominique towards the table under the baobab tree where the men of the station were standing.

"We're having our first official town meeting," said Antonio. "Legacy wants to talk to you before it gets started."

187

L. A. Johnson Jr.

Legacy came around the end of the table with out-stretched hands. "Glad to see you, Dominique," he said. "I'm glad you got here today. We're organizing a militia, and electing a captain for it, we can use your help."

Dominique glanced towards the gate through which Liana, and Yolanda had disappeared. "First I should see how Yolanda's doing. I mean the girl I took from the Zulu's. Liana must have told you about her. You could never guess the trouble she can get into."

Legacy didn't feel that there was a problem at this moment. "I understand a little from what Liana told me. She told me what Mario told her. The women will look after Yolanda; it's their duty, anyway." He grabbed Dominique's arm firmly and led him around the table to the side facing the assembling crowd. "Take a look at them," he whispered. "Before the day is over you will understand what I mean about needing some help."

Dominique looked, trying to understand the position he should take. These men were going to be his neighbors for some time. They would be closer than neighbors, as people were bound to become when they were crowded together within the walls of a settlement station. Summoned from their various leisure activities by the bell some of the people came running, others walked. There was a lot of nudging, shoving, and playing. Some were drunk and noisy.

Dominique was familiar with the difficulty of handling jungle men, whenever any great numbers of them were gathered together. Each had to be as in dependent as the next. He could sense the restlessness in the crowd while gathering, many were not happy about being summoned by a bell. Others were talking, some were thinking, some were arguing as usual, as they did in every jungle town meeting.

Very few of them were real, jungle-men, they were farmers. Most of them had come from a part of Portugal, where not since their grandfathers were young, people had to hunt for their keep, or fight to stay alive. They were all fast-talking, gritty, ornery men that went with jungle living. No matter how hard a man tried to control his temper where he came from, the minute he entered the jungle he carried a chip on his shoulder. The bell stopped.

Yolanda The Enchantress

"Big circle," shouted someone. "Down in front," yelled others. "We can't see Legacy," shouted a voice.

The last complaint bought several laughs. The men in front sat on the ground, behind them the nudging, shoving and shouting continued. Legacy seemed to ignore the foolishness.

"Before we start," said Legacy, putting his hand on Dominique's shoulder, "You have heard enough about him, he is joining us, and this is Dominique de Salvo. He came to Congo Basin before the first settlement was founded. He knows the country better than most white or black men do, he was with Novas at Zambia, Tanzania, and Mozambique.

He's a man that can challenge any African on his own ground. As an example of that, here's what just happened to him. Zulu warriors stole his horse from him. He followed the thieves into Zulu country, when he saw they were keeping his horse where he couldn't get near it; he took something away from them they valued much more. He stole a young woman they had inslaved for years, and bought her back with him. She's in the stockade now."

Dominique stirred restlessly. The Gomez plan was working. A number of women on the outskirts of the meeting turned, and rushed towards the gate, immediately more interested in getting a look at the surprising new arrival than in the future procedures of the meeting. Leaving Yolanda on her own among strangers was as safe as leaving a hungry lion in a cage with an unarmed man.

"A woman," exclaimed a young man standing in the back row. "Ask if he knows where I could get one."

Legacy joined in with the laughter, while guiding Dominique to his seat on the bench at the table. Legacy took his seat at the head of the table.

"Now, to our meeting," he said, his manner was as easy as if this were no more than a conversation, among friends. "Since we've been here, it's been our way, whenever we've had to make up our minds about something; we talk about it, and give everybody their say. Somebody has to start the talking, and I know you're used to me doing that."

"We surely are," said someone.

"We like it," said another, with good nature.

189

"What we're here to talk about today," Legacy went on, "is the right way to defend ourselves. We have been working hard building and planning. Everybody's been doing his share even more than expected, but having enough to eat and a roof over our heads won't do us much good if we let Africans come and take everything away from us." The crowd was sobering and getting serious. "How to protect this settlement can't be left to each man to do whatever he wants to do. We all agreed, we must organize a military company to which every man, and boy over the age of thirteen will belong."

There was a general murmur of agreement. "The next thing I feel we must keep in mind is this," Legacy continued. "When we have differences of opinion on any matter, we will discuss these problems until we reach an agreement. We will talk as long as we need to in order to reach one. That will not work when it comes to defending ourselves. When we are attacked it will be too late to stop to talk. Therefore, it seems to me that the first step in organizing ourselves into a military force is to elect a man to command it. Does anyone have a different point of view?"

Dominique could see the motion of one-man rule was none too welcome, but each man present was waiting for the other to raise the first open objection.

Dominique could see the motion of one-man rule was none too welcome, but each man present was waiting for the other to raise the first objection.

"I'm sure we all agree on that," Legacy continued after a brief pause. "That makes the selection of a military commander the most important decision we can make. We shouldn't rush to elect that man without a debate. Whatever talking we have to do, let's do it now and get it over with. I suggest we recess for three hours, than come back with our minds made up on the man whom we can all give our full support."

Everybody was surprised by this postponement. They had expected Legacy to push his agenda right through. The meeting broke up into groups, which drifted away, men arguing thoughtfully and vigorously among themselves. Monty, Antonio and Diesel walked away, leaving Dominique alone with Legacy.

"We could have gotten our man elected by bringing it to

head without a problem," said Legacy. "We have the votes, but we don't want it to look like we are forcing him on them...because we want everybody to cooperate."

"Who is your man?"

"Diesel, Diesel Avila. At first we thought of backing Monty or Antonio. Both have been military officers with plenty of political and command experience, but there are some that feel the Gomez's are taking too much on them-selves. Some are angry because we own two thirds of the land, and have leans on the rest, that only makes it worst. Diesel has an advantage. He's a doctor, not a soldier. Most of the men here have served in the army, or navy, they had, had their fill of military officers. On the other hand, the position is too important to let it be filled by just anybody that can get the votes. That is why we bought Diesel out here. He's smart, and we can trust him?"

"Who dislikes him?"

"Nobody, everybody likes him, but there are a few against giving any one man so much power. There's been some talk of a town council, instead. Brandon De Jesus, the merchant, that tall fellow over there with the keen nose is going around talking, and whispering his reluctance. He wants a town council or a board of directors. Look over there, that tall thick heavyset man in the black shirt coming through the gate into the stockade. His name is Ammonia Nervy, the priest. He wants the church to be in charge of everything. Because we haven't given him all the power he wants, he's against anything we are for."

The fight for power that Legacy was concerned about happened in every new settlement. If a family ever, was able to handle this sort of thing the Gomez' were. Dominique would be glad to see Diesel get the title of captain. A man could hardly take on more grief than that of a military command of a new set-tlement.

"I'll vote for Diesel," Dominique said, getting up. Legacy laughed. "We're expecting a lot more from you than, your vote. People will listen to you. You're a stranger; you haven't been around to take sides. They know you fought with Novas, and you know African's, and what it takes to defend this settlement. They will listen to you. The problem isn't Diesel. It's convincing them to give him the power, and authority he needs. You can make them understand, that if there is ever a place that needs one-man in control it is a new settlement."

Dominique nodded; his eyes were still on the gate, the Gomez women and nearly half the women of the settlement were swarming around Yolanda.

Legacy's eyes twinkled. "If you're worried about Diesel, don't give it another thought. Liana's known Diesel a long time. His getting command of a army of farmers wont impresses her."

"I'm not worried about Diesel," said Dominique.

The chance to ask Legacy any questions vanished, when a woman rushed through the gate. She pushed through the crowd, heading straight for Dominique. She was stunning, rosy-cheeked, redheaded, nearly as tall as Antonio glowing with the same enthusiasm, and in fact, looking a good deal like him. She grabbed Dominique by the arm.

"I'm Carla, Antonio's wife," she announced. She stepped pass Dominique and spoke to Legacy. "I promised Brittany I'd bring him. She wants to see him."

Legacy was about to object but his face slackened, the moment Brittany's name was spoken.

"How is she today?" he asked. "She was asleep when I left this morning."

"She's fine," said Carla. "She ate all her break fast."

Brittany eating her breakfast seemed to overshadow this special day with Legacy. "Don't keep him long. He has work to do. Tell Brittany I'll come home, when I can."

Carla pulled Dominique towards the gate. "Brittany's Legacy's wife," she explained. "They've been married over thirty years, for the first time she's pregnant. She's resting in bed to keep from losing it. She will spend every moment in bed if she thought that would help." Four boys, ages from six to ten were playing, and glancing over their shoulders at Dominique. "My four oldest. You rode with Paul O Dais Novas that makes you a hero to them, to all of us, for that matter. Even Legacy's im-pressed." She gave Dominique a quick, intent look and nodded critically. "Now that I have met you I'm beginning to understand what started Liana worrying. In her own way she is just as stub-born as the Gomez men."

"I've noticed that," said Dominique.

192

Yolanda The Enchantress

"You're a little stubborn yourself," said Carla. "Bringing your wild Zulu woman here." She smiled. "Nothing could have upset Liana more," She smiled again. "What you have done is worst than some of Antonio's tricks I can remember."

Dominique blinked. After having braced himself to listen to the disapproval of the Gomez women, to be greeted by their amusement was like walking into a den of hungry female lions, when your thoughts were somewhere else.

Inside the gate, the first three in the row of huge houses were twice the size of those beyond. "Ours, Legacy's and Monty's," explained Carla. "Liana's living with Monty and Crystal. That is where she took your little heathen." From two to six children were sitting on the steps of a huge, house. We have ten." Dominique looked at her. She couldn't be more than twenty-seven and the blush on her face was that of a teenage girl. She smiled than laughed. "Disgrace and scandals. They seem to keep coming, one every year." From within the house there came a fierce wail. "My baby must have heard me, he's hungry. Come in a minute."

The huge kitchen had a pleasant smell of new pine. The fireplace was brick instead of stone, pots and kettles were neatly placed on the shelf above it, and all were brass and copper. The long table running down the center of the kitchen had been built with old seasoned mahogany. It was so large and heavy no animal smaller than an elephant pulling a huge wagon could have towed it over Congo Road. A smiling African woman lifted the baby from the cradle. "Sit down." Carla said to Dominique. She sat on a low stool in the corner so that when she opened her dress, and took the baby only her head and shoulders were visible over the cradle. The child's yells ceased with a sudden gurgle. Dominique was grinning, and nodding while Carla was talking. He examined the mahogany table and the bricks that were used to build the fireplace.

"Antonio took the table apart and put it together again after we got here," Carla explained. "It took an elephant pulling a huge wagon, to haul it over the mountain. Antonio likes to see us sitting around it. He found plenty of clay to make bricks on that slope beyond the upper spring. He fired enough to see how they would do. They came out fine. Once the Africans clear out enough so that we can build brick homes, all of us can have brick houses if we want."

Dominique reflected, no white family had ever come to Congo with the ability to plant instant, and stronger roots equal to that of these Gomez's.

"Faster, Brady," said Carla, glancing down. "If we keep Dominique more than another five minutes, Uncle Legacy is going to start ringing that bell, of his." She looked up again to smile at Dominique. "You are Dominique to everybody else in this family, Mr. de Salvo, so I'll call you Dominique, too."

"Good," said Dominique. He didn't mind being a friend to such a fine woman. "I've never met people I really wanted to get along with."

"I wouldn't say that welcoming outsiders into the Gomez family homes is a Gomez family tradition," said Carla. "They liked you when they met you. That's the reason Brittany and I had to meet you. Hurry up, Brady. There isn't time to be polite, Dominique, or even civil, so I'll come right out with it. Brittany and I know what the Gomez men have decided about you. We also know what they think about you bringing that half-breed Zulu here. We think this problem is far too complicated for them to handle. We have made up our minds, Brittany, Crystal and I, we'll handle this problem ourselves."

To Dominique it was like catching a glimpse of a fleeing impala. He knew as he slowly lifted his rifle that his next step would bring him into view. At last he could know what he was facing, all he had to do was ask. He did.

"What do they want?"

"They're waiting to who Liana wants. They want her to have anything she wants."

"You Gomez women have different ideas?"

"Not this time. If what Liana wants, is a man, we want her to have him. The Gomez brothers' wives would like to see Liana with a man of her own."

There it was. After all his worrying it was as simple as that. The men were willing to wait and see what position their wives would take. What it came down to was that everything depended on Liana.

"What makes you think I'm a better choice than Diesel

Yolanda The Enchantress

Avila?"

"We're not sure. Liana never talks much, as for all we know she hasn't made up her mind. That's another reason Brittany and I wanted to meet you. We wanted to see if we agreed with Crystal; but even before meeting you the odds were all in your favor. Diesel's been after her for years.

First he lost her to Edwin Copula. Since she's been a widow he's been trying hard again, and still hasn't been successful. Listening to the rumors at Thousand Oaks, you had the advantage from the very first moment you met her, that night at Plato's dance. "Carla seemed to be reading his mind. "Her brothers like you, but they will turn on you in a second if they thought you meant to harm her."

"Well," said Dominique, "I don't, perhaps the sooner I tell her the better. You said she's at Monty's house, next door?"

"First you've got to meet Brittany," said Carla, placing the baby in the cradle.

This kitchen was much smaller. The fireplace was built with colorful stones, and the table was oak. Brittany lay on the couch by the window. She was stunning in spite of streaks of gray in her jet-black hair. There were red lines revealing suffering on her pale face. She was beautiful. She looked stern, bitter, even cold, until you noticed that glow of happiness in her eyes. She turned her head on the pillow with slow, careful movements, to preserve her energy.

"It is a pleasure meeting you Mr. de Salvo. It was nice of you to come to see me." She exchanged a glance with Carla.

"I'm not surprised," Brittany continued. "Legacy likes you; he's seldom mistaken in his judgments. Please sit down, both of you, where I can see you."

"Have you seen your Zulu woman yet?" asked Brittany.

"Liana bought her in for a minute," said Brittany, smiling. "She's such a shy little thing, but she took a most sympathetic interest when she learned why I was in bed. She advised me to eat plenty of gorilla meat, so that I would have a strong baby, as gorillas do."

"All her life she's lived among African's," said Dominique quickly. "In most ways she's the same as one."

"Well, she's not among African's any more," said Carla.

L. A. Johnson Jr.

"Legacy wants Dominique back right away. So I'll tell you what I think." Said Carla. "I don't think her being here has to be a problem unless we make it one. She's here. We can't help that, but we can make the best of it. There's only one-way to do that, and that's to make her feel like she belongs, just as if she were any other young woman who's just escaped from heathens. So how about this?"

"With all my children I could use some extra help. I'll hire her to work in my house. That will give her a home with us. That is certainly better than letting her go on staying with Liana at Crystal's. It won't take long to teach her, good manners, everything else will come. She can learn and she's pretty. With as many strapping young bachelors as we have it won't take long before she'll be taken by a man, and settled in a place of her own. You bought her here, Dominique that makes you responsible for her. Is there anything wrong with our plan?"

"She has relatives in Kingdom of Buganda," said Dominique.

"Relatives she's never seen," replied Brittany. "That has most likely forgotten her. Why should she go to them?"

"You don't know her," said Dominique. "She's a problem. Didn't Mario tell you about her torching Median's house? She'll be no help to you. She'll give you nothing but trouble."

Again the women exchanged glances. "Why did you bring her here, Mr. de Salvo?" asked Brittany.

"Taking her from her Zulu relatives was an accident, but once it happened there was no reason to hide what had happened."

"It wasn't because you felt sorry for her?"

"Sorry for her? She's a wild cheetah. Nobody could be around her very long, and feel sorry for her."

"Would you object to her living with one of our men?" persisted Brittany quickly.

"Why should I object?" said Dominique, getting up. His temper was beginning to flair. So much interest, and support from Liana sister-in-laws was an advantage he hadn't counted on, but he wasn't a slave tipping around the house politely with his fate to be determined by the entire Gomez family. "I don't care who she lives with. I have my own wedding to think about.

Yolanda The Enchantress

You said everything is up to Liana. That's how it will be." He turned in the doorway smiling at them unapologetic-ally.

"You have been frank, and mighty honest with me, both of you. Probably a whole lot better than I deserve. Could be I'll come running back asking for your help."

Outside, he walked towards Crystal's house next door and came to a disgusted halt. Half dozen women were standing on her porch, and steps. They chatting laughing, gossiping, and giggling, like schoolgirls. Unexpectedly Crystal caught sight of him from the window and came running to him.

"Oh, Dominique," she whispered, "I'm glad you have come." Her voice dropped to a whisper. "I don't believe your Zulu woman is going to make a difference. Liana is trying to be patient, even though inside she's upset, but it has never been her way to let any thing keep her from getting what she wants, I know, I just know, Dominique, I hope nothing goes wrong."

She squeezed his arm and rush back into the house. Dominique didn't like the idea that something could still go wrong. Perhaps, now was the time to go in and talk to Liana, no matter how many women were in the house. Women were on the porch and steps staring and whispering at him. The door was ajar, and Dominique was so anxious to get away from the staring whispering women, he didn't knock. He pushed the door open and walked in.

Standing in a huge living room. Yolanda was setting on a chair by the fireplace. Standing over her was the Catholic priest. He was over sixty, short, broad across the chest, very large, with deep yellow eyes behind wire-framed spectacles. His face didn't match his priestly black coat, white collar, and deep overbearing voice. "Confession, repentance and prayer," he was preaching to Yolanda as if from a pulpit, "these are the steps by which the most confirmed sinner may return to grace."

Crystal entered quickly, from another room. "Reverend Father Ammonia Nervy, Mr. de Salvo," she said. The priest gave Dominique a quick searching; very hostel look, while stepping forward to shake his hand. "A very great privilege has been granted you Mr. de Salvo." His voice echoed throughout the living room, his grip was firm, and strong. "Rescuing this poor creature from the clutches of those heathens you not only saved her life, you have opened the way to saving her immortal soul as well."

"Who is this man?" Yolanda asked Dominique.

"He is a white voodoo priest," said Dominique. "The head of the local Catholic church."

"Do I have to listen to him?"

"Yes. He wants to help you think like white people think; you have to learn how we think as fast as you can."

Yolanda folded her hands sternly in her lap. "I will lis ten. I want to learn how your people think, but I do not know what *I* will think."

Dominique stared at her impatiently. It was obvious to him that she had been trying to cooperate because she had given him her word up on the hill. Still, it wasn't safe to leave her alone here with this priest. If the preacher kept at her, as he had every intention of doing, she would attack him with any thing that she could reach. He had to find Liana. That had to come first.

"Well," he said to Yolanda, "whatever you do, stop and think before doing it." He turned to Crystal. "Where's Liana?"

"She went somewhere with Monty. They wanted to talk."

Talking with Diesel. She was talking with anybody but him. Dominique started for the door.

"Dominique," called Yolanda.

"Yes?"

"You come back?"

He swung around saying. "You have only two things to worry about," he snapped. "One is to stay out of trouble, and the other is to do, whatever you're told."

Again she was pleased by his anger.

"Yes, Dominique," she said submissively.

He was still angry when he reached the gateway. In the meadow beyond, the turkey shooting, the camel and horse racing had restarted again. Most of the men had gathered around the rum barrel, and the barbecued pit. Others were just sitting on the ground arguing. Children dashed in and out among groups of elders. Several of the more impatient women had persuaded some of the younger men to help them get the dancing started. More than three hundred people, counting their slaves, were

walking around, slaves were serving their masters. Then he saw
Liana. She was far away, sitting on a log, leaning against the
fence in-closing the horse pen, near the corner of the camel pasture. Sprawled on the ground around her were Legacy, Antonio
and Monty. All were talking earnestly.

He started for them. These Gomez's seemed to think that
everybody should go on being polite, and friendly while their
women sit around plotting ways to help them out if they make a
mistake, giving their men time to sit, and study whomever, and
talk about which they think is good enough for Liana. She was
talking to her brothers about what she thought of him. He wasn't
going to hide or stand in a corner and wait to be invited when he
could walk over to see what they were planning for him, but after a few strides he stopped. He decided it would be wiser to
wait until he could talk to her alone. He had waited this long he
could wait a little longer.

Men standing near Dominique, were watching him, others glanced at him. The bolder men walked over, and introduce
themselves, shook his hands. Others followed and then more. He
remembered that he was supposed to tell them to vote for Diesel
Avila. The Gomez had given him a job to do for them, while
they were making up their minds, about him. Whether he liked it
or not he couldn't avoid giving his opinion. They asked him what
he thought. They valued his judgment. There were many ways
African's would attack a settlement, and since this was going to
be his home he told them what he really thought, weather or not
it helped the Gomez family. The advice he gave was repeated
again and again as new groups came up.

The same story he told each time was: "You need a captain. Someone has to be in charge. Some-body has to keep track
of whose turn it is to stands guard, and to watch the stock, and
send men out to look for African signs. It's a nasty job and any
man's a fool to want it, but it is a one-man job, one man can do it
better than a town council full of rich men. You don't have to
worry too much about who you elect. When African warriors
come, you'll turn to old Rosario Vales, anyway. He'll be able to
tell you how many of them there are and whether there are so
few that you can run out and chase them of, or, so many you
should bring all the settlers into the palisade. He'll know what to

do and how to do it. Mario's another man that knows."

Always as he turned away, some men followed him whispering. "He's the man for the job." And always someone else had an answer. "He's too close to the Gomez's it'll be just like putting one of them in charge." No one ever asked him directly if he wanted the job. He never turned around to confront the whispers this only stirred up talk that might have otherwise died out. He certainly didn't want it and wouldn't take it. He never wanted to be an officer with Novas, because the responsibility of command was a never-ending annoyance, and when the shooting started it was worst than an annoyance. He didn't want that kind of responsibility, again. On the other hand he couldn't help taking notice of these men. Most of them were respectable-good men. In most new settlements, they generally were full of a great number of troublemakers with a large population of no-good men. He should have known that in selecting settlers to bring out with them the Gomez's wouldn't have included any outright imbeciles. Most of them were willing to listen to advice from anybody they thought knew better than they did.

They wanted to do what was best, they were trying to figure out what they didn't know, and what it might be like, on days when spears and arrows flew threw the air and plunged into the stockade walls. They wanted to know what to do when bodies of their friends lay by the edge of the maize-fields full of spears or arrows. They wanted to know what to do when Africans warriors howled, hiding in the jungle. They wanted to know what to do, when their women and children were on the roofs with buckets of water putting out fires. Even the mighty Gomez family, who had thought of almost every-thing, likely, hadn't thought about that day.

The men questioning Dominique started arguing with a drunk that had lost part of his ear. His ear had been chewed off in a life and death fight with two cannibals, in the jungle. When Dominique looked towards the pasture again, Liana and her brothers were not in sight. On the other hand, the barbecued pig, and fried impala, and roasted crocodile had at last been pronounced done. The slaves preparing the food finally announced that the food was ready and started cutting off huge hunks. Mario joined Dominique on his way to the gate with a plate of hot meat.

"Come over here by the lake and eat with us," Mario said. "You haven't met Cindy."

Cindy was sitting on a log. She didn't look around or attempt to stand up until they were beside her. When she did she seemed to keep rising. She was nearly a foot taller than Mario. She was very thin with brown hair.

At first glance she was the homeliest looking woman you could meet anywhere. Still there was something about her that made you take a second look. She had very large breast, and larger butt than most skinny women had. Her lips were full and her eyes were green. She was in love. When she looked at Mario you could tell what she was thinking.

How she appeared to other people, Mario didn't care. He was as pleased with her a king with his queen.

"This," he said, "is Cindy." His face saddened when he noticed the way Cindy was looking at Dominique.

"So you're Dominique de Salvo," she said.

Dominique was confused. If there had been anyone in the settlement, other than Mario, upon whose support he had relied, it had been Mario's wife. He wondered uneasily if she knew something he didn't know yet. There were all those women swarming around Yolanda, and the priest, too. On the other hand, Cindy might only be trying to make Mario angry. A new bride didn't always like her husbands' friends.

"Mario's my oldest, and best friend," he said. I'm not willing for Mario's sake to let this moment pass without saying something."

"Say what?"

"I'm not a monster. Wasn't that what you were thinking?"

Mario tried to repair the situation. He gave Cindy a gentle nudge. "Think about what you're saying. You better make friends with him; nobody can tell you more about me."

She gave Mario's arm a playful slap, and as she looked at him there was a glow in her green eyes indicating that ordinarily such little exchanges often erupted quickly, and Mario always put out the fire immediately. However when she looked at Dominique her glance was still as cold as before.

"Mario tells me you're his best friend," she said.

"He's my best," said Dominique. "We have been friends a long time."

"What I don't understand," she said, "If you're such a good friend of his, why is it when he was getting along so well you had to bring that woman here to make trouble for all of us?"

Mario grabbed her arm and shook it sternly. "Here comes Monty. Sweetheart, Dominique's staying at the lumberyard with us. You can have it out with him tonight. Save it for then."

"Always we have to worry about what the Gomez's might think. I suppose now you'll want me to start worrying about what Dominique might be thinking. You can do what-ever you wish, Mario Goalie, but...."

Mario shook her so fiercely that she stopped. She jerked away from him, but she didn't say anything else.

Monty joined them. "Hope you have eaten, Dominique." He smiled at Mario and Cindy. "Sorry to take him away from you." He took Dominique's arm guiding him towards the gate. "We've received a mysterious summons from the church."

"What's wrong?" It was a mistake not to get back to Yolanda sooner.

"All I know is," said Monty, "the spiritual shepherd of our flock sits glowing, and bewildered in Brittany's living room. He requested the presence of the entire Gomez family. He asked for you, too."

Crystal met them at the door, and paused to whisper to Dominique. "She won't wear any of my clothes, though I'm nearly her size, in every other way she's been cooperating. Nearly every woman in the settlement came to see her, they were all so curious; she was polite to all of them. I took her over to see Maria Renaldo's baby. She was very interested. The priest came twice to talk to her. She listened to him talk. She's asleep now, she's worn out."

Bewildered and glowing, Reverend Father Nervy sat at the head of the table. All the Gomez's were seated; Antonio and Carla side by side at the table, Legacy was sitting on the floor beside Brittany's couch, but Dominique saw only Liana. Sitting on a stool, back in a corner, leaning forward, her finger laced above her knees; her dress pulled tight over her the roundness of

Yolanda The Enchantress

her thighs and hips, her body drawn into a series of gracefully submissive curves. She was in deep thought but calm. She smiled faintly when their eyes met and gave a slight nod of her head as if warning him to keep calm. He followed Monty and Crystal to assigned places at the table.

"Make this as brief as possible," said   Legacy. "Brittany shouldn't be stressed more than necessary."

Father Nervy stood, clasped his hands behind him and paced up and down as if to gather his thoughts. "This is a matter of utmost urgency," he pronounced. "Otherwise I would not have insisted that every one of you come here."

"Well, stop walking in circles and say what's on your mind," said Antonio.

"Ignoring Antonio, Nervy said, Congo Basin is a godless land. I am the only priest in the Congo. Throughout this unholy wilderness, in this settlement I enforce the rules for the church. It is my duty to make certain that the church demands are not challenged, that this holy candle in the jungle is not extinguished, or infected by voodoo worshiping witchdoctors."

"If you're bringing up the church question again," said Legacy, "we can only say what we've said so often before. As soon as the other two mills are finished, we'll build your church."

"A place of worship is indeed the most essential building of a Christian community," said Father Nervy, but that is not the protest I'm here to make. We can hold services in God's open air, or in a stable, or anywhere that people gather together. What I am protesting is the sudden appearance of a heathen in our very midst."

"He must be talking about Yolanda." said Carla.

"I am, indeed. My heart breaks for her. I pray constantly that light may come to her, but the truth is that in giving her refuge we are sheltering a sorceress, she's a voodoo priest, and a mistress of witchcraft. The Enchantress. The witch of witches."

The Gomez women, gasped. The Gomez men were smiling in equal disbelief, but the nature of the charge wasn't a surprise to them. Dominique knew what was happening. They had sent for him to defend Yolanda's, for them it was a double advantage. If he quieted Father Nervy, he would save them the

L. A. Johnson Jr.

trouble of doing it. Meanwhile, they realized what slippery ground this put him on; they were watching how he handled himself. They had him in a tighter spot than when they first started looking him over the morning he reached Monty's house, or during the land survey when they took so long to make up their minds. He couldn't just jump up and give the priest the clout he was tempted to give him. His real opponent here was the Gomez family?

"A witch, her grandmother," he replied. Don't know what she's told you or anybody else has told you; she's not a witch. Let me help you get everything straight, her ways may be strange, she may be a little ignorant because she's lived with Africans all of her life, she's no more a witch than you are."

Father Nervy shook his head sadly. "None is as blind as those who refuse to see. The truth is, Satins always trying to spread his evil works through strange things, and she is such a thing."

"Nonsense," said Legacy. "What evidence do you have?"

"I have indisputable evidence, I regret to say, and I myself have questioned the young woman at length. There is, I'm sorry to say, the testimony of Maria Renaldo is damning and unmistakable. When the young woman was permitted to see the new infant she noticed the cradle was lined with gazelle-skin. She immediately asked if the child was a female child. When she was told that it was a boy she became strangely excited. She said the child must be taken from the cradle at once. She told the mother she was spoiling the boy. She said a girl baby should be laid on gazelle skin so that when she grows up she would be shy, pretty and graceful. A boy baby must always be cradled on leopard or lion-skin to make him flexible, and strong, and capable of making massive and deadly leaps upon his enemies.

She didn't stop there she criticized Mrs. Renaldo for remaining in her bed in the midst of her family. She said this had infected all of them. She said that childbirth was unclean, and Mrs. Renaldo should have withdrawn to a hut in the jungle, and remain there for weeks, or until she had purified herself using pagan rituals. In failing to do so, she insisted, she had bought misfortune upon her other children, and upon her husband, and all who were near to her. When I saw Mrs. Renaldo, she was in

204

Yolanda The Enchantress

tears, and suffering from an acute disabling spell, which that heathen had cast on her. Make no mistake my brothers and sisters what I have described to you is sorcery, black magic, voodoo, witchcraft, and its being practiced among us by that, Zulu woman. The work of the Devil."

"Nonsense. Foolishness," said Dominique. "Everything you have said. She's an African. Gazelle-skin, leopard and lionskin are ordinary things. That doesn't make her a witch...nor does she practice witchcraft."

Reverent Father Nervy paid no attention to Dominique. His attention remained fixed on Legacy. "Seems to me it's an opportunity for you," suggested Legacy. "It's your sworn duty to convert her."

"I have spoken the truth, struggling towards that end; but she is unyielding, shameless, and hardheaded. Nevertheless, I shall continue until I have saved her troubled soul."

"That settle it," said Antonio. "That's why you have summoned us?"

"I'm coming to that." Father Nervy stepped forward pointing his finger at Dominique. "There is the man I am here to accuse."

"He's not standing," said Monty. "He sits."

"Don't point at me," said Dominique. "I don't like it."

"There set's the man," continued Father Nervy, not at all disturbed by the interruption," who bought this heathen among us, and how we have received him? We have taken him to our bosoms. We have covered him with honors, and this family; I am trying to understand." He looked about the room in sudden triumph, "the leading most respected family, God forgive us. This whole community has forgotten that this family is planning to make him one of them. "

"And there," said Monty, "Now we understand."

"You see, Dominique," said Legacy, "he's attacking us, and placing the blame on you. I think I told you he wants a greater part in running this settlement. Now he thinks he can make us give in to him"

"He stands a poor chance with me." Dominique stared at the Father Nervy until the priest looked at him. "Whatever you have to say, say it."

L. A. Johnson Jr.

"That's what I have come here to do." Father Nervy addressed the Gomez's again. "There is but one stand we can take, if we are honest men, and women with a regard for the sanctity of family life which dwells at the heart of Christianity. We must give this man his choice.

For weeks, he's lived in a cave with this Zulu woman. Now he's bought her here with him. We must insist that he take her as his lawfully wedded wife, so that hereafter we may hold him responsible for her conduct, or we must cast them both from out midst." He glanced at Dominique solemnly. "You shake your heads, and smile. You don't agree with me, before you give me your final answer, reflect, think and talk among yourselves."

"I've already thought about it," said Dominique. "I think you're crazy. Do whatever you're threatening to do. What's next?"

Father Nervy continued to ignore Dominique. "I feared that you would harden your hearts. Once more I have held open the gate to my Lord for you. If you will not enter I must still do my duty. I shall make this subject the first order of business when the meeting reassembles this afternoon."

"They'll shout you down," said Legacy.

"Some may try, but the seed of righteousness will take root. It will grow", his face covered with perspiration and his voice cracking, "it will flourish, it will spread like the tree of life which had sheltered this community from that heathen that was bought among us."

"It's a fact," said Antonio with a chuckle, "he can create a lot of problems for us."

Dominique stood. The Gomez's had been holding back to see how he would deal with this. The time had come to show them. He started around the table. Father Nervy didn't retreat. Instead he gathered himself as if prepared to fight if violence was necessary. "Don't worry preacher," said Dominique softly. "I'm not going to attack you, but you better listen, even if you're not use to listening. You call this a godless country, perhaps it is; but this is not a lawless settlement. One more word out of you in this house, or anywhere near me; I'll kill you."

Father Nervy looked around silently at the others in the room.

Yolanda The Enchantress

"Sounds to me," said Monty cheerfully, "He means what he says."

Father Nervy started for the door, and Dominique stepped aside. By the time he reached the door, he had recovered a tiny shred of his dignity. "I forgive you," he said, raising his hand in benediction, "I am certain you know not what you do. I will pray for you." He went out and Dominique returned to his seat and sat down.

"Would you have shot him?" asked Antonio.

"I may still have to," said Dominique. "He's the kind that won't quit."

Dominique noticed the Gomez's weren't shocked. They were watching him with approval. Liana's eyes brightened. He himself was ashamed of his display of violence, but the Gomez's were willing to allow the killing of a priest as long as the threat was made in their interest.

"I think Dominique is going to be helpful," said Legacy,

The incident seemed to be closed.

"Now that we can talk reasonable again," said Carla, "what does everybody think about Yolanda moving to our house?"

It was a general question but everybody looked at Liana.

"Don't look at me," said Liana. "Let Dominique make the decision, he knows her better than we do. What do you think, Dominique?"

Everybody looked at him now. They had pushed him in a corner again.

"Ask Yolanda what she thinks?" he said.

That's true," said Legacy slowly.

Legacy called Brittany's slave and sent her for Yolanda. Carla and Crystal started talking about Carla's oldest boy refusing to eat dates. Legacy and Brittany were talking in low whispers. Brittany leaned her back against the wall and closed her eyes. Antonio was whistling under his breath. Monty began telling Dominique about a baby gorilla that had ripped Rosario Vales pants off. Yet the waiting was as awkward as if they were sitting in an uncomfortable silence. The door opened and Yolandawalked in.

"My church dress." whispered Crystal to Dominique. "

L. A. Johnson Jr.

Yolanda walked slowly into the room. She was no longer wearing the crocodile-skin outfit, and her braids were arranged across her head, making her look taller. Crystal's aqua green-colored dress fit her to perfection, and she looked good in it, making her seem suddenly as much a lady as any woman present. Legacy stood, as did Antonio and Monty.

"Who told you to put on that dress?" Demanded Dominique.

"Nobody," said Yolanda. "I wear it so everybody can see I do not belong in it."

"You certainly don't," said Dominique. "Go and take it off."

Yolanda was addressing the Gomez's, she pretended not to hare him. I do not belong in this dress. I do not belong here., and I do not like it here; I am Zulu..."

"You are here," said Dominique. "I don't care whether you like it or not."

Yolanda continued talking to the Gomez's. "I do not come here because I want to come. My home is with Zulu. I would have never left my person, that is where I wanted to be; but Dominique took me away. He tied my hands. He tied my feet. He carried me long way on raft. He carried me on his back, when I want only to go home."

"I've wished a many times, I'd let you get away," said Dominique.

She turned to him. "You bring me here. I do not want to stay. I want to go home to Zululand. I am Zulu. That is where I belong."

"The hell you do," said Dominique, getting up.

There was a slight gleam in Yolanda's eyes. Liana's quivering voice broke the silence. "Sounds to me as if Dominique has made up his mind."

Dominique turned from Yolanda to face Liana. He was trapped, and he had trapped himself. "I haven't decided anything," he said. "I haven't had a chance to. Tell me where you think she belongs?"

In these crises, the Gomez's seemed to move according to plan, as if each knew what the other thought. Neither Monty nor Antonio glanced at Legacy. Yet they immediately moved

Yolanda The Enchantress

towards the door.

"We don't have to settle everything right now," said Legacy. Glancing at the window, "It's getting late, its time to get the meeting started again." He linked his arm with one of Dominique's. The men walked out of the door. Monty and Antonio walked ahead. Legacy still had his arm through Dominique's, and Dominique felt like a prisoner.

"Liana's a little sensitive about that girl," said Legacy. He was talking man to man about the unpleasant situation, though on the whole mysteriously pleasing. "You can hardly blame her, but she will be OK, if you give her time. Carla will take the girl off her hands. When Liana's had a chance to think she'll realize there's no reason to make too much of it. My sister has a temper, you must have noticed, still she can be very understanding, too.

I think the best thing you can do is to leave early in the morning, take your merchandise to Sea Pen. I heard yesterday from Sable Buena, the storekeeper there. They're short of mineral salt at Sea Pen. Take it to him, and you'll get whatever price you ask, by the time you get back Liana will be okay." A slightly stocky old man in a red shirt with a nearly white beard, and was waiting at the open gate. "Excuse me, Dominique. Meet Shameless La Paz, my overseer. Well, Shameless, what do you think?"

"Good, Major," said Shameless. "Good." He thrust an upward thumb and glanced at Dominique.

"After he talked to them, all were willing to go along with the one man government."

"Good," said Legacy. He took Dominique's arm again and walked on with him. "Well, that's one thing off our minds, thanks to you."

Everything managed to suit the Gomez's. Everything was going the way they wanted. They were sending him to Sea Pen, too get him out of the way. Making Diesel captain and giving Liana time to make up her mind...who she wants. Dominique pulled away from Legacy, and walked over to Mario who was walking with a group of men moving toward the Africa Tulip tree. He drew Mario aside.

"Tell as many people as you can before the meeting," he instructed Mario, "Tell everybody, I've had an argument with the Gomez brothers over Yolanda. Tell the storekeeper first."

Mario's eyes glowed with confusion. "What are you talking about? Legacy was just walking' with you. I saw him with you."

"Don't argue," said Dominique. "Trust me. Just do it."

Dominique watched Mario catch up to Brandon De Jesus. Mario whispered to him. The storekeeper grabbed the man next to him. Other men entered the circle. The circle broke up, each man becoming the center of another circle. The news spread though the crowd moving slowly toward the African tulip tree like waves thrashing against the shore.

The buzz of excited whispering kept on. Dominique knew what was coming, Dominique stood on the back row, and the bell stopped ringing. He knew men like these better than the Gomez's could ever hope to know them, because he was one of them, but it came sooner than he had expected. The storekeeper stuttering in his haste, and excitement with his sense of importance spoke before any-body could say a word.

"Mr. Chairman, Mr. Chairman. I move that we now form a military company, and elect a captain giving him full authority. As a part of this motion I nominate the best man for the job, Dominique de Salvo." There were yells from the crowd most of approval, and some of surprise from those the news hadn't gotten around to yet. Dominique was watching Legacy. Legacy's expression never changed. His eyes swiftly scanned the crowd until they met Dominique's, and afterward they still remained fixed, and thoughtful. Dominique met his glance with his own calm stare, giving no sign of what he felt. A sense of being free and fully alive flowed over him, as if he had just come out of a burning house to take a long breath of fresh air.

Shameless La Paz turned around from his position up front and faced the crowd. He had been told that his main job was to keep the election from getting out of hand. He was more than a little confused by what had happened, but he dutifully did what he could. He spoke out as soon as the crowd settled down enough to give him a chance. "I think Dominique de Salvo is a good man, but when it comes to electing a leader we should stop to think. We should pause long enough to figure out if he is the right man for the job. I like how he looks and act, but how do we know, for sure, whom we are voting for? To most of us he is a

Yolanda The Enchantress

stranger."

Monty was lazily leaning against the trunk of a tulip tree. He spoke without straightening up. "Very smooth, he gives orders without hurting any body's feelings" The remark bought a nervous laugh. Nobody could be quite sure of weather he was making fun or questioning Dominique's qualifications, or agreeing with Shameless La Paz's argument. A number of men yielded on the spur of the moment loudly, protesting openly when they thought the Gomez's were disapproving.

Mario stood, he was solemn, but there was no doubt about the person he supported. "Dominique ain't a stranger to me All I can say is, we couldn't do better." This bought laughter, and open disapproval of the Gomez's, in which an undercurrent of relief was clearly evident. Mario was known to have been a firm supporter of the Gomez's. His switching so easily made many of them think that they could oppose the Gomez's without getting themselves too involved in the risks of an argument with them.

Antonio stood up, putting an end to all doubt. "I move," he bellowed, "that this nomination be closed."

"All in favor say aye," directed Legacy.

Many of the ayes were little more than gasps of amazement. Several of the slower witted had been completely taken by surprise by the lack of confrontation; but this is what the Gomez's wanted all the time. They were strangely glancing at Mario, and he was looking as suspiciously, and bewildered at Dominique.

"The ayes have it," ruled Legacy.

Dominique knew there was a struggle for power, it was between him, and the Gomez's, this time, and he had won. He became aware of Diesel at his elbow.

"I've told you," said Diesel, smiling, "You're a bold fellow. My hope is that your duties will keep you away from home most of the time, somewhere in the jungle, far away."

"If it does," said Dominique, matching Diesel's wit, "I'll take a doctor with me."

He began to push through the crowd to meet Legacy who had started towards him. Everybody stepped back and then moved closer again to observe the meeting. Legacy's gray eyes were teary until they met Dominique's, then they warmed with

211

approval.

"The birth of the democratic process in the Congo," he said, offering his hand. "Thing's happen often very mysteriously to bring the right man to the right place, at the right time. Captain de Salvo, we are at your service."

They hadn't foreseen losing control of the election and they didn't like it, especially to him, but they couldn't make a fight of it. They were protecting Liana's possible future husband. They were preparing if necessary, to close ranks around him, if the time came to make him one of them. Their devotion and their generosity impressed, and confused Dominique. He felt the need to make some concessions himself.

"I still have to go to Sea Pen in the morning," he said.

Chapter 13
I'll Hang The Door

Dominique spent the remainder of the afternoon drifting among the crowd, talking casually, memorizing each man's face, and name. He was finding out what weapons they owned, and how well they could use them. He wanted to learn what they knew, and how well a man could hunt. As he walked by he observed how men held their liquor, and deciding in each case whether, or, when it was the man's turn to serve his time on guard, or what to do with him, or if he could be trusted. He wanted to know if he was one of the few that could search the jungle with Rosario.

The dance had finally started. Carla and Crystal came out to mingle with the women for a while. Practically every woman in the settlement had come, but Liana had not, and no Gomez approached him with a message from her. Once he saw her in the gateway, talking to Diesel.

"Put Diesel on the first watch at the camel pasture tonight," Dominique said to Mario, who was helping him prepare the guard roster. If he happened to see Liana tonight he didn't want Diesel around. At dark he ordered the dance stopped, insisting that everyone come into the stockade, rounded up couples

Yolanda The Enchantress

lingering in the shadows and ordered the first watch at the horse and camel pasture.

"What's the chance of Africans attacking you on the way to Sea Pen?" asked Diesel cheerfully.

"Not as good as them attacking you here tonight," said Dominique. "Keep your eyes open."

"I always do, but sometime I don't like what I see.," said Diesel. "

Dominique placed the Mendoza brothers on the first watch in the stockade, Chi-co at the gate, and Caspar walking the rifle platform. Having learned from Mario that both were courting Rebecca De Jesus it seemed a good idea to assign them to the same watch, to keep the one on duty from leaving his post to see what the other was up to. Then he took the guard roster to Monty's house for Monty, as his lieutenant, to keep for him while he was away.

Crystal let him in. She and Monty were alone in the kitchen. Crystal noticed Dominique's quick glance around.

"Yolanda moved over to Carla's," she said. "She was quite willing to go. The children over there love her, and Liana was tired. She's gone to bed."

"Been a long day for you, too," said Monty. He reached for a jug. "How about a nightcap?" His smile was not quite as warm as usual but he was friendly enough.

"Thanks," said Dominique. "But I'd better get some rest, myself. I want to get an early start in the morning."

"Sea Pen's quite a distance to travel alone with four pack donkeys moving slowly. Aren't you taking any help?"

"I'll make it. Rosario Vales, and Dyer Capsules, and the Andes boys are going to River Head to hunt rhinos tomorrow. I'll have company till noon. After that there will be stations every twenty miles. Then, I'll be able to rest the donkeys, and travel faster from station to station."

Crystal walked with Dominique to the door. "Nothing has happened yet, she hasn't change her mind about the person she wants," she said, squeezing Dominique's arm, "hurry back."

"Before she changes her mind?"

"Oh, no. I only mean, why complicate things if you don't have to? Anyway, return quickly, trust me it's important."

213

L. A. Johnson Jr.

Dominique glanced at the door beyond in which Liana stood, possibly sleeping, or lying awake thinking and listening to the whisper of their voices.

"Perhaps I should go in there and get her up, and ask her if she's changed her mind."

"My God, no," said Crystal, pushing him out the door.

Starting for the lumberyard, he remembered the problem now before him. He still had Cindy's strange bitterness to face. Silva Hernandez was sitting on the porch outside the closed door of the lumberyard.

"Sit down," he invited, cordially. "They will call us when dinner is ready."

Behind the heavy oak door Dominique could hear Cindy complaining. Her voice was too low for the words to be understood, but the tone was bitter. Dominique sat down beside Silva.

"I leave when they start arguing," said Silva. "Mario handles her better when there's nobody watching."

"Do they fight much?" ask Dominique.

"Not as much as most," said Silva. "But, when they go at it, generally it's a pretty good battle." He turned his head towards the door. The low drone of Cindy's complaint had ceased. "Mario has her under control. Now listen."

Oddly dragging footsteps retreated from the kitchen, and then from somewhere beyond there was a slight squeak. "That's their bed room door. He'll give her what she needs, after they've finished, it won't be long before we eat." Silva leaned forward; spat out his chunk of tobacco and with a finger began scraping the remnants from his teeth. "It never takes Mario long too get her under control. He handles her better than I was able to handle her mom." The two men waited. The silence inside continued. Though Dominique's mind were memories of Mario's earlier shyness with women. After a while Silva turned his head again. The door squeaked once more. Silva stood and Mario opened the door glancing out.

"Why are you guy's out there in the dark? He asked. "Dinner's been ready and waiting', I'm hungry whether you're or not."

They went in and followed Mario to the table. Cindy was bent over the pot that swung on a hoist in the fireplace. There wasn't much of a fire but her face was red. She started serving them. She never looked directly at Dominique or said anything to him; the plate she gave Dominique was heaped with large choice pieces of stewed impala.

"Give him more," ordered Mario.

Cindy gave Dominique a strange look, blushing more than ever. "Dominique knows he can have more," she said, "whenever you say sweetheart."

She gave Dominique another strange look, this time accompanied by a yielding smile. Dominique stared at Mario.

Mario laughed. "What was wrong with Cindy was, she thought you were keeping that crazy Zulu woman in the jungle for me. She thought you bought her here so I could have her whenever I wished. What gave her that idea was my sneaking off three times in a row to see you, and not telling' her nothing about Yolanda before you showed up here with her. Took me a while to make her understand that Yolanda is yours."

Silva kicked Dominique's boot, but there was only a faintest twinkle in his eyes as he watched Mario. "It's a fact," he told Dominique, "nobody can tell Cindy that Mario can't have any woman he wants, she thinks that every woman in this settlement is after him."

"I remember a few that were," said Dominique, gravely nodding his agreement with this point of view. "Every place we went. Only reason some of them aren't still following him around is that he always told them they were wasting their time."

Cindy didn't laugh. She was listening with glowing eyes, believing every word. She sat down at her place with a contented sigh, glancing at Mario. She blushed, while picking up her spoon, and plunged it into the broth, and leaned towards Mario. She spoke with sudden uncontrollable passion. "Now he's mine."

"Only yours," Mario said firmly.

From outside came the sudden, very clear, broken call of a goose. Dominique stood. So did Mario and Silva. All were reaching for their rifles.

"Acting as if he saw nothing out of the ordinary in her being outside of the walls. It's Yolanda," said Dominique, "I'll be back." He glanced back from the door. Silva and Mario were exchanging masculine grins.

"Take your time. Don't hurry," said Mario. "Cindy will re-warm your stew."

His loud laughter faded as he encountered Cindy's stare.

"Who is she signaling for, in the dark?" she demanded. "Answer me Mario Goalie."

Dominique closed the door behind him. His eyes had to adjust to the darkness.

"Yolanda," he whispered angrily. "Where are you? Why are you out here? What's wrong?" He walked around piles of boards and beams stacked in the sawmill; most of it was freshly cut lumber for the construction of the gravel mill. He could hear her, but he couldn't find her. Her laughter caused him to look up. She was above him sitting on a crossbeam. Her shapely figure loomed clear against the moonlit sky. She leaned over and her braids fell forward.

"Come down here," he demanded.

"You' take me back," she said.

"First I want to talk, then I'll take you back." He started to climb up after her.

She sprang to her feet, and ran fearlessly along the beam, swung around the corner upright and ran along the adjoining beam, pursuit was useless. She kept ahead of him, circling continuously around the framework beyond his reach. He climbed down and sat on a stack of boards. She returned to her perch above him, and stopped laughing.

"How did you get out?"

"It was easy. White people sleep very hard."

Dominique stood up. "The very first night, eh?" That idiot at the gate is going to wish he had stayed awake."

"He is not asleep."

"The how did you get pass him?"

"I not go near him. I came over wall in back."

"What happened to the guard there?"

"When he walk, he look only where he walk."

Dominique sat down. "You've come to talk. Then, talk."

"You go to Sea Pen in morning?"

"Yes."

"Take me with you?"

Yolanda The Enchantress

"No."

"Because she would not like it?"

"Because I wouldn't like it.

"When you come back?"

"Possibly five or six days."

"Then we go to Kingdom of Buganda."

Dominique paused before answering. She leaped from her perch and sat beside him. Glancing up at his face she nodded her head thoughtfully. They were talking, but subject was not good, even worst than she had expected.

Yolanda said, "When I first look at her I know."

"What did you know?" asked Dominique.

"For long time she would not let you take me to Kingdom of Buganda."

"Now, wait a minute. I told you, I'm going to marry her. That you can count on."

"You're a fool." She picked up a branch and struck him furiously. He blocked the blows, and took the stick away from her and held her until she had   quieted.

"What makes you think so?"

"Many hours I watch her. Her flesh is smooth, she has the shape men like to see, but she is more than that. In Zulu Land I have seen women who are like her. Such a woman has something that is different, something most women never have. It makes every man want her. Every boy, every warrior, every old man, they come to her. Men come from other villages; all want her."

"You're saying I'm a fool for wanting a woman that other men want?"

"Yes. It is better to have a woman that is only for you, you do not want a wife that is wife to other men."

"Perhaps among your people women stir up strangers and invites them into her hut."

"There is no difference to you if she takes men or if she does not take men. You want her for the same reason other men want her. She will not be for you alone." Yolanda became strangely calm. "I do not like it when you act like a fool. There is one thing you must do."

What is that?"

L. A. Johnson Jr.

"You promised many times, to take me to Kingdom of Buganda."

"I know that."

"Then you must do it"

"I will."

"When?"

"I'm not sure, yet."

"I do not like it here. I will not stay here long."

"You'll stay 'till I'm ready."

"I will go to Zulu."

"No, you won't. I'll catch you and bring you back."

"When will you take me to Kingdom of Buganda?"

"After the rainy season.... Something happened here I didn't count on. They've made me head of the militia. I can't leave now. This is the season there's the best chance for trouble. When the rainy season comes, I'll take you."

"That will be to long."

"Why? You're being well taken care of."

"Before we go you will marry her."

"You might as well accept it, nothings going to stop it.."

She stood up. "Only one thing is sure."

"What's that?"

"Talk is no good." She stared away.

"Where are you going?" She paused as if she had not before considered this. "Back over the wall," she said.

"Wait a minute. You will get yourself shot."

She started running. Forcing her to walk he grabbed her wrist. They approached the station with caution. They crouched in the shadow of the stockade until Jasper Mendoza, who was walking the perimeter of the rifle plat-form above, walked by. Dominique lifted her up by the ankle until she reached the top of the palisade.

He watched only long enough to be certain that she had dropped down on the other side. He ran to the lumberyard and called Mario. Mario stepped out of the door, closing it behind him looking around suspiciously.

"What did you do with her?"

"I helped her over the wall, I haven't any doubt that the next time she'll run away. I need your help."

218

Yolanda The Enchantress

"You mean, right now?" asked Mario.

"Yes, now."

"What will I tell Cindy?"

"The truth or make something up."

"She will never believe it."

"Be a man," said Dominique. Mario reluctantly opened the door announcing. "Dominique wants me to go with him to take a look at the guard post."

"I don't care where you go," Cindy replied.

Dominique pulled the door shut, and pulled Mario off the porch. "No time now to argue with her," he said. Besides, it won't be long before she will be leaning against that door listening and waiting for you."

"And suppose she ain't?" said Mario bravely. "A man's got to let a woman know who's running the show, or she'll run all over him."

"Come on," said Dominique, pulling him away from the door. The two ran around the huge wall to the far side.

"You take the far corner," whispered Dominique. "Keep out of sight, I want to catch her in the act."

"You ain't planning' on us staying here all night?"

"No. Just a little while, if she going to escape it'll be right away. She'll wait until she thinks I've had time to get back to your house."

Mario grumbled while rushing off towards the other side. Dominique sat on the ground. Above him the sharpened tops of the palisade logs loomed clear against the night sky. From time to time he could see the head, and shoulders of the guards pacing past along the rifle platform, but no matter how hard he stared during the intervals between these fleeing minutes she didn't attempt to escape. After an hour he gave up, and crept in the shadows towards Mario.

"She tricked me," he admitted. "I thought she would come over that wall again tonight. Let's go home."

"Sometime you act like you're smarter than everybody," said Mario. "But lately you haven't been."

He didn't say any more until they were almost to the lumberyard. "What makes you think she wants to run away?"

"She said she would."

L. A. Johnson Jr.

"There's only one way to handle this situation, pat her on her big round behind; and let her go." He glanced at Dominique's face. "Why are you hanging onto her?"

"Not tonight. If she turned up missing tomorrow it will look like she's gone with me to Sea Pen?"

Mario smiled. "That's a fact." His smile became an unsympathetic laugh as the problem became clearer to him. "You tell me to be a man. You don't want her, and you won't let her get away. Let her go."

The kitchen was empty and lighted by a burning wick floating in a tub of grease. Mario locked the outer door before running for his bedroom. He stopped after a step or two away from the door.

"Silva's room is behind the office," he said, gesturing towards the office beyond the kitchen. In his impatience to get away from Dominique he kept gesturing in the direction of the door. "Cindy put a mattress in a storeroom for you. Take a lantern to light the way, don't want you fallen' on the saw, or stumbling' around in the dark." He laughed briefly at his own joke. He was trying hard to be polite and courteous to his friend, but where Dominique slept tonight was the last thing on his mind. A thought, something important came to him. "I'll help you load up when you get ready to leave. If you decide to leave before daylight, call me. Sometime I'm a little slow getting' up in the morning." He smiled as if he were joking; he picked up a lantern, and handed it to Dominique. Something else came to him. "You didn't have time to finish your dinner. If you're hungry, meat and potatoes, in the pot."

"I'm not hungry," said Dominique.

Mario sighed with relief. With the first step Dominique took in leaving the kitchen Mario rushed to his bedroom door.

"Sweetheart, I'm back," he called through the door softly.

His hand gripped the latch. It resisted. He pushed at the door. It didn't yield. He threw his shoulder against it. The door was barred. His smirk was replaced by an expression of rage.

"Sweetheart," he whispered, pounding on the door.

"Don't put up with that," advised Dominique. "Get an ax." When Dominique entered the kitchen just before dawn there was a fire burning in the fireplace. Cindy was bending over a

Yolanda The Enchantress

skillet frying bacon, humming happily, and Mario was eating a huge breakfast.

"Eat a good breakfast, and drink a cup of coffee," advised Mario. "You'll need something' that will stay with you." Peace had again descended upon the Goalie household. The two men were halfway to the pasture before either said another word.

"That Cindy," Mario said. They don't come better than her. Sometime she acts like she's real mad, but she's not mad at all."

They glanced up at curls of smoke from chimneys in the stockade that were rising in the clear tropical air, above the green meadows. Even greener fields of maize in the valley bottom glistened with dew. A few patches of mist bordered the edge of the jungle. Old Rosario Vales, and his fellow rhino hunters had completed their early morning search of the valley; they were riding over the hills to the west on their way towards River Head Settlement. Young Nippy Gavels, who had been on guard the second shift at the horse and camel pasture, glanced at them.

"Looks like they didn't find sign of Africans," Nippy said, almost regretfully, to Dominique and Mario as they approached. "Ain't seen none since we've been here."

"They'll be coming soon enough," said Dominique, "One thing you can do while I'm away, Mario. Make sure Monty doesn't stand for any slacking off. You know how Africans like to test a new settlement station. Their holding off this long is a bad sign, not good at all." They caught the donkeys, and started back with them to pick up the magnesium sulfate at the mill. The stockade gate was open, and Carla came running out. She had a green cloth tied around her head; her red hair was flowing down her back, revealing the first rays of the rising sun. Her face was flushed and her eyes bright.

"Yolanda's gone," She watched Dominique curiously to see how he took the news.

"When did she leave?"

"I don't know. Nobody saw her leave; it must have been just before dawn. I was up with the baby before the sun rose. She was still in bed then; I thought she was sound asleep. She's not in the stockade, my children have searched everywhere."

"Take the animals," Dominique ordered Mario.

221

L. A. Johnson Jr.

Mario stared at him. "What are you doing?"

"I'll find her and bring her back."

"Want me to help you?" Mario's tone of voice indicated he thought that Dominique's present frame of mine had left him without enough wits to pick up the tracks of a heard of elephants.

"Load the donkeys. I know where she is." Carla was also staring at him. He dashed around the lumberyard, jumped into the stream and ran along the bank. Bushes and trees on the bank from the view of anyone screened him higher up the hill to the southwest. He crossed the upper falls; with hardly more than a glance at Liana's huge black slaves building her mill, he kept running up the stream. When he reached the upper section of the jungle he circled wider to the west, and came out of the edge of the jungle again. He looked down the slope at the settlement station, and at the road he would take when setting out for Sea Pen. It was a section of hilly land from which both directions of the road could be watched. He was certain that Yolanda would be in this area.

If she were going home to Zululand, she would have left last night. He let out a gasp of satisfaction when he saw her. The delay and annoyance was worth the delay to have her at such a great disadvantage. She was hiding in tall grass watching the trail heading west. She had chosen a spot from which she could slip into the jungle, the moment she saw him coming up the trail to look for her. On the other hand, had he started out before hearing she had gone, she could have run ahead, and waited for him somewhere, or follow his caravan as long as she pleased before showing herself?

He sneaked up on her so noiselessly that he was standing over her before she realized he was there. She was chewing a kola nut and smiling. She was certain she had the advantage, and she was enjoying it. When she saw him she spat out the kola nut disgustedly and sat up.

"You catch me," she said.

"Come," said Dominique.

She rose without an argument, and followed him. They climbed down the hill. He could hear the pounding of her sandals behind him. She had never before been so submissive. His

222

out-maneuvering her had taken the fight out of her. Perhaps it had been a lesson that would last a little while. It hadn't cost him a great lost of time, either, and it had been worth something to prove to people at the settlement station that he didn't have to take any nonsense from her. Around the settlement below, the day's activities were getting under way. Several men with their slaves carrying farming tools over their shoulders were heading towards the maize field. Another group of slaves were digging, ditches; others were preparing to cut down trees. Legacy, Antonio and Monty were riding off somewhere. Dominique noted that every man who exited the gate had a rifle with him. They had listened to what he said yesterday. He was getting everything under control, even Yolanda; everyone except Liana, and that would come.

Again he was approaching Liana's mill. This time he looked with interest. Osceola and his sons maintained a high quality of workmanship no matter what they took on. The second floor and the interior partitions were being constructed. There were matching tongue, and grove. The outer walls were square, carefully fitted along lines that had been drawn by a ruler. Dominique could see that the lower section of the building was the business, with living quarters for the help. The upper story was larger, with more rooms.

He paused to stare. Evidently Liana was planning to live in the upper story. A gust of excitement rushed over Dominique. If so, standing before him, half constructed but still with the clearly indicated shape of walls, floors, windows and doors, were the very rooms in which Liana and he would someday live together. There were the stairs they would climb, the hard wood floors across which they would walk the walls to shut out all but themselves. Looking at the actual boards and rafters made the meaning of their life together suddenly real, much clearer than it had ever been before.

Always before, his thoughts of her had been in dreams. Painful efforts to remember how beautiful she was, and his desire to have her, but here something more substantial stood than any dream. This was the place they would live someday as man and wife. They would share details of daily companionship as real as the chairs, tables and bed they would be using.

L. A. Johnson Jr.

Here he's a member of the company, a landowner, a commander and in every respect he would be equal to her brothers, for him, this place was only a start. Before long he would own Diesel's land, he would join his land with his, then they would own everything around the head of the valley. Next year he would build a huge mansion on their plantation for them to spend the rest of their lives in. The entire prospect to him was as clear as the door opening Osceola was cutting in the head of the stairs. The dream was a reality that might as well start taking shape right now. He would give her time to think while he went to Sea Pen, but before he went anywhere or did anything he would talk to her and make sure everything was settled, up to and including the date of their wedding. He became aware of Yolanda's, gaze fixed on his face.

He shouted at her and walked on, veering away from the mill as he passed. Then, forgetting Yolanda's curiosity, he stopped again to stare. Osceola and his sons had stopped to eat. They were being served not only by Old Else, but also by two young African women of a stature very near as impressive as that of the men in the family. One had skin the color of golden-brown, the other was a very dark-chocolate, but otherwise they looked like twins, and they were more than just tall. Their bodies' arms and legs were beautifully shaped and their faces were beautiful. Full chest, and broad hips, they were tall and gracefully slender. They smiled and spoke in low voices, carrying themselves with pride and dignity. In their elaborately printed dresses, with matching scarves on their heads and huge gold rings in their ears, they looked like African goddesses.

"That is Hannah and Yuma," said Yolanda.

"Who?"

"Wives of, Ababa, and Oki."

"Ababa, and Oki?" Then Dominique nodded, oh, Osceola sons. "How do you know so much about them?"

"They sleep in the stockade. I see them last night. People talk to them. I hear."

"You hear a lot of things."

"Because I listen." She looked thoughtfully at the young goddesses. "They are new wives. For long time she looked for women for Ababa, and Oki. Other women she find are too small.

224

Yolanda The Enchantress

She looked more and more far away. Finally she fined these two. They come this spring through the jungle from a place call, Mali."

"Mali?

"Mali," said Yolanda, "Where is that?"

"West Africa near Senegal on the Atlantic Ocean."

Sudden anger seized her. "Always she look-no matter how far-for what she want."

"What's wrong with that?" This refined African family worked hard to make the kind of home in which Liana belonged. Dominique approved of the quest for Hannah and Yuma.

"She like only what is best for her," Yolanda mumbled.

"Come on," said Dominique impatiently.

The frown was still on her face. Instead of following him, she sat down. "No," she said.

"Get up."

She shook her head. She was at peace again, as she always felt when she resisted him. He bent down, grabbed her by the arm and lifted her to her feet. She didn't struggle. She let her body go limp. He threw her over his shoulder and turned to start on. Only then did he realize what she had seen behind him before she sat down. Liana was coming up the path from the stockade. It was too late to avoid the meeting or the manner of it. He walked towards her leisurely.

She stepped out of the path to allow him to pass with his burden. She was wearing a starched, pink dress and a pink bonnet that shaded her eyes. As he moved closer he noticed that she was pale, but she was smiling.

"Didn't take you long to catch her," she mumbled.

"She wasn't running away, she was hiding on the hills; she wanted to go to Sea Pen with me."

"I think she till wants to," said Liana. "You must be doing something she likes, or you wouldn't find her so easy to handle."

A hiss of anger came from Yolanda. She reared up and began to struggle to escape his grasp. Not even during their first fight she struggled so violently. She struck him, clawed at his face; and tried to bite him. Her panting breath accompanied by cheetah-like cries. Restricted by his rifle he found it impossible

225

to control her. He thrust his rifle into Liana's hands while grabbing Yolanda by the base of her braids, holding her away from him while he took off his belt. With his belt he bounded her arms to her side. Lifting her with one arm he took his rifle from Liana, and quickly started on. Yolanda kicked furiously.

When out of Liana's sight, Yolanda stopped kicking.

"She see the trouble you take with me," she watches. "She knows you will never take so much with her."

"There will never be a reason to," shouted Dominique, realizing that the outburst was an attempt to destroy his relationship with Liana. "She is a sensible, cultured woman. She's not like you. A miserable, little creature like you." He dropped her down to her feet and jerked his belt off of her. "I am though. Go where you please. Go hometo your Zulu relatives."

She looked up into his eyes with a slow, reluctant but satisfied smile. "You get very mad with me," she said softly.

"Go back to your people," he repeated. "I won't stop you."

"I do not want to go back to Zulu."

"Where do you want to go?"

"I want to go with you to Sea Pen."

Mario and Silva had the donkeys loaded in front of the mill. Cindy was standing in the open doorway. All were watching with interest. Dominique grabbed Yolanda by the wrist, and dragged her over to them.

"That room I slept in last night," he said to Mario. "I won't need it for a few days." He pulled Yolanda another step forward. "Lock her in there, and keep her locked up until I get back."

Cindy spread her arms across the doorway. "No, you don't, Mario Goalie. You have told me this, and told me that, have always believed you up to now. You're not bringing a woman into my house as long as I am alive, you aren't.."

Mario walked over to Cindy; she braced herself in the doorway.

"I have never told you anything but the truth," he said. "Nobody's been fooling' you and nobody's been trying' too, you have been doing' all the fooling' too yourself."

"She's not coming' in here," screamed Cindy.

Yolanda The Enchantress

Mario was pale around his lips, and tiny round beads of perspiration flowed from his forehead. "No good arguing' or yelling'," he said. "Whatever you think I've been doing before, I ain't joking', you better listen. Dominique's my best friend and he's in trouble. I'm going to help him just like he would help me, if it were the other way around. We are going' to keep the girl for him while he's gone, If it isn't here it'll be in that hut by the grove of orange trees near the stream. I'm going to keep her one place or the other. Have it whichever way you want."

Cindy, sobbing wildly, ran across the kitchen and slammed the squeaking door. Mario took out his handkerchief and mopped his face.

"You have been holding back, now she knows who's wearing' the pants," said Silva, shaking his head in approval of is son-in-law. "Wish I'd had that same stern hand with her mom, things would have been much better."

Dominique pushed and pulled Yolanda resentfully. "She's raised enough hell for me," he said to Mario. "No use letting her ruin your family, I'll fine somewhere to leave her."

"No," said Mario. "She's staying here."

He led the way to the storeroom. It sat in a corner in the warehouse, if was used as a blockhouse. A ladder was leading up to a rifle platform and holes near the ceiling, which let in air and streaks of light. Dominique released Yolanda. She walked calmly forward into the room and looked around with surprising approval.

"I like it better here, than in the stockade," she said. "You will return in a few days?"

"Five or six or however long it takes me."

"I will stay here." She seemed satisfied with her situation. She acted like she gained some kind of new advantage over him. He turned in the doorway and looked back at her suspiciously.

"That is right. You're here and you're going to stay here, and don't try to get out."

"Why should I? You know I am here. You will come back."

Dominique went out and slammed the door. Mario went to get a hammer and nails, and attached strips of wood to the

227

door and frame. Walking ahead, Mario crossed the kitchen without glancing at his bedroom door, and sat on the front porch steps. Dominique stepped over him and sat down beside him.

"You and I have always taken care of each other," said Mario gruffly. "Now we're standing' together against a couple of women, and our friendship is even stronger. Get going and get back as soon as you can."

Dominique placed his hand on Mario's shoulder for a second, then untied the lead rope, picked up his rifle and rode off with his pack train. The first thing he saw when he turned the corner of the lumberyard was a pink bonnet, bright in the sun, up by the falls. Liana as sitting on a log, with her face in her hand, staring at the lake. He tied his horse, and donkeys under a fig tree behind the mill. Osceola and his sons glanced down, while hammering, and sawing on the second floor. Dominique started towards the falls, but Liana had come to meet him, and their meeting was in the middle of the construction site. With Else standing around, and Yuma, and Hannah watching, each as strong as a man, handing boards to their husbands above.

"I'm glad you decided to stop," said Liana. "I wanted to show you what we are doing here." Speaking politely She continued, as if what interested her most at the moment was showing off her new house and business. "The main workshop will be where we are standing, the forge over there; and the gunsmith shop there. Osceola's family will live behind the kitchen. Next summer Osceola will put in a water wheel so we can power hammer alongside the forge there. I will live up stairs."

She ran ahead of him up the flight of stairs. The floors above had been laid, and the outer walls were going up rapidly. "This will be the dining room," continued Liana. "There will be a fireplace, one like Antonio's. The bedroom will be there with another room behind it, and a combination sitting room, guest room, and of fice." Her gestures included the whole living area with very enthusiastic approval. "It is not very big, but it will do for a while, because everybody has to live within gunshot of the stockade."

"Osceola," heard Else's high pitched voice from below bellowing. "You, Ababa, and Oki come down and eat breakfast."

Dominique had seen them eating breakfast only a little

while ago. They couldn't stop to eat every few minutes. Without saying a word, Osceola and his sons laid down their tools and rushed down the stairs. For the first time since they said good-by nearly a year ago Dominique and Liana were alone. She was looking at him, thoughtfully.

"Well?" she asked.

He was trying to control his feelings as long as she was able to keep hers under control. "I'd like to know where I stand?" he asked.

"Where do you stand, Dominique?"

"Tell me. I don't know, and I don't like it."

"Have you made up your mind, who you want?"

"I can't make up my mind? I can't?" I've spent nearly twenty years thinking of no one but you. I all but deserted to travel to Eagle Landing to see you .I traveled all the way back to Congo to look for land for your family. I have run through the jungle to Surrey, and paddled hundreds of miles down the Yoruba. I have boiled mineral salt and bagged magnesium sulfate in a cave all winter to have enough money to build a house for us to live alongside your brothers. Don't talk to me about making up my mind. Not when everybody from here to Beguiler Ferry Crossing is standing around, whispering, with a finger to their lips, whispering, don't move, don't make a sound; don't do anything, Liana is thinking. "

"Do you understand? I should know what we are doing."

"If you're talking about Yolanda and me in the jungle, let's settle that once and for all. I told you before, up there by the lake, and I am telling you again. Nothing happened between me and Yolanda there or anywhere."

"Whatever happened, it doesn't matter." It's in the past now, along with other women you have had, and, the husband I once had. After all you, and I, are mature adults, I hope."

He was puzzled. "What are you saying?"

"You might get restless and want to leave. I've come too far, to far too make a fool out of myself. I have given up every plan I ever had. I've moved out to this untamed godless jungle, and created a new life. We finally saw each-other again yesterday morning after all those months."

"Are you saying that after coming out here, you're not

229

sure of whom you want?"

"Are you sure, Dominique, you know who you want?"

"How many times do I have to tell you? Stop playing games and let's get everything straight right now. I'm sure of whom I want. Will you marry me?"

"Yes," she said. She was beginning to smile. "Don't look so surprise. We're probably not for each other. I'll try to control you, and, you'll try to run over me. I would be better off with Diesel, but he's not the man I want."

"No," he said slowly. "He isn't." She said yes before thinking. Her answer was strange, yet as clear as his questions. This was clearly no moment of triumph for him. Everybody had been trying to tell him the way it really was. She *had* been taking her time thinking. She had carefully considered everything in her mind until she decided he would make a better jungle husband than Diesel. He was the man her brothers liked. The man best able to implement her plans, and fit them into the other Gomez family members plans. Now after having made up her mind, she was making him crawl to her. Worse than that, she was going to control him completely. She was standing in front of him, smiling, waiting, as she had appeared, in his dreams waiting for him to reach for her. And that was what he was doing, and he knew it, but he couldn't help it. No matter how much time she spent scheming, or how little she wanted him, he had to have her.

He grabbed her. Their embrace was sudden and aggressive, nearly violent with as much passion as that night, that moment under the incense tree or on the hill. Only this time there was nobody around to interrupt. Here there was no need to think of others. He held her firmly against him, hugging her, kissing her passionately. He prolonged the kiss savagely; ready to take her if he had to. He wanted to make her feel something because he was feeling so much. She was no longer resisting, nor was she drifting away. She was embracing him. Now suddenly she was becoming aware of the distance. Her eyes were closed. Slowly they opened. She stared into his, at first they were only startled, then they started widening with surprise, with what amounted almost to panic, self-control, and over-whelming fear. His sudden triumph was so great that he began to laugh. Her face moved and saddened but she didn't avoid the question.

Yolanda The Enchantress

"Don't laugh," she murmured fiercely. "How was I to know? Something like this has never happened to me before." He had won, after all. She never thought this would happen. She hadn't planned this genuine and passionate surrender. He couldn't stop his cynically laughter. Not until she placed her lips on his. Her response was now as urgent as his demand, her arms and lips responded as eager as his.

"When?" he asked.

She laid her head on his shoulder. Her voice was calm. "Today, if you want, but I think we wouldn't enjoy, starting our life together in Monty, and Crystal's house. You still have to go to Sea Pen, or have you forgotten? Let's get married, the day *my* house is finished."

How long will that be?"

"About a week, according to Osceola. Perhaps a little longer than it will take you to go to Sea Pen and back." She pushed away and looked up at him. She was smiling, but her eyes were no longer calm, and peaceful. "There will be a door at the head of the stairs when my house is finished. The day my house is finished you can open the door, and come in, if you are coming to stay."

"When I get back I'll help Osceola and his boys finish the house, and I'll hang the door myself." He kissed her again. Her embrace was so delightful he didn't want it to end, but it had to end, at once, if he was going to leave today. This time he pushed her away. He had to go to Sea Pen .

"Such strength of character," she mocked him.

"Joke while you can," he warned her. He kissed her once more and ran down the stairs. Osceola and his sons were watching them, not so much inquisitively as hopefully. He smiled at them with affection pride and approval.

Chapter 14
They're Taking Her Home

It was so hot in the stockroom that perspiration poured in streams off Africans unloading the donkeys. Sable Buena thrust

L. A. Johnson Jr.

his hand into one of the open sacks, and let the white crystals flow through his fingers.

"H-m-m-m." He grunted once expressing his doubt that the magnesium sulfite was of insufficient quality to give it any value at all, and at the same time to his astonishment that it was as good as it was.

"Test as many as you want," said Dominique. He walked to the doorway where the air was less suffocating, and looked out at Sea Pen. The place had far more people than when he last had been here. Most of them lived in shacks, tents, or bush huts outside the walls of the stockade. Every one of them was making as much noise as he or she could. They were firing rifles, lighting firecrackers, the air had the scent of gunshots. They were singing Portuguese songs, and striking pans. They were celebrating the news of Nova's latest victory.

The word had just come from Port Eden Ton; another Masai leader had been captured. King Nearby and his fifteen hundred warriors had been defeated. According to the story Novas and his army were traveling fast, and alone; they had reached the banks of the Nile. Dominique doubted everything hadn't been quite as simple as that, but there was no question the siege of African Oak had been lifted. The advance upon Xhosa Country was over, and the threat to Congo had been removed.

The warriors were in headlong retreat, heading for those distant jungles in the north and west, from which they had come. People, who had been too busy to listen to Novas' appeals for men, were shouting in his honor, howling with pride because he was a Portuguese officer. They were calling him the savior of Congo settlements. You could be sure that when he returns most of them would be too busy to listen to him. Novas couldn't go on performing miracles with a handful of soldiers with no better backing than he was getting from people he was defending

Dominique walked over to Sable; the storekeeper brushed off his hands, sat down on a sack, and took off his wig. With his sleeve he mopped the few gray hairs on his balding head. The wig was his only extravagance, he looked twice his age Sable was nearly sixty. With his black wig on his head, he was handsome. He thought he looked like a dashing young man well able to win female companionship. He was the richest man

Yolanda The Enchantress

in Congo, but he was too stingy to marry a woman, or have a long lasting romantic relationship. He hated spending one penny more on useless things, but he didn't mine spending money for a good wig. At the moment there was a large spider crawling among the carefully combed strands of his wig. Sable snorted with rage when he saw the spider, caught it and crushed it with his thumbnail. He looked at Dominique, his frown switching to a grin.

"You have worked hard, I'd like to see you make something from it," he said while plunging his finger into one of the sacks. "I'll give you double the value of what your stuff is worth. The only reason I can do that is because I happen to know some folks that want it bad."

"You mean half of what you will get for it."

Sable looked distressed. "I mean an escudo a pound, and that is twice what I ever heard of magnesium sulfite ever sold for before."

"I'll take it," said Dominique. "You're paying with gold."

Sable jumped as if a bee had stung him.

"Gold," he cried. "You must have been walking around with your eyes closed, and your thumbs stuck in your ears since you came out of that cave of yours or you would know there is no gold in Congo; no silver nor copper neither." He was waving his arms wildly. "If you don't believe me go find out for yourself. Then come back and maybe we can talk business."

"You might be right," said Dominique. "Everybody acts that way, for a fact, including some that have plenty, but I have to have gold. I didn't work all those months for nothing."

"There is none, beleave it or not. Try finding some. Go to Port Eden Ton. Go to Nova Gala or Sierra Leone. They are harder up than we are here. Who do you think has gold?"

The Spaniards," said Dominique. "This stuff is no trouble to pack around; it's barely half a dugout-load. I can get silver or gold for it at African Oak, or for sure at Mali."

"Then that's where you should go," said Sable. He stood and marched into his office with an air of disgust.

Dominique untied his donkeys and led them to the watering trough. While they drank he took off his shirt and plunged his head into the cool water. He was taking his time, waiting for

233

Sable to follow him. He was thinking. Everybody talked about Sables' stock of maize. The back of his warehouse is piled high with stacks of it. Sable had shipped a dozen boatloads down river to Surrey. People were nearly starving right after the hard winter, they had to pay any price he demanded, but the spring was surprisingly warm, and new crops were flourishing. Now no one was buying more than he needed, and the price was falling daily. Sable must be nervous about being stuck with such a large surplus.

Dominique had an idea, with people moving to Congo Basin, most of them were arriving too late to plant crops of their own, by fall maize would be in short supply again. But whether that proved true or not, maize right now had a value for him as tangible as gold or silver. His agreement with the Gomez's was payable in the terms of bushels of maize, the set rate was twenty-five cents a bushel. Sable, overloaded with maize, might let some of his go at half the value. If he could work Sable up to, say, twenty-five hundred bushels, in exchange for the magnesium sulfate, then he had a safe deal. The sum he had to have would then be in sight.

After the proceeds from the sale of the watch, and Prince Kudzu's shirt, and Colonel San Diego's pants were all sold, he would need only a small loan from Mario to have the full thousand escudos, or its equivalent, four thousand bushels of maize. He sat on the edge of a log to dry in the sun. When he noticed that Sable was strolling out to join him he turned around and began putting on his shirt.

"I've been thinking'," said Sable. "Perhaps I could help you."

"I'm listing, but not for long."

"This is what I can do," continued Sable. "If you're thinking of going to Mali, you might as well take a full cargo. You can travel on the river with a barge-load of maize just as easy as you can with a half loaded dugout of magnesium sulfate. I have a proposal. At Mali they have plenty of mineral salt, but they never have enough maize, and when they have a surplus, they ship it to markets in North Africa."

Sable had fallen into his trap. "I would have never thought of that," said Dominique. "You could be right. The

234

problem is, I have magnesium sulfate, not maize."

"I have a little maize," said Sable. "Just to help you out I might trade you some."

"Thank you for the offer," said Dominique. "I'll think about it." He paused, frowning, pretending to think. "Of course, it would keep me from having to go all the way to Mali. I could sell my merchandise at African Oak? But nobody there ever needs maize."

Sable was trying hard to show a friendly, concerning interest. "Would it be worth your time to go all the way to Mali, if you had enough maize."

"How much is enough?"

Sable's lips moved in the processes of his thoughtful calculation. "Just to help you out, I might consider three thousand bushels for your merchandise." Sable waited, smiling, for Dominique's eager acceptance of an offer so generous. Dominique was thinking, he didn't answer. Sable certainly wanted his merchandise bad, he would probably trade even more to get rid of his excess maize. Dominique was calculating, too. A bill of sale for three thousand bushels would keep him from having to borrow anything from Mario. The thought of Mario, reminded him of the way Mario negotiated a trade. "Never take the first offer," Mario always said.

"That sounds to me like a fair proposition," Dominique conceded. "Just about what my magnesium sulfite is worth. There's only one problem. That much maize is not a boatload. I'd have to hire two men to help me with the boat, same as if it was a full load. That cost money."

All of Sable's pretended friendliness vanished. "Take it or leave it," he said.

"I guess I'll have to refuse your offer," said Dominique.

Sable walked back into his warehouse. Dominique watched him, angry with himself. His bluff had backfired. He had talked big about African Oak and Mali when in fact he didn't have time to take his merchandise as far as Port Eden Ton. He had to sell his merchandise to Sable for whatever he could get, and return to Rhino Creek. A faint relief came with the thought of the watch shirt and pants. He had to sell them to Sable, too. He would give Sable an hour. Then he would come back, not to talk about the magnesium sulfate, but about other things he had to sell, and when they started bargaining again he would take what he could get for the lot.

He led his horse and donkeys back to the warehouse. Sable's helpers had disappeared, so had Sable. Dominique slowly closed, and secured the open sacks, carried them out and loaded them on his donkeys. He took his time and still Sable remained out of sight. Dominique secured the last sack, and started around the corner of the warehouse with his donkeys. There wasn't enough grass in Sea Pen to feed a small goat in any pasture within half an hour of the town. He purchased some hay for his donkeys and horse to feed on. He decided to wait an hour before returning to bargain with Sable again.

Sable stuck his head out of his office window, and started talking to Dominique's donkeys. "A man can bargain so hard he defeats himself."

"Happens like that some time," agreed Dominique, still walking.

"Never like to see a man try hard to get ahead and some-how manage to make a fool out of himself."

"Neither do I," said Dominique, pausing.

"Four thousand," said Sable. "That's my last offer."

"Four thousand, eh?" said Dominique, still clinging to his pose of thoughtful consideration, though the figure was ring-ing in his ear like the loud clang of a bell. Not thirty-five hundred, but four thousand. The amount he needed. It was the result of his friends' wisdom; the need of borrowing from Mario was no longer. He would have the shirt to get married in. It even left him the watch to trade for the kind of riding horse, a wealthy landowner and militia officer should have. "Perhaps I should take your offer."

"Get in here and sign the bill of sale, before I realize how big a fool I'm makin' of myself."

The workers popped out of nowhere and began to unload the donkeys again. Dominique went into Sable's office.

"I can't load that much maize on my donkeys," he said. "Write the order to deliver on demand, I'll send for it."

Sable grunted and started writing on a second piece of paper. Dominique signed the bill of sale for his magnesium sul-

Yolanda The Enchantress

fite and folded Sable's note and placed it in his leather pouch where he kept his flint and steel. An order from Sable Buena was as good as gold, better than money floating around in Congo.

"For a season's work, you have done well for yourself," said Sable, still grumpy.

"Not bad," said Dominique.

He went out to his horse and donkeys tied at the rail. A man and woman were looking them over with favorable, analytical interest, feeling on their legs, flapping a bandanna in front of their eyes and, peering into their mouths. An Arab from Sudan The man was tall, big, and black. With a black beard and thick black eyebrows, he had the aggressively stern authoritarian look of royalty, or, perhaps that of an overseer who had been in charge of a big plantation where slaves were kept under control. The woman was tiny, with straight blond hair, red nose blue eyes and a never ending sniffle.

"Nice donkeys, for this part of Africa," said the man. He had a deep scratchy harsh voice, which boomed the sound of authority.

Dominique nodded and began loosening the nearest tie rope. He didn't have time to stop and gossip with strangers.

"My name is Taboo Ikea," said the man. "This is Mrs. Ikea. Heard these animals might be for sale."

They're not," said Dominique. My friend, Mario might be willing to sell, since he has little need for pack burros any more, but if so he had want to handle the sale himself.

"Buy 'em, Taboo," ordered the woman. Her voice was weak and scratchy.

Taboo turned hastily back to Dominique. "We will give you a real good price for 'them," he said.

"They belong to a man in Rhino Creek," said Dominique.

The answer had no apparent effect on Mrs. Ikea.

"Buy them, Taboo," she repeated.

Taboo edged sideways a little, as if a firecracker had exploded near his foot. "You see, it is this way," he addressed Dominique passionately. "Fiona, she's sick of this part of Africa. She wants to leave, but we need good donkeys to pack out."

Dominique grabbed the horse's mane, to swing up in to the saddle. In spite of his impatience he was amused by the tall

Arab's fear of his tiny German wife.

"Been here long?" he asked.

"Too long," said Fiona.

"We got here this morning before dawn," said Taboo, anxiously hoping that Dominique would understand the situation. "We came from Port Eden Ton by boat. We can't afford to throw away the few things we have left. The only donkeys other than these we have been able to find, are worn out."

"No good at all," said Fiona, "like the people in this settlement."

"We need good donkeys and a wagon," said Taboo. "Fiona she likes to travel fast."

"A person can't walk fast enough," said Fiona, "getting' away from here."

Dominique mounted and glanced down at her. "What is it you don't like about Congo?"

"Everything," she said. She covered her nose. A faint breeze was stirring the stagnant dusty air, bringing with it the unpleasant odors of Sea Pen, where hundreds of people lived huddled together among accumulated waist, in dirty campsites, and filthy stock pens. "The smell."

Dominique laughed and jerked the lead rope to get his donkeys started. "Sea Pen has quite a smell, all right, since the snow melted, but before you give up you ought to take a look around and see some of the country. There's still plenty of fresh air in this part of Africa."

"See some of the country," repeated Sable from the warehouse doorway. "From the story they told me when they came to me for burros this morning, there have never been people that have seen more of this country. They came down the Indian Ocean with Colonel Suarez last winter, but that new settlement in Swaziland, everybody else speaks of so well wasn't good enough for them. They traveled down river to Yoruba, and then up to Port Eden Ton, and then to Flamingo Grove, and now they are here. They have seen the best there is out here, and none of it is good enough for them." His righteous indignation grew on him. "What's wrong with Congo?" he demanded of the Ikeas. "Tell me."

Taboo shifted uneasily but his wife was ready with an

Yolanda The Enchantress

explicit answer. "You people-mostly. Dirty, lazy, shiftless, white trash, setting' around all the time with your long red noses stuck up your big white asses, gossiping about Africans while stealing' their land, and none of you have gumption enough to farm one acre yourself, or fight off Africans when they come to take your cows. So far as this part of the country goes, it might be bigger than Kingdom of Buganda, but it's not better."

Dominique stopped laughing and pulled in his horse and donkeys. "Kingdom of Buganda? That's where you come from?"

"And that is where we are heading' back too," said Fiona.

"Anywhere near Rotshidzwa?"

Fiona stared suspiciously. Taboo quickly replied before she could make another offensive statements. "No! We came from a small village beyond the jungle to the south, on the Zambezi River."

"Ever happen to run across anybody from Rotshidzwa?"

Taboo grinned. "Yes sir, you might say that I surely did, once, and I married her." He repeated himself while glancing at his wife. "Fiona's family owns a small plantation on Spring River," he exclaimed with more caution.

"Taboo he's done more than what you might say run across me," added Fiona, giving her husband a sudden, smug smile which obviously confused him. "He followed me around for nearly a year."

Searching for his pipe and tobacco Dominique laughed cordially. Suddenly willing to sit, and talk awhile. "When you lived in Rotshidzwa, ever know any Qukeza's?" he asked her.

"No," said Fiona. "But there's a Qukeza Village down by Drivers Fork."

"I mean, Rendi Qukeza."

"He died nearly twenty years ago, but last I heard, his son's still live there." Dominique leaped to the ground. "Perhaps I could help you purchase these donkeys."

"Be careful," advised Sable. They'll have you eating out of their hands."

"We will pay what they are worth," said Fiona, but she was still on guard. "Now what do you want?"

"Only this," said Dominique. "There's a woman at the settlement I came from who's related to those Qukeza's, a niece

239

of Rendi Qukeza. She's been living' with Zulu's all her life. I'll make sure you get a good deal for the donkeys if you'll take her to Kingdom of Buganda with you, and make sure that she arrives safe, and sound to the Qukeza family."

"That we would be willing to do whether we got the donkeys or not," said Fiona. "She belongs with her family."

"She may not be too easy to handle. She's only been away from the Zulu's a little over a month, and she's always talking' about going back to them."

"We'll take her to Kingdom of Buganda," said Fiona. "I promise we'll take her home."

"Where is your stuff?" asked Dominique. I'll pack you over to Rhino Creek with me, and you can talk to my friend."

They stopped to eat at dusk. When the moon rose they started on again, and kept on until well after midnight. By the third hour of daylight the next morning they had crossed a crest of huge hills. Below they could see the huge beautiful valley of Rhino Creek.

"Lovely, mighty pretty," said Taboo.

"Looks like a prosperous settlement to me," said Fiona.

Dominique rode on ahead leaving them to lead the donkeys. It was hard for him to speak without letting out a yell to relieve the uncontrollable pounding in his chest. Suddenly his confidence in his luck had returned. He had worked hard farming the magnesium sulfate, and had sold it for a good price. But running into the Ikeas had been nothing but luck. A man might take satisfaction in overcoming difficulties but there was no satisfaction like the feeling that things had started to break his way. Nothing could make a man feel as good as that.

He lengthened his hordes stride, weaving in and out among clusters of vine covered fallen trees uprooted by angry cyclones of other years. Suddenly he came upon Diesel, sitting on a log with a double barrel shotgun across his lap. Diesel wasn't making the slightest pretense at hunting. He was sitting there watching the path from the west. When Dominique came into view he gave his usual cheerful smile.

"Behold, the groom cometh," he called out. "I was hoping something would happened too you, I didn't want to leave until I was certain nothing had."

Yolanda The Enchantress

"Nothing had so far," said Dominique. "When are you leaving?"

"Before the wedding."

"That's what I would do, if it were the other way around," agreed Dominique. He was too excited and impatient to put up with Diesel's snobbish humor.

"I'll leave the deed to my land on the altar," said Diesel. "Or wherever Father Nervy decides to marry you, and, by the way, he has become your newest friend. First time in his life he has approved of anybody but God. What in the world did you do to him? Amazing! The way you took this entire community without trying. Some drag their feet. Now don't give me any argument about the land. You would have done the same, if it had turned out the other way."

Dominique didn't want to argue. He wanted only to go. "Going back to Eagle Landing?" he asked.

"No. They need doctors everywhere in the Congo. I'll hang my shingle in some settlement not too far away, somewhere where I will be within shouting distance. After all, something unforeseen could still happen to you. Liana's been widowed once already."

"That's a fact," agreed Dominique. "Well, better luck the next time." He started to past.

"You're impatient, and no wonder. I will keep you no longer. I have convinced myself once more, you're made of real flesh, and blood, and you're not just a bad dream. Now go. Liana's house is nearly finished, if you're interested, except for a door. Ah, ah, that does interest you. For some reason I cannot understand why they placed the door on the roof."

"Far from it," said Dominique. "But something will happen to me right here, and now if I linger hear much longer. I've got to see that door." Rushing down the slope, coming out of the jungle approaching from the west, he saw it. Even if he hadn't been warned he would have seen it. He began to run and laugh as he had laughed with Liana in his arms; suddenly he realized she was surrendering more than she wanted too. It was clear to him, that she wanted everybody to know she belong to him.

The house was a beehive of activity; slaves were carrying

in furniture, cleaning up around the yard, nailing the shingles on the roof. All the Gomez's had come to help. Getting the house ready in time had become a family project. As he reached the nearest corner Liana was running to meet him.

"It didn't take you long," she was shouting."

He dismounted and watched her, enjoying the sight of her running to him. "You have returned, too soon?"

Want me to go back?"

"No," she said softly. "Come and help." Breathlessly she threw herself into his embrace, slowly leaning back looking into his eyes.

"No use looking so smug," she said softly.

He glanced at the door leaning against the chimney. "I better hang that where it belongs before the wind blows it away."

"Tomorrow," she said, "hang it tomorrow."

"Tomorrow?" he repeated.

She nodded, her eyes not leaving his for a second. Slowly he leaned towards her lips. She lifted her head, and her lips parted.

From somewhere just above came Monty's voice: "About time." Followed by cheering, and applause.

"He's right," shouted another happy person."

Dominique looked up and saw all the Gomez's, except, Brittany, and Antonio's children, watching from the windows above.

"Most interesting view when looking down on you like this," said Monty. "Kiss her again."

"The way they are carrying on," said Liana, "you might think you're marrying the family, but you're not. You're marrying me."

"If it's up to me," said Dominique, "we'll see them at church on Sundays, or at family gatherings."

She took his arm and walked with him towards the door. The Gomez's came rushing out to greet him with affectionate jeering of congratulations. Men were shaking his hand, and patting him on his back. Crystal and Carla kissed him.

"You never had a chance," said Legacy. "Not since that first dance with her at Plato's."

Yolanda The Enchantress

"Feels good to have some competition in the family," boomed Antonio. "Of course, I've got a head start of ten strapping children, but the way you get around I'll have to keep moving to stay ahead of you."

"I'm so happy I could cry," whispered Crystal.

He barely heard what they were saying. He saw there smiling faces through a haze of sympathy, and forced cheers of good will, through dancing golden dust in a sunbeam.

The Ikeas stopped the donkeys on the slope nearby, and waited. Legacy noticed them at once.

"Find you a tenant farmer?" he asked.

"No," explained Dominique. "They're on their way home to Kingdom of Buganda. I bought them here thinking Mario might want to sell them his donkeys. The woman used to be a neighbor of the Qukeza's. They are going to take Yolanda to Kingdom of Buganda with them."

Linda squeezed his arm. "Really?" She seemed pleased, but no more so than she might have been by some unexpected gift he had bought her from Sea Pen. "Thank God for that."

The other women were more openly vocally suspicious.

"Sea Pen is hardly full of Qukeza neighbors," said Antonio. "Who told you about that odd couple."

"Nobody. Just happened to run across them."

"Luck like yours, Dominique, is more than luck," mumbled Monty. "Its divine intervention."

"Well, I better get along with them and get the donkey trading under way," said Dominique. He glanced up at the door and then down at Liana.

Dominique pointed at the lumberyard, with excited gestures, motioning to the Ikeas, and walked on ahead, again. The shrieking sound of the saw in the mill blocked the sound of his approach. He stood in the doorway unnoticed. Cindy was bent over her spinning wheel. Yolanda was beside her, watching, holding the yarn.

"That is right, Zulu Woman," said Cindy. "You catch on fast."

Yolanda was wearing a pink and white dress that was once Cindy's, it had been altered. The tailoring had been done so neatly that it fit her well. Around her neck hung a gold chain and locket, also Cindy's. Her hair, no longer in braids was wrapped on her head, and across her brow, its curliness had been pressed out with a hot curling iron into a wavy fringe, which made her face look even more beautiful. She saw Dominique and stood with her hands touching her breast in a shocking feminine ges ture. All of her stubborn savage qualities were gone.

The thumping of the wheel stopped and Cindy, also, looked around. There was no hint of welcome in her glance. She jumped up standing as if she were protecting Yolanda. Dominique stepped into the kitchen.

"Well, well, this is fine," he said, as forcefully as he could. "She's been behaving so well, you let her out?"

"There was never a reason to lock her up," said Cindy. Thrusting an arm around Yolanda's shoulders gripping her tightly.

"Where's Mario?" Dominique asked, backing away.

"He's in the back working. You hear the saw?" Dominique started for the door.

"Dominique?"

It didn't sound like Yolanda at all. Her voice had changed as much as her outward appearance. It was shy, timid, and nervous, almost trembling.

"Well?"

"You marry her today?" asked Yolanda.

"Tomorrow." Replied Dominique.

He waited for what she had to say, bracing himself for the outburst, but she closed her eyes and smiled. Cindy glanced at Dominique.

"You're my husbands best friend," she said. "That's the only reason I'm letting you step in the door."

Dominique found Mario in the sawmill.

"God all mighty," said Mario. "Back already? You must have flown." He gave Dominique a quick jolting nudge with his elbow. "Something on your mind?"

"Want to sell your donkeys?" asked Dominique.

Mario shook his head. "Not enough money in this settlement worth one good donkey."

"Want to talk to a man and woman, who has money?"

Mario stopped suddenly with a jerk. "Who?" Where?

Yolanda The Enchantress

How much?"

Dominique escorted Mario around front and introduced him to the Ikeas. Then he backed off, and sat down on the rocking chair on the porch. Mario's bargaining would give him plenty of time to think about how to deal with Yolanda, and Cindy. He took out his pipe, and pouch. He had just started to break up a leaf of tobacco, when to his astonishment; he saw Mario and Taboo shaking hands walking towards him.

"A deal that quick?" Dominique asked.

"The price is right," said Mario, "No reason to argue."

"We might as well get started, Taboo," said to Fiona. "We can make it to Nova Gala before dark." She turned to Dominique. "Where is the Qukeza girl?"

"These people are taking Yolanda to Kingdom of Buganda with them," he explained to Mario. He noticed how quick Mario's grin changed to a frown. "What's wrong with that?"

"Nothing," said Mario. He leaned over and looked through the open doorway. "If you can work it out."

"What's to be worked out?" asked Dominique. "Come in and we'll discuss it."

Yolanda was standing beside Cindy, and Cindy's arm was still protectively around her. Yolanda's eyes were downcast; she was trying to look shy and frightened. Cindy couldn't have been showing more anger at the strangers coming in behind Dominique. She or more likely, Yolanda must have been listening. "Yolanda," said Dominique. "This is Mr. and Mrs. Ikeas. They are from Kingdom of Buganda. Mrs. Ikeas use to live near the Qukeza's. That makes her almost the same as a neighbor to you."

"No, it doesn't, said Cindy. "Who invited these people into my house?"

"I did," said Mario gruffly.

Fiona seemed not in the slightest disturbed by Cindy's hostility. She walked over to Yolanda and studied her carefully.

"She's got the Qukeza people look, all right," she uttered. She continued to study Yolanda. "I have never seen your father, but I have heard tails of the time nearly twenty years ago when he left to go to Tupelo. Nobody knew what happened to him, but that's all over now. We have come, Taboo and me, to take you to Kingdom of Buganda."

Yolanda raised her eyes, not to look at Fiona but pass her at Dominique.

"I do not want to go to Kingdom of Buganda."

"And nobodies going to make her," Cindy burst out. "She can stay right here in this house as long as she wishes. Tell him, Mario. Tell him. This is our house. She can stay here with us."

"She can stay with us, sure enough," said Mario. "There is no doubt in my mind where she belongs."

Yolanda moved away from Fiona and clung to Cindy.

"She'll stay where she wants to," said Cindy.

"Yolanda," demanded Dominique.

"Yes, Dominique."

"Come here."

She walked over to him, timidly and obediently. He led her out the door.

"Cindy," said Mario, equally forcefully, "gets those people something to eat. They have a distance to travel before night falls."

Dominique stopped in the yard and faced Yolanda. She looked uncomfortable in the pink dress, with the locket dangeling below her her throat with her hair braided, her face had become unyielding, and expressionless, more Zulu-like than ever.

"Now," he said. "Let's talk."

"Talk, it is no good."

"You're going. Home to your family."

"Not with that woman," said Yolanda.

"Why not?"

"Many times you said that you would take me to Kingdom of Buganda ."

"That I have, but this is just as good a way to get you there. Finding these people to take you is the same as taking you myself."

"No. It's not the same."

"Whether it is or not, you're going."

She looked at him, "If I go to Kingdom of Buganda now,

Yolanda The Enchantress

I never see you again."

"Doesn't matter? I'm getting married, tomorrow."

"That is in my head all the time." She said.

Why do you want stay here?" he asked

She was looking thoughtfully at his face. "You will not stay with her."

He laughed. She was as bad as Diesel. "What's your real reason?"

"She will not like it if I stay here."

"You're going," he shouted. "You're going, if I have to tie you up and pack you as far as Gun Road myself."

She was delighted, as always, by his anger. "Every time you get very mad with me," she gets angry.

Suddenly Yolanda began to laugh, as maliciously and spitefully as ever she had laughed on the raft, and rushed into the house. He went after her. Instead of running to Cindy she kept on towards the room in which she had been locked. He came to a stop, deciding it would be more sensible to wait until she and he, had calmed down before continuing the conversation.

Cindy glanced at Dominique as she walked by him rushing after Yolanda. Dominique gestured impatiently for Mario to follow Cindy, to keep her from interfering. Mario followed reluctantly. The Ikeas were sitting at the table eating, paying no attention to what was going on.

Dominique went outside. Mario came to the door. He never looked so worried.

"Come in here," he said.

Dominique followed Mario through the kitchen. The Ikeas's were still eating. Mario led the way to the storeroom. Yolanda was in Cindy's arms, her face hidden against Cindy's breast.

"Their, their, little Zulu woman," Cindy was uttering.

"What's wrong now?" demanded Dominique.

Cindy glanced up angrily, quickly looking away, blushing and breathing hard. "Tell him, Mario," she demanded.

Mario coughed a couple of times and finally spoke.

"She said she's pregnant."

"Who is? Cindy?"

"No. Yolanda. She says it's yours."

"She just told us," added Cindy, her voice trembling.

"Why are you lying, I've never touched her." Dominique said carmly. He pushed Mario aside, and pulled Yolanda away from Cindy and began to shake her. "Look at me," he shouted. She raised her downcast eyes. For an instant, he saw in them a flash of deceit, and enjoyment of his frustration. That same frustration she saw in them when she threw her clothing in the river. He shoved her away and turned frantically, facing Mario and Cindy.

"Are you crazy, too," he shouted. "You can tell that she is lying, and I am not. Mario, you know me well enough to know that I would never deny a thing like that if I had done it. I have never been with her. She is as much a virgin as she was when I first met her, believe me."

"I belive you," said Mario gloomily. "But nobody else will, look at her; little, sad and crying, moping, around in the corners pretending' to be with child, and everybody knows she has just come from weeks in the jungle with you-who do you think is going to believe you other than me? Nobody but me. Beginning' with that preacher. You scared him once, and now he is going to enjoy a chance like this to get back at you! After he is finished every woman in this settlement will help him. They're all going to act just like Cindy. Most women think a man's always wrong, even if they know he's not." He glanced at Yolanda. "Look at her drooping' like a flower that needs a drank of water. The way she's acting' doesn't matter to you but it will to our neighbors; she's got you, and you know it."

Dominique turned around, grabbing Yolanda's wrist. She looked at him, smiling this time, expecting physical violence from him, rejoicing in her triumph. He pulled her out of the door.

"Stop him, Mario," screamed Cindy. "Stop him. Help her. He's going to kill her.

"Shut up," ordered Mario. "She doesn't need help no more than you do."

Yolanda made no effort to pull free or even to hold back. She ran beside Dominique, smiling, as he crossed the kitchen with her and out of the door. They circled the horse and donkeys and started up the path that led upstream past the stockade. It was only when she realized they were going to Liana's house; she started struggling to get away.

"Dominique Where are we going?"

"You want to tell your lie, don't you? You can tell it to everybody that will listen, starting with Liana. She's the person you want to believe it, isn't she? Her whole family is up there with her. You want them to hear it, too, don't you?"

Yolanda was listing to what he was saying; trying to understand what he was about to do.

"What is the problem?" Afraid to tell her?"

"I'd like to watch her face while I tell her."

"Then come on."

"Wait, Dominique."

"For what?"

She was studding his face, trying to make up her mind about something.

"They will laugh at me? That is what you want?"

"I don't know what they'll do? Perhaps you do, possibly at me. It won't take long to find out, will it? Come on!"

"You want them to laugh at me?"

"What is all this talk about laughing?" Nobody has ever felt like laughing, except you."

"Wait, Dominique. I need to think."

"It'll be the first time."

"I think you're sure now."

"Sure of what?"

"That you never want to see me again."

"Never will be too soon."

She continued to confront his anger with a strange peaceful calm coming over her.

"Now I am sure, too."

"Of what?"

"That you want me to go."

"I've been telling you that a long time."

"I will go."

She turned and started walking quickly back towards the lumberyard. He started after her understanding that everything was finally resolved, and had ended suddenly and simple. He was dazed and confused. Seconds ago he was filled with rage.

Now he felt empty.

Mario came running out cool, calm and collected. "What did you say to her to make her understand?"

"They will never make Nova Gala before dark, walking, leading those donkeys," said Dominique.

"They'll need horses or camels to ride, you and I need to go with them at least that far. When they reach Congo Road they can join up with some other movers. They'll be traveling alone until they get to Nova Gala."

Mario stared at him, all he said was: "Somebody's got to go to bring those camels back." He went to get three camels.

The Ikeas's came out. They weren't bothered by the commotion. After deciding in Sea Pen to take Yolanda with them, Fiona had taken it for granted, that was the way it was going to be.

Dominique caught a quick glimpse of Yolanda while standing in the open door. She was dressed in her Zulu clothing, and her hair was still in braids. She had stopped pretending. She was herself again. Now she looked just as she had the day he had first seen her.

He walked over to the horse, and removed his saddlebag, and the leather bag containing the printed shirt, and other things he had left in the bag among the Ikea's goods.

"I placed something in your pack, I want you to have," he told Taboo. "It is a shirt that once belonged to Prince Kudzu. If you run into somebody that can afford it you can get a good price for it."

"Why are you giving' it to Taboo?" demanded Fiona.

"Might be that when you get to Kingdom of Buganda it could be more trouble than you think, finding her people, and getting her to them. I want to pay you so you'll feel obligated to do whatever you need to do."

"We told you we'll take her to her people," said Fiona. "All in one piece." She was studying his face. "You can give my husband the shirt, if that makes you feel better."

When Mario came back with three camels, Cindy started weeping frantically, losing control of her senses, but she kept out of sight in the kitchen. Yolanda's face was covered with paint when she came out. She mounted, and sat without emotion waiting for the caravan to get under way.

Dominique rode ahead, up the long path through that same wild berry patch, and passed the same grove of orange and date palm trees. It didn't seem possible that little over two weeks had gone by, since he had been here.

There was the spot where Liana slipped down from her horse into his arms, the hut that he and Yolanda had spent the night; and the lake in which Youlanda had bathed. He wondered what Yolanda might be thinking now. He resisted an impulse to signal to her to come up and ride with him. There was nothing he could say to her if she did. Everything had already been said.

He kept moving; retracing the course he had taken with Mario and Yolanda when he packed in the magnesium sulfate and before that with Legacy and Monty on their way here to see Rhino Creek for the first time. Presently he was crossing the meadow where he and Yolanda had been over-taken by rain that afternoon of his second approach to Rhino Creek. There was the rock beside which he had stopped the donkeys to tighten a pack rope. He kept his attention on the trail ahead. Beyond the meadow was the stretch of incense trees, clusters of elephant grass, bamboo, and cane, and then the hills from which you could look down on Nova Gala Settlement. From there, the Ikea's and Yolanda could go on without an escort.

In the elephant grass Mario galloped up beside him. He glanced over his shoulder towards the travelers behind.

"Want me to lead the way for a while?"

"Why?" asked Dominique?

"Just asking'."

Mario dropped back to wait for the others. At the foot of the hills Fiona came up to ride with Dominique. "We'll stay at Nova Gala, until we can join a party going east," she remarked, more as if thinking aloud than addressing him. She pulled away without waiting for his answer. It was early evening when Dominique rounded the shoulder of the hill, which entered an open ridge from which they looked down on Nova Gala Settlement below. Looking down there was an old rhinoceros trail leading to the riverbank skirting the town. They could see children playing, guarded by men with rifles, while driving stock from remote pastures to pens near the stockade for the night. The ferry was being pulled across the river. The others came up. Everybody dismounted. Mario stringed the camels together, that were to be taken back.

Dominique walked over to Yolanda. Her face was painted red and white, without any expression. She was shivering, though the weather was blistering warm.

"Talk," she said, "is no use."

There was no answer to that or to anything else either that could be said. He took out his watch and thrust it at her. The suddenness of the moment broke her calm. She wept.

"Why?" she asked.

"I want you to have it. That's why. There will be things you'll need. Clothes, maybe. It's a gift. No need you being a complete burden on your relatives. You wouldn't like that."

She stared at the watch. She closed her hand, and looked up at him. Into his eyes, which had always been so unafraid. There came a look of fear, like the sudden panic or terror of a child awaking in the darkness of an unfamiliar hut. She whirled, clutching the watch tightly, and started running, her braids swinging.

The Ikea's had already started on with the pack donkeys. She passed them running ahead of them down the trail. A few steps beyond there were clusters of thick, green, bushes at the head of the curve. When she was out of Dominique's sight she hid behind th

e bushes. Like the first time she had stepped into his sight it had began out of such a thicket. It began to seem to him that all that had happened between them from that first moment to this second, in which she had suddenly vanished from his sight, was as if it had never happened.

Chapter 15
Equally Responsible

No cooling came with the coming darkness. The heat of the day changed to blistering of steam. Mario rode ahead, leading the three other camels. A stifling hazy fog covered the sky, it became too dark for them to see, still they kept giving their mounts their heads, now that they were homeward bound they knew their animals would show them the way. Dominique rode at the end of the line with no concern, other than to keep his camel's nose close to the tail of the camel ahead. At last, everything was settled. He could stop worrying about Yolanda. He relaxed avoiding low branches that kept striking him in the darkness. He gave up making the slightest effort to take notice of their progress; he became aware of how far they had traveled only when they came out into the open meadow. For a moment he could see her again, standing here on this spot tightening the pack rope. The raindrops glittering on her face had made his emotions rise until he moved closer. He should have known better. There wasn't the slightest hint of a tear in her eyes, not even doing that last moment before they parted.

He rode up beside Mario. "No use you doing everything," he said. "I'll lead for a while."

"Didn't mean to make you mad," Mario called after him.

"You didn't," said Dominique.

It must be after midnight. If so, then Mario was right; this is my wedding day. As time passed the fog began to clear. They could see a little now, and hoped to make better time by guiding their camels around fallen trees, and rocks, which would keep them from wasting time. The camp was just ahead. In spite of Dominique's bouncing on the saddle of the trotting camel he was getting sleepy. He had ridden this trail many times. Beyond the berry patch and grove of orange trees, was the ridge of the hill. The hill from which he first looked down at the huge valleys running threw, Rhino Creek. There he had crouched in the rain in the darkness. He had stared towards the stockade and tried to imagine how Liana looked at that moment, and what she was doing. She was down there tonight, this time he knew what she was doing. She was waiting for him.

Entering the wild berry patch his camel snorted, and came to a sudden stiff-legged stop and stood trembling. His ears cocked forward, his nostrils widen. Dominique couldn't smell what the camel smelled. But he heard rustling in the midst of the undergrowth beyond the thicket. Then a stick snapped. No animal other than a lion or a gorilla could have frightened the camels. The rustling was too gentle to be a gorilla or a lion. The weight that had broken the stick was not that of a lion or gorilla. There was a chance that the unseen presence was an African warrior.

Dominique recovered from his exhaustion when he felt a sprinkle of rain. There could be one African or fifty. However few or many it was too late to retreat. He gave the low, sharp signal that Nova's men used in the jungle, where they could see neither friend nor foe, to charge straight ahead. He heard the sudden thump of Mario's rifle butt against the rumps of the other camels. All five camels plunged forward. He let out a series of wild yells, Mario quickly joined. The camels crashed through the tangle of vines and undergrowth. The commotion might have been ignored if not for the onrush of whooping camel-men. Dominique caught a whiff of the grease and pain African warriors smeared on their bodies. There were no cries, no blazing spears or glowing arrows. The camels plunged through the wild-berry patches, passing the grove of orange and date trees, and over the top of the hill. They were halfway down the slope before he and Mario were able to get the animals under control.

"What spooked you?" demanded Mario.

"There was at least one African back there in the bushes," said Dominique.

"You don't say." Mario leaned back in his saddle. "Come daylight I'll take some men and find them, and we'll put them in a cage to celebrate you wedding."

"You mean to help you work up some courage."

Mario laughed. "You're thinking' about Dominion Medina's wedding' night, the night he married that Spanish woman, and we dropped a black mamba in his bedroom window."

"No. I'm thinking of you! Osceola and his huge boys will throw you in the lake if you come too close tonight."

After having a scary encounter with an African, the mocking, down to earth talk lifted Dominique's spirit. The men of the settlement would undoubtedly celebrate the wedding night of their captain. Right now he was thinking about what it would be like in their bedroom, with Liana beside him in the darkness, listening to the outer blast of gunshots, banjo playing, and stones clattering on the roof, accompanied by Portuguese songs and shouts of congratulations.

The first glimmer of dawn was in the eastern sky, but the valley was still dark. The stockade was shroud in silent. There was no one in sight, or a sign that anyone had been disturbed by the uproar on the hill.

"Looks like the guards could use some discipline," mumbled Dominique.

Then, as the camels splashed into the lake, shots rang out from the stockade. Bullets struck branches over their heads.

"Hold your fire!" Dominique yelled. "This is Dominique de Salvo and Mario Goalie."

A low babble of many voices flowed along the rifle platform. The station wasn't unguarded; it sounded as if every man in the settlement was up and armed. Above this unexpected chatter rose Antonio's angry bellow: "Who fired that shot? You have been told not to shoot 'til you see whom you're shooting at. Come on in Dominique."

"After we put the camels away."

"No. Bring them in here," shouted Antonio.

The gate swung open. It was still too dark to see much, but Dominique could tell everyone in the settlement station was wandering around, and all the stock had been driven in. He dismounted, and found Monty beside him.

"Did you hear that yelling in the jungle?" he asked.

"That was us," explained Mario. "We were scaring' a heathen before he could scare us."

"They must be here already," said Monty cheerfully.

"Who?" asked Dominique?

"Come. Talk to Legacy," said Monty. "He knows more than I do. I've been helping Antonio drive into the stock. Legacy's in Antonio's kitchen."

All around them were huddling, whispering groups of women and children. On the platform above, barely visible in the dark, loomed heads and shoulders of the men of the settlement lining the platform. The lantern in the kitchen flickered, by contrast to the outer darkness casting a glare of light. Diesel, and Shameless were lifting old Rosario from the floor, and Carla was shoving a mattress under him. Rosario lay limp, breathing heavily. Diesel dragged the mattress with old Rosario on it, into the adjoining room.

"Good to see you back," said Legacy to Dominique. "Old Rosario's not hurt, just tired. He ran nearly fifty miles without stopping, that's quite an endeavor for a man his age. His heart skipped a few beats a second ago, Diesel said its ticking normal again. Just before he collapsed Rosario warned us to get ready for what's coming. Earlier today he decided to visit Torres's Station, to find out if that band of Africans living in the jungle, along Yoruba River had seen anything, he never got to Torres's. The jungle up that way is swarming with angry Africans. By the number of boats, and barges on that part of Lake Tanganyika he said there's over a thousand of them."

"What kind?"

"All kinds, but mainly Lozi, Zulu, Ashanti, and Masai. Quittance, Wagnerian and Mandingo with then?"

"Fifty or more marching across a meadow."

Here again, as at Figueroa Station, were echoes from another world, this time echoes that thundered and reechoed. He imagined warriors leaping, bending, twisting, and dancing, and saluting their Chiefs. This seen was familiar, but on this occasion, many Chiefs. He could feel the earth trembling from the thunder of drums. He could see warriors thrusting their shields forward, and others waving their clubs and violently thrusting their spears into the earth. This familiar image of jungle warfare haunted him. "That's bad, mighty bad," he said. "Means the whole thing was planned in Elephant Falls. Could be why they're coming' to Congo Basin is because they can count on King Babysit Masai warriors to keep Novas and his army penned down on the Zambezi River."

"I'm no judge of African tactics," said Legacy. "If they are operating according to a military plan, they wouldn't be coming this way. They'll head for Port Eden Ton to cut Novas completely off from Congo Basin. "

"Some of them came this way," said Monty. "Dominique and Mario ran across at least one of them not to long ago in the jungle."

"That doesn't tell us much," said Dominique. "If they have crossed the Yoruba with a army as big as Rosario says, they'll send spies over the mountain to keep track of what we are doing'."

Antonio broke in, excitedly. "Let them come. Most of our men can hit a moving target, with one shot. We have plenty of maize and meat, water and gunpowder. We can hold them off, we'll make them suffer every minute they attack this settlement."

"We'll keep them out," said Dominique. "If we can't we'll be the first Portuguese stockade that had to surrender. We have other people to think about. We have to find out how strong they are and which way they're moving. We can't just sit here waiting for them to come. They could be heading the other way to Flamingo Grove or Rotshidzwa, or even to Port Eden Ton."

Legacy was listening; his eyes became fixed, and watchful. "That's true, but our first duty is to protect this settlement?"

"It's every settler's first duty to make sure he protects his settlement first," said Dominique. 'But that is only a small part of building a new nation. According to what Rosario saw, this is more than just a big raiding party. You don't need a thousand warriors to steal livestock, and kill a few settlers. It could be they are trying to run all of us out of Africa. That's what they have been talking about in Elephant Falls for the last couple of years. Now they think they can do it. No settlement can withstand that kind of attack forever. We have to help each other. We have to know where they are, and which direction they're moving. We need to bring all of our people together, from every settlement at once, and run those warriors back across the river. The only way to find that out is for somebody to go out and look for them, and make sure that the news has gotten to other settlements. Mario and I will do that." All three brothers were staring at him.

"The news must have spread to other settlements already," said Legacy.

"We don't know that," said Dominique. "Torres's Settlement Station could have been attacked before they knew what was happening. Thanks to old Rosario's run we may be the first to hear anything about it. We have to find out for ourselves whether or not they are coming this way, and find it out in time for us to send for help."

"How long will you be gone, presuming you're able to

get back?" asked Antonio.

"Sometime tomorrow before midnight."

"I can see the advantage in sending out scouts, all right," stated Monty. "But you're our commanding officer, and Mario's our second most experienced man, send someone else."

"We haven't got anybody else, but Rosario, who can get anywhere near them. If they got close enough to see anything, they wouldn't know what to look for."

"Come in where you can hear this, Liana," said Legacy, looking beyond past Dominique. "It concerns you as much as anybody."

Dominique turned and saw Liana in the open doorway. She must have left her bed without pausing longer than to throw on a blue robe; in her haste she had forgotten one of her slippers, because one of her feet was bare. Her eyes were wide and teary; her pale face looked even whiter because of the arrangement of her hair dangling above her shoulders. With every step she took forward into the flickering light she looked too him even more beautiful.

Antonio nudged Dominique and whispered loudly: "Since the first alarm she has been up on the rifle platform watching, and listening, because she knew you were due back."

Liana moved slowly towards Dominique until they were standing face to face, confronting him, her questioning gaze fixed on his face. As always, when she was near him his only impulse was to hold her. He reached out but she pushed his hands away, angrily.

"*Why do you have to go?*" she demanded. "*Why?*"

So unlike her usual self-control Dominique was shocked by her coldness, before he could answer her brothers hastily took upon themselves the burden of trying to make her understand. "Somebody has to," said Legacy. "Nobody else can do it."

"Old Rosario's the only other man who could," said Antonio. "Look at him! He'll be worn out for perhaps a week."

"It's Dominique's duty," said Monty. "You know that."

"I don't," she shouted. "His place is here, you know that, you know he should be here."

"You were outside the door listening before you came in," said Legacy. "You heard what he said, didn't you?"

Yolanda The Enchantress

"I heard everything, and I saw how anxious he was to take the whole war on his shoulders; but I didn't hear a good enough reason. What makes him think he has to be the one to go?"

Monty turned to Dominique to explain. "Liana is singing a familiar tune, she's afraid. She has always been afraid." She thinks her brothers welcomed every excuse to rush off to war. What I think. It appears that she had even less patience with you, her future husband."

"No." said Carla sharply. "That is not what she means."

"He knows it isn't," said Liana. "Dominique knows it."

"I know how to fight Africans," said Dominique stubbornly. "I know how to do that better than any of you. I know what I should do. As long as I'm in control of the militia, no one will make decisions for me."

He looked down into her upturned face. Her eyes met his, she was no longer angry. She was making a silent appeal meant only for him. A button on her robe had fallen away from her throat revealing the swell of her bosoms, but when she raised her hand it was not to button it, but to brush back her hair. She was offering herself to him, silently begging, pleading, and pleading for him to stay with her. He understood. Tonight, she would have come to him, in that blue robe with her hair falling over her shoulders. Her eyes were glassy as the last gleam of lamplight slowly dimmed, before Carla blew it out. She could have been lying in Dominique's arms in bed tonight listening in the darkness to the singing of happy settlers.

Instead, tonight he would be miles away, creeping through another kind of darkness. Listening for a different kind of turmoil, accompanied by the sound of war drums. The sound of a single snapping twig meant, approaching danger, enemies approaching, not of a friend, but a mortal enemies. He was filled with resentment of this sudden unpredictable turn in his life. He didn't want to leave her. He wanted to stay with her, but a strange force was seizing him filled with excitement. He was being controlled by an urgent since of duty to rush away into another kind of darkness. His mind and thoughts were already leading him in the direction of that danger, with which he would confront before this time tomorrow.

L. A. Johnson Jr.

"I have to go," he said.

She turned away from him abruptly, walked to a chair and sat on it with her back to him. Carla placed a comforting hand on her shoulder; Dominique wasn't as sympathetic towards her. His main impulse at the   moment was a growing irritation with her, to use a time like this as an excuse for a display of female pride. Crystal came running in and stared with concern from one face to another.

"Dominique has to go," explained Carla.

"No, oh no," cried Crystal unconvinced. "You can't, Dominique. You can't! Not today."

"Can you think of a way to persuade the Masai, or Zulu to wait until after the wedding," said Monty.

Monty drew Crystal against him, and began stroking her hair soothingly, shaking his head slightly, warning her not to say anything more. Then he was startled by something she said, in her expression as she looked up at him. Though she hadn't been in the room she had the same feelings as Carla, there was something the women knew, and there men didn't know. Monty looked at Dominique, his eyes narrowing, forming vague conclusions. Legacy and Antonio were watching Monty's, suddenly stiffen. These Gomez brothers were able to share each other's thoughts without the need of words.

"If you must go," stated Liana harshly, without turning around, "go now!"

Dominique was beginning to understand. They weren't objecting to his going but to his eagerness to go, as though in some way he was leaving her. They thought he was giving her far less than she deserved. More than that, he wasn't respecting her wishes. His irritation changed to annoyance and then into anger. He couldn't win. There was no winning. Wars don't start and stop to suit the whims of the Gomez family.

"Legacy, you're in charge while I'm away," he said. "Turn the stock out to pasture during the day to save maize. Send scouts out four or five miles every morning and evening. When Rosario feels better, let him range farther depending on how well he can get around. Post six men in each mill. Keep everybody alert every second as if you're expecting a battalion of angry African's to be coming at you any minute. Send a man to

Yolanda The Enchantress

Nova Gala to tell Rosario's story. They may send you some help, but you don't need help to hold this stockade, but you could use a few men that know their way around the jungle."

"I accept your instructions my captain," said Legacy, very formally. "I also, I completely agree with them."

Dominique picked up his rifle, which he had leaned against the wall when he came in. He turned to face the Gomez's once more. He paused a second. Liana didn't turn around. No changes of expression came over any of their faces. He went out. It was light enough now to see clearly, horses, camels, and elephants. People were standing in the open square, and sitting between rows of houses. On the platform riflemen could see a greater distance, with the coming light. They were lowering their rifles beginning to relax, and talking in low excited tones with friends and neighbors. There was no sign of an enemy.

Mario was not in sight. The moment he heard about Old Rosario's dash he knew what had to be done. It was only natural for him to hurry home to break the news to Cindy. Dominique headed for the lumberyard. The stockade gate opened for him, and quickly closed behind him, he heard the pounding of bare feet, and he turned and saw Liana dashing towards him. She threw herself into his arms, and clung to him passionately.

"Oh Dominique, my love," she cried. "I'm so stupid. I'm always doing things to make you hate me. I know you have to go." She leaned back to look up at him, tears streaming down her face; still she was laughing, and flaunting her usual, unyielding self-control. "Come back to me, more than that, you have to want to come back, you have too. I have to believe you will. We can accomplish so much you and I. We can't throw our love away, no matter how stupid I act or how impatient I get with you being so slow to understand what *I've* been trying to say."

While you're away please don't think of me as a woman that is spoil, someone that has to get her way; I'm not like that. Think of me as I am." She took one of his hands and guided it beneath the opening of her robe, and pressed it against her breast. "Think of me like this." Her low laughter and smile looked genuine now, but insulting. "Don't think of me so often, that you let some African kill you. Only think of me when you're safe, and relaxing, hurry back."

L. A. Johnson Jr.

The touch of his open hand against the soft warmth of her body made him rise in his pants, and it aroused in him a surge of sensation so strong, it was painful. Glancing over her shoulder he became aware of grinning riflemen looking down from the platform over the gate. He glanced up at them and quickly looked away. When he looked down at Liana he realized that she was angry again.

"I'm making a fool of myself," she whispered.

She pushed him away. His right hand was entangled in her robe and the other was holding his rifle. Before he could grab her she had torn completely away from him and was running back into the stockade. He watched as the gate closed behind her. He should have rushed to overtake her. She deserved the reassurance for which she seemed to need so much, and they both deserved the solace of a more private farewell embrace. It would be unfair to her if she were subjected to another public more painful farewell embrace. To take her into his arms again for one more moment would be a wonderful privilege for him, but not for her. She had chosen to inject something tragic into their separation. She might as well be spared another unhappy separation. He turned walking towards the jungle thinking.

Silva Hernandez came out of the sawmill, rifle ready to fire, he was working his way along the riverbank, peering into open windows, searching behind banana, coconut, and palm trees. Silva was old enough to remember unfriendly Africans on the border of   Eagle Landing, he knew that first light was the time to make sure there were none crawling around, looking for a chance to hide in an unguarded building. The door to the sawmill was barred, but Mario opened it before Dominique knocked on it. Cindy was cooking pancakes pouring maple syrup into a small jug, and stuffing food into Mario's game sack. This was the familiar war ration, one of the many jungle tricks they'd learned from African. A man could carry enough to feed himself for days without his needing to hunt to keep going. She knew Mario was going deep into the jungle. She was biting her lips, and her face looked a little pale, but she was trying to show no outward sign of her anguish. Mario walked over to her and picked up the sacks, she lifted her head staring at Dominique.

"For once," she said, "I'm glad you are as mean as you

262

are, Dominique de Salvo. You're meaner than any African, I've ever seen. If anyone can bring my husband back safe its you."

"Dominique and I, we've been in tight spots before," said Mario with forced enthusiasm. "We'll take care of each other. I'll be back before you clean and cook that shoulder of impala. We're counting on you having it ready and waiting for us."

He leaned over and gave her a playful slap on her behind. She grabbed his wrist and hung on to it so tight that her fingers nearly locked. Backing out of the doorway Dominique turned to face a cheerfully grinning Diesel. Diesel was wearing old scuffed up boots, a black shirt and a wide brimmed hat.

"I'm going with you," he announced.

"No way," said Dominique.

"I'll save you the trouble of stating all your objections," said Diesel. "I know them. You think that I'll be of no use to you. You think I'll be a hindrance. You think you and Mario will have to spend unnecessary time babysitting me, to keep me alive. Nevertheless, I have something to offer too. I don't know much about Africans. I have hunted all my life and I can get around in the jungle without making any more noise than you. If something goes wrong and you get into a fight, three guns are better than two. I can run faster, and farther than either of you. When the time comes to bring the news back three will stand a better chance than two."

"Whatever gave you such a foolish idea?"

"It's not a foolish idea; it's a bit of wisdom. Think, lawyer. Perhaps you seldom stop to think these days, but I have all too often recently been required to think. At any rate, even you can understand that I can't sit at home, and hold Liana's hand while you bravely explore in the jungle. If something happen to you, my friend. My desire and only remaining hope, even that would vanish. Neither she nor I could ever forget that I had not gone with you to confront our enemy's."

"What enemy could you confront with that little shotgun?" said Dominique, pointing at Diesel's custom made short-barreled folding double barrel gun.

"This little shotgun," said Diesel, "may not shoot as far as that long-barrel rifle of yours, but its double barrels are loaded with buckshot's. At any critical moment, such as our getting trapped in a gully at close range, you'll be surprised how many will fall with one blast."

Mario came out, red in the face fumbling with the leather straps on his powder horn, throwing his game sack over his shoulders.

"Let's get going," said Dominique.

Mario looked at Diesel. "He's going with us?"

"That's what he says."

"Are you crazy," remarked Mario, showing no surprise, "that three's a crowd. We might need him if we get trapped, than we'll need another gun."

Dominique set out at an easy trot, the other two following, in single file. He took a short cut through the jungle, down the valley heading north away from Rhino Creek, rushing by coconut trees. Monkeys had abandoned this section of the lake after the settlement was built. For some reason, today, the lake was full of impala's, giraffe's, flamingos, and an occasional aardvark. This morning there were dozens of ostrich's, and zebras on each side of the path. Dominique swung wide of the lake to avoid startling the ostrich's; he didn't want to send them into instant flight.

At the estuary where Rhino Creek dumped into the south fork of Lake Tanganyika, he paused to survey the jungle and hills across the lake, and talked to Mario. "According to Rosario they came up Lake Tanganyika in boats. Coming that way they could have been planning to head for the settlements near Flamingo Grove. I think after coming as far as Torres's where Rosario saw them, they would never head east. They wouldn't come down Gorilla Passage to attack our settlement, or Nova Gala. I think we can be fairly certain that if they're coming through the jungle, they'll be on the other side."

"You can never be sure about Africans," stated Mario. "They don't think like we do, but you're right about straying' on this side. If we don't run into them, sooner or later perhaps we'll stumble on their campsite, and if their tracks circle to the east we can get back to the settlement before they can get there."

Diesel had no comment to offer while listening to the brief discussions of men acquainted with the many secrets and mysteries of the jungle. He listened closely to every   word and his eyes brightened with interest. Heading north, along the western slope of the valley approaching the south fork, Dominique followed the crest of the ridge, where ancient rhino trails made going easier. The height gave them glimpses of distant sections of jungle across which they looked for smoke, or the unusual behavior of animals in open meadows. They ran with long smooth strides. Their body's leaning slightly forward glancing, scanning constantly the ground, and to the limits of the horizon, permitting nothing to escape their attention. They stopped, and examine a deadly black mamba snakes slivering tracks in the grass, and studied the sudden flight of vultures, just, over the ridge beyond the lake.

No warning signs appeared as they raced on mile after mile. As they ran, their eyes were constantly watchful. Dominique's thoughts kept drifting back to his parting with Liana. He might have handled the situation better. A woman often became emotional when her man is suddenly snatched away from her, and because it was her wedding day, that had made it worst. He should be glad that she took it hard, but Carla and Crystal had acted just as foolish, even the Gomez men. Others too. Cindy called him mean. That was because of the way he handled Yolanda, but there was no other way to deal with her.

Perhaps, Cindy was right. For more than a month Yolanda had been with him every day, nearly every minute. He had gotten to know her better than most men would ever know their wives; because he had to think all the time about everything she said or did. When she disappeared behind those bushes he felt empty. He stopped as suddenly as if he had run into an invisible wall stretched across the trail. In the path at his feet were prints of a gazelle, which had been galloping along peacefully, after watering at the lake a mile or so back. The tracks revealed that the animal had come to a sudden stop. He had stood here without motion for a few seconds and then, wheeled, and dashed down the slope to the west.

He could have seen no more than Dominique could see now through the thick wall of shrubbery. Some sudden sound or scent had spooked him. There was something, down the slope towards the lake that had scared him, whatever it was, sent him into instant flight. Whatever it was could be near or far, because the wind was gusting in all directions.

Mario came alongside, and took one look, grinned at Dominique and glanced down at his rifle. Signaling Diesel to keep a few paces back, Dominique turned from the rhino trail and rushed down the eastern slope.

The three men started running. This was no time to be cautious. They had come out to find unfriendly people; the sooner they found some they would know what they had come out to learn. New energy and life suddenly flowed back into Dominique. He was aware of the faintest breeze against his face. His senses sharpened no sound was to indistinguishable or so faint that his ears didn't pick it up. His eyes spotted the slightest tremble of the most distant leaf.

Mario moved to the right where he could see behind trees as Dominique approached. Dominique was likewise watching the thicket in front of Mario. They depended on each others keen eyes and ears for their protection. Their tenseness and sharp sense's mounted with caution, and excitement. When you get right down to the truth there is no excitement you can share with anybody else equal to what you felt when you know your life is in the hands of another person. Nothing heightens the senses on a man like danger.

Chapter 16
Warn Our People

Out of the corner of his eyes, Dominique caught a glimpse of Mario's face. Mario was as watchful, and as tense as a lion hunting his prey, beneath the tenseness was patience and self-control. He had left behind a devoted wife and a lovely home. He should have never come, he should be getting off work around this time of day, dashing for the fishing hole behind his house. There came a peaceful feeling over him, he could be shot any minute, but this minute he could breathe easily, that was when he relaxed. He felt as if he had shaken off a heavy burden. It was like being a soldier again. From that moment every step he took was timed by the beating of a silent drum. He

Yolanda The Enchantress

was free as only a warrior could be.

Just ahead, a coconut tree had fallen carrying with it a number of smaller trees. The massive entanglement of trees and outstretched branches, covered with vines were an ideal spot for an ambush. Dominique and Mario stopped and approached with caution. First one and then the other, watched, rifle ready, one hiding behind a tree while the other moved closer. Diesel hung back and watched, but all their caution and wariness was unnecessary.

The huge pile of brush was empty, for miles beyond stretched a thicker jungle. Ahead stood, a mile-wide grove of fallen trees with straight branches, rising from an untamed jungle floor, on which there was no trace of undergrowth. Still in some sections you could see through the jungle as far as you could see across open grassland.

"Could be," said Mario, "that gazelle, imagined danger like you imagined that African last night."

Diesel laughed. Dominique swore. "It was necessary to search this area before they went further." It took over an hour's circling before they located the first footprint, and then another hour to read signs left by Lozi, and Zulu warriors who had reached the west bank of Lake Tanganyika by boats. The warriors had climbed to the top of the ridge, and returned to their boats, and pushed off again. The mission of these Africans had been to examine the trails west of Lake Tanganyika. Two lost hours was a huge price to pay to learn no more than that. They spot ted more clued along the shore of the lake revealing that the main war party was somewhere to the north, moving west. If they were heading for Rhino Creek they would have sent more scouts out this way and kept them out.

The three men headed north. The silent, pounding drums were timing Dominique strides, but it only pounded. It didn't show the way. The marshland bordering the lake where the next tributary emptied into the south fork was impassable. They discovered this after spending hours trying to find a way through. They were forced to retreat, to take a different route making a wider circle on higher ground. Returning to the course they had decided not to explore, they came upon an expanse of burned land. Beyond new undergrowth was so thick it nearly denied them passage, and the canopy above was so thick, they couldn't see the sky, in any direction.

"Might as well be traveling with sacks over our heads," grumbled Mario. "If our enemy's were camped twenty feet ahead we would stumble into their camp."

"Old Rosario knew his way around patches of thick jungle like this," said Dominique. "You have been at the settlement for months. Ever talked to him about the general lay of the land up this way?"

"Rosario, doesn't talked much," said Mario. "I haven't had time to do much more than work, and when I was off, I was running' back and forth looking after you."

They pushed their way through entangled bushes and vines. They traveled nearer the lake seeking easier going, but instead they found walls of cane and bam boo growing in the lake, that was even worst. With the gradual widening of the lake, and its low ridges, they traveled further west. They had traveled miles out of the way, searching for more open country. The afternoon was blistering hot. The canopy above their heads blocked every breeze of air. They tramped persistently and stubbornly on, Dominique and then Mario taking turns leading the way. They were making paths by throwing their weight forward, or crawling when necessary. Hours went by, their lack of progress made them seem even longer.

"Give me a crack at leading for a while," asked Diesel. "You have been doing all the work."

The others grunted and stepped aside, mopping their faces. Diesel began chopping and leading the way. Twenty minutes later, his blade struck a low flat vine-covered stone, high enough to allow them to stand on, to see over the bushes. The three stepped up onto the stone. The whole valley to the north was exposed to their view. In Dominique's head the silent drumbeat seemed accelerate to a sudden threatening unpredictable, emotional roll. Fifteen miles or less to the north in the direction of Torres's Station, hundreds of vultures were chirping hovering and circling in the sky.

"Something is dead," said Mario. "A lot of some-thing."

Diesel was watching the grim faces of the two men, seeking a clue to their conclusion, "The Africans could have suf fered heavy losses," he suggested.

"Don't know." said Mario, "I hope eight or nine hundred of them died last night, from some contagious disease."

"If they had taken the station they would have burned it, there would be smoke?"

"Vultures wouldn't be circling over head," said Mario.

"Africans carry off their dead," said Dominique.

Recording the direction and approximate distance across the intervening valley, Dominique led the way back into the bushes and down the slope. At the foot they came to the end of the brush. They entered the beginning of giant plants of cane, and bamboo, which now extended all the way across the lake bottom. The new green growth was nearly as thick as the bush. The old dry stalks that had been killed by last winter's cold weather were as hard as a stone, and rattled like a baby's rattler when brushed against it.

"We should fire a shot now and then," said Mario. "So every African within fifteen miles will know we're coming."

"Doesn't matter," said Dominique, pushing his way between stalks as big and rigid as a heavy fence-post. "At the rate we're going, it will be tomorrow before we get close enough for anyone to hear a shot."

Despite the fact that it was now dark, they could tell the direction they were heading by glancing up at the stars. Sars were visible through swaying tops of towering bamboo, and the thick canopy above. They could tell they were making little progress. Now approaching an old rhino path that led to the lake, they followed it. On the other side the going might be better. It couldn't be worst. At the waters edge they crouched and listened. Waves and curls of mist were rising from the dark water. Not a sound other than thrashing of waves broke the stillness. Now even jungle animals seemed to have retreated from the quiet jungle. They decided to build a raft to ferry their weapons, ammunition and food sack, to the other bank.

They found the bamboo was much thicker, this side was worse. The jungle floor on this side was flatter, and the growth was wilder and thicker, but they didn't return to the other side of the lake. Torres's Settlement Station was on this side. They pushed on northward making as little noise as they could. Sooner or later they were bound to come out in a cleared valley surrounding the settlement station. By midnight Dominique estimated, they had traveled only half the distance between the flat rock from which they had seen the circling vultures, and the valley in the distance. The next time he glanced up he realized the difficulties under which they had been laboring were being multiplied many times over. The canopy of mist was thickening. A thick blanket of fog had formed over the top of the trees blocking out the stars, they were tramping around wild maze, giant plants, and bamboo. They were guessing the direction in which they were trying to go.

To follow the shoreline of the lake was no good, because the lake twisted and turned. To follow its course would add miles to the distance they had to travel. Already they could barely hope to arrive by dawn. Occasionally they crossed elephant or hippo trails running through the thicket, but any one of them was as likely to lead in one direction as another. After hours of struggling Dominique was certain that they were headed south instead of north. They plunged on.

"We are traveling in circles," said Mario. "Chances are we're not going south, just in circles. That's what people do when they're lost."

"We have to keep moving," insisted Dominique. "Even if we don't come out where we want. We can't just sit and wait for daylight."

"Right," said Mario. "Let's keep acting' like we're going somewhere. Diesel came along to watch how a couple of old soldiers like us get around in the jungle. You think he doesn't know we're lost?"

Diesel cleared his throat. "Would a compass be of any use?"

"Yep," said Dominique. He glanced at Diesel. "You have one!"

"Of course," admitted Diesel. "You acted like you didn't need my help. I bought it with me because I knew I'd need it, if I got separated from you."

"First the rock, now a compass," stated Mario.

They knelt around Diesel's compass. Dominique struck a spark from his flint, while blowing on the ignited wick until they

Yolanda The Enchantress

could see the quivering needle. They walked nearly a hundred yards west, and repeated the procedure. They were traveling no faster, now they were moving in the right direction.

An hour went by. There was no change in the thickness of the bamboo, or the makeup of the lakes bottom. They cut down clusters of cane and bamboo. They walked in the swamp, struggling, forcing their legs forward, and brushing against rubbery growth poking out from stalks. They were on slippery, swampy ground, soon long dawn would break, and time was running out. Suddenly Mario hissed. All paused. The fog had settled just above the ground. Mario was so close to Dominique, his shirtsleeve touched Dominique's shoulder, but he couldn't see him.

"Don't hear anything," whispered Dominique.

"Me neither," replied Mario. "I smell something."

He took a few slow cautious steps forward, sniffing at the warm moist air, and then paused again.

"Give me some light."

Dominique crouched beside Mario and blew on the smoldering wick. The object on the ground was the reason for Mario's intense interest, became visible.

"Cow dung," murmured Mario with satisfaction. "Never expected to see some I'd like."

Delighted by the proof that they were near the grazing range of the settlement, they pushed on, moving slowly and silently. The bamboo began to open up. They had reached an area that had been heavily grazed by feeding stock. Mario paused, sniffing again. Dominique too, was aware of the disgusting odor in the heavy wet air. At first this smell was elusive, but still of fensive. They kept moving. There was another scent that was faint, and even more disgusting. It was the odor of decaying flesh. Suddenly there was rustling in the bushes, ahead, followed by swishing. The beating of wings drove the stale air against their faces.

Disturbed by the approaching men, the vultures rose from their feeding. The three men crept forward, and huddled together on the ground.

"A goat," Diesel whispered, relieved.

This was grass eaten by domesticated animals, now it

271

was only short stalks. They could see nothing through the surrounding fog, but they could feel their feet sinking into plowed earth. They were at the edge of a maize-field. The men crouched and listened for minutes, no sound warned them of what might lie ahead. Mario nudged Dominique. He looked up. The fog overhead was becoming, various, shades of gray. Daylight was about to break. They crept on into the maize-field. They were searching for cover, a spot from which they could see what was beyond the maize. The fog slowly melted enough for them to see shapes and blurry outlines of each other.

Some of the maize had been trampled as if stock had been driven back and forth through it. The odor of charred timbers, mingled with the heavy stench of death. The vanishing fog was concealing a nightmarish horror that would soon be revealed. There was another rustle ahead. Shadowy-winged shapes rose into the air, flapping their wings awkwardly. The sharp smell of soured milk mingled with a heavier, stronger unpleasant odor of decaying flesh. They saw the carcass of another cow; this one was covered with spears and arrows.

There were more carcasses scattered through rows of maize, hyenas and lions were feeding by the dozens. The men knew the risk of continuing, could startle the feeding predators into sudden flight that would reveal their approach. Despite that it was normal for animals to retreat, and return. After a night of gorging the hungry vultures had attracted leopards, and other predators. They crept around the carcass of a camel that had been killed with spears, and then came to an instant stop. They had reached the edge of the maize field. The three men lay flat behind the last row of maize and listened. The frightening, silence continued.

The fog vanished as suddenly as if a curtain had been drawn aside, not more than forty feet away there was a woodpile, and beyond it a fence. Across the woodpile was sprawled the body of a woman, scalping had left her only fringes of bloody gray hair. Her garments had been torn from her, exposing her naked body.

Beside the fence lay the bodies of three young children, two girls and a boy. They had been killed by being swung, and slammed into the woodpile. Their heads had been crush. Several heads had been cut off of bodies, and placed upon a huge stone, all waiting to be mounted on bamboo poles.

"Every now and then," whispered Mario, "something happens that makes you hate people."

Diesel was observing and examining the bodies from a distance, with a professional eye. "Those children appear to have been dead probably, two days," he said. "Perhaps a few hours more or less considering the heat. The woman, they kept her alive. They broke her arms and legs and raped her. When they finished, they threw her on the logs. She died about an hour ago."

Watching the fog drift towards the lake Dominique stood up behind a cluster of maize-stalks to scan the area. The whole area around the settlement was coming into view. The building and stockade were heaps of ashes. The number of dead cattle scattered about was in the hundreds. More fearfully revealing was the arrangement of naked people; their bodies were mangled and mutilated. Torres was capable of defending itself; it was a big prosperous settlement. There were corpses of men, women and children. All had suffered more grievous wounds than had been required to end their life. Their twisted limbs suggested they had been broken in ways, that death itself had bought no relief from their agony.

Nothing moved among rows of dead, except vultures, hyenas, and lions feeding, slowly shifting and ripping huge chunks of flesh from lifeless bodies, moving from one leg to the other. The African's appeared to had gone.

"They must have gotten in the stockade with some kind of trick, most likely at night," muttered Mario. "This was one of the best stockades anywhere, and they had nearly three hundred men. They could have fought off every African between here and Elephant Falls, until their gun powder ran out."

"Whatever the trick-it took all the fight out of them," said Dominique. "They surrendered. Noticed how many were beaten with clubs, and how they're arranged in rows. They were prisoners, and they'd been put in groups, before they were murdered."

"Some of them might be alive," said Diesel. "I'll check them."

273

L. A. Johnson Jr.

"No!" said Dominique sharply. "Stay out of the open. Other settlements in Congo haven't been taken yet. They are the settlements we have to think about, we don't know which way they're heading."

The fog was lifting slowly dissolving with the warmth of the rising sun. Dominique scanned the area looking for a place for them to hide if the need arose. The most interesting features of the area were the mile-long maize-fields and rows of pineapple. Mangrove trees were growing along the riverbank. The maize-fields stretched in a semicircle revealing the ashes of the settlement. Points of the semicircle flowed towards the lake leaving a small strip of open pasture. Beyond the fence and woodpile was a narrow bush covered ravine. The gorge zigzagged and cut a diagonally path across the clearing. Then it-surged south to the river. They went that way.

They could see through the thicket, pineapple, and mangroves trees. Looking over the river, they stood with an air of satisfaction. Dozens of dugout canoes, and huge black and white striped barges, were beached along the west bank. Curls of smoke rose in the jungle beyond, from campfires of warriors left behind to guard the boats. The war party was moving west towards an area where the settlements were thickest. They were heading where an army of settlers could be more rapidly gathered if the alarm were spread in time. Before crossing the river the three men stopped to talk, because they needed to know how many Africans were guarding the boats. Handing his rifle to Mario Dominique climbed an acacia tree. He climbed down the branch of the Acacia tree, until it bent enough to climb onto a branch of a pineapple tree. He pulled himself up into the pineapple tree until he could see over the river, and valley on the other side.

The first Africans he saw were on this side. Fifty or more were sprawled out on the beach lest than a hundred yards up river. Some were on their stomachs, some on their backs, a few in the water; some in such odd positions that for a second he thought they were dead. After taking another look, he realized they were sleeping. Every warrior was wearing Portuguese clothing, some had on w omen's aprons and petticoats. Even from a distance Dominique could see the blood now dried. They

274

had eaten the station's beef, and drank the settler's whiskey, wine, and rum. The excitement of burning the fortress walls had led to a greater excitement. The warriors had slaughtered cattle, which led to the ultimate excitement of murdering, people. Now exhausted by their own excesses, these Africans were not able to march on to new attacks, it would take a day, possibly two, and even then it would be nearly impossible for them to catch up with the main force.

Dominique wondered who was in command of the main force. The mission was too important to have been given to lower chiefs, like Mohammad Sotto, or Kwanzaa Bissau. The command had probably been given to a Mandingo Chief. Whoever he is, his warriors were giving him more trouble than any leader deserved. However he felt about the massacre of prisoners, if he had any kind of military training at all, he had to be disturbed, by the need-less killing of livestock. To manage a number of warriors was a challenging task for any chief. Hundreds of heads of cattle, if kept alive, and driven along on hoof would have fed his army for months.

Keeping the trunk of the tree between him, and the men below, Dominique turned to search the other bank. His grip tightened suddenly on the branch he was holding. A very loud booming, blasting sound came from across the river, it was the the unmistakable boom of a cannon. It came from the direction of Gasper's Settlement, which was nearly ten miles to the west; the booming sound, was followed by the firing of a second cannon. Before the second explosion echoed through the jungle, the three men knew what they had set out to learn. They knew where the enemy was and what they had done, and what they were doing. They knew that for the first time in Congo's history, Africans had cannons. The surrender of Torres's Station was no longer a mystery. The settlers had no choice but to surrender. No stockade of wood can withstand artillery fire. Those same cannons were now attacking Gasper's Station. It, to would surrender, and they will be murdered. Every settlement they attacked would fall, if they waited to be attacked. The only hope was for an alarm to be spread in time for every man to come out from behind his stockade and fight in the open.

Dominique took a second look, he saw another African, this one was awake; he spotted him. He was running about, vigorously kicking his sleeping companions. He kept pointing down the river towards the pineapple tree. Dominique scrambled down to the ground, there was no use wasting words on the cannon shots. The others understood their meaning as well as he did.

"There's about fifty Africans on the other side," he said. "They'll be coming after us in a few minutes. If we get separated, remember this: You, Mario, and you, Diesel, return to Rhino Creek. Tell Legacy to send women and children to Nova Gala, and to get ready to march his men wherever they are needed, when word comes of wherever that is. Tell him whatever happens; don't get trapped in the stockade. I'm going to Gasper's Station, Flamingo Grove and Sea Pen."

Mario and Diesel nodded. Dominique led the way back. They were half the distance up the ravine, when it suddenly became all too apparent that more than one African had seen him. A group of six became visible against the morning sky on the bank just above. Dominique raised his rifle, and according to a long established understanding with Mario, in the event of such a choice of targets, he shot the one on the left, and Mario shot the one on the right. Still four remained. Staring down at the two white men desperately reloading, the Africans understood their advantage. Preparing to attack they lifted their weapons. One had a spear two had bows and arrows, and the other a huge knife. Dominique thought he was going to feel the sharp blade of the spear.

Diesel still a few pace back was hidden from the view of the Ashanti warriors by bushes. The sudden book of his double barrel shot gun surprised Dominique almost as much as it did the Ashanti warriors. Two of them dropped in there tracks. The other two doubled up falling forward into the ravine. With the butt of his rifle, Dominique killed the one that had fallen near his feet. Before Mario plunged his knife into the last one, the warrior had raised his arm and threw his knife. Dominique climbed to the top of the gully and looked towards the river. The Africans that were on the other side of the river hadn't reached the pineapple trees. He continued reloading and slid down into the ravine. Mario was standing reloading, but Diesel was sitting down reaching for his shotgun.

"Come on," urged Dominique. "We have time, and none to waste."

"Diesel's been hit," said Mario.

Diesel struggled to his feet, keeping all of his weight on one leg. The other was drenched with blood; the knife was in his leg.

"How bad?" Dominique demanded. "Kneecap's smashed, said Diesel, as calmly as if he were diagnosing a patient's injury. "I can put a little weight on it as long as I keep it straight but I can't bend it." He sat down with the leg sticking out with his shotgun across his lap.

"You and Mario better get going. What you have to do is too important to waist time fooling with me."

"We didn't bring you along to tell us what to do," said Dominique. "You will do as I say, exactly what I say. Don't argue. Mario and I will hold them off for a while from here. Walk as fast as you can, climb up the ravine, crawl through the maize-field. When you've had enough time to reach the bamboo, we'll run and catch up. Then we will worry about what to do next."

"Yes, my captain," said Diesel with a conciliatory grin. He struggled to his feet again, and handed Mario his shotgun. "This will slow me down." Grabbing bushes Diesel hobbled up the ravine. Dominique and Mario scrambled to the top of the gully and saw three Zulu warriors running down the riverbank. They were just about the right distant to hit a moving target. Two dropped as the rifles cracked, and the third dashed into the jungle. There was a sudden mix of signal whistles, and animal calls all along the edge of the jungle, but the recently awakened Ashanti warriors remained for the moment none too aggressive. They were more concerned with telling one another what to do. Dominique shot at a moving bush, and heard a yell of pain. Mario shot into the same tree Dominique had climbed, and a warrior fell headfirst.

"Some of them are coming up the ravine," said Dominique.

This advance was protected from any direct rifle shot by a curve in the lower ravine.

"Just what I've been waiting' for," said Mario.

L. A. Johnson Jr.

He picked up Diesel's shotgun and aimed it high. After a moment of frowning, and careful study, and several thoughtful changes in the angle before firing he squeezed the trigger. The blast of buckshot went just far enough to scatter before plunging down into the lower ravine. Yells of outrage, mingled with susprise burst from the Africans, and the waving brush tops indicated the haste with which they were retreating.

"That's a hell of a gun," said Mario, holding the shotgun fondly.

"Let's get out of here," said Dominique. "Diesel's had enough time to get quite a ways; if we wait too much longer they'll be entering the maize-field."

They crawled up the ravine to the end. Dominique glanced back. The African warriors hadn't come out of the jungle. They were resting before making the short dash past the woodpile when Mario grabbed Dominique's arm. "Look." Diesel was hobbling out of the northern section of the maize-field into the open field beyond the ruins of the station. He had not only taken an opposite route to the one he had been ordered to take, he was deliberately heading towards the warriors in the jungle, and he knew exactly what he was doing. He was holding up his hands to show he was offering himself as their prisoner. Dominique jumped to his feet.

"You fool," he yelled. "Get back. Don't do that, run."

"You run," yelled Diesel in reply. He had never sounded more cheerful. "Don't argue with me. It is too late now for you to do anything except what you should be doing. Get out of here, go, and warn our people."

Dozens of Yoruba warriors were running out excitedly surrounding Diesel, there was nothing Mario or Dominique could do.

"Don't argue, he says," whispered Dominique. "He certainly made sure we had no chance to argue. He made up his mind the minute he got hit."

"He's a good man," stated Mario. He's as puzzling as his little shotgun. Two times in a row he saved our life."

"He was thinking about saving more lives, than our," said Dominique. "There's nothing we can do. Well, let's get out of here, and fast, too."

278

Yolanda The Enchantress

At the end of the maize-field they paused.

"I'm circling to the north here, I'll have a better chance to get around the war party at Gasper's that way. Tell Legacy I'll send word to him about what's going on when I get to Sea Pen."

"Be careful," said Mario. "Don't worry about anything. I'll look after Liana, same as I will Cindy."

Dominique stared away. The thought of Liana was as far removed from him as if she were still in Eagle Landing, as she had seemed before he left Mozambique. Everything else in his past life seemed that far away. All he could think about was what had happened at Torres's, and what was happening to Diesel. And what would happen at Gaspers before the day was over. The pounding drum was alive in side him now. He swam the river and climbed out north of Gasper's Station. Occasionally yells in pain drifted towards him, from a distance, but there were no cannons fired since those first two shots. That must have been all that was needed to bring surrender. By now people there were beginning to suffer. They were enduring the same kind of needless brutality as people had at Torres.

Beyond Gasper's, he headed for Chimpanzee Trail, which stretched across northern Congo, from Lake Tanganyika on the main Sahara River, to Chimpanzee Valley then to Congo River. Thousands of years of elephant migrations had trampled the soil down to the underlying limestone. In places the hard wide road was about seventy-five yards wide. From the shelter of the jungle's edge Dominique scanned the wide pathway for a moment. Then he stepped out into the open, and started running. Ordinarily in traveling through the wilderness he would have never exposed himself in a manner so dangerous. He knew there was a far greater chance of him encountering Africans now that he was west of their main force. He knew they had sent out scouts to watch the trail to prevent news of their advance from reaching the settlement before them. Still he stayed to the road where he could travel much faster.

Taking to the jungle only occasionally, when approaching a stream crossing, or a hilltop. On hilltops or hiding in bushes near a stream, were places scouts would probably be hiding. Another dangerous place was when crossing expanses of grasslands he could be seen from a distance. An hour passed, a second and then a third. He noticed that jungle animals seem nervous, but not unusually disturbed. This is a big country he kept telling himself, no matter how many Africans were trying to watch the trail, one man on foot could travel a long way's without encountering any of them. He decided not to go south to Zebra Valley Settlement. That was the most exposed settlement, after Gasper's; the Africans were surely preventing any approach. Even if he were lucky enough to get through to the station he wouldn't be able to get out again. His news was too important to the rest of Congo to take that risk. He kept to the road until he knew he was north of Flamingo Grove, now running down an old rhino trail.

The country was more open now, and it was more difficult to keep within reach of patches of jungle. Finally a mile wide belt of grassland stretched south. He had to cross it. He stopped to take a deep breath and then started. Lifting his knees high to be lest impeded by the tall grass, crushing the grass he ran as fast as he could. He was half way across when the first Hausa camel-man appeared over a ridge to his left. It was too late to hide in the tall grass, because the African had seen him and was blowing a piercing blast on his war whistle. More mounted Hausa galloped over the ridge, pulled up for a moment alongside the first and yelled with satisfaction at sight of a white man stranded in the open. Whooping and jerking their dancing mounts into a gallop, they swept down towards him; leaning forward avoiding their camels' bouncing necks, continuing to yell.

Dominique turned and dashed back towards the woods he had left; leaping, running, zigzagging like a fleeing gazelle avoiding spears and arrows. They started shooting, but their marksmanship was off because of the jolting of their camels, luckily he was not hit. They veered to the right when they saw where he was heading, and raced to cut him off from the jungle. Calling upon deep-seated stores of reserved energy, he found a final burst of speed, and entered the shelter of the trees by a margin so narrow he could hear the swish of arrows and spears whirling past. When he entered the jungle he could move faster, with more freedom on foot than they could on camels. They wheeled back into the open, spreading out encircling the thicket.

Yolanda The Enchantress

Since he had foreseen this, instead of trying to hide, he dashed towards an adjoining meadow. While the Hausa warriors were retrieve their spears, and loading their bows, Dominique dashed into another section of woods unseen. While the Hausa were searching the adjoining section, he crawled into a brush-covered ravine. He entered another section of the woods, where he had more room to hide and maneuver.

The warriors had guessed his plan to make a dash for Flamingo Grove. All but two fanned out across the open country to the south, to keep him from going in that direction. Two dismounted, and started tracking him. The deadly search continued for hours, he was forced to travel farther west. It was after noon before he was certant he had escaped, he headed south again. He had traveled miles in the opposite direction, and he had lost three precious hours. He was north of Flamingo Grove. Furthermore, once freed of the excitement of escaping, he began to realize how fast he was tiring. He had twenty miles to go he walked slower to save his strength, seting a pace to which he felt he could keep until he got there.

An hour went by without a new alarm, now there were signs of human use on the trails. There were a number of marked trees, which had been marked claiming the land. There were groves of maple trees that had been tapped; he was approaching the outskirts of Flamingo Grove. Then his luck, which had taken an unpleasant turn when he was spotted by that Hausa camelmen, took almost as sudden a turn the other way. He saw another man riding a camel, this man was white, and the man was riding out of a marsh with a string of bamboo traps rattling, and jangling. He was old, with a nappy white beard. His beard was so long it touched his camel's mane. The man was dirty caked with mud and the muscles on his face twitched because of some kind of a nervous disorder. Never had Dominique been so pleased by the sight of another white man. The trapper pulled in his wild-eyed camel and watched Dominique's approach with interest.

"Flamingo Grove, how far?" demanded Dominique.
"Nearly thirty miles."

Dominique reached out steadying himself against the camel. Coming to a stop seemed to take a greater effort than to keep on running. He could barely stand. "Give me your camel,"

L. A. Johnson Jr.

he said.

The old man shook his head patiently. "No sir."

Dominique grabbed the man by his belt, and pulled him from the saddle. The old trapper offered no resistance, nor did he seem to be angry after being handled so roughly.

"I have to have him," said Dominique. "My name is Dominique de Salvo. I'm from that new settlement over on Rhino Creek."

"Shameless Chandler," murmured the old man politely.

"Listen to what I'm saying," demanded Dominique. "I've got to get to Sea Pen as fast as I can to warn them that a war party is in Congo Basin. You can save me a couple of hours, if you take the news to Flamingo Grove. Now listen closely, tell them what I'm telling you. Over a thousand warriors have crossed the south fork of the Sahara. They have taken Torres' and Gasper's. They were able to defeat them easily, *because they have cannons.*"

An unexpected spark of energy appeared in the old mans eyes. "Field guns?"

"Guns big enough to knock down a stockade. Make sure people at Flamingo Grove understand that, and make sure they send the news to Smithfield, and other settlements, too. Take the news to Flamingo Grove. I'm going to Sea Pen to warn them, and get some help for your people here." Shameless glanced up handing Dominique the reins.

"From what you've said there's nothing else, I can do, I've got to let you have him. You'll never make it afoot."

Dominique pulled and struggled until he was sitting in the saddle. Shameless still seemed none too excited by his roll in their common mission. He stepped back, pawing at his beard, looking sadly at his camel.

"His name is Bones, no use calling him one name or another. He's too mean to pay attention to what you call him, but he's a good animal. When you get to Sea Pen, if you make it, leave him with George Hazelnut, he's married to one of my daughters."

"Flamingo Grove," Dominique reminded him. "Remember? That's where you're going." He pulled Bones around and got him started.

282

Yolanda The Enchantress

Shameless called after him. "If Bones stops or lay down under you, bite his left ear, the left ear, remember, the left ear. You can chew the other off and eat it for dinner; he'll pay no attention, at all."

"Flamingo Grove," Dominique yelled.

Bones set off at a clumsy awkward gallop. His feet stuck the ground at unexpected intervals. Unless pulled aside with brutal strength he would run head first into the nearest tree rather than go around it. Dominique found the going more demanding than if he had been on foot. He clung tightly to the saddle, and counted the miles. For the first hour Bones hadn't balked once. Then as he approached a narrow stream, after having gathered himself for the leap across, he froze. Dominique was thrown out of the saddle into the water. Climbing back on, Dominique remembered the warning to bite his left ear. He did so. It worked. Bones plunged ahead. He threw up his head vigorously, violently, striking Dominique in the face making his nosebleed so bad that he had to return to the stream to stop the flowing blood with cold water.

Mounting again, Dominique worked Bones into his clumsy gallop and kept on. Dominique was careful to avoid the camels tossing head. Worst than the unpredictable balking was Bones' way of walking down hills. It was with irregular, unexpected, jarring jumps. Then he swerved a little. Dominique wished for another encounter with Hausa warriors, in which Bones would become the target of a warrior's arrow. The advantage in riding Bones. He would had never have had the strength to keep going, without stopping to rest, on foot. Approaching Sea Pen road, Dominique knew his destination was only miles away. Passing travelers on the road every once and a while, gave him a chance to spread the news. Each person to whom he told it, made it that much more certain that the news would be spread widely.

He had little confidence in the old trapper telling his story, and Dominique's confidence in the trapper grew less ever hour he rode Bones. Would the trapper remember what he had been told to say when he got to Flamingo Grove? The ignorance of the threat to Congo made the danger more obvious, it bought Dominique a kind of comfort, and he was determined that Diesel's sacrifice would not be wasted. To make things worst, no one Dominique met on the road had the faintest hint of an African invasion. By nightfall Dominique begun to wonder if he was going to make it. He kept falling asleep and catch ing himself, as he was about to fall from the saddle. Bones, stubborn as ever, seemed to be growing stronger, and galloping on harder than before. Each jarring impact of the camel's hoofs seemed to attack Dominique's nervous system. His mind was as tired as his body. He forgot what he was doing and why he was doing it. What would happen, if he didn't get there in time, or they didn't believe him? What would happen, if he couldn't remember what he had to tell them? He wasn't so sure, even now.

It seemed that whatever he had to say would be said too late. Days must have passed since he swam the river below Torres's. It could have been weeks, or some other season. It could have been some other African conflict that had long since been dealt with. He was becoming more confused. His eyes closed. He sagged forward, clanging on to Bone's mane. This time he didn't catch himself in time. Striking the ground awakened him. He had tied the end of the reins to his wrist so that the camel couldn't go on without him, because he didn't have the strength to climb back on. There was an embankment near by. Bones was profoundly suspicious of it. With much difficulty he edged Bones near enough, and crawled up onto the hill and dropped into the saddle. It was only then that he realized, he was in sight of Sea Pen.

He stared straight ahead not understanding. He was very confused. He thought he was asleep and dreaming what he was seeing. Huts and sheds outside the stockade were in flames. Men with torches were running about setting fire to the others. They were expecting an attack and they were denying the Africans the use of the outbuildings as cover for the assault. That made no sense. They couldn't know here that a war party was coming, because he hadn't told them yet. The gate open, his confusion was multiplied many times. He fell off his camel into the arms of two Africans. Reflections from the flames gleamed on their faces. The mud on their faces was pealing. The men grabbing him were patting him on the back, and calling his name, weren't Africans. They were old friends he hadn't seen since Mozambique. This made the least sense of all. They couldn't be here. He had enough wit left to know that, they were with Novas. They didn't belong here. This is Sea Pen; he knew that because he had struggled so hard to get here.

"You're not Africans," he said, accusingly. "You're Hector Moralize, and, Peter Hernandez."

"Captain de Salvo, the lawyer, he's just as smart as he was before he became a farmer," said Hector to Peter. He grinned at Dominique. "We only look like Africans, at least Peter does. In the section of the jungle we've been traveling through it was much safer."

"We just got in from Fort Novas," explained Peter. "Old Raven Mateo's cousin in Elephant Falls told Novas what was comin' at you Congo Basin folks, so Novas, Hector, and me came to help you."

"Novas is here?" stammered Dominique.

Behind them in the guardhouse, came happy voices from the crowd of men gathering in the town hall. Dominique slipped from the grasp of Hector and Peter. He sat down on the ground saying Novas is here. Novas has come; Novas will take care of everything now. That was a big relief. There couldn't have been a greater relief, than an equally great depression settled over Dominique when he thought about the ignorance of the threat to Congo to most settlers that made the danger even more obvious. But Novas being here gave Dominique a kind of comfort, now more than ever Dominique was determined that Diesel's sacrifice wouldn't be wasted. His own desperate effort to get to this settlement with the news was unnecessary. Foolish perhaps, but now he could sleep.

"Was that Dominique de Salvo I heard?" Novas walked over to the doorway of the guardhouse. "Bring him in."

Hector and Peter picked Dominique up. Inside, twenty or thirty of the most influential men of Sea Pen were lined along the walls. Their eyes were fixed on Novas as if he was the pope and they were his followers. Novas looked odd with his red hair cut low. He had washed off most of the paint, and someone had given him a shirt. Novas glanced at Dominique, sagging between his two friends, revealing the seriousness of his condition.

"You've been traveling hard. Got some news?"

"Only what you already know," mumbled Dominique.

"Goldie, a Mandingo prince, left Elephant Falk with five hundred warriors or more. Mohammad Sotto and three hundred of his warriors joined him a few days ago. They are joining seven or eight hundred Lozi and Zulu warriors in Charka Land. They are heading for Congo Basin, that's all I know. What do you know?

"Has he crossed the Yoruba River already" Dominique pulled away from Peter and Hector and stood. He had something to say, to make a difference. He had for a listener the one man in Africa who would know what to do about it. He spoke softly and clearly, afraid that he might not have the strength to say it again.

"They have been on this side of the Yoruba, nearly a week. They came up Lake Tanganyika in boats and barges. They took Torres's, nearly three days ago. This morning they took Gasper's. I think they are heading for Zebra Valley next. The settlements stations have to surrender on demand, because they have two pieces of field artillery. When you decide what you're going to do, send word to Major Legacy Gomez at Rhino Creek? I promised to give the camel I rode to a man here, a man named, George Hazelnut."

He was starting to fall forward. Novas caught him by the shoulders and helped place him on a bed, he was asleep.

Chapter 17
You're The Hero

Dominique headed north, over the same trail he had traveled so painfully when struggling south with his news, but it was different now. He had a night's rest and he had been loaned a horse. He wasn't alone; Hector and Peter were with him. Other than Mario, they were the men you would want to travel with you in the jungle. Also with him were a dozen young militiamen from Sea Pen. Making the most difference of all, Novas was behind him. The settlers in Congo were aroused and ready to fight. Men were leaving their farms, plantations with huge mansions, and their stockades by the hundreds to join Novas.

Yolanda The Enchantress

"Find Prince Goldie," Novas ordered. "Keep me posted on where he is, and what he is doing. I want to be able to move the moment Figueroa gets here, and those from Nova Gala. I'll hit him so hard; he'll never cross the Yoruba River again."

Dominique rode on, feeling more at peace with him-self than he had been for some time. Not much longer than a year ago he had been set on leaving Novas, at Mozambique, he was willing to stoop to any trick, to get our of the army. Since then he hadn't worried once about returning, but all the time it must had been gnawing inside him to account for him feeling so good about working with Novas again. He had already made up for the time he had taken off. Novas had made a great fuss over the news he had bought and over the effort he had made to bring it. Now, Dominique was in command of the advance guard of Novas' army. With all the Congo settlers for the first time rallying around Novas, a greater blow would be struck than any since the taking of Zambia and Mozambique.

The silent drumbeats were now constant reassureing taps. Everything Dominique had to do from now on would be ordered, even his return to Rhino Creek. That might not come for quite a while, but he felt good about the delay. When he returned all of the things he had set out to do, would be done. After Novas and Prince Goldie clashed there would either be no settlements in Congo to worry about, or Rhino Creek would be as safe as Beguiler Ferry Crossing. Even Yolanda could fit into this new system. She must be halfway to Kingdom of Buganda by now. Of course, that couldn't be. It had been only three days ago; he watched her run down the hill towards Nova Gala. He could still see her braids swinging, and her hand tightly clutching the watch.

Dominique would be wise to keep his eyes, and mind on what he could see down the hill ahead of him. Most any time they would be getting into country where there could be warriors watching every trail, or, chasing settlers. The main trail north from Sea Pen was still deserted. Nobody in the northeastern tier of settlements had started running. The people of Flamingo Grove and the neighboring, French, Belgian, Spanish, British, and German settlements were just as stubborn. They were going to defend their homes and protect their stockades, cannon or no cannon. As it was turning out with Novas coming with help the decision was wise. Every settlement was saved, except Zebra Valley, their fighting served a purpose. They had slowed Goldie's advance.

Dominique kept moving, without stopping to look for African signs. He wasn't interested in cattle thieves that preceded most invasion. Nor was he interested in scouts that had been sent out ahead of the main body. He was moving fast, only slowing a little at every stream crossing or narrow gorge. They didn't have time to stop or worry about an ambush, no matter how bloody the battle. The hot summer morning wore on. From time to time Dominique slowed down to a trot. There was need for haste, but a greater need to save the horses for the demands the day might yet bring. The peaceful calm of the jungle remained unbroken even after they had crossed Congo River. Hippopotamus, secretary birds and gazelle were grazing within sight of the trail. War and the movements of armies could not have seemed more distant, or more unlikely.

The first evidence, that something was wrong appeared, when they were within a mile of Flamingo Grove. Five Belgian men rushed from a thicket yelling, with yells of jubilation. They said they were one of the scouting parties sent out from Flamingo Grove to search the surrounding jungle for Africans. The settlers were delighted to see a group of horsemen riding towards them from the south.

"It was so quiet last light," reported their leader, "that folks, they begun to think old Shameless was crazy when he told us about cannons, and Africans by the hundreds. Since we came out at daylight, we've picked up tracks upward more than fifty warriors were crawling' around during' the night, but we couldn't find any of them this morning. They've gone."

"How about Zebra Valley Settlement's?"

"We ain't heard from nobody at Zebra Valley since yesterday, and we haven't heard a cannons blast neither; and its less than eight miles."

"Novas is back in Congo," said Dominique, "settling his horse. He's raising men, and on his way. Get your militia ready to join him, and send mews to the other settlements. We've got to keep moving until we find where they are. When we do we'll let you know."

Dominique led his command on through the Flamingo Grove valley, past the station and on along the trail to Zebra Valley. Another group from Flamingo Grove was searching cautiously through the jungle up the slope from the eastern edge of the pasture. They were startled by the sudden appearance of riders from the rear, and were speechless as Dominique's men passed. The failure to use cannons at Zebra Valley puzzled Dominique. If the Zebra Valley station surrendered without the firing of a shot, by now Flamingo Grove should have been attacked. Instead, the warriors that were posted around Flamingo Grove settlement station were there to prevent the people in the settlement from sending for help.

Now they had been withdrawn. The withdrawal made Dominique ride his sweating, panting horse even faster. If Prince Goldie, after taking Gasper's, had suddenly headed west towards, Okapi Trail, to Chimpanzee Valley, or, Zebra Valley instead of towards Flamingo Grove, there was more need than ever to get some quick and definite news to send to Novas. The trail broadened enough for Hector and Peter to ride beside him; he glanced at their faces. Traveling fast and blind through the jungle was bad because, at any moment warriors could surround them; they would have to fight to stay alive. They glanced at each other and grinned, because this was something they had to do.

The trail narrowed again. Dominique's attention was fixed on every overgrown bush they approached. For the last hundred yards there had been no question about how many warriors had recently been in these woods, as recently as a few hours ago. The ground was covered in all directions with foot, and hoof prints. Any moment they expected a volley of blazing arrows, spears, or an outburst of war whoops. Even if Prince Goldie had turned west he would have left Bushmen or Pygmies warriors to protect his flank. Just as Dominique was about to head another way, there wasn't time for caution or even common sense. The trail curved around a huge date palm tree. Suddenly they were out in the open pasture surrounding Zebra Valley Settlement Station. The snug little stockade was still intact, closed up tight, and bristling with riflemen. Dead cattle scattered about indicated the fort had been nearly taken by surprise; there was no time to drive in all the stock before closing the gate. A loud cheer came from the defenders at the sight of horsemen. Dominique pulled up beside the stockade. The faces of the men peering down were pale and worn. Tyler Johnson leaned over the wall to answer Dominique's questions.

"Do you know where they went?"

"We're not sure they've gone. All night hundreds of them were howling in the jungle, like they thought they could scare us to death. They only stopped long enough for Judo Kenya to tell us we should surrender, if we knew what was good for us." He motioned pointing at the edge of the pasture. There stood a post with a man tied to it, still smoking. "They burned Blink Jones, one of the prisoners they took at Gasper's. They killed him where we could see him and listen to him scream for mercy. At dawn they stopped whooping, for the last two hours we haven't seen nor heard anything. There are not many of you. You better come in here with us. Most likely they're around somewhere waiting for us to come out."

"They could have had you," said Dominique, "if they wanted to. They have cannons."

Peter and Hector were searching the edge of the pasture. Peter let out a yell Dominique joined him. He had found the tracks. The cannon had been dragged down the trail from Gasper's, and wheeled into position. Then, some time before daylight, they dragged it off again in the direction from which they came. The deep grooves stretched through the jungle, skid marks could be seen as far ahead as you could see roots of trees. They were blazing a new trail, but where were they going. Prince Goldie's sending scouts to Flamingo Grove last night could have been part of a plot to confuse the settlers to keep from revealing his plans. Dragging the cannons to Zebra Valley and dragging them off again has cost him valuable time and labor. It couldn't have been a trick. There must have been some sudden change in his plan. At the speed of which the cannons could be moved they would catch up with them within the next hour or two.

There was no use telling Novas Prince Goldie's position had been established within fifteen or twenty miles unless, Novas could also be told at the same time, the direction Goldie was

Yolanda The Enchantress

moving. Dominique divided his men into two groups, leaving Peter with ordrrs to follow, a hundred yards behind. He had to be certain that his whole scouting party wouldn't be destroyed in one battle, with no one to carry Novas the news. The closer he got to Gasper's the more impatient he became. He signaled his first group into wide spaced single file. If they encountered danger, the soldiers in the rear could retreat successfully no matter what happened to those in front. He stayed in the lead, because he trusted no man's eyes as he did his own. Watching and studying the landscape ahead, he kept moving, first trotting, then galloping when the jungle opened.

They pushed forward expecting at any moment to find the silent pounding to change into a violent throbbing pounding roar; but nothing happened. The tracks left by the cannon led into a deserted blackened clearing. Then on and beyond to the south fork, they were heading in the direction of Torres.

Dominique told Hector. "Wait here with the horses for thirty minutes, look around for signs. Peter and I will go ahead on foot. We will probably run into them between here and the river." Torres's wasn't a large settlement. The heap of ashes that marked its site was awful small. Skirting the edge of the clearing, Dominique noticed there had been too few cattle carcasses left for lions, vultures, or hyenas. Only chewed bones remained after the cannibals had satisfied their appetites. Eating mainly human bodies. The other people here had been taken somewhere else before they were killed or eaten.

He reached the trail and walked between the cannon tracks. These were no longer clear and sharp; the footprints of hundreds of bare feet or sandals had trampled them. The whole African nation seemed to have assembled for this march. Some of the footprints were less than an hour old. Gesturing for Hector to drop back fifty yards, Dominique ran on. The trail entered the grasslands and nothing had happened, now there was no chance of an ambush because the cover in which Africans could hide was a short distance away from the path. His mind was not as occupied with danger as with the deepening mystery of the sudden withdrawal of the enemy, after the success of the first attack was successful. All of Congo was open to them.

Already it was clear that they had not marched west

along the Okapi Trail. Soon he would know for certain if they were catching up with their main force. The signs they had left were as deeply entrenched as by the passing of a heard of wild elephants. The south fork was just ahead. In another minute he would know something. They rode threw a cluster of banana and palm trees, now at the river's edge he knew little more than before. They dropped to the ground, Hector beside him, speakingsoftly scanning the two shores. The tracks ran to the water but the boats were gone. There was no sign of tracks or then getting off on the other side. The whole African army had taken again to the river. He considered this fact, and what it might mean.

The south fork was too shallow for barges carrying cannons to travel upstream. Dominique was thinking they were heading for Rhino Creek, or Nova Gala. They were in boats again, and drifting down river with the current. Prince Goldie could land where he pleased. He had his choice of landing, anywhere along three hundred miles of jungle shores on Lake Tanganyika or the Yoruba River. The pounding of the silent seemed now to be mocking him. After all his reckless searching he had little news of value to send to Novas, other than, Prince Goldie could be expected to attack at almost any place at any time. The others arrived. Dominique stood up speaking to Peter and Hector. "From the beginning it's never made sense, their attacking Torres's and Gaspers way back here in the jungle. Something's wrong, why are they wasting their numbers, their cannons, and their surprise?

They could have accomplished more if they had attack Port Eden Ton first. It could be they've finally realized that, and now they are back in their boats. They can make it to Port Eden Ton before dusk, and everybody in Congo is heading this way looking for them."

The answer didn't come from Hector or Peter; it came from another familiar voice.

"Would you like to know where they went?"

Dominique turned and saw Diesel sitting on Peter's' horse, his wounded leg thrust out stiffly.

"My gracious," cried Dominique. "You're alive!"

"Barely," said Diesel. "Three miles riding sidesaddle

with my leg slamming against bushes has convinced me, that I'm still alive."

He was naked except for a blanket wrapped around his middle; most of his body was smeared with black paint, his head was plastered with red clay. He had been beaten by Waggish, and Quittance warriors, that is what they do to a prisoner they were getting ready to kill. His fingernails had been ripped from their sockets. The other fingers had been bitten. His whole body was covered with deep gashes, and bruises, but his most severe injury was still his leg. It had swollen nearly twice its normal size. Unless he kept on being as lucky as he was to be alive he would loose it. His body ached, and he was shivering in constant unyielding pain.

"Found him buried under leaves at the edge of the clearing', back there at Gasper's," said Peter. "Wouldn't have known he was there if my horse hadn't stepped on him."

"Right on my good leg, too," complained Diesel.

"Where do you think they went?" demanded Dominique.

"Back to where they came from, each to their own village about that, I'm sure."

"Are you certain, or guessing?"

"Perhaps it will save time if I tell you what I saw and heard, then you can figure it out yourself."

"Do that," said Dominique. "And don't leave out anything, whether you think it is important or not."

"My friend, everything that's happened to me lately has been important, but this story will take me some time to tell. Please help me out of this uncomfortable saddle, that's sticking to me in places, I've been struck the hardest."

Diesel was lowered to the ground. He stretched out his leg with a sigh of relief. "Start with what you saw and heard. The warriors that ran out to welcome me were extremely happy to have me in their possession, especially after they were told what I did to six of their friends in the ravine. They lost interest in chasing after you and Mario. All their interest and anger was focused on me. They took me to the other side of the river where they were joined by an equally excited group of warriors. They stripped off my clothes without concern for my, wounded leg, and started smearing black tar and paint on me. They rubbed wet red clay in my hair. The black tar, if I remember was an extremely bad sign, but the clay puzzled me."

"That was to protect your scalp from the fire," said Dominique.

"Ah! For people who are so primitive that's oddly considerate, but you must be right. Because other warriors were throwing firewood near the base of a tree, all this was happening so fast. The expressions on their faces were as bright, and eager as a young boy about to fly a kite for the first time. At that moment one of their many chiefs rode over on a camel. I learned later he was Mohammad Sotto, the butcher. He is a skillful Ashanti scoundrel and a fierce warrior, but I'll remember him in my will. For some reason Sotto began to yell angrily at his warriors, and immediately a frightening alarming, argument began. All this was in Lozi and Ashanti tongue, in spite of my curiosity I didn't under-stand a word they said.

Later I learned the reason for the argument, was because a Mandingo chief named Prince Goldie was in disagreement over the killing of prisoners at Torres's, because he had personally guaranteed their safety before they surrendered. Now he refused to permit further use of his cannons unless all the chiefs and kings swore to observe the terms agreed upon on all future treaties.

The warriors holding me captive wanted to kill me, but Chief Sotto, to my great satisfaction argued for my life so eloquently and persistently. Eventually I was taken to Prince Goldie's hut. He had set up his headquarters in the pasture at Gasper's, which had quickly fallen. He was already engaged in a furious argument with other African chiefs and kings, trying to save this new crop of prisoners, my fate was entangled with theirs. The other terrified prisoners were huddled on the ground around him. Yelling warriors occasionally killed some unfortunate prisoners that were unprotected, and carried them away. They stopped only when Prince Goldie drew his spear, I moved as close to him as I could. The Lozi and Masai side of every argument had to be interpreted to him, at that time I was able to understand some of what was said.

While arguing over the fate of prisoners, there were many outbreaks, and interruptions. All with out warning by

Yolanda The Enchantress

Chief's and King's that disagreements. The King's and Chief's didn't like taking orders; they had to be persuaded to cooperate and they argued about the most trivial decisions. Prince Goldie argued with them for days, he argued so fierce and so long, he nearly lost his voice. His face was grim, his eyes as were red. His eyes were as red as if he had a fever. As a commanding officer, he hated the murdering of prisoners, as a warrior he was even more disturbed by the needless killing of cattle, at Torres's. This had left his army hungry with the necessity of scattering to hunt in order to survive.

As another example of the difficulties, which constantly overwhelmed his authority to command, the other tribes refused to help drag the cannons to Zebra Valley. They said this kind of work was for women or animals. The Wagnerian warriors, frustrated, were forced to drag the cannon without help. Tribal disputes and arguments, endless, passionate augments continued throughout the afternoon and into the night. Accompanied by periodic returns to the subject of the prisoners. Because of my injury's I wasn't watched, when darkness fell I was able to slip into the jungle, where I found a shallow depression in the earth and covered myself with leaves. I expected to be discovered and returned with the coming of daylight, but after nursing my injuries many hours I fell asleep and slept until that horse of my friend here stepped on me."

"Prince Goldie was having no more trouble than you have with any soldier," said Dominique, "What made you think that he suddenly decided overnight to break off his whole campaign?"

"This, I have not told you, there was another argument. Towards evening two men came to Gasper's. They had ridden hard, and long. It seems we harbor a number of renegades in our settlements that make a practice of running to the Ashanti with information. These two told him that Novas had arrived in Congo Basin with his army."

"You're right," interjected Hector. Peter smiled and said, "It was us."

"The news had an amazing effect on the Africans. Where before, they had been excited and boastful, the mere mention of the name Novas put fear in them. With the grave sensibility of wise old chiefs and kings, warriors became calm, sober, and more inflexible. Chiefs and kings started discussing the military disadvantages of their situation. They were without food, without enough ammunition, and without numbers to dream of confronting Novas.

Prince Goldie raved until his face turned from black to blue-black. They stared at him in disbelief. Chiefs and kings, grieved in silence looked at hin as at a friend who was loosing his mind. Crawling away, I heard Prince Goldie calling them cowards, and old women, while they, becoming angry, too, called him a fool and a madman. It was hearing that and nothing this morning. After hearing that, gave me the idea, they have gone home. "

"I think you're right," admitted Dominique.

Hector and Peter had been whispering while listening to Diesel's story.

"Looks like the war's over," said Hector. He glanced at Dominique, warily. "Since the doctor's from your settlement you can take him back there. Peter and me we'll scout down river a ways to make sure Prince Goldie keeps going."

"Scout down the river," said Dominique. "I'm going with you to make sure you do. This war barely started, it is not over. After what they've done, Novas is going to hit them twice as hard as they hit us. Now there's even more need than there was before to tell Novas where he can find Prince Goldie. Novas will follow him, no matter how far he has to chase him."

Diesel was cringing slightly watching Dominique's face with a serious, very thoughtful expression.

"Go and get them my two legged friend. Unhappily and in pain, I will limp home while you rush off to be a hero. What do you want me to tell Legacy about your militia, and what do you want me to tell Liana?"

"Tell Legacy to send my men to join Novas, and tell Liana I said... you're the hero." Dominique paused. "Tell her when I come home I'll run every step of the way," he added, and then turned abruptly to the men on horses. "Get down off of your horses and pay attention. Remember, everything you've seen and heard today, especially what Doctor Avila told us. Remember what I'm telling you now, so no matter whatever the questions is asked, you'll be a able to answer."

He counted off the six horses that looked the most tired. "Take three extra horses and build a litter to take my friend home, to Rhino Creek. Take it easy; go the long way around Smithfield. Six of you are going, because I want my friend to have a safe trip, He deserves one, keep your eyes open, the jungle is full of angry warriors."

He counted off the next three. "Take Okapi Trail to Chimpanzee Valley, and go to Port Eden Ton. Tell Colonel Costar Prince Goldie's army is traveling in boats, they are on the Yoruba, but they could change their minds, and still head for Port Eden Ton."

He turned to face the last three. "Ride as hard as your horses will take you, and tell Novas what you know. Tell him we think that Prince Goldie is crossing the Yoruba, we'll let him know something within a day or two." He turned to Hector and Peter. "While they are riding their heads off, all we have to do is build a dugout canoe, and float down the river."

"You got that right," agreed Peter, grinning.

Chapter 18
Good Intelligence

After climbing the tree he could see every hut in the valley. The village Novas will attack first. The distruction accomplished by Figueroa and Cordoba, when they burned this village down a year ago, hadn't lasted. The Ashanti, Masai, and Mandingo helped them rebuild. Nearly every hut was of soil and reeds, but the big one at the lower end of the village was built like a blockhouse. When Novas attacks his main force should ride in from the upper end, using the other huts for cover when approaching the fortified hut.

While waiting for Novas to build a strong army, we'll keep him informed of everything that's happening here. Count the number of warriors that's present at any given time, and note when, Mohammad Sotto, or any of the Kenya's come to talk to any of the chiefs. We'll know if the news is good or bad, by the way everybody acts.

For days the warriors celebrated, the capture and destruction of Torres, and Gasper's settlement stations. The warriors begun to settle down a little, they hadn't killed a prisoner for the last two weeks. Most of the prisoners alive were women and children.

Dominique dropped to the ground kneeling in the hollow section of the tree. For minutes he rubbed his legs and knees until he was able to use them again. Glancing through the roots and vines, he realized that darkness was rushing in. He had rubbed soot all over his body to keep from being seen in the tree, and he was armed with only a knife. Carefully moving the vines he stepped on the exposed root of the tree. He paused and listened until he was certain there were no unusual sounds in the darkness. Then he stepped from root to root, onto a huge rocks submerged in the river. From that rock onto a fallen tree; and stepped on another tree. He jumped on huge entangled pieces of driftwood, and slivered silently into the water without leaving a footprint.

Now came the part that made up for the hours of misery in the tree. Floating slowly down the river, enjoying the peace and quiet of the tropical night, while warm water washed off the filth, and relaxed his cramped muscles, was extremely pleasant and relaxing but it never lasted long enough. He swam a mile downstream towards a pile of driftwood that had slammed against a huge, submerged rock in mid-river. This collection of branches and fallen trees had taken root creating a tiny island. He crawled through the entangled bushes and uprooted trees into the nest, in the interior where he kept his clothes, weapons and food sack. This was where he met Peter or Hector, after they had traveled back and forth across the Yoruba River to take the information he had gathered to Novas. They also bought him news each time.

From day to day Dominique followed the movements of the army. He knew Novas was coming up the Yoruba River from Port Eden Ton. Quintile, with the Sea Pen militia was coming down the Congo River, and up the Yoruba. Figueroa was marching across country from the south, and Rhino Creek militia was with him. Serrano, Hernandez, just about every male settler

Yolanda The Enchantress

was coming. Dominique had expected to find Peter waiting for him tonight, he was disappointed that he wasn't. He dressed, ate his cold impala jerky, then, and Peter still had not come, he when to sleep. Long before dawn he was awakened, to his satisfaction Peter was coming.

"Novas, has crossed the Yoruba," said Peter. "He's going' to attack Mamba Valley, day after tomorrow, first thing in the morning'; then he will head for Shanty Land."

"Go back and tell him I think they know he's coming," said Dominique, "but they don't seem to have any idea how strong he is. They are worried, because they don't know what he's going to do. Tell him that since Prince Goldie left with some Ashanti warriors, and a few northern Arabs, two weeks ago, none of them have come back. They must have gone to Elephant Falls. Novas will have only the people that live here to deal with. I'll go and take another to see if everything there is still the same. You or Hector come back, about this time tomorrow night."

Peter nodded and cleared his throat. Something else was on his mind. "I saw Mario," he said. "They made him lieutenant of his settlement station's militia. He wanted me to tell you something, he made me say it over and over 'til I got it right." Peter paused to clear his throat again.

"What did he tell you?"

"He said. A door on the roof is not nailed down as tight as you think?"

When you see Mario tell him thanks."

Dominique watched as Peter lowered himself into the water and swam to the bank. Then the water turned black and glossy again. He was alone. The words Peter had spoken had been Mario's that was Mario's idea of humor. But the message was from Liana, as clearly from her as if it had been delivered by one of her brothers. The message had come with a warning; so unpleasant it startled him, as when a silence is broken by a sudden crash that was unexpected.

Now that he had time to think about it he was still startled. She consider their parting at the gate, as a breakup between them, in order now to be sending him such a shallow message, that if he comes back, she would think about letting him in again. He had taken it for granted; when he got back she would

299

be waiting for him, and everything would work out as they always did when people are so strongly drawn to each other. Instead she was saying if he returned she might give him another chance. He didn't like what he was reading. No good could come from his shutting his eyes to the fact. He had to have her, on his terms, or not at all. She knew that. He would rather spend his time thinking about what he knew he wanted instead of what he couldn't have. He began to single out, and dwell upon the things about her that pleased him most. There were so many. Slowly, and deliberately he let his imagination drift back to her, up the stairs and through the open door.

Slowly, working his way northward towards Shanty Land during the hours before dawn, he became so absorbed in the detail of these thoughts that he lost his way; but from daylight on there were things in the village to watch that demanded his attention. There was little question the Lozi were greatly disturbed about something. It seemed that they were having trouble making up their minds, what to do. From noon on they held council in front of a burning fire. The fire pit was beside the fortified hut, which was much larger and stronger than the fortress at Mamba Valley. The council was interrupted for a while in the afternoon by a war dance, and the beheading of a prisoner and then they resumed their discussions, every man present waited to have his say. Like most Lozi councils this one was slow to come to a conclusion. After dark Dominique crawled closer to make sure the council was still continuing, afterwards he returned to the island in the Mamba River. There he found Hector waiting for him.

"Novas, is still going to attack before dawn."

"Tell Novas something is going on at Shanty Land. I don't know what it is yet," said Dominique. "He'll have eighty or ninety warriors to deal with at Mamba Valley. I'm going to

sleep. I need it."

Once he stretched out he was too sleepy to take advantage of the opportunity to think, about Liana. Before dawn he woke up thinking about Novas, and his army pressing forward in the dark through the jungle last night. Keeping under control, over a thousand angry men speaking six or seven languages, in

Yolanda The Enchantress

the jungle at night, was a challenge even for Novas. He was too restless to sit. He decided to go back to the tree. He was thinking, he might see something before the first streak of light that could help, even if Novas were informed of it at the last minute.

He didn't bother swimming upstream, because there was no longer any need to worry about leaving footprints. He ran up the riverbank climbed the tree and looked out. At once his effort was yielded a rewarded. Lozi, and Dung warriors were dancing, and chanting war songs. Dung and Lozi, women were chanting and waving their hands in the air. The earth trembled with the sound of war drums.

The Lozi, and other inhabitants had become aware of Novas' approach, but they had learned of it too late to send to Shanty Land for help. It was light enough to see women running out of huts with bundles, putting them down, picking them up again, forgetting where they had put them, chasing their dogs, and arguing at their children. Even warriors were running about as wildly, and aimlessly as people do who have just discovered something horrible is about to happen. The villagers had decided to run, and burn their homes, before the attack. Some were running around catching and killing their dogs, or locking them in burning huts, anticipating immediate pursuit. They were taking steps to prevent the possibility that their dogs excited barking would betray the route of their flight. Every hut was burning, and dogs were howling, and moaning in pain.

Dominique saw two brass cannons being rolled out of the burning, fortified hut. He hadn't guessed their presence there during all his watching. Prince Goldie must have left them there with some hope of their being used again, against other settlers. Lozi warriors rolled the cannons onto a barge, and poled the barge to mid-river, and pushed them overboard into deep water. Several bags of cannon balls followed. Dominique smiled. When he tells Novas where they are, he'll have them dragged ashore within an hour. Suddenly a group of warriors came dashing through the maize field; they were carrying sacks of cannon powder. This too, was being hid for later use. They dug a hole near the base of the kola tree. Yells followed by moans, whistles and animal calls burst from the jungle just beyond the village. Lozi scouts came dashing in, accompanied by flurries of rifle

301

shots. Novas' first line of soldiers came into view. The people still in the village rushed for their canoes, and paddled across the river. A second line of riflemen was now sweeping through the maize, and another was closing in on the upper section of the burning village.

Dominique glanced down at the Africans digging at the foot of the kola tree. They had the hole just about filled. Two of them were nervous because of the nearness of the advancing soldiers and fled. The others stayed until they had smoothed over the earth, and carefully removed all traces of their digging. They had stayed too long. Another of Novas' columns came into view. They were coming from the south, along the riverbank. Realizing they were being surrounded in danger of being killed, the three warriors hid in the bushes surrounding the tree. By the time they had gotten themselves settled, their feet and legs were stretched through the hole at the base of the kola tree, below Dominique. He was a prisoner trapped in this tree and Novas army was only yards away.

This time his rifle and ax were on the ground, leaning against the kola tree. They were inches from the out-stretched feet of the Lozi warriors. Any moment a warrior could move and knock down his rifle. Or, one of them could crawl or squirm back into the concealment hollow tree, and look up and see him. Dominique thought of dropping down on them. Thinking that the suddenness of his appearance would give him the advantage, but he decided that was a foolish idea. To reach them he would have to crawl through the shrubbery. While he was doing that, they would kill him.

The advance continued into the village. The Sea Pen militia companies made rafts to furry their weapons, and swam across the river to be certain that the fleeing villagers kept running. After a brief pause to rest, Figueroa's militia reassembled. Dominique could see Mario and the three Gomez brothers. They turned and marched up the river. Dominique knew Novas had ordered Figueroa to circle Shanty Land. He had planned to attack the village from both sides at once. The remaining two divisions of the army, he knew, Novas had ordered to cut down the maize, even though it was too young for good eating. As all this activity continued, not one of the soldiers came near the tree

Yolanda The Enchantress

Dominique was trapped in. Looking down he could see brown legs with out motion, as still as if they were, an outgrowth of the kola tree. Again he was on the verge of leaping down on them. If he did he would be risking more than his life. He had to tell Novas about those cannons, and he had to make sure that he lived to tell him. He knew those cannons would make a difference when Novas attacked that blockhouse at Shanty Land.

Novas was preparing to cross the river, and go on. He had given Figueroa the time he needed to get into position beyond Shanty Land. Desperately Dominique thrust the blade of his knife through an opening in the branches, hoping it would glisten in the sun, and attract a soldier's attention, but no one saw it. The army crossed the river. The burning smoldering village, surrounded by burning maize-fields was suddenly deserted, when the last militia company rushed into the jungle. The Lozi warriors below kept as silent and as motionless as before. Ten minutes drifted by. Finally at last the warriors move into a nearby thicket. When they vanished from sight, Dominique climbed down and picked up his rifle. Thrust his head out of the bushes, and through the vines; but the Africans were still hiding.

The sudden appearance of a Portuguese soldier, leaping from a tree not far away startled them, it was too much after the long strain. They dashed, from the thicket, and plunged into the river. The sight of their sudden appearance, had scared Dominique at first, then he stood, with a sigh of relief.

After an hour of hard running Dominique caught up with Novas at the head of the column. Novas wasted no time talking about how pleased he was about the cannons.

"Take Valeria's company," he said, "go and get them."

When Dominique watched the Lozi warriors dump the cannons, he watched carefully. He lined up the spot between two mangrove trees across the river. They had no trouble finding the cannons on the bottom, but it took time to twist enough rope made of vines, and even more time diving to attach the line. Even with the elephants pulling, there was trouble getting the cannons to shore. The riverbed was covered with large boulders against which the axes kept catching. It was dark before the cannons were on bank. Everybody cheered when they saw the dripping, brass cannons. They had traveled a great distance since their use had first been planned in Elephant Falls. They had been dragged and floated for hundreds of miles. They had made it possible at Torres's and Gasper's the striking of a terrible blow against those settlers. Now men were swearing, and shouting in their delight because they belonged to them.

Dominique sent men ahead to widen the trail. The rest of the company grabbed the lines attached to the elephants and pulled. The cannons rolled forward, lunged and skid. The wheels of one of the cannons plunged into the earth. The same cannon wheels plunged into the ground, again, halfway up the hill pushing and pulling the soldiers and elephant. The soldiers struggled to free the cannon. They approached the top of the hill and started down, on the way down the wheels of that same cannon plunged into the ground again. The wheels locked and started siding. The cannon was sliding sideways, and twisting. The wheels struck a huge rock, and unlocked themselves. Without a warning, there was a sudden unexpected thrust, and a burst of speed.

The cannon overran its human pullers and elephant. It swerved from the path and wedged its self between two huge trees. After freeing the cannon over and over again, the straining and struggling continued, up and down the next hill. In the darkness small trees and bushes were overrun. The wheels of that same canon bounced over a root, and sank nearly a foot in the ground. A storm drifted overhead as the laboring convoy was in the midst of the swamp between the third, and forth hill. They cut logs to make ramp to keep the cannons from sinking into the earth. Using brute force, and elephants up to their waist in mud, dragged the sinking cannon on through the storm. Novas sent back another company to help, and later he appeared at Dominique's elbow.

"We'll get them there," said Dominique.

Throughout the night, they heard rifle's firing to the north. Novas' men were occasionally, firing and reloading. The rain had increased the chance of them being attacked during the night, with useless rifles. Two hours later the rain stopped, but the ground was so soggy, that with every jerk the cannons sank, even deeper, so deep at times the barrels sunk undet the mud. Morning came, and the cannons were not within sight of the ad-

Yolanda The Enchantress

vancing war party. Then, instead of scattered firing came brief volleys, which changed into an outright assault.

The battle had started. More men were sent back to help pull the cannons. At Shanty Land the warriors didn't run, they attack the invading army. Figueroa's army had much farther to march, because the storm had slowed him down. The warriors from Shanty Land outnumbered Novas' army, and they had the advantage.

Novas had a barge waiting at the bank of Dung River. The cannons were pushed aboard. The river was shallow and swift. The barge slammed into submerged rocks and began to come apart. Some of the men jumped in, and guided the barge towards the bank. Approaching the crest Dominique could see the battlefield. Sections of the jungle was smoldering with the smoke of hundreds of wishing arrows defending the the village. A frontal attack on the jungle below was made impossible by flanking fire from the big blockhouse. The most numerous African lines outnumbered whites so much they were beginning to stretch around Novas' outer flank. Either the jungle in front or the blockhouse had to be stormed at once or Novas army would be defeated.

The sweating grunting men pulling the ropes pulled the cannons to the top of the hill. A platoon of Novas' regulars ran up to help them. The cannons were wheeled around and loaded. Novas himself fired the first shot. It ripped huge logs from a corner of the fortified hut. The Africans defenders came running out and seconds later the building was on fire.

Dominique sat on the ground watching as cannon balls splintered trees in the surrounding jungle, others plunging into the burning huts in the village. Warriors, seven and eight at a time, were fleeing the jungle, heading for the maize-fields. Then by overpowering numbers of white riflemen appeared and swept towards the village. Dominique picked up his rifle to join the advance. Peter Hernandez came running.

"Novas want to see you."

Dominique found Novas on horseback, organizing his militia for a final assault to clear the fighting Africans from a section of the jungle on the far flank. Spears and arrows were whispering through the air. Being mounted, Novas was the most prominent target in sight, he was standing high in his stirrups for all to see. He swung his horse around, leaned down, and grabbed Dominique's shoulder.

"The cannons did the job, just in time, too. We will keep them on the run now. Most of them will get away before Figueroa arrives to cut them off, but we'll burn their village and destroy their maize. They'll have to hunt to eat for 'til next year's crop grows, that will keep them too busy to make trouble in this part of Africa, for a long time. That's the news I want taken around Congo as fast as we can spread it. Too many settlers are moving back to Portugal. Nothing will stop that quicker than good news. That's why I'm sending one man to every settlement today, right now, to spread the news around quickly. You will find the others waiting, where the barge with the cannons landed. Get going, you're taking the news to your settlement."

All the time Novas had been watching the course of the battle, which had developed into a sudden, frantic warrior retreat. His eyes met Dominique's for a second. He frowned saying. "From what I heard you won't be objecting to this order like you did the one last spring, when I ordered you to go to Eagle Landing", before Dominique could reply he wheeled his horse, and galloped off towards the village.

Dominique stood looking at Novas. Thinking perhaps he had done enough. The trouble with Novas was he always left you wanting to do more. He turned and walked towards the river.

Coming up the trail was a camel caravan carrying supplies for Novas' army. Dominique stepped off the trail to pass. The man riding the lead camel glanced down. Dominique came to a sudden stop.

"Taboo Ikea," he exclaimed! "I thought you were on your way to Kingdom of Buganda."

"That's were I wanted to go," said Taboo. "Fiona, she changed her mind. When she heard about Congo being' full of so many unfriendly Africans, she said this is not the time for white or black folks to be
running around Congo, especially couples like us. I was drafted into the Nova Gala's militia."

"Then Fiona and Yolanda-they're still at Nova Gala.

Yolanda The Enchantress

Fiona is, but Yolanda-she took off."

"She what?"

"She ran away. When she heard we were staying in Congo for a while, she didn't like it."

"Where did she go?"

"Not even Fiona knows. Worst part of it was, she took that backpack you gave to me with her, the one with Prince Kudzu's shirt in it. How's the war up ahead going?"

"A draw," said Dominique rudely, he strolled on towards the river.

Chapter 19
She's Gone Home

Dominique came to a sudden stop in ankle-deep grass upon which the first sprinkles of rain were falling. He was walking threw high grass that spread over the hillsides for miles around. On each side the thicket, and under growth had been trampled down by elephants. They had nibbled on it while passing, but above his head the thick canopy blocked out the sky. In some places the thicket had been ripped away by feeding giraffe.

Then he noticed the most recent footprints were nearly a week old. Looking ahead he sighted the station a little before dusk. He slowed up to avoid getting there before the sun rose. It angered him to have to creep towards his own stockade. He was returning from a war to the place he was the sole authority. He tramped down the creek, and came out near a corner near the grove of orange, and palm trees not far from the lumberyard.

"Where is Mario?" shouted Cindy's sharp demand before he had reached the door.

He saw her rising in the darkness from a bench setting against the wood and brick wall of the lumber mill. He had a feeling she might have been sitting there, listening, and watching the trail from the north, the way Mario had gone.

"Still with the army," explained Dominique, quickly. "He was OK when last I saw him, his militia company didn't fight at Shanty Land so he should be OK."

"How soon?"

"After they finish burning, probably within a week."

"Another week, eh? That Mario. Whoever comes back last, that will be Mario." Her voice was sad with longing.

"He's as anxious to come home as you want him to."

"Maybe." She drooped, and leaned back wearily on the bench. "All the same I get just as angry at him when he's away, thinking he's with some woman enjoin' himself."

Dominique leaned his rifle against the wall and sat on the bench. There was no use trying to avoid the problem when talking with Cindy.

"Where is Yolanda?"

"Don't have the faintest idea."

He questioned her briefly thinking Cindy might be lying to him. He stopped. That wasn't her way.

"She ran away from the Ikea's, don't you?" he asked.

"Yes."

"She must have come here; perhaps she's hiding in the jungle, waiting for me to return."

Cindy slowly but emphatically shook her head. "She's not in the jungle, not around here. This is the one place we know she's not." She paused and shook her head again. "Figueroa was here, he had to lay over a day, waiting for Novas to send him orders. Whether he should go north, by way of the Old Lozi Trail, or by Gator Ridge. He had his whole army out looking for her. Anita Figueroa wasn't satisfied 'til nearly six hundred men searched every inch of ground for miles around."

Dominique's mouth dropped open.

"Anita, was here?"

"She came back with me and Fiona," explained Cindy impatiently.

"Perhaps you should start from the beginning."

"You're right. It's because of you. You might as well know about it. You started it. When Yolanda ran away, Fiona came here to tell me. I knew how much Yolanda admired Mrs. Figueroa, so, Fiona and I went to Figueroa's home to see if she were there, she wasn't. Anita came back here with us and stayed until she was satisfied Yolanda wasn't anywhere around here."

"You, Fiona, and Anita, too," marveled Dominique. Not

Yolanda The Enchantress

in all of Congo could you get together a search party more likely to find whatever they had decided to look for. "Not one of you has the slightest idea where she's gone?"

"All we had to go on was something she said, once to Fiona." She said, "She's going home."

"Home," said Dominique. "That's it. I told her home' is with her family in Kingdom of Buganda. That's where she's gone. She's that stubborn, once she had started there she was determine to keep going whether the Ikea's did or not."

"That's what Anita and Fiona said, but I think, she's gone back to Zulu Land. She's gone somewhere. She won't bother you no more," said Cindy. She leaned her head against the wooden wall. "You'll find your woman in her mill. You can sleep with her tonight. The preacher's gone, so you don't have to wait for him to say some words."

"You have no right, to talk about her like that."

"What's wrong with what I said? That's how Mario and I did it. You've been around long enough to know, there ain't no other way to get married in the jungle. What counts is that you come out the next morning, you tell everybody, you're there to stay. How else can women get husbands in settlements where there's no priest? She's no better than the rest of us." Cindy stood. "You might as well go home, and hit it a couple of times. I'll tell everybody, especially those folks over at the stockade, what you said about Novas burning, Lozi country."

He wanted to run up the path towards the upper falls, bot not while he was within sight of Cindy. Even out of sight every step was slow, and deliberate. The dark outline of Linda's house appeared before him. The wooden shutters were tightly closed over the windows. That was sensible. Osceola and his sons had built a huge formidable fortress, and by now Novas had probably chased the last, prowling, unfriendly African across the Yoruba River for the rest of the summer, but still you couldn't take any chances. You never knew who was hanging around. The hammer of a rifle clicked, and then came a swishing sound as it was drawn back.

"It's me. Dominique," he called out.

Osceola stepped from behind a huge rock near the path, his silver hair and balding head glowing in the starlight.

L. A. Johnson Jr.

"Thank God," said Osceola. "Come, Miss Liana will be happy to see you."

Osceola hurried up the path in front of him. Else unbarred the door. The red glow from the lantern cast a pattern of warm light and shadows across the room. Osceola's sons and their wives were eating.

They rose, smiling and bowing, when they saw Dominique. The door at the head of the stairs opened.

"Dominique?" There was a hint of surprise in Liana's voice. "Is that you, Dominique?"

"Yes."

"Her voice cracked," why has it taken so long?"

He rushed up the stairs. She retreated from the doorway, watching him as he came in. He placed his rifle against the wall and closed the door behind him. She ran to him, but she didn't let him kiss her. She only clung to him, pressing her face against his chest, while sinking her fingers into his shoulders as if trying to convince herself that he was really there.

"I'm here, all right," he assured her, grinning. "Let me go, I'll make you believe it."

She released him and backed away. She was glad to see him. Yet there was a nervous tension like when they had parted. It was like they were standing at the gate again.

"I'm beginning to believe it," she said. "You've changed. Are you hungry? I was about to have dinner, you have come at the right time."

She walked around him to open the door. "Else," she called. "Set another place?"

When she returned she left the door open. Maybe it was only natural for her to seem so nervous. When last he had been with her so much had gone wrong. He was very conscious of the door she had left open.

"Please sit down," Liana insisted. "You must be worn out as well as starved." She was getting control of herself. "Don't say a word-not yet. Just sit back and give me time to think."

Walking across the room he walked pass her bedroom door. It, too, was open. With one quick glance he saw her bed with the covers turned down; the white linen sheet was showing. He hadn't slept between sheets since the time he had visited

Yolanda The Enchantress

Mali. On the foot of the bed was a pink silk nightgown.

"You can have me tonight." She said.

He sat in the chair across the table from the place set for Liana. It was an elegantly carved oak chair that fitted him in all the right places. Sitting down felt good, he hadn't sat in a chair for quite a while. The table and cabinet were of the same polished oak. Osceola must be as good at carpentry as he was a blacksmith. Linda poured two glasses of wine from a decanter on the dining room cabinet. She gave him one and clicked hers against his.

"Pleasant company," he said softly.

"Pleasant company," she repeated.

He hadn't had a drink for weeks. He felt a warm tingling feeling rush down his throat. He looked around, nearly a dozen or more candles brightly lighted the room. The bright light gleamed on the cast iron pot in the fire-place, reflecting on the display of brass and copper bowls on the mantel, them he noticed that same reflection on the finely carved display of crystal glassware in the dining cabinet. She was wearing a peach dress. The brilliant candlelight changed the peach into the color of a ripe mangrove, dangling from a tree in the sun, the brightness, made her hair look more reddish-brown, and her eyes seemed to glowed when she looked at him.

"It's bright in here," she said. "When I'm alone I like it that way."

She walked around the room blowing out the candles. When she lifted her arm, and cupped her hand at each candle the motion drew the dress against the curves of her breasts. He became even more conscious of the two open doors. Perhaps it meant nothing, or was she expecting some one else?

Else came in with a tray with thick tender slices of juicy gazelle. She returned with a platter of sweet potatoes browned with sugar, and crispy biscuits. The butter splattered on the biscuits dripping with honey, looked and smelled delicious. Else stepped back.

"Don't come back for the dishes," said Liana smiling. "Take the night off."

"Yes, mama. Good night, mama. Good night, sir."

Else closed the door carefully and walked away. Liana

met his glance with a slight smile.

"Eat," she demanded.

"The gazelle, ham, and everything else tasted as good as it looked and smelled. He was hungry and the food was delicious, but something was wrong, it didn't seem real. Nothing seemed real.

"How's Diesel?" he asked. "He's quite a man."

"He's doing very well," said Liana. "He's a very good doctor. He saved his leg, but he'll always limp a little, and do you realize, I haven't asked about my brothers?"

"They were well when I saw them. They still are, without doubt. There was little resistance at the first village; Figueroa's division didn't get there in time."

"Legacy sent me a letter. He said you were spending most of your time, sneaking in an out of Lozi villages, gathering information to send back to Novas."

He told her about the kola tree, She told him how the women in the absence of their men had organized a female militia company, elected officers, and drilled twice a day. They finished eating, and she placed the dishes on the dining cabinet.

"Smoke if you wish," she said.

He took out his long pipe, and started fumbling at his pouch before he remembered he'd used up the last of his tobacco.

"I have some," she said, bringing him the jar. "Lonely as I am, I'm always prepared for gentlemen callers."

She sat down in her chair across the table from him. They continued talking as if they were only friends who had little to talk about. He was getting more and more uncomfortable. . More uncountable than he was when he was hiding in that kola tree. She was just talking and smiling, watching and waiting. She was probably thinking of the strange manner of their last parting, and still holding that against him. She was making him come to her. She wanted him to beg, plead, and crawl. There was more to it than that. He put his pipe in his pocket to avoid fumbling with it. There was something wrong and he had to face it. He didn't want to face that fact, because that would make him angry or feel even more uncomfortable, because she was right. He had been here for hours, and had tried only once to kiss her. He was just sitting there, fidgeting and squirming with the table between them. They talked about nothing. They talked about how good this year's maize crop was growing, and now they had stopped talking.

"Yolanda," he said abruptly. "I heard she ran away from those people that were taking her home."

Liana grew pale, suddenly. There was a strange look around her eyes and mouth.

"I don't believe it," she said. "I don't."

"Believe what?"

"Don't try to avoid the subject."

"Something's aren't so easy to avoid. I told her many times that I would take her to Kingdom of Buganda."

"You did everything you could to help her. It is not your fault she ran away while you were fighting her people."

"I should have never mentioned it."

"Don't you dare, don't dare for an instant, talk and act as if I'm being unreasonable. We haven't seen each other for weeks. I didn't know if I'd ever see you again, now that you're here you sit for hours moping over a woman you don't care about."

"I can wonder, cant I, or is that wrong, too. Whether she's gone to Kingdom of Buganda, or back to her Zulu family, or if she's dead in a some valley somewhere?"

They had risen to their feet and were leaning towards each other in bitter, brutal, aggressive, confutation across the table not as lovers but as rivals.

"Well?" she asked, and waited.

"What do you want me to say? I don't give a damn about what happens to her?"

"No." She was intentionally keeping her voice calm and steady. Then suddenly she lost control. "Oh, Dominique, Dominique, what is happening to us? What is wrong with us? Nothing could be so wrong as what we are saying and doing." She regained some of her composure. "More than us, and how we feel, there are others to consider. There is Mario. He's your best friend, and a more devoted friend no man has ever had. My brothers have accepted you as one of them. And the people here have made you their leader. This past month they have been so proud of you. They worship you. How can you give up every-

L. A. Johnson Jr.

thing to go wander off to heaven knows where to look for that little crazy Zulu?"

"Who said anything about me going to look for her?" What would happen if I did? Are you saying don't come back?"

"I'm saying, you can't come back to me. Not long ago I told you, you could come in that door whenever you're ready to stay. I meant it then and I mean what I'm saying now."

Her words came at him like blows. She was telling him what he could do and what he couldn't do. She was rendering the terms upon which he could have her and all that came with her. Worst of all, her terms were not unreasonable; she had every right to her demands. He had given her every reason to be standing there like a vengeful wife, measuring him, pressing rules, and enforcing her demands. Her eyes flashed glassy and angrily at him. Her body was trembling. The intensity of her emotion had exposed all the passion in her. Never had she appeared to him so beautiful. She was controlling him again. In no other way could he defend himself against her. Only by controlling her, or taking her, making love to her could he ever win her.

He bumped recklessly against the table getting around it. Her eyes widened, at first in disbelief, she swallowed, when she realized what he was doing. With a gasp of relief she threw herself into his arms.

"How hard we work at making fools of ourselves." As she whispered he could feel the movement of her lips on his neck. "We always argue, and it always seems to happen on our wedding day." An unpleasant sound of soft laughter simmered, and interrupted briefly threw her low murmuring voice. "There is no reason for it. No reason, none at all, the truth is whatever you want to do, Dominique, I'll let you. Tomorrow sometime, we can discuss what you want to do about her, perhaps in the morning."

She laughed again, unpleasantly and deceitfully. After a night with her, she was certain that she would be able to control him in the morning. Over her head he saw the turned down bed. She was saying this is our wedding night. Their marriage bed was but a step away. The sound of her words and what she had demanded crept over him. When he awakened in that bed in the morning it would be too late to talk about what he might or

314

might not do. He wouldn't be free to deside whether he should stay or go.

Chapter 19   Part 2

Today the early morning silence was that of silence, the silence of a wasteland. People who traveled Congo Road hung around this area waiting for company. Most of the time Congo Road was as empty as it now was. He could see and read the most recent footprints. They were no more than a week old. He stood still, breathing deeply, because he had been running. He had to stop surrendering to waves of disgust and anger that flowed over him. The sudden feeling that he couldn't stay with Liana had been so clear, and strong that there had been no deny-ing it. Even though it still persisted, he hadn't once felt the impulse to turn back.

He might as well give up trying to understand himself. A man who had spent nearly twenty years trying to get a woman only to run away from her again was beyond understanding. The desire for her that had been with him so long was still haunting him, and his emotions were beyond his understanding; still he wasn't going back. There was no good his spending the next twenty years feeling the need to drive his fist into the nearest tree. Sooner or later he had to start settling down, and it might as well be now. Before he took another step he had to stop, and do some thinking, about where he was going and how he was going to get there. He had already committed himself to looking for Yolanda. Now, he could get on with that.

Standing at the foot of Gun Road, where the west-bound trail forked to Nova Gala one way, and Figueroa's the other, he could close his eyes and see Congo Road stretching eastward all the way to the Niger River, and Kingdom of Buganda beyond. He had traveled this road often; he knew every step of the way. He could foresee the end of his journey. Once he found the Qukeza family there was one or two things he could learn. He could learn that Yolanda had arrived safely. That would mean his concern for her had been foolish, and that would make his journey meaningless. That would surely mean that his journey had been a waste of time. The wrong guess would cost him weeks, probably months, and would leave him with a trail that was too cold to follow. He had to guess right.

Eight weeks ago Yolanda stood where he was standing now. She had come south from Nova Gala; here she could have stood as he was doing. Perhaps she was trying to make up her mind which road to take. Did she take Congo Road east to Kingdom of Buganda? Did she go south over the mountain to Red River and into Zululand. He tried to put himself in her place. When talking to Cindy he had argued that home was Kingdom of Buganda, because that was where he wanted her to go. Actually, from the beginning she had taken little interest in the existence of her Kingdom of Buganda relatives. The only home she had ever known was with her Zulu relatives; Home for her is Zululand, not Kingdom of Buganda.

He grunted and smiled with sudden satisfaction. An idea had come to him, a way to find out within a day which direction she had taken. Had she decided to go back to Zulu, she would have swung east to Gorilla Passage. She would have known there would be too great a risk, taking that route of running into some northern Africans. Who would be far more likely to treat her as a stray animal than a woman on her way home? After thinking about it, if she had started south she would have swung wider to the west towards the big bend of Redwood River Trail. Redwood River would have bought her within an hour's travel of the cave. She wouldn't have gone past without stopping there to rest. There was that same cunning of the average woman in her. All he had to do was to go and look in the cave. If she had been there he would know she had gone back to her Zulu relatives. If she had not then he could set out for Kingdom of Buganda with the feeling that he knew where she had gone.

As soon as he broke through a vine riddled section of the jungle, into an open valley it started raining. After an hour of hard rain, it stopped. By early afternoon he entered the creek he searched. He remembered the time he crossed the ridge to look for Mario. The time he lost Ruddy to those Zulu warriors. The thought of his beautiful horse stirred new resentment in him. She had caused him to lose everything that belonged to him. Now he

Yolanda The Enchantress

would be spending more time and effort for more months, more time than he could predict ahead. It wasn't that he had anything more important to do; he had to be sure, no matter how long it took. He had to know what happened to her.

It was easy to blame her for every wrong turn in his life. It was a relief to realize that when he reached the cave he would know which direction she had gone. That brought the time closer when he would be able to make her sit, and listen to his complaints about what she had done to him. She would probably laugh. She was always happier, the angrier he got at her.

The sun was setting as he climbed down the slope past the waterfalls. Vines that covered the door revealed that someone had recently been there. He stepped into the stream....in knee-deep water. The new green growth of bamboo, and cane was above his head. The hard winter had killed bamboo and cane here, as it had in other parts of Congo. Off to the right he head coughing and grunting of a heard of elephant feeding. Further away he heard a party of giraffes bellowing. He spotted a baboon chasing a chimpanzee. Then he saw a heard of rhinoceros running. Just ahead of him it was still light enough to see crocodiles darting through the water.

The last time he walked down this stream he was carrying Yolanda on his back. It was after that she stopped fighting him. He left the door unbarred that night, but she didn't run away. His life wouldn't be so complicated if she had escape. Grass was beginning to grow again. The rail of the horse pen and most of the shed was covered with sprawling vines. Unless you knew about the door to the cave under the falls you would never know that it was there. Moss had grown all over it; the edges of the frame were covered with new growth of fern. The fern around the door would reveal whether she had been here or not. It was nearly impossible to find a footprint in the rhino trampled meadow.

In a few minutes it would be too dark to look for any kind of sign. He took a handful of maize out of his game bag, tossed it into his mouth, and strolled across the meadow to the door. Even in the fading light he could see at once that the fern around the edge of the frame was frayed. Somebody had opened the door. They were careful not to touch the outer coating of moss over the face of the door. They had avoided stepping in the soft sandy earth in front of the threshold; still opening the door had disturbed the fringe of ferns. He pushed the door open. The outward serge of stale air, brush against his face. Among the familiar smells of his cabin was that of charred wood in the fire pit. There had been a fire there since his last time here. Whoever had opened the door stayed long enough to cook at least one meal. The darkness of the cabin was like a blanket across his eyes. Instinctively he stepped sideways out of the doorway.

He ran his fingertips along the wall of the cabin, and stopped; staring at the darkness and listening. He could see nothing at all, and could hear only the splash of the stream in the cave, but there was a familiar smell. Incense leaves had been added to one of the beds within the last few days. Whoever had come to the cave had spent the night. Most likely it was Yolanda. She had decided, after all, to go back to her Zulu relative. Suddenly, a ticking sound came out of mid-air, and the watch struck the hour.

"Yolanda," he cried. "Yolanda." There was no reply. The watch stopped striking. "Yolanda," he repeated. Still she didn't answer. Dominique held his breath listening to hear where she was standing, but he could hear nothing. "Yolanda," he cried again, beginning to get angry. He reached out for her in the direction from which the sound of the watch had come, but only slammed his hand against the wall of the cabin. Still she didn't speak. He set his rifle against the wall, and reached again. Not able to find her, he became more infuriated and started lunging about the cabin with outstretched hands searching for her. From time to time he came to a sudden stop, listening, hoping to hear her move, some movement that would reveal her location. He was angry because she was making a fool of him. Yet revealing her presence with the watch, and afterward hiding from him.

Waving his arms finding no one while lunging forward, sometime slamming his hand against the bare wall. He shouted in his anger, when he stepped into the fire pit, stumbled and fell headfirst. He lay there for a moment, breathing hard and listened for her laughter, but no laughter came. He thought that she had run into the passageway leading to the cave. He scrambled to his feet and felt his way along one wall until he felt the cold, damp

Yolanda The Enchantress

air of the main cavern. He stopped thinking. She couldn't be hiding in that dark, damp cave. Not unless she were really afraid. She knew it was he who had pushed open the door, because she had held the watch to his ear. She was amusing herself at his expense. She was making a fool of him, if she were in the cavern he would need a torch to look for her. He started back to the cabin.

The outer starlit sky framing the open doorway was bright in contrast to the darkness within. More likely than anything else, he decided, she had fled through the open door, because when he first reached for her, she must have slipped pass him, and gone outside. He walked to the doorway. It was dark, so dark that she could be sitting only a few feet away, in the middle of the meadow and he would never see her unless she moved. Or she could be perched in the mangrove tree right over his head. She was hiding somewhere out there, crouched; listening to the commotion he was making in the cave while trying to find her. "Yolanda," he said, holding his voice to a calm but firm conversational tone. "Come here." She didn't answer. Perhaps she was farther away. He tried the broken signal geese call. That should mean some-thing to her, but it didn't. There was no answer.

He surrendered to his anger again. He wasn't going to give her the satisfaction of him running around in the dark looking for her. He backed away from the doorway where she couldn't see him if she was watching, and ate another handfuls of maize. He could see no movement in the meadow, or around the horse pen. Tired and disgusted, he felt his way to his bed, and stretched out on it. She'll come in when she gets tired of sitting out there. He didn't want to give her the idea it made a difference to him weather she did or not. There are two sides to a joke.

He wriggled and squirmed into a comfortable position. The fresh incense leaves had been carefully laid to make a soft bed. She couldn't have been expecting him to show up. She must have been sleeping here herself. He could smell the faint scent of fresh grass that always clung to her clothes and hair. Suddenly and curiously, he stood, and felt his way along the opposite wall. The floor had been swept bear where her bed was supposed to be. She had slept in his bed while he was gone. He began to

L. A. Johnson Jr.

wonder why she was still hanging around more than a month. For what reason could she be here so long? She must have started for Kingdom of Buganda and changed her mind. He returned to his bed. He smiled. Sleeping in her bed was a joke on her. When she decides to come in, she'll have to find another place to sleep.

The daylight in the open doorway awakened him, as it had that first morning, when he thought she had run away. That morning he woke up with a sense of relief. He was certain she had gone, but this morning he wanted to see her. He was relieved to know that she was here. It had saved him from looking further for her. Just as she had done that first morning, she was bathing in the stream; soon she'll be coming home, with a string of fish, and fruit in a banana leaf. She'll come in without saying a word. She'll build a fire, and start cooking his breakfast. He would pretend to be asleep. He'll close his eyes; he wouldn't have to say anything. It would be as if they had never been away from here. All this seemed so certain to him that he rushed to the doorway to watch for her approach.

A gazelle and her fawn were grazing in the meadow. The gazelle lifted her head at the sight of him, and galloped nervously away. There was no sight of Yolanda and the doe was proof that she was not anywhere near.

"Yolanda," yelled Dominique. He ran down to the stream, he yelled until he was hoarse. Finally he managed to get himself under control. He went back to the cabin and settled down. Standing in the doorway, he scanned the area surrounding the cave. Painstakingly examining the area in order to pick up her trail so that he could follow it. She had thoughtfully paid attention to the slightest detail when coming, and going. She had left as little evidence as possible that might attract the attention of some passing hunter to her living in the cave.

After an hour of searching the ground, he was able to identify only a few faint imprints of her sandals, but they were there before yesterday. She couldn't have slipped out the door last night. Even if she had leaped from the threshold to the tree, and climbed it, which was unlikely, she couldn't have leaped from He had traveled this road often enough to know every step of the way, he walked on the ground without leaving a footprint.

Yolanda The Enchantress

Earlier the dew was heavy. She hadn't left the cave after he had entered it. She had run into the cavern. There was no logical reason for her to hide in there this long. She didn't know about the exit on the far side of the mountain. Even if she did.... why would she make; that long dark dangerous journey? It would have taken her hours of walking, and crawling through those dark, narrow, damp crevices. She would need a torch; she didn't have enough time to light one.

More likely than anything else she had blindly run into the cavern, and become confused in the darkness. She could have gotten lost somewhere in one of its endless passages. Perhaps she had fallen and hurt herself in one of those damp musty chambers. He ran into the cave twisting a torch made of rags. He plunged it in a tub of oil, lit it and rushed into the cavern. The light from the burning torch revealed at first glance everything she had been doing except where she was now. In the nearest dry corner where his sacks of magnesium sulfate had once been piled was the pack roll, with Prince Kudzu's shirt, and the crocodile-skin pants and shirt she had made him. Beside it was a row of baskets. One was filled with dried berries, another with salted fish, and another with smoked ostrich, and others with wild potatoes, dates, rice, coconuts, reddish, palm nuts, seeds, peanuts, and green bananas. She had been at the cave a long time.

She must have come here, when she left Nova Gala. She never had any intention of going anywhere else. She had planned to stay here indefinitely. She had stored enough food to last the dry season. The flickering light revealed something else, far more important to him at the moment. Since his last firing, new deposits of magnesium had fallen on the floor of the cavern beyond Yolanda's hoard. She could not have crossed that floor without leaving footprints. There were no footprints. She was not in the cave. Dominique tossed the torch aside and ran back into the cabin. He no longer thought that she was hiding from him. A sudden overwhelming deepening concern replaced his anger. He had to keep his wits in tack to figure out what could have happened. Running around and yelling like a crazy man wouldn't help. If he was ever to make use of the sense's God had given him, he had to settle down and use them now.

Last night she stood beside him, an arm's length away,

when she held the ticking watch to his ear. Since then she hadn't left the cabin by the door or gone back into the cave. Nor is she here now. All three things obviously couldn't be true. The most logical one to doubt was that he hadn't heard the striking or ticking of the watch, but that wasn't true. He heard it. It had startled him. It was the last thing in the world that he had expected to hear. He didn't imagine that. He could still hear that ticking sound coming out of the darkness near his ear.

He walked over to the spot where he was standing last night. Just above his head was the hole in the wall where he always kept a wooden box. He took a deep breath reaching into the cubbyhole. His fingers closed upon the small wooden box. He took out the watch and stared at it. It wasn't running. He shook it. It ticked a few times. He fumbled in the box and found the key and turns it several times. The watch started ticking with precision. Last night it was ticking. The ticking and striking he had heard must have been its final effort before it stopped running.

The truth rushed over him. Sometime, probably day before yesterday she set the time, and put the watch back in the hiding place where she kept it. It was probably yesterday, early in the morning before it started raining. He thought after studying her footprints, she had left the cabin; she hadn't planned on going anywhere. She had intended to come back. Otherwise she would have taken the watch with her. She would never leave without it, perhaps she had gone out to pick more berries, or gather wild onions or check animal traps; something happened that was keeping her from coming back. He picked up his rifle and walked swiftly to the doorway. His fear was a shield that hung between him, and what he could see of the meadow. He hesitated a moment glancing around thinking but he didn't see anything, he needed to think. He had to use his imagination. He had to guess where she might be, she couldn't have gone a great distance. He wouldn't have to look very far, but he would have to search with extreme care. He would search within a circle of the first two miles of jungle to the mountainsides. He'll search the cliffs, shallow caves, and deep pools of water, around the quicksand. Then he would search within that same circle, under uprooted and entangled trees. There were hazards out there for

Yolanda The Enchantress

any kind of accident. The most unpredictable mishap could happen to anyone alone in the jungle. A foot wedged under a fallen tree could keep you pinned there until you died.

The thought of old Rhino Gonzales haunted him. Rhino was one of the most experienced Jungle men. He walked out of this same cabin one morning, and never returned. One mistake and he was gone. Dominique began to run. There wasn't time to look carefully for signs; whatever happened to her must have happened early yesterday. Perhaps he was already too late even if he found her. He searched in ever-widening circles, moving each time deeper into the jungle and higher up the mountainside above the falls and climbed down again to search the lake. Every few steps he gave the broken geese called or shouted out her name. No reply ever came. He searched long into the night, always returning to the cabin hoping that she had come back, but the cabin was always dark.

The next day he searched another section of the jungle near the cave. He examined the section inch by inch, section by section back and forth, like an old experienced hunter. He systematically, carefully, searched each patch of thicket. She had taken every precaution during her time here. She had never twice taken the same rout when going, and coming. There was not the slightest clue indicating, where she was going. Even between the cave, and the stream she hadn't left the slightest trace. Still, from time to time he found places she had been. Places she had picked berries, dug roots, cut vines for baskets, and set traps for small animals. There was no sign of anything unusual; there wasn't the faintest clue to reveal her disappearance?

The third day he serched another section of the jungle. The forth day he searched another. He had lost all hope of finding her, but he had to know. He searched in low spirits, imagining what might have happened. He had carefully searched the ground within the natural limit of her ranging around the cave, until he was certain she had not been a victim of any ordinary accident such as a nasty fall or a snake bite, or perhaps a deadly encounter with hungry lions. There was a chance that she had been carried off. Zulu, of course, wouldn't harm her. Still at times, Quittance, Xhosa, and Ashanti sometimes wandered this far and could have stumbled upon her. And there was a type of

L. A. Johnson Jr.

white man worst than any African. So far he had no evidence or reason for thinking that. Any such encounter would have left traces and there were none. No footprints other than his had been found within miles of the cave. Slowly he was becoming hopeless and kind of helpless.

The evening of the fifth day it rained. The drizzling rain became a drenching downpour that continued through the night. So heavy and prolonged it was ripping and flattening leaves on the ground, breaking branches, crushing twigs, and beating down every blade of grass. Afterwords if he wanted to continue searching there would be nothing to search for. All signs of footprints have been washed away. All traces, tracks or signs were rendered meaningless. The realization that his search had ended without a reward for his efforts bothered him. He ate only berries or chewed on roots that he had picked or dug. He slept very little. He sat down in the bamboo where the rain had overtaken him. The weight of his misery was so overpowering that he was barely able to move. He sat there, in the rain, with his head sagging between his knees most of the night. He moved slowly, with the instinct of a sick lion crawling towards his cave, struggling. Because of the rain, and darkness with his own carelessness it took him a long time to muster the strength to search for his stream. Tramping through the jungle he stumbled upon his stream.

He tramped down the stream, staggering with weariness, falling repeatedly tripping on rocks and logs that covered the creek bed. Striking his head against a huge branch, he stumbled and fell; his head slammed against a submerged rock. He lay there stunned and nearly drowned, face down in the water, before he could recover enough strength to crawl onto the bank. Morning came. The rain stopped, the clouds began to clear. He struggled to his feet and stumbled on. The sun rose, the glare hurt his eyes, because of the beaming rays he kept his eyes slightly closed. He walked by the flat rock without seeing it. He crawled, dropped, and rolled under the bush where he slept the morning of the cyclone's approached.

Increasingly vivid memories of her swept over him. He could see her laughing in triumph on the raft. Limping rebelliously behind him down Redwood Trail. Handing him his watch

324

Yolanda The Enchantress

at Median's, and, leaning down towards him from the rafters at the lumberyard. Always he had scolded her, insulted her, and pushed her away, keeping her at a safe distance. He had deceived himself, tricked himself into thinking he didn't want her, because he didn't feel about her the way he felt about Liana. Now, he wanted her. He wanted her and no one else. He wanted most of all to tell her he never wanted her to leave him again. He couldn't do that now because he watched her run down the hill towards Nova Gala. At that moment, all he had to do was to kick his heels into the side of his camel and go after her.

The sun was burning his eyes. He placed his arms over his face and leaned back. He had barely enough strength left to move the slightest effort. He squirmed sideways leaning into the shadows of the bush. His body was sore all over and unable to move without pain. He had given himself a terrible beating falling so often, and slammed his body so violently against rocks in the stream. No wonder he was so weak. He hadn't eaten a good meal since that night at Liana's, nor anything, since that hand full of maize that night he arrived. There was some maize left in his game bag in the cabin. He needed to crawl to the cabin and eat something before falling to sleep. If he falls asleep before eating when he woke up he would be too weak to eat, but nothing was worth the effort.

The sun was beaming across his eyes, for hours because it had drifted above his head he must have slept a little. He was in so much pain he could barely move, but the same dream was recurring. Struggling with a much greater effort, he sat up. This dream was more confusing than any he had ever had. Not even a dream should be so real.

"She's gone!"   "She's gone!"   Yolanda's gone!"

The End

L. A. Johnson Jr.

Mamba Books & Publishing
"Where Knowledge is Wealth"

www.ingramcontent.com/pod-product-compliance
Lightning Source LLC
Chambersburg PA
CBHW071058250626
47159CB00002B/513